The Red Death

Book One in the Duology

M. Kenzie

To those who never gave up.

Prologue

Caged

Roux

Being trapped in a cage isn't the worst thing about being in prison. Sure, there's the actual cell. A small, dank space with stone walls covered in mildew and a thin line of a window high above me that lets through a sliver of light. There's even a nice wall of rough metal bars to frame the black hall beyond. Yet eventually it simply becomes another cage. Another room. Even the rats can be good company after enough time. Especially if you catch one in time to satiate your growling stomach.

No. The worst part is the cold.

It's inescapable. This particular prison, the Prison on the Mount, is nestled high in the snow-covered mountains where winter reigns year-round. You can distract yourself from the hunger, the loneliness, even the hopelessness, at least for a little while. The cold, however, seeps into your very bones to shake you as if to keep you from forgetting the icy chill. One becomes grateful for the dirt, shit, piss, and gods know what else simply to put more distance between skin and stone. The slabs might as well be cubes of ice. There are no fires here. No tapestries to keep in warmth, no blankets tossed to the prisoners, and we were certainly given no clothes to replace whatever rags we had on when we were brought in.

Only the thin window above tells me when it's night or day along with the rise and fall of temperature. The chill becomes so fierce at night that when I eat, I'm no longer sure if I'm eating stale bread or the chipped pieces of my chattering teeth. Cold breeds desperation. Moans or shouts echo down the halls from people trading the only thing they have for a little extra food, a blanket, a torch. Perhaps they're grateful for the few moments of body heat.

My stiff fingers slide over my toes to count each one. "Seven, eight, nine, ten." I blow out a slow breath, knowing it's a puff of mist in my cell even if I can't see it in the lowlight. Two years I've been trapped in this dung heap. For two years, I've been caged. Not all of it in this high mountain prison, oh no, I'd been moved five times. Each after a rather brilliant catastrophe orchestrated by me. I've been in this cold hell for a little over eight months now. At least, I think that's how much time has passed. The longest I've been in one place yet. Two years in captivity out of twenty-three years of life may not seem like much, but it feels like a small eternity. I've learned that having ten toes is something to be grateful for.

A loud click rings through the hall and chains clatter as the other prisoners drag themselves towards the bars for breakfast. No chain clanks as I tug myself feebly towards the middle of my cell. At the first prison, I used a bone from a skeleton roommate to release myself from my bonds. At the second, I used the chains to strangle a few of my jailers. They'd decided not to furnish me with any this time.

I sit cross-legged on the stone floor with my head bowed. My legs are little more than toothpicks and my arms are thinner still. *Yet I still have ten toes.* And when I escape from this rancid place, I will find a house with a fireplace big enough for ten men to warm them by.

Staggered footsteps grow closer as the group nears my cage and something in me manages to be satisfied by that. They still fear me. Even if it's only a little. Solid strides interrupt the soft scuffs and I only deign to tip my chin up when they stop outside my cell. Their torches nearly blind me, but I manage to see the person before me. There stands my jailer in all her glory; pale, scarred skin, angular face, dark eyes, and a dark soul, in my experience. A slow smile creeps over my face. The woman has the good sense to take a step back without taking her eyes off me. The nervous soldiers at her side do the same.

Yes, I will get out of here. And they're afraid because they know it.

Chapter One

Escape

Silvanus

I never like visiting the Prison on the Mount. It's cold, muddy, and carries a foul stench in the air as if the souls trapped inside the mountain prison are rotting. I sigh as my eyes scan the towering stone guards on either side of the grand door. Two soldiers etched into the dark stone of the mountain stand over twenty stories tall guarding the entrance with grim mouths, cold eyes, and swords held up against their shoulders. In ancient times, rumor was that they were the only ones to guard the prison. If a prisoner tried to escape, the soldiers would come to life and eat them whole. They would then live out the rest of their life in the stone belly of the guards. Some stories say that the guards allowed some to escape, something about a pure heart, true remorse, or similar. It's been a while since I've had time to read for pleasure.

I heave another breath as I turn towards the doors. "You sighing isn't going to make time pass any faster." Henry, my guard and best friend, comments at my side with an amused tilt to his full lips.

I huff again just to make him roll his brown eyes. "It took us long enough to travel here and now he's wasting time gossiping with the warden." Impatience has me drumming my fingers on my arm and I shift from foot to foot as my father chats to the woman across the muddy yard. A servant shivers next to them waiting nervously for their next order.

"Gossiping? Is that really what you think they're doing?" Henry raises a thick brow and maintains a soldier's stillness and vigilance. The opposite of my constant fidgeting.

The corner of my mouth lifts. "Plotting is probably more accurate, but I thought gossiping added some much-needed levity."

He chuckles and looks over the prison ahead of us. "Not much of that found here, that's for sure." I watch my father glance over at me and I hold his gaze until his brows furrow with displeasure. We look alike, much to my chagrin, but I've always taken solace in the little differences. Our hair is red and wavy, but his is darker than mine and easily tamed into a coiffed wave. Our skin is pale and freckled, but my freckles are darker and far more prevalent. The major difference is that I'm lean and he's broad, but I treasure each difference.

Not only are the long trips to this horrid place exceedingly boring, but every moment the awkward weight of spending time with my father hangs over us like a noose ready to slip around our necks. Not unlike the lanterns around us. They spread faint gold light through the early morning mist and hang from ropes reminiscent of the gallows. Even the lanterns look eerily like human skulls. My father is the overseer and usually takes these trips alone, but he wanted me to come along this time. My mother pushed me to go as well, so I knew there was going to be something special about this trip.

A groan is gathering my throat before he finally shakes the warden's hand and the small group begins heading in our direction. The servant scrambles to follow and accidentally bumps into my father, sending him stumbling a half-step towards the cliff edge. Henry begins to say something else, eyes still on the Prison, but I'm already heading towards the group with anxiety building in my gut.

My father whirls around to face the young man who has gone pale as snow. "*What* are you doing?" He hisses and the boy at least has the courage to meet his gaze.

"I-I'm sorry, my Lord—"

"Sorry." He repeats, his voice colder than the wind as it howls in the ravine below us. The warden crosses her arms and watches the scene with a disinterested stare. "You could have killed me. Sent me over the edge into the canyon. How do you think your apology would soothe my wife? My son?"

He swallows. "Poorly, sir." My father nods and begins to turn as I pause a few steps away, hoping that'll be the end of it. "I hope you'll forgive me, sir. We were nearly ten feet away from the ledge anyway." Nerves shake the young man's voice as he wipes a hand over his dark blonde hair. My eyes shut a moment as Lord Lurec freezes. He could have accepted the fearful apology or the plea for forgiveness, but not the dismissal. My father expects his word to be accepted as law. If he said he was in danger, then any opinion other than that is a challenge to his authority.

His hand shoots out and curls around the man's throat before he drags him to the ledge, holding him over it so only the tips of his toes still touch the black rock. He's gasping for breath and my father's nose wrinkles as his ink-smudged hands crease the fabric of his sleeve—the only thing he has to hold onto. "Any risk to your lord's life is unacceptable. No matter the…probability." The man's eyes bulge as my father's hand squeezes.

"The good news is that you're safe and no such apology or message is necessary. Shall we spare ourselves the same chore by returning the man to his feet?" I slide to the opposite side of the warden as she sighs at the show. "I think your point has been made."

"Has it?" He questions without taking his eyes off the man whose feet are desperately scraping at the rock beneath him. A few pebbles tumble off the edge and ping down the cliff's sharp edges as the servant nods his head as much as he can. My father pulls back until the man's feet are flat on the ground and his hand laxes so he can suck in a few breaths. "This man may have learned his lesson, but what about others? Tales spread so far so easily. What will they say?" His thumb brushes over his jugular as tears gather in the servant's eyes.

My hands clench even as I keep my tone light and conversational. "Perhaps that their lord was understanding and showed mercy after a lesson learned."

"Yes. Please. Please, have mercy." The man whimpers and I stiffen as my father's gaze turns to me. His eyes are almost as dark as the rock of the cliffs below and he doesn't hesitate a moment more before pushing the man from the ledge. I move to step forward before I feel Henry's hand snag one of my belt loops under my cloak. My eyes flash to his and he gives me a sharp look even as screams echo from the gorge until coming to a merciful stop. The hard thumps of his body hitting ledges and spikes, however, continue until out of range.

"I have no desire to be known as 'merciful', Silvanus." My father's cold voice breaks the silence and I turn back to him with trembling fists. His eyes scan mine casually, as if he hadn't just murdered a man. "Mercy is weakness masquerading as kindness. It's a foolish lie that we sometimes tell others for advantage, but not one we can ever believe. It doesn't exist."

"It certainly doesn't exist in you." I hiss just as coldly back. The only thing keeping my father from joining that poor soul down below is Henry holding me back. Not to mention we're surrounded by witnesses.

"We have work to get to today, gentlemen." The warden reminds us, not at all phased by what's happened.

My father leans down and I feel Henry slide a hand around my belt. Whether to continue holding me back or to prevent him from tossing me over as well, I'm not sure. Lord Lurec gives me a half-smile. "I'll bleed it out of you too, soon enough." I lean forward, but Henry keeps me still. Lurec waves a hand toward the warden before beginning to walk away from us. "He's yours, Warden."

The warden sighs as she turns to me. "Your father has other business to attend to, so you'll be coming in with me today. There's something he wants you to see." My anger simmers as he walks towards a line of traders coming to drop off supplies to the left of the prison. His business takes place outside the prison, of course, so his fine silk clothes aren't stained with the stench within. Part of me wonders if he fears that the stone guards will sense his rotting heart and gobble him up if he gets too close. Still. As his only heir, this place will eventually be my responsibility.

I pull myself together, tucking the anger away to be sharpened into something better later. "I'm sure his…business is terribly pressing." Her eyes narrow while I take a steadying breath. "Lead the way, Warden." I lock my jaw while following a none-too-happy warden through the tall iron doors with Henry just behind me. A chill slides down my back at the screech of the closing doors and the solid bang as they clang shut behind me. Somehow, they remind me of a creature's maw sliding closed to trap prey within. But I'd been inside the prison a couple of times. Nothing is new, out of the ordinary, or unexpected.

Except her.

We climb and climb and climb to the highest room in the tallest tower. Sweat beads on the back of my neck and cools in the chill as even fit Henry huffs with effort. Prisoners reach out of their cages cajoling or pleading with us and I can't help flinching when the warden slams her foot down on a woman's hand as she reaches for her boot. She doesn't even scream as her fingers bend and crack from bones shattering. A whimper is all that can be heard from the cell and I try to shake off the feeling of her eyes on me as we continue.

We and most of the few soldiers around us are panting by the time we finally reach our destination. The warden opens a door and I peek around her shoulder only to see a single cell on the far wall. There's so little light in the room that I can't see if there's anyone inside it, but there must be if we're here. Some in our group have torches, so we bring light with us and I blink a few times before I can see clearly. The prisoner doesn't look up, but I can see her clearly. I think it's a her anyway. She barely looks human at all.

My first impression is that she looks like Death. Matted hair, black as night, shrouds her head like a hood. The cell reeks like all the others and patches of her pale skin are nearly black with filth. The very sight of it has my nose crinkling before she tilts her face up as we come to a stop in front of her cage. Her eyes stay closed, more than likely to shield them from the onslaught of light we've brought with us, but I'm thankful for the small mercy. I'm not sure I want to see what those eyes hold. The only window or source of light in the room is a slit at the very top of her cell, so small I doubt two fingers could slip through, but a slice of light finds its way. No wonder the bits of her skin not covered in dirt are pale as snow.

Her face is skeletal. Lips that must have once been pink are chapped and tinted blue. The point of her chin looks sharp enough to cut and those closed eyes sink deep into her skull. I'm worried her paper-thin skin will rip over her cheekbones should she speak. Boney fingers are clasped neatly in her lap where I see too many gaps and strange lumps from skin stretched tight over bone. Yet when the warden takes a step back when the prisoner hardly moves, I know she is no ordinary prisoner. Perhaps they truly have caged Death. She smiles and a chill dances down my spine.

"Still haven't found what you're looking for?" Her voice grates and scratches on its way out from disuse. Or from screaming. "What a pity." Even with a voice like gravel and a body barely there, her tone is cloying. Teasing. I keep to the other side of the soldiers, hidden in the shadows.

The warden juts out her chin. "Seems like you're the one in need of pity." Her nose scrunches as she walks back and forth in front of the cell like a predator that can't reach her prey.

The prisoner hums, content to take her time to respond. Her pale lids lift and I find myself leaning forward to try to catch a glimpse of her eyes. Or to make sure they aren't just sunken, empty pits. "As you can see," she stretches her spindly arms out to the side, "I have no collar around my neck and no leash for someone to tug." Her head cocks as her smile slants, sharp as any blade. "Yet I can practically see the red around your neck from your master yanking yours. What a disappointment it must be to have a dog unable to sniff out the one thing you're sent out for."

The warden locks her jaw and on any other day, I'd be endlessly entertained to see the stoic woman so bothered. But this environment isn't exactly one for entertainment, although the woman in the cage seems to think otherwise. "Better a dog on a leash than a pig in a stye." She takes a daring step towards the bars while her soldiers shuffle in clear unease, including Henry behind me. Death's smile widens. "And you can easily be fitted for a collar. A spiked one."

The prisoner shrugs. "You're welcome to try, Annaliese Warren." The soldiers around us whisper and their shoes scuff on the floor. My brows raise. No one in this shithole speaks the name of the warden. No one knows it. Her title is her name here. The prisoner tilts her head back just enough so that the torchlight catches a sliver of green irises. I'm instantly reminded of the deep emerald vipers that lurk in the trees far down the mountain. As a child, I watched and admired how they would wrap themselves around a branch before going still to wait for their prey to make the mistake of coming just close enough. Her invitation strikes me as a spider coaxing a fly into her web.

"Another time." Annaliese grinds out and steps within a foot of the metal bars with a hand resting on the hilt of her sword. "Once upon a time, you could have been the sniffer dog. Do you think about that while you waste away? How you could be out there, free, traveling the world, if you'd just taken the offer?"

The woman in the cage stiffens, the only sign that the words hit their mark, before the flicker of emotion vanishes. "Freedom on a leash isn't freedom." The cloying tone is gone. Her voice cuts through the air like glass shattering in a silent room. "I'd rather rot inside this shithole than bow down to lick the boots of someone who thinks themselves my master." Her words clang through me, the truth of them staining the inside of my head like blood splattered on a white canvas.

"Wish granted." Annaliese chuckles, Anna, as she insists upon outside this place. "Although I almost hope you'll one day take the deal. Just so I can see you finally break." She leans close to the bars, letting her hands wrap around the cold metal despite a soldier tugging on the back of her charcoal-colored cloak in warning. "To see the great Roux brought to her knees. See her beg." My body goes still at the name. No. It can't be.

Roux. One of the most prolific assassins ever known. They surfaced around five years ago when four public officials were found dead, hanging from a bridge by their bowels. Almost instantly the name was born; the Red Death. Or Roux, to those who didn't want to be caught saying the name lest they come find you. The assassin never meant a quiet, painless death. They only brought screams and streets bathed in blood.

And this woman is apparently the prolific killer that vanished two years ago.

The woman doesn't move but stares unrelentingly at Anna with those round eyes. "It'll never happen." The promise is soft, but solid as the mountain beneath us. A soft breeze winds its way through the hall despite the windows being few and far between. The hair on the back of my neck rises as I try to keep a shiver at bay and pull my cloak tighter around my body.

Annaliese shrugs with a smile tugging at the edge of her thin lips. "I'll watch your death with just as much relish. And the day you die—" She doesn't finish because, with a flash of movement from the assassin, the warden is covered in shit. Pale brown, putrid sludge covers the warden's face, and her grey uniform, as well as already beginning to dry in the heavy ruff of silver fur around her neck. It must have taken all the strength the woman had to throw it since she now sags from her straight-backed posture.

Still, Roux cackles so hard, she has to hold a hand to her stomach. "Even after all this time, I still have perfect aim!" She gasps between laughs as Anna snags the end of her cloak to wipe away the filth. Despite myself, despite it all, a soft laugh leaves my lips at the absolute outrage scrawled across her face. Heads whip towards me, but the pair of eyes that I look to belong to the assassin.

I'd run into a mountain lion during a hunt once. She'd been stalking us the moment we entered the wood and I'd only caught her because my horse got spooked. The mare wouldn't move forward, so I glanced up to a small cliff where the cat waited. My eyes met the bright yellow of hers as we both froze. That's the only way to describe the feeling that shoots through me now.

The feeling of being appraised by a true predator.

My body locks up, my palms start to sweat, and my heart starts to thunder in my chest. Yet I don't move. I just wait with my eyes locked on hers. Hers narrow as she looks me up and down despite the shadows cloaking me. "You never bring me new toys, Annaliese." She says, so sugar sweet I almost laugh again just because of the shocking change.

The warden wipes herself off as well as she can before spitting a gob of saliva which lands in front of the woman. "He's not a toy, he's—" She cuts herself off before she reveals my identity. "Forget the deal, Roux. I hope the next time I come here your body is cold and the rats are chewing your face off." Anna snarls and marches towards me, flicking her chin towards the door.

"Think I'll stay a moment." My gaze stays on the woman sitting on the grimy floor. "This is what you brought me here to see, isn't it?"

Annaliese hooks curled fingers around my arm, thin lips curling into a sneer. "This is not a game. She will toy with you until you're close, then she'll rip out your throat."

Black eyes burn into me, but I simply turn my head to address her. "You stain my clothes; you pay for them." Her face contorts with fury before she seems to remember who she's talking to.

Carefully, her fingers peel away one by one before she straightens with as much dignity as one can when covered in refuse. "You have a few minutes before I come to fetch you for your father."

"Fetching isn't exactly what you do best, Annaliese." Roux comments. I swallow my chuckle as the warden rolls her shoulders and her jaw ticks. Her soiled cloak ripples behind her as she struts out of the room with a few guards. The caged predator reclaims my full attention.

I step out into the torchlight a bit more as the soldiers assigned to me keep to the door in a silent plea to leave. Henry stays at my back with his hand on his sword. Her cell is in a tower. One way in and one way out with barely a window, so the light from the soldier's torches lights her face, but keep mine in the dark except for a line over my eyes from the slit above.

There's fear welling in my stomach, but along with it is a sliver of something else. Curiosity. "I've heard you don't treat them very well," I comment, lifting the edge of my grey-blue cloak where the warden touched, wrinkling my nose at the smeared dirt there. I go on as my eyes return to the seated woman. "Your toys."

She snorts, the reaction so knee-jerk it makes me blink. Dirty hands and feet push her back against the wall so the icy stone can hold her up. It seems this interaction has drained all her energy. "A lord's son would certainly know a lot about toys, wouldn't he?"

I raise a brow, but it's easy enough to guess who I am with my fine clothes and my access to such a high-security prisoner. "Yes. Although mine were taken when I was barely more than a boy. Not beheaded, like some of yours."

She cocks her head. "Aw, you poor rich boy." My jaw locks at the condescension, but she goes on. "I did to them what they would have done to me. Perhaps with a little more flair." The edge of her lips turns up as she gifts me a wink. There's less open hostility on her face than when the warden was here. Her eyes are penetrating, gauging, figuring out whether I'm a friend or foe. "None of them were as pretty as you, anyway." It's pure instinct to let a crooked smile leak onto my face and she purses her lips while surveying me. "I think we would have had quite a bit of fun back in the day."

I take another step towards the bars despite the soft noise of dissent from Henry behind me. "Your kind of fun? Or…" I trail off and find myself leaning forward at her flash of teeth barely resembling a smile.

"Oh, definitely my kind of fun. But not my professional fun, if that's what you mean." She assures me with a feeble wave of her hand. "I'd never waste a pretty face like yours. That's all you lord's sons are good for anyway. Well, that and maybe a little bit of my professional fun depending on the man."

I bristle at the delegation while she grins, seeing the discomfort flash across my face. My teeth graze over my bottom lip as I take a moment to reel myself in and observe her. I look her up and down as I try to imagine what she could look like when healthy and strong. All I see is a breakable body wielded by an unbreakable will. And that body happens to have a smart mouth. Perhaps the former is why I wanted to stay behind. That and the small moment of understanding combined with the way her earlier words rang true not only for herself but for me, a lord's son trapped under the thumb of his father.

My gloved hands clasp in front of me. "The deal the warden offered you." I preface, watching her spider leg fingers knit together in her lap either to subconsciously copy me or to consciously mock me. "What was it?"

"The same deal she always offers me." The answer is vague, but her eyes shimmer with interest. "But you have to give information to get information. Tell me something, lord's son." She leans forward a bit and my eyes flick to her back as if I'll see the bones of her spine breaking through her skin. "What is your father's name?"

I smirk even as I feel the heat of Henry at my back as he steps nearer in silent warning. This is valuable information. If she wants it because she plans to hold me for ransom, it won't work. My father may drag me on trips like this at my mother's insistence since I'm due to inherit, but that's the only amount of fondness he holds for me. And I for him. The choice of whether to answer or not isn't a hard one. I want to know what he's doing here and why she's here getting personal visits from the warden. "Lord Lurec. This heap of rock falls under his jurisdiction, so he manages to drag himself from fingering coin to visit it every few months." My tone is bored, but her eyes glimmer at gaining new information.

"And why has he brought you on this particular visit?"

I cross my arms over my chest and raise a brow. "What deal were you offered?"

She grins at the counter offer. "Yes, we would have had a lot of fun." The hair on the back of my neck stands on end, but I find myself leaning forward as she does. "The warden's employer offers me the guise of freedom in return for my help in finding a certain object of value."

"What object?"

Her grin slants. "How far is it from here to your estate?"

Henry now moves to my left. "We should go." As insistent as his tone is, I don't spare him a glance. He's been stuck with me since my teenage years. Now that we're nearing twenty-five, he should be used to my antics.

"Approximately three days as the crow flies."

She nods slowly and sighs at my expectant expression. "A book." My brows furrow. A book? Someone would release this murderer to find a book? "Come now. You must have learned in all your time in fine classrooms the power of knowledge." Her scold calls me from my thoughts while her stained hands rub stiff feet, fingers pausing over each toe. "In history, winners must have more than armies and gold, lord's son. Knowledge is the true currency of victory." Her eyes shine with the promise of success. "Do you love your father?"

I huff a laugh. "No. And if you ask because you plan to kill him, I wish you luck." Her smile widens and I take in the minute movement. If that is indeed her plan, and who could blame her for wanting the head of this dung heap dead, then all her questions would make sense. But she would need to escape to stand a chance.

"We must go. *Sir*." The sir is mocking and pointed, something he only calls me when annoyed, but I hold up a hand for more time as I stare at her for another moment.

"One last thing. And I don't ask for information in return." My hands lift to unclasp my cloak as her eyes follow my every movement. "When you come for your prey…" She swallows as I drape the fabric over my arm and step close to the cage. Only a foot away. "Take only that which you came for. The woman chained to him is innocent." I toss the heavy fur cloak in, careful to avoid touching the filthy bars. I've barely taken a single step back before her hand has claimed the cloth to wind it around her body like a cocoon. Still warm from my body, I'm sure it feels like a raging fire compared to the icy air now raising goosebumps on my neck. Potent relief blooms on her face, the first soft emotion she's shown, before her closed eyes snap open. The only thing left to see are those vivid eyes peeking out from a gap in the cloth.

"Rare for a man to bargain not for his own life, but for another."

A rugged smile cuts across my face. "I'd consider it an honor if you came for me, Roux." A flash of yellowed white is all I see of a smile before it is time to go. My head tilts toward her as a sign of respect. Dangerous as she is, she's just as magnificent as that mountain lion that stalked us in the woods, just as admirable as the vipers in the garden. "Until next time, Roux." I straighten and gesture for the guards to walk out which they are more than happy to do. Before I walk after them, I hesitate one more moment. I can feel those viper eyes burning into me even though I don't turn around. "Never break," I murmur before following the fading light through the door and down the winding stairs.

*   *   *

The heavy door that separates the world from the prisoners shuts behind me and I take a deep breath of the clean, crisp air. It's not even noon yet, which is the time I prefer to get up. The stone guards don't move to swallow me and something in me uncoils at the fact. My eyes take in the clear blue sky before Henry steps forward to impede the view with a shake of his head. His skin is dark as the sodden earth beneath our feet with eyes a few shades lighter. "That was foolish." I shoot him a look out of the corner of my eye while swallowing a heavy breath. Sometimes it still surprises me when I glance over at him and find him a couple of inches below eye level. I'm used to the days when we were shoulder to shoulder, but as we grew, he broadened while I shot up. He adds on a sarcastic, "*Sir*?" just to be an asshole.

I roll my eyes. "It's fine. What is she going to do with a cloak, anyway? Escape by twisting the threads into a yarn key?" I chuckle and bend down to scoop up the last bit of pure snow from the muddy ground to rub over my gloves to clean them. The mountain is nestled high in the mountains, so while winter in the valley is mild, this place is perpetually caught in ice and high winds. My nose wrinkles at the state of my filth-covered boots. I might as well burn these clothes. There's no chance I'll ever get the stench from this place out of them. Henry sighs and follows me down the cobblestones towards the bridge. On the other side of it lies our carriage waiting to ferry us back to the estate as soon as my father is done talking to the warden beside the doors. No doubt plotting. *Again.*

The black monolith behind me looms like a shadow with small carts scattered around the bottom carrying cargo to and from the far-off city. Soldiers are stationed here year-round, so products have to be ferried in or else they'll waste away along with their charges. Cobblestones surround the prison in a u shape embracing the towering stone while the opposite edge drops down in a sheer cliff. The only way across is by the drawbridge leading to the road down the mountains.

Gods, I hate it here. The cold bites at any bit of skin left in the open air like an arrow finding a vulnerability in armor. Especially without my cloak. Yet even with the frigid air, I don't regret the choice. It was already soiled by the warden and the look of relief on that woman's face was worth it. As is the possibility of earning her mercy. Even if she is Roux.

My head shakes at the fact. She was different than I'd imagined. In truth, she can't be more than twenty-five. The same age as me. Younger, more than likely. To be that age and to have already wreaked so much havoc…I wonder what drove her to it. Perhaps even more interesting, how was she caught after years of evasion?

Henry opens his mouth and I ready myself for the lecture, but he doesn't get the chance to say a word. A blood-curdling scream rips through the air and I turn around just in time to see a man being vaulted out of a high window. "Shit," I swear as the body slams into the cobblestones with a couple dozen cracks and a big *splat*! My eyes lift back to the window to find Roux leaning against the window frame with a wide grin on her face. She wiggles her fingers at me in an affectionate wave before she vanishes back into the prison with a sweep of my cloak. "*Shit*." I rush towards the fallen body, but of course, nothing can be done. The guard was dead the instant he hit the pavement.

There's a moment of silence and shock before the world bursts into noise and chaos. The warden is shouting commands as traders mount their carts or escape in their carriages in a mad rush. I yank Henry out of the way of a cart as the horses swerve towards the bridge. "We have to go!" He yells above the din and I nod, pushing him towards the bridge. We sprint across only to come to a screeching halt in the middle.

"Son of a bitch." My father slides into our carriage, smooth as a cat, then waves the driver on without a glance behind him. Henry snags the back of my shirt before shoving us both to the side and nearly off the edge of the bridge to avoid another wildly careening carriage. The next moment, one of the wheels breaks off and the carriage slides to the edge of the gorge. The horses whinny in panic as it tugs them backward. There are only moments to decide what's to be done and I don't hesitate. Metal sings as I draw my sword and bolt to the ties.

"What are you doing?" Henry shouts as I mount the piece of wood between the panicking beasts. I sway on my feet before bringing my sword down on the straps connecting the horses to the cart. Vaguely, I hear the carriage door open as someone shouts for help, but there's nothing to be done for them. They're too far away to reach and in too precarious a position. The horses though, don't have to die. Two swings cut loose one side and luckily one swing slices through the other. They bolt forward, free, while I leap to the side towards Henry as the carriage falls into the canyon. My hands scramble for Henry's as I dive, but my aim is a little off. I slide toward the deadly drop and our fingers graze one another as I pass.

Screams rip through the air as the carriage shatters on the jagged rocks and I hope I'm not destined for the same fate. Fear and panic slice through me as my hips slide from solid ground into open air just as Henry grabs onto my hand. I hold on for dear life as Henry manages to draw his dagger, then slams it down into the wood of the bridge to act as an anchor. "Pull, Silva!" For once, I obey and use him as leverage to tug my body back up onto solid ground. I've never been so grateful to be covered in dirt and mud. But there's no time to feel relief.

My hands take fistfuls of Henry's shirt as I tug him to his feet. "Find a cart, carriage, or horse, and get out of here. Do not wait for me and do not turn back!"

His brown eyes go wide. "But, Sil—"

"That's an order!" I shove him in the opposite direction as we move back across the bridge towards the prison. We'll have better chances of finding something separately. I only stop a moment to snag my sword from the ground and sheathe it before continuing to run back towards the prison. There are still stragglers trying to get away as fast as possible, but many left things behind in their haste. My eyes zero in on a cart filled with hay and a pale horse shifting uneasily in front of it. I make for it while hoping this cart's wheels are sturdier than the last.

Screams still cut through the air. There are wails from people bent over the bodies of trampled friends and family, but I don't pause. I sprint to the cart and look over the harness on the horse. The buckles are complicated and I don't have the time to undo all of them. Not to mention these ropes would take forever to cut through. It'll have to stay connected to the cart for now. I sling myself into the seat and tug the rope keeping the horse stationary from its post.

"Raise the bridge!" The warden's sharp command rings over the yard just as I snap the reins for the horse to move. It seems the mare has been waiting to be free as she bursts into a full sprint towards the slowly rising draw bridge.

20

Henry appears on a brown stallion and makes it across with barely a jump, then turns back to wait for me. Exactly against my orders. "Come on!" He waves, urgency lining his every limb. I snap the reins again and the horse snorts but pushes harder.

It'll be close. Terribly close.

"Come on, girl, come on." The mare's sides heave with every breath, muscles flexing, nostrils flaring, until we hit the edge. We become weightless as she jumps and all the air in my chest leaves me in one sudden *whoosh*. The canyon below stretches out to our sides with the jagged walls jeering and the crystal river miles down glinting in the patchy sunlight. For a moment, it feels like my soul leaves my body.

Then it slams back in as we crash into the ground on the other side with barely an inch to spare. The wheels clatter onto the road as we swerve towards a curve before everything settles and we continue in one piece. The horse slows to a trot as we move further away from the cliffside with Henry keeping pace alongside. I take a look back at the prison, then immediately empty the contents of my stomach into the hay laid in the cart behind me.

Disgust fills me at the taste and smell. So much so that I nearly vomit again, but I force myself to turn back around and urge the horse to go a little faster to keep the breeze blowing the stench behind us. I address Henry to keep myself distracted, "I told you to go."

His eyes roll. "And would you like me to list all the times you've disobeyed my orders in chronological or alphabetical order?" I shake my head as he pulls ahead slightly. "I'd never leave you in a place like that, Sil." His voice has a rare edge in it and his jaw flexes as I glance over at him. I'm sure we're thinking of the same memory.

"Well. Too bad we can't say the same of my father." I tease and he scoffs, but the air around us lightens.

"We'll see what he has to say for himself when we get back."

"No." I refuse without an ounce of levity in my voice. He looks over at me with furrowed brows and mouth open. "Don't even think about it. Nothing good ever comes from confronting my father."

"Sil, you could have died. Or worse, you could be stuck on that mountain with a loose lunatic!" Henry's voice raises and his horse snorts disagreeably.

I wave an unconcerned hand. "But I didn't and I'm not. That'll be punishment enough for him." Henry huffs but doesn't push the issue. After his temper dies down and he remembers what happens when anyone moves against my father, he'll agree with me. We fall back into companionable silence. A few minutes pass of shocked quiet as we move down the mountain and absorb everything that just happened. Yet when the silence breaks, it isn't Henry or I who shatter it.

A sharp point presses into my lower back. "Turn or stop the horse and you die." Goosebumps burst to life over my entire body as that voice I only heard from within a cell speaks right beside my ear. "I'm still debating killing you anyway since you just puked on me." Her voice is light, but irritation colors each word. I glance to Henry trotting beside us and the fear and shock on his face says it all. Regret fills my stomach along with more bile, but I swallow both.

"We didn't exactly realize we had a guest." I posit, fighting a shiver as she laughs.

"Well, I do have you to thank for giving me an opportunity." She holds out a shimmering piece of metal in front of me that I slowly realize is a piece of the clasp from my cloak. The perfect tool for picking a lock. I'm an idiot.

Henry is more than likely thinking the same thing even as he defends me. "Then perhaps you can repay him by removing the dagger." She hums, pondering the decision, before I feel her body and dagger pull back. I snap around to look at her. A dagger about the size of her forearm stays pointed at me and her other hand clings to a sword belt that looks a lot like—

I glance down at my hips and find my sword is gone. My jaw locks as I look back at her while she grins, settling back into a clean patch of hay. Her eyes are half-shuttered to keep out the bright sun and blood is splattered over the few rags covering her, but a wide smile stays on her face. "Hello, toys."

Chapter Two

Predator

Roux

I'm in the sun again.

Even with the layers of dirt and blood blocking it from hitting my skin, I can feel its warmth. Gods, I'll never take the sun for granted again. The light is almost blinding after two years in the near dark, but I can see well enough to watch the shock ripple across the men's faces. "If it's any assurance, I've no desire to take your lives at the moment."

"Already had your fill today? You caused plenty of deaths back at the prison." The soldier spits before the lord's son scolds him with a single look. One might guess that it's the silent command from a superior to an officer, but I'd say they aren't like a high-born and servant. There's real worry on the soldier's face. More than if he were simply concerned about employment. These two are more akin to friends and if that look is any indication, they've been friends for a long time. It feels so good to stretch my mind again, to read people like I used to.

I shrug a shoulder. "Only a few at my hand. You can blame me for the rest, but that's rather unfair considering I wasn't driving the carts that ran people over." I believe his cheeks darken even though his skin is already dark as a chestnut. His jaw flexes, but he says nothing more as his friend holds out a hand to tame him. My eyes shift to the lord's son as I spin the dagger in my hands, letting it threaten them for me.

"What if I turn the cart around instead?" Even squinting, I can see the brilliant red of his short hair. The color isn't like wine or blood, but shimmers and gleams like shades of copper or a fox's rich coat. It stops a few inches from his scalp while the back and sides are trimmed a bit shorter. He has a straight nose, clearly never broken, and an angular chin under a sensuous mouth. The very look of him is high-born even without the fine clothes and perfect posture. Jealousy strikes me at his sun-kissed skin covered in freckles. He is…disgustingly beautiful.

My head cocks as I consider him, unblinking. "You'd be dead before the horse turned its head and your man would never risk your life." The soldier beside us swallows, but neither of us blinks. Thoughts fly through eyes so blue and clear they almost seem transparent.

"And if we shove you out onto the road? You're weak. We could overpower you."

"I did just escape a high-security prison."

"But not with brute force." His eyes narrow at me while I flick dirt out from under my fingernails with my blade and nothing but innocence in my eyes. "You no longer have my cloak. I'd guess you made a show of pushing that guard out the window so they'd see what you were wearing, then ditched it. Swapped it for a guard's so you'd blend in with the others storming the prison." A smile tugs on the corner of my lips. Smart. Very smart.

He copies the movement even with the fear in his eyes, taking it as confirmation that he's right. "I was sorry to get rid of such a fine gift, but I'm afraid it was necessary." I'm regretting the loss as the cold of the mountains sinks into my bones, but it's better than the cold walls of that cell. "Once again, you have no weapon. I could kill you before you made a move towards me."

He scans me for a long minute before holding out his hand to his companion. "Cloak."

The man blinks, opening his mouth to object, then shuts it at his friend's imploring look. He hands him his cloak with curled lips and the lord's son considers it a moment. "Seems there's a deal to be made here, Roux."

I raise a brow. I'm not particularly fond of deals, but I am weak and depending on what he offers me, it might be easier to have them around. The best cover is one I can wear in plain sight. He takes my silence as permission to go on. "I'll keep you with us. Feed you, house you, clothe you. Get you a bath." It's a struggle to keep silent instead of snapping at him to get to the point, but I let my mind imagine the simple pleasure of the few things he listed. I'd kill for a bath alone.

There's a slight smile on his face as if he can see my longing and I scowl to cover it up. "And what would I have to do for all these lovely things?"

He takes a breath, drawing things out for dramatic effect. Typical lord's son. "Simple. Kill my father."

The man beside us makes a loud noise of disagreement that the son rolls his eyes at. "Come now, Henry. He's a cruel and greedy master who is running the estate and its people into the ground. It'll be ruined in two years. One, even." Henry does nothing to combat this other than locking his jaw, so those clear eyes return to me. Caution and curiosity lurk in my heart as he goes on. "Do that and leave nothing to implicate me, my family, or Henry, and bring harm to no one else living on my estate. Afterward, you will be free to leave without a word from me or mine. Besides," He half-smiles, "I have a feeling this is a goal you'd like to accomplish anyway and I've just made it easy." He holds out the cloak to me, a peace offering, but I spare another moment to stare at him.

This is a golden opportunity. There's no arguing that, but there's also no guarantee of an honest agreement. Betrayal is rife

26

in the world. I know that firsthand. Yet I see no ulterior motive in his eyes. Just as there was none when he gave me his cloak in the prison. "Why haven't you killed him yourself?" He blinks, surprised that I've asked.

Still, he doesn't balk and hesitates only a moment before answering. "I don't want to get my clothes dirty." I snort. There are plenty of ways to kill without getting dirty, but I accept the answer. For now.

I take the offered bundle with a sharp smile. "Done." I'd planned on killing his father anyway, but he seems to know that as he smiles back. There may be no guarantee of an honest agreement, but I gave him no assurance on my end either.

"Good. We're going to get you a bath first. You reek." He turns away but keeps his body angled towards me with his leg coming up to rest on the seat beside him. I'm flattered that he doesn't turn his back on me.

I wrap the cloak tight around my shivering body, popping up the hood to shield my eyes from the sun as well as my face from any passers-by on the road. "You try sitting in shit and dirt for two years. See if you come out still smelling like jasmine and sandalwood." I can still smell his scent from wearing his cloak, the sweet aroma clinging to my skin like drying mud. The other man's scent is more natural—the product of everyday life; the salty tang of sweat, the musty smell of a barn, and the slightest hint of citrus more than likely from aftershave.

His head turns slightly. "Are you an Enhanced?" An Enhanced; a being who has magic swirling in their blood making them better, stronger, and faster than any other. Even their senses are sharper.

I shoot him a critical look as Henry's gaze turns more concerned. Funny, considering one look at the two and one would think the broader man with rippling muscles would be more inclined to risks and fights. Rather than the almost gangly lord's son, anyway. "What fun would it be if I told you?" His head turns a bit more and I grin. "But I wouldn't want you to think my skills were the gift of some higher power. No. I'm not Enhanced. Just naturally talented." I wink at him while his man frowns. I slide closer so I'm tucked in the corner across from the lord's son. There is muscle there. Leaner, more athletic muscle rather than the kind used to protect. He shuffles to the side a bit and my first guess is to get away from me, but then he flicks his chin to the cliffs ahead where the mountains part.

"It'll take us about a day to get out of the mountains. We should hit the foot by nightfall and there's a river not too far off the road. Chilly, but warm enough to bathe in for a short period of time." His nose wrinkles and I fight the urge to shove him off the cart.

"You have a real problem with dirt." A strangled laugh barely makes its way out of Henry's throat that he tries to turn into a cough. He shoots a half-wary look my way as if I'll kill him for laughing. I wiggle my fingers at him instead.

The redhead sighs. "I like to be clean. I like my fine clothes that cost a lot of money to be clean. I don't know why people think it's such a big deal."

I pick up a piece of hay and poke his hip with it, grinning when he winces as if it were a blade. "I'm not sure if you've noticed, but the world is kind of…dirty." He rolls his eyes while Henry seems to be fighting a smile.

"I understand that. Hard work and toil are things I'm not unused to, nor do I shy away from them. But excuse me if I prefer lounging in the sun on my balcony or walking through the gardens instead." Memories of me doing the same drift through my head and after years of waiting and loneliness and darkness, I find myself looking forward to something.

A few minutes pass with the soft sound of hooves hitting dirt filling the silence. These mountains are all black rock with long falls into pine-filled valleys or ravines. Not much to look at even though I drink it all in as if it were the finest painting, but I have more interesting entertainment. My head tilts to look up at the lord's son. He's tall, even sitting down. From the image of him standing outside my cell, I'd say he's just over six feet. Four or five inches above my middling height. His gaze flits over me watching him before he rolls his shoulders. "So...what am I to call you? Since we'll be stuck together for a while now." Nerves lace his words, but I take it as a compliment.

"Give something to get something."

He sighs. "Silvanus. As for my title, I prefer to go by my mother's name Dinnsesk." He glances over at me with a small smile. "You're welcome to call me Lord Silva Dinnsesk." My eyes roll, but the corner of my lips flick up. His eyes remain on me expectantly and I turn to look at a vulture gliding over the pines a little way off.

"You already call me Roux."

He shrugs a shoulder. "Yes, but I doubt you want me calling you that with people around."

I think for a moment as I spin my dagger in my hands to catch the glinting sunlight. "Call me whatever you like." He turns a little in his seat with his mouth open and I stop my ministrations to smirk coldly at him. "There are few alive that know my true name, lord's son, and the only reason they aren't dead is because I haven't had the time to go after them. Yet." I was caught before I could complete what I set out to do. The reminder sets my teeth on edge and he seems to realize it's wiser not to push me.

His man shakes his head at the exchange, so I let my hand idly reach out towards him. "Are you feeling left out, soldier?" He jerks his reins to guide the horse away from me and, luckily, he isn't on the cliffside lest the sharp movement drive him right over. His movements are sharp and controlled though. I know I'm right in assuming he's been a soldier. No doubt he was called back home to babysit this lord's son.

"Of course, we've been excluding you." Silva grins at the warning glance the man gives him. "This is Henry Cascarra. More than a pretty face, he also has rather nice hair."

Humor flits through me, so sudden and shocking that it takes me a moment to respond. "Stunning," I add, watching the man look up to the blue sky with a long-suffering sigh.

"Insufferable." But his hand reaches up to run over his soft, golden brown curls as Silva glances at me with humor dancing in his eyes. Gods, it's been so long since I've seen something like that. Felt it. I slide so my back is to the side of the cart and shut my eyes while turning my head to the sun. My senses remain sharp in case one of the men reaches for my weapons, but neither tries.

The ride down the mountains is cold and quiet, but all that matters is that I'm free. Free. Free. *Free.*

I finally start to thaw only for night to begin drawing its dark curtain over the world. The chill hardly registers since I'm taken with the first sunset I've seen in...well. A long time. We stop a mile or so from the road under a towering pine that has covered the ground with discarded needles. A slow-moving river lies only a few meters away colored gold in the setting sun. I'd be jumping into it at a full sprint if I could run at all. Silva was right. The only way I got out of that place was by disguise. I barely have the strength to stand, much less fight. Or run.

My knees nearly give out as I drop out of the cart and use it to hold me up as I walk toward the pale horse. Sword and dagger tied securely to my thin waist; I take my time disconnecting her from the cart. The men keep their distance, but I feel their eyes on me. Under the guise of guiding the horse, I let her ferry me to the water while using her as a crutch. A moment passes as I look her over, feeling her muscles, her breath. She stands between the men and me, so they can't see my appraisal. My hands slide over her moonlight skin as I feel how strong she is and breathe in that distinct horse smell. Sweat left dark lines where the cart was hooked to her, turning her pale hair a dark grey. She's far too strong and her back is still straight, so I doubt she's usually pulling carts. Probably a filly they hooked up to break her in. I trace the sweat marks while thinking of how strong she must be to have ferried people and cargo to the prison, then still had the energy to get us here. She's a fighter.

I don't speak, but let my hand rest on her neck. My skin isn't far off from the pale color of her. At least, under all the filth and grime of the prison. "She doesn't have a name." Silva's voice is soft as he slides into place on her other side. His clear eyes reflect the gold of the sky and the water as if they were mirrors. He slips off his black gloves and tucks them in the pocket of his forest green pants before running a hand over her flank. "Or if she does, I didn't exactly pay attention to that when we were rushing to escape." Something else this beast and I have in common then.

I run my hand down her neck again. "I'll name her," I state, meeting Silva's gaze as he glances over at me. "She's mine." Surprise flits through his eyes before the corner of his lips tugs up.

Henry sighs heavily as he attends to his own horse a few feet away. "She belongs to the prison. Or to whatever sod lost her bringing goods there."

My sharp eyes cut over to the soldier. "You could say *I'm* the property of the prison, dear Henry." He swallows and busies himself with his work while Silva smirks.

The future lord shrugs. "We have more than enough room in the stables. I don't see a problem with it."

"I wasn't looking for permission," I snap.

"Of course not." He inclines his head towards me before backing up towards Henry. My teeth grit as I watch him, then I relax and go back to watching the mare.

She bends to take a long drink and doesn't seem keen to move away, so I sink to the ground with my dagger falling to the grass beside me. I shove my hands into the water, gasping softly at the chill. Running water, no matter the temperature, feels amazing.

My hands cup the molten gold in my hands and I drink less than I want. I'll have to drink and eat carefully to restore my body to its former glory. Bathing, however, can be done at any time. I dismiss the background noise of the boys talking about a trip into town as I fold up my cloak with the dagger tucked carefully into the folds. Then nothing can stop me as I slide into the water.

Small pebbles dig into my thinly covered skin, but I think of them like little brushes scraping dirt off me. "You'll want to wait—" Silva attempts and stops himself as I pay him no heed. The water is only about waist deep, so I'm up to my shoulders when I crouch. Only then do I turn back to the men. The lord's son is staring at me with a raised brow and amused smirk on his face while his friend shakes his head disapprovingly. "I was planning on getting you some soap."

I wave them off. "Please do. It'll take far more than one dip to clean me." My hands slide over my body twice before I realize the rags covering me are also gone. Seems dirt was the only thing keeping them on. "I'll need clothes as well." Irritation flits over Henry's face, then vanishes as my eyes narrow at him. I tip my head back into the calm water so my hair can soak. All sound narrows to the soft rushing of water past my ears and even as I start to shiver again from the cold, I realize it might be my favorite sound in the world. My head snaps to the side when my horse turns her head to find Silva kneeling by the waterside. The opposite side of my weapons and cloak, but my eyes will be on him until he leaves that spot.

"What do you want? From town, I mean." He keeps his eyes on my face even though most of my naked body is more than likely on display. I'm sure I'm not much to look at right now, but the respect he shows me makes me...not like him exactly. Tolerate him, I suppose. I sit up and let my long, matted hair cover what's left of my breasts.

That question...such a privilege. What do I want? Many, many things, but I can settle for a small few for now. "A brush." I start, going on when he waves a hand. "Clothes. A child's will more than likely fit better. Food. Potatoes, apples, and meats would be best. Unscented soap." When it seems I'm finished, Silva nods and turns to Henry who crosses his arms.

"I should be the one to stay, Sil."

Silva sighs and stands to face his friend fully. "I'm more of a public figure, my clothes will attract attention, and I said you're the one going." Henry doesn't move. "Fine, I'll go." He grabs the small sack of jingling coins before heading to Henry's brown gelding. "Roux, promise not to eat him while I'm gone?"

I flash my teeth at the soldier and wiggle my fingers. "I make no such promise."

"Alright, alright." Henry all but leaps for the reins of his horse, taking the money as he swings onto its back with an effortless grace that I envy. "I'll return soon." He promises and glances at me as if it's also a warning. I lax back into the water while trying to tug my fingers through the thick tangles in my hair. Thundering hooves tell me of his leaving and after one last scrub, I leave the river in deference to the fire Silva is building. All I've got is my cloak, so I wrap it tight around me before sitting as close to the fire as I can get. My hair is heavy with water and matts and it's extremely tempting to chop it all off, but that can wait. Silva has loosely tied my horse up to the tree behind me and she lets loose a high-pitched whinny as if in protest.

"She's certainly got a pair of lungs." He mutters while stoking the fledgling flames.

The words run through my head a few times before I smirk. "She should. Her name is Banshee."

Clear eyes flick to mine before he chuckles. "The harbinger of death. Well, no one can say you don't have a sense of humor." My smile grows as he settles across from me with the fire dancing in those mirror eyes. "You've been starved before." Positive emotions vanish at the statement and my smile disappears. "The foods you said to get. Specific."

"Perhaps you're more than a pretty face, after all." I coo, watching irritation with my tone war with gratification at the words. High-borns are so easy to play with. Seems not everything about the world has changed. "But you have no idea what you're talking about." My words are ice cold and he huffs at the assumption.

"And why should I not?"

I lean closer to the fire so it flickers in my eyes. "I can tell. You've never known hunger. True hunger. The kind that strikes you so deep you feel sick, the kind where your stomach turns on you, feasting on itself, your muscles, your body, because there's nothing else. The kind of hunger that has you pondering whether it's worth it to try and eat a finger or a toe simply to stop the pangs of pain shooting through you from your empty gut." My fingers dance over my toes under the cloak wrapped tight around me, counting them one by one. Silva's face is pensive and his eyes are wide as he stares at me. My head shakes. "There's a look that others have when they see someone starving when they've suffered the same. You don't have it."

I relax back and close my eyes for a moment to shut out the pain still lacing my body. It's sharper now after all my activities. *Soon*, I assure it. Soon we'll have real food instead of stale bread, oats, or crumbs. Silva tugs in a breath and my eyes snap open to see him nodding. "You're right." I blink, surprised. "I've never known hunger like that, but we have met." His eyes flick to mine and I remain silent to simply listen. "There was a farmer on our land who was falsely imprisoned. When he was released, he looked thin as a wraith and had to follow a special diet to regain his strength. The same food you asked for were the first things healers gave him."

My head cocks and my eyes narrow as silence stretches between us. Usually, a person would shuffle or look away, giving away their discomfort or fear. Silva doesn't back down. In the prison, I could practically smell his fear, yet he didn't back away.

"How did your farmer get out?" I doubt it was in the same fashion as me.

His eyes flit to the fire gaining strength between us. "I took the rest of his punishment. Two weeks in his cell." I keep my expression smooth, but I know he notices the way I go still. A sardonic smile appears on his face. "He'd already served two months without my knowledge. When I found out, I had to get him out. He wouldn't have lasted another week. Much less two."

I push myself back against the trunk of the towering pine, too exhausted to sit up anymore and hating how my vision blurs from my lack of strength. My fingers itch to spin my dagger between my fingers, but instead, I keep it close along with the sword. "You must have loved a grimy cell."

He laughs, dry and short. "It was my own personal Under." His head shakes before his eyes lift to meet mine once again. "And I was only there for two weeks. I can't imagine longer." Like two years.

"No, I doubt you can." Offense doesn't appear on his face this time. He only watches me curiously with more questions swirling in his eyes. I ask him one instead as I fold my thin legs under me. "Why aren't you afraid of me?"

"I am." His response is immediate and without an ounce of shame.

A genuine smile tugs at my lips as I shake my head. "Yes, but it doesn't rule you. You're aware of the fear you should feel because of who I am. You're mindful. You aren't afraid." At this point, I know the difference.

Silva takes a deep breath, frowning as he picks a speck of dirt off his white shirt stained with mud. "I've always had respect for predators. The skillset they have. They hunt and kill to protect, to defend, to eat." He looks me over and shrugs a shoulder. "It would be different if you were a murderer. A killer without reason. But you're a predator. I figure, so long as I don't give you a reason to kill me, we'll coexist."

"And how do you know what I kill for, lord's son?" The question is loaded, but his expression remains curious.

"I don't. I just know you kill for something."

"How?"

"You haven't killed me yet." A smile cuts across his face and I allow myself to return it.

Sighing, I look up to the stars starting to peek out of the fading blue of the sky. "I have no intentions of killing you or your man," I admit, sliding a finger down the flat edge of my blade. "But if that changes, you'll be dead before you realize it."

Chapter Three

Enhanced

Silvanus

She isn't how I thought she'd be. Out of her cell, I figured she'd taunt us mercilessly or remain completely silent to unnerve us. Which she does. But she also keeps up conversations and when we aren't talking, she seems taken with the environment. She stares at the sky, runs her hands over the grass, over the dirt, in the water, and takes a deep breath every few minutes as if memorizing the world all over again. It wouldn't surprise me if that's exactly what she's doing. The torture she's been through…I wonder if she hasn't truly seen the world in two years. The soldiers and the warden balked at coming close to the bars of her cage. I doubt they took her on walks outside.

I take the time to look her over now that the water has washed away some of the grime. In addition to her skeletal frame, she's covered head to toe in scars. On her face alone there's an elongated x under her left eye and another line on the right that cuts from just under her nose down past her barely pink lips. From the barest look I got when she was in the river, those are the least of her collection.

It's still a shock to find this legend can act so…human. She's good at hiding it, but I'd be blind not to miss the light in her green eyes when Henry lays her bundle of goods in front of her. He's quick to move back to my side as if he'd laid a bomb and I only chuckle at him a little. Food comes first and she eats slowly, conscious that she has to pace her weak body lest it purge the food the instant it slides down her gullet. Her hands tremble with each mouthful she brings to her lips and I fight a surprised smile when she sneaks Banshee an apple.

Afterward, she washes her hands before sliding thin fingers over a mahogany tunic. Black pants lie underneath with brown boots and a simple bone comb to the side. A white bar of soap and a toothbrush are the last of her treasures along with a small blue bottle. Her hand freezes as it hovers over the glass, then plucks it from the grouping.

"It's only a ten-pound potion," Henry says as he settles down at my side to eat his own food. "Figured you'll need to gain weight quickly with all that's planned." He shoots me a firm, disapproving look before diving into his food. He may not approve of my arrangement with Roux, but he's a good man who would give anyone the shirt off his back if they needed it. Well, maybe not if Roux needed it.

She twists and turns the bottle in her hands before unplugging the cork. "Thoughtful of you, Henry, but I don't need strength to kill someone." Her voice is sickly sweet as her eyes flit to Henry's food as he gulps audibly. My eyes dart to my own food before I turn my focus completely on her. She tilts the drink until a single drop falls onto a red-capped mushroom beside her. A test. To see that the potion maker wasn't lying or that we hadn't poisoned her. There's a little twinge in my gut that she thinks we'd attempt it, but of course, she would. I doubt she survived this long by being trusting.

A few seconds pass and I'm relatively sure that Henry isn't breathing before the mushroom triples in size. My friend deflates in relief and the assassin nods before downing the entire bottle. There are potions for nearly everything; weight gain, weight loss, invisibility, and even invulnerability for the rare few who can afford it. Magic is rarely found in people, and even rarer are those who can wield it. In the time of the gods, magic was prevalent, but that time has long passed. Since the gods left this plane and humanity ruined the guardians they left behind, magic has slowly died out. The few that have a little in their blood discovered that while they can't cast spells, they can add a little magic to potions. Usually for an exorbitant price. None last forever either, but the better the potioneer, the longer they last.

I watch Roux carefully as she sets the bottle back in the bundle, waiting for her to spontaneously gain ten pounds before she catches me and snorts. "It doesn't happen like the mushroom, Silva. It's more gradual."

My body laxes in its vigilance as I shrug. "I've never seen someone take one before." Although, I have seen people take weight loss potions in court. The process isn't a pretty one. Their skin turns sickly, faces go gaunt, and some turn so weak they can barely stand. I saw a girl die from one not too many years ago. The image she saw in the mirror didn't match what she thought of herself, so she just kept taking more. Until she couldn't.

Roux sniffs the soap before nodding satisfactorily at the lack of smell before her eyes cut to me as she continues. "Adding is easier than removing. The body takes to it like hunger to food. Especially an emaciated one like mine." After our conversation earlier, the words have more weight than they did before. She heaves herself up by a tree branch while holding the cloak loosely around her. "I'll gain the weight over the next few hours without ill effect. Ten pounds isn't much. I'll have to gain a lot more for it to be noticeable." And for it to make a difference, I'd guess.

I watch her carefully stagger over to the river, dropping my eyes when she drops her cloak before sliding into the water. Her earlier dip barely removed any of the grime covering her, but did wash away the blood from earlier today. Hopefully, this time will be more fruitful. I find myself curious about how she truly looks. The face and body, emaciated as they may be, of the fabled Roux.

"What are you thinking, Silva?"

I face Henry's bushy, furrowed brows. We'd been together since we were teenagers, put in place by my father to try to keep me out of trouble and preserve his only heir. The result was me pulling Henry into whatever trouble I stirred up, but he's managed to keep me alive through all of it. Although things got a little dicey during his year away as a soldier. His crooked nose is evidence of punches he's taken for me and I believe he shattered that square jaw of his once. A lovely scar slices diagonally off his right cheek and I've repeatedly told him it adds to his good looks. Even if I don't carry signs of it, anyone who thinks I'm not as loyal to him as he is to me is a fool.

"I'm thinking that I'm solving a problem." My voice is hushed, not that I'd particularly care if Roux heard, but Henry seems more inclined to secrecy. "My father is a drain on the estate. He throws money to the side like slop to the pigs, money that we need to provide for the estate and our tenants." Heat sneaks into my voice and Henry nods, but his disapproving expression doesn't shift. He'd seen first-hand the golden encrusted carriage my father ordered, the ridiculous expensive paintings he'd ordered just because of the high cost, and not to mention the jewels he fingers when bored.

"But kill him, Sil? You want that on your conscience?" His deep-set brown eyes glitter like amber with the flames dancing inside. No matter what, I know he'll back me, but I know this is him showing concern for me.

I clap him on the shoulder. "It's something I can live with." I hope. "He didn't mind if I was killed earlier today. Why should I care about his life?"

"Because you're a better man than him, Sil." He levels me with a look and I take a deep breath, letting the playfulness and teasing fall away so he can see how serious I am.

"That's why it has to happen." My hand on his shoulder squeezes. "I'm not holding a grudge because he's been a terrible father. I'm not doing this because he doesn't care if I live or die. He is killing the estate. This means all the people we employ, all our tenants, the servants, will lose everything. Not only their jobs but the land they grew up on and their dreams for the future. Everything will be gone." I let my hand fall as I straighten up a bit. "I've tried speaking with him for years to no avail. The only solution is to remove him." Not to mention the other problems that will be solved with him gone.

A teasing smile makes its way back onto my face. "Besides, I'm not the one who is going to do it." We glance over to Roux in the water yanking her brush savagely through mangled knots in her hair. I hope she uses more finesse than that when we arrive at my estate.

Henry flicks my ear, snapping my attention away from Roux and back to him. "And that absolves us of guilt?"

"I feel no guilt in protecting my people and their livelihood from a cruel, greedy man with no thought of anyone but himself." My words are sharp, but once they leave my mouth I soften. "What are you thinking, Hen?"

His pouty lips screw up to the side. "I feel no fondness for your father and wouldn't mind him dead, but you orchestrating it doesn't bode well. Neither does releasing Roux out into the world with no recourse." Wariness drifts through his eyes as he glances over at her.

I shrug a shoulder. "Technically, I'm not orchestrating anything." He spares me an irritated glance for the technicality while I go on. "I don't know anything about what she's going to do. Just the result. As for no recourse, she spent two years in that dungeon. Afterward… afterward isn't my problem."

"Uh, it kind of is because whatever havoc she causes once released is directly connected to us." He insists, but I can't raise a bit of concern about it. The world is a dark place. Maybe it deserves to have someone terrorize it in return for the havoc it wreaks.

I pat my friend's shoulder again before laying down beside the fire. "Sleep. We'll be home soon."

He sighs. "That's not reassuring." A grin cuts across my face as my eyes shut listening to the water slaking off Roux a few meters away.

*　　*　　*

When I wake, the sky is tinted a dusty blue as dawn peaks over the horizon. I can barely see it, however, because Roux's light body is hovering over me with her knife against my throat. Green eyes edged with urgency and flecked with gold appraise me as I freeze. Panic slices through me and I start thinking if I can wake Henry before she gets to him—

But she removes the knife and holds the flat side against her lips before she glances to my right. Tentatively, I follow her gaze into the early morning mist but see nothing. My lips part as I turn back to her only to find she's gone. Looking around gives me no clue as to where and even her bundle of goods has vanished.

Still, I'm not one to ignore a warning.

I kick Henry's foot and swallow a laugh when he sits up, sword in hand like he's been holding it all night. "What—" I shake my head and he falls silent. He glances over to where Roux settled down for the night and his eyes widen at her not being there. Banshee whinnies quietly, so my head turns back to where Roux looked earlier.

They slip from the mist like ghosts, or like the banshee Roux's mare is aptly named after. White horses gleam in the morning light with completely pristine coats. No dapples or imperfections like Banshee and the perfection feels wrong. Unnatural. All riders are dressed in the pale color as well and their bone white hoods are pulled low over their faces. There's nothing but darkness within the hoods, not a flicker of color or a face, and their hands are covered in white gloves.

Enhanced.

I'd only ever seen groups like this once or twice as they passed the estate hunting their target. Never have I been this close and I don't particularly want to be this close right now. If they were to find out we had something to do with Roux's escape…I'm not sure what would happen. There are stories of them sweeping through and taking only those they were sent after, but there are other, darker tales of massacres left in their wake. They never leave any mess—just bodies laying still with eyes staring endlessly upward.

The five Enhanced come to a stop on the edge of our campsite as Henry and I hurry to stand. "We seek a girl." A female voice drifts through the air without seeming to come from any of the figures before us. The air feels charged with energy as if the beings before us hold all of it within themselves. Like storm clouds holding back lightning. The Enhanced in the middle, the leader I'd guess, has silver lacing wrapping around the edge of her sleeves and hood. Almost like a crown and bracers.

I stand quickly, back straight, sleep forgotten as my instincts prick up in the presence of danger. "I am Silvanus Dinnsesk, son of Lord Lurec. There are no women here. We're headed for Ayncuarst Estate only a few days ride from here." I try not to shift on my feet with unease as the riders dismount and begin to search our meager campsite. All are careful not to touch us. Part of me wonders if it's because they're ghosts. I'd read what I could about the beings, but all the information on them is inconsistent and vague. The only thing all the texts agree on is that they're descendants of one of the goddesses. The Huntress, if I'm remembering correctly.

The only noise they make is their deep breathing as they try to scent what has been lost. Roux's unscented soap now makes sense. She must have known Annaliese would send Enhanced after her. Henry stiffens as one crouches, skimming a white-gloved finger over the engorged mushroom Roux sat beside just last night. It's tempting to step over to distract the hunter, but I don't dare. That might as well be an admission of guilt. No, the best course of action is to say as little as possible.

One rests her hand against the cart and I watch Henry's throat bob. "This is from the prison." The ethereal voice says while my arms cross over my chest.

"I was forced to improvise when an escapee caused mass chaos and my father slipped away in our carriage without a care for me or my guard." Real irritation coats the true words as the events replay in my mind. Selfish to the end, my father. An amused hum fills the air as that seemingly empty hood turns to me. A chill slides up my spine like an icy hand. She takes a measured step towards me and I brace myself for another question that isn't a question, or worse; a touch.

But I speak before she does. "I've always wondered something, Enhanced, if you'd humor me." She pauses in front of me while all hoods swivel towards me, Henry's head included. My body is held tight, the instinct to fight or flee warring with my mind telling me to stand my ground. If I can hold their attention, then perhaps they'll miss something important. Her hood inclines to me and I take that as permission. "Are you born with your abilities or taught?" Soft laughter drifts on the wind from the Enhanced around us and this time I can't keep myself from shifting from foot to foot.

"We are born Enhanced, but our abilities are then nurtured so we may reach our full potential."

I nod. "At the war colleges." Intrigue begins creeping in over the fear swirling in my gut. "And are you all…female?" I'm a bit tentative with this question, having nothing to go off of other than their voices.

Laughter drifts through the air again before one of the others slides behind me. "I like this one. You wouldn't let us keep him as a pet, would you, L?" The hair on the back of my neck stands up as the Enhanced glides away. I'm not sure I want to know what being their pet would entail. Then again…

The hooded figure before me shakes her head. "No, I would not." Amusement tints her voice as she turns back to me. "The majority are born female, like the Huntress herself. There are a few male Enhanced, but none in my troupe." She waves a gloved hand to her soldiers.

After a quick moment of deliberation, I bow my head to her. "A privilege to witness you, Huntress." I can feel Henry's shocked eyes burning into my skull as I make myself vulnerable to her. She hums and my head snaps up as the sound seems to come from under her hood. For a brief moment, I think I see the glimmer of dark skin and violet eyes before the darkness falls again.

"Huntress." She repeats, her voice still emanating from within her hood. "I do like that." Another step closer and we'll be nose to nose, but I can't bring myself to turn away. Her foot lifts, then—

"Leader." A deeper female voice drifts over from the riverside. A soft sigh escapes the woman in front of me before she slides to the side. She glides over with supernatural smoothness to pause beside the gurgling water. I don't dare let my eyes wander to look for Roux lest one of them notice my wandering eye while Henry stands firm at my side with a hand on his weapon. Two stay by the water gesturing over it, across the water, and downstream. They must be speaking, but their words are kept too quiet for my unenhanced ears to pick up.

Concern strikes me as I wonder if Roux jumped into the river to be carried downstream. It would be the quickest way to get away from here without carrying her scent. However, she's too weak to swim far and it would be inconvenient to hunt her down only to drag our assassin's dead body from the river.

The leader nods and the group floats to their horses before mounting them with ease. "Perhaps we'll visit your estate when our horses require rest," I swear I can hear a smile in her voice.

I incline my head. "You're always welcome. Huntress." A deep chuckle leaves her before they gallop back into the mist only to vanish the next moment.

Henry and I are quiet for a few minutes as we make sure they're far enough away to not overhear us. Then he's striding over to slap me repeatedly on the arm with his empty scabbard. Each slap is punctuated by a word, "Stop. Inviting. People. Who. Can. Kill. Us. To. Our. Home!" I grab the scabbard on his last blow and spin around, swinging it against his ass. He yelps, scowling as I laugh, and grabs the item back.

"Technically, I only accepted their suggestion." He rolls his eyes at yet another one of my technicalities. "And would you rather I denied their request?" Henry gulps at the thought while I start gathering our things. "Let's head out. We'll need to find what we lost before heading back out on the road."

"Unless she finds you first." Roux's voice drifts over and I spin on my heel to find her casually sliding down the trunk of the tree she'd rested under last night. Her green eyes are brighter today. I wonder if it's because of the slight weight gain on her face or from the excitement of this morning. She'd changed into the clothes Henry brought back and while they hang off her like billowing sails, they're better than only a cloak. Her hand slides over Banshee while she shakes her head at me. "You have a death wish." Yet the half-smile on her face makes me think she doesn't disapprove.

Henry's jaw is half-open as he looks at her. "How did they not sense you? One stood right under that tree!" He points to the engorged mushroom and I'll admit I'm curious as well.

She shrugs a bony shoulder. "Several scrubs in the river, unscented soap, a strong-smelling pine, being still, and this." Her thin fingers reach up and drag blissfully untangled hair over her shoulders. It's still dark as night and dull, but it's also shorter. Yesterday, it came down to her hips. Today, it falls to the small of her back in half-hearted waves. "Tossed the mats down the river for them to follow. It'll take them a little while to figure out the scent is faked and they'll have no clue where along the river I was." I blink, staring at her as she unwraps the food she didn't eat last night and slips a few bites into her mouth.

"Brilliant." I breathe without meaning to, but her face alights with a playful grin.

"Get used to it." She wraps up the food again and tucks it away in her pocket. "We should get going. It'll take us longer since we'll be straying from the roads. Better to keep your assassin safe." She winks at us before untying Banshee from her branch. Henry looks at me incredulously, but I wave him on to follow her orders. I move to her side as she walks to the cart with Banshee and reaches for the halter. "We won't be using that."

I drop the halter and straighten. "No?"

Her head shakes. "We don't need it and the weight will slow us down."

"And if you have to hide?"

"Hiding in plain sight is usually the best course of action."

"And what am I to ride, assassin?"

A sickly-sweet smile stretches across her face. "You'll be riding behind me, lord's son. Nice and close."

I lean against the cart and raise a brow. "Is that to make sure you don't fall off?"

Her eyes go cold, but that grin only widens. "Or to make sure you don't run into another beast keen to swallow you whole."

"Good luck with that," Henry mutters and my eyes roll before I meet her sharp gaze again. We stare off for a few seconds, seeing who will look away first. "Can we go?" Henry walks past us already settled on his gelding that nudges past us. The assassin and I sigh at the same time, then frown at one another. I move forward before she presses a hand against my chest. I can see those gold flecks in her eyes again as she shakes her head.

"I'll be in the front."

I stare her down, hating being told what to do. "You don't know where you're going."

"Henry does." She flicks her chin towards him astride his horse. "We'll follow him."

I search for an argument for that until Henry huffs with impatience. Giving in, I move to the side and gesture to the cart with overexaggerated grandeur. "Ladies first, then." Amusement and irritation flicker through her eyes before she steps forward, puts a foot on the spoke of the cart, shoves herself up using my shoulder, and then slides smoothly onto Banshee's bare back. It'll be rough riding with two passengers and no saddle, but Roux has given me little choice. I doubt things would be more comfortable with Henry on his horse.

Sighing, I let my eyes rove over the campsite for one last check before using the cart as a foothold to sling myself atop Banshee. To her credit, the beast only shifts slightly as Roux and I slide together. Shock hits me first. I knew she was skin and bones, it's obvious just looking at her, but it's different to feel it. Her hip bones poke into the sides of my thighs and this close, my tall frame dwarfs her. I could rest my chin on her head easily. I'm by no means a stout or thick man, yet my thighs are nearly twice the size of hers. Gods, I need to get her a full meal. As soon as she can stand it, anyway.

We amble onto the road with Henry leading before we slip into a worn path cutting through the woods on the right. Dappled sunlight slides over the path ahead and our heads, but I note that Roux's dark hair seems to gobble up the light. Hopefully, if we move quickly and cut through the woods, we have less than two days between us and home. Two days before Roux is close enough to kill my father.

Chapter Four

Sanctuary

Roux

All of us are quiet for a while as we take some time to wake up since the Enhanced stole part of our morning. They'll be on my tail soon enough, but there are multiple ways to avoid them. I've done it before. My body aches from exhaustion and hunger as well as the cost of magic. It doesn't take much to disguise scent. Just a few simple hand gestures. But all magic has a cost and while most spells only take a little energy like any other muscle, my body is weak. I may as well have lifted the weight of a fully grown man.

No, I'm not an Enhanced, but they are not the only ones who have magic. Potion makers have enough to imbue their brews with special properties, charmers have enough to calm animals or trick people out of their coin, and I happen to have enough to get by when I need to. It feels good to use magic again. Feel the vibrancy and energy of it coursing through me like life's blood. All the prisons were warded against it, of course, the very foundations probably whispered over with enchantments. The weight of the protective magic burdens my shoulders still and my hope is that it'll fade before we reach the estate.

Who knows what tricks I'll need up my sleeve when we arrive?

The sun is on the rise when I decide to speak to my passenger keeping his arms loosely wrapped around my waist. For now, I'll keep my magic to myself. The more I can keep from them both, the more power I have over them. "You know, you might want to avoid tempting danger to toy with you." I draw my cloak a bit tighter around my shoulders to keep the morning chill off my bones. It'll also keep any other travelers from seeing my frail body which may stoke concern or suspicion. "A poor little lord's son like you might get himself in over his head." I feel his answering grumble deep in his chest behind me and fight a smile.

Silva leans into me a bit, the warmth of his body seeping into my back as if he were fire itself, while his mouth idles next to my ear. "Why? Have you made that your occupation?" His voice is smooth and husky like a draft of whiskey. Honestly, I wouldn't mind a glass right about now.

"Toying with you or tempting danger?"

"Both."

A deep chuckle leaks out of me without resistance before I flick my hair behind my shoulder, casually hitting Silva in the face. He pulls his head back out of striking distance but leaves his body close. I don't scold him for it because I could use the heat. "I don't toy with danger, lord's son, we dance." Nostalgia drifts through my chest for the complicated moves and the thrill of every step.

"You miss it." His comment has me tugging in a sharp breath. He sees more than most and I've fallen out of habit with concealing everything from everyone. After so long in a cage in the dark, it's strange to be seen.

My breath slips out, long and slow, dancing in swirls through the chilly air. Spring still has yet to escape winter's clutches, it seems. "I was a prisoner for two years. Trapped in a cell. I missed my freedom every day." My grip adjusts on the mare's mane and my chin lifts to see the trees swaying above us. "Now that I'm out, my weak body is my prison." Frustration laces every word, but I don't mind that they hear it. They should know that I'm angry. Everyone will know soon enough.

Silva's arms adjust slightly around my waist. "A temporary state."

A crooked smile appears on my lips. "Will you hand feed me peeled grapes in the gardens of your estate, lordship?"

He scoffs. "A poor, little lord's son does have better things to do than feed a needy assassin."

"Needy?" My voice jumps up a few octaves and he laughs, the sound shaking his chest behind me before I dig my elbow into his ribs.

He's saved from being murdered by Henry dropping back beside us. "What's the plan when we get there? We can sneak her in easily enough, say she's a traveler who needs food for the night, but what about after that? How are we going to hide her in the estate or, gods forbid, justify her being there to your parents?" They're all good questions, but I'm not a fan of being talked about rather than with.

So, before Silva can speak, I say, "Lurec has never seen me. He has an idea of what I look like from stories and reports from the lovely warden, but he's never laid eyes on me himself. After I gain weight and strength, I could arrive as anyone and no one would be the wiser." Silva's lips flatten at being interrupted, but I plow on. "And how long I wait depends on the way I decide to kill him." The men are silent for a moment as this sinks in.

"What's the delay? Feeling out of practice?" Silva teases, but I only smile.

"Not at all. It's a…principle, if you will. I kill people the way they deserve; a painful death, an ugly death, a quick one. I need to know my target to decide their fate." My hands itch slightly as they hunger for a blade, a bow, or simply to do the job bare. I have missed this.

"We'll keep to that then." Silva's voice is more sober than before. "I'll hide her with me, tell the servants we found her on the road, and offered our assistance. They tend to mind their own business anyway." I nearly scoff at that.

Raising an eyebrow, I glance over my shoulder. "Do you host so many women that the servants have become blind to them?"

His cheeks brush a light red while I smother a smile. "Women in the house aren't unheard of and I prefer to think my servants respect my privacy rather than assume they're blind." On that at least, he's wise. Most of the information I got in my old days of doing this was from discontented servants. They may not show that they care, but they store each piece of information away in case it's of use at a later time.

Henry's brows go sky-high. "Hide with you? Are you mad, Sil?" The nickname nearly makes me smile. It's cute. A sign of closeness between friends.

My head turns just in time to catch a flash of a smile on Silva's face. "Thought you'd have learned that long ago, Hen." The man shakes his head, though I glimpse his small smile, and pulls ahead once again to lead us at a faster pace as if getting there faster will make a difference. Based on what I know and have heard from Silva, the contrary is true. I'll have to come up with a particularly creative way to kill his father and that takes time.

*　　*　　*

We manage to avoid any incidents over the next two days and arrive at Silva's estate as the sun sets on the third day. A few hours ago, the land had turned rolling rather than steep and farms dot the area along with patches of forest. Cresting one of the hills is when Ayncuarst Estate comes into sight.

Naturally, it's sprawling and grand, like any other estate. It towers over the green hills and trees around it, tan stones glimmering almost gold in the fading light with spires reaching up towards the pink sky. The whole of it is rather uniform and symmetrical; three floors, with spires separating the body from the arms, and windows with diagonal panes dotting the entire golden building. "Not bad, eh?" Silva comments and I can feel him sit up a little straighter at the sight of his home.

I shrug a shoulder, doing my best not to fall asleep on Banshee's back. "It's no palace, but no, it's not bad." It's better than the palace since I'm more relieved to be here than there. My only desire is to sleep. I don't even care if it's in the barn, so long as I can rest my head somewhere safe.

"Pales compared to a cell, hm?" Henry scoffs at my blasé response before galloping down the road with a happy shout. We follow right after and I find a wide grin lighting Silva's face as we go.

The road leading to the house is lined with grand trees whose branches stretch like arms welcoming whoever passes under them. There's a large square drive littered with pebbles for carriages, but we don't touch the rocky road. A quarter mile off lies the stables and that's where we trot, tired and hungry. "I'll handle things. Stay close and quiet. If you can." The last bit is said as a tease and I resist elbowing him as we enter the warm amber light of the stables.

It's a large rectangle with openings in the front and the back. The one opposite us leads back out to the green hills to a pasture and paddock for training. The buildings around us are the same tan stone as the house ahead but with dark green roofs. Being two stories, I'd guess they have quite a few farmhands and stable personnel that are witnessing us enter. The hair on the back of my neck prickles as I feel eyes on me. I tug my hood lower over my face before Silva tugs it completely off my head.

My hand is instantly on the dagger at my hip before he whispers. "It's fine, this is my home. Trust me."

"I don't." I spit, fingers wrapping tight around my blade's hilt. It's half-drawn when a spindly man comes limping out of the stables to meet us with a gap-toothed grin on his face.

"Master Silvanus! So good to see you home, lad!" His voice cascades easily over the quiet din of horses, but the man's visage has me releasing my weapon. I'm not Roux here. I doubt word of my escape has reached this place yet. No one here is seeking me or wishes to lock me up. I'm just a strange girl. Silva slides off Banshee and walks to the man who hasn't even made it a quarter of the way across the stables because of his bad limp.

He clasps hands with the man and grins happily. "Pleasure to see you too, Mr. Geoffrey. Although you should be in bed, by my count. Your wife will have my head." The older man waves off his concern as I grow more and more relaxed. Henry hops off his horse as we arrive next to the older gentleman who shakes his hand as well before looking up at me.

Milky blue eyes scan my face while I tug my cloak a bit closer to conceal my thin body. "And who have you brought with you, sir?" Silva searches my eyes and seems to be satisfied with the lack of murderous intent there. Smirking, he reaches for me. My eyes narrow at him, but I set my hands on his shoulders and let him help me down off Banshee. He wraps my arm around his even as I keep a hand on Banshee so she supports most of my weight.

"This is…" Henry struggles and my mouth opens to answer instead, but Silva beats us all.

"Clytemnestra." My head whips towards him. "We found her in some distress on the road and brought her here to be cared for." His eyes swim with humor as he turns to face me while I look at Geoffrey.

Gritting my teeth, I give him what barely passes for a curtsey. "A pleasure to meet you, Mr. Geoffrey." Henry's mouth nearly falls open at my polite response. "Though please, I prefer Nestra."

The old man, however, seems overjoyed. "You must surely be tired if you're curtseying to the likes of me, Miss! You have the speech of a lady!" His smile is bright as the sun even as I note his smile isn't gap-toothed at all, but missing a tooth entirely.

"Come with me and we'll set you up with a bed, a bath, and some dinner." He offers his hand to me, palm up, and Silva is passing me over before I've said a word.

"She'll stay here tonight, but afterward I'll find her better housing in the big house. Keep her from my parents, would you? I'd rather they not meet her until she's ready." Silva speaks as if I'm not there and clearly enjoys every second of it. Henry is looking between us all, slack-jawed. This isn't exactly the plan.

Geoffrey nods. "Of course, sir."

"I look forward to a visit from you tomorrow, *sir*." I remind Silva who only smiles brightly at me.

"Wouldn't miss it. Goodnight, Miss Nestra. Henry?" The lord's son turns on his heel with his soldier following close behind while other workers take Banshee along with the brown gelding deeper into the stables. The one upside is that Geoffrey's staggered pace matches mine since I'm shocked that I'm still standing. I'll need more weight potions soon. Maybe even one a day to get some strength back.

Geoffrey pats my hand kindly. "You'll be ravenous, of course, my dear. My wife and I will set you up nice in one of the worker's spare rooms. It won't be much, but it'll be warm and private." Sounds like the blessed Above to me. He goes on, clearly the kind to chat whether one is paying attention or not. I find it's nice to simply be talked to as a woman rather than an assassin, murderer, or prisoner. "Master Silvanus and Master Henry are kind men. Good you came across them and not some vagabond or ruffians. Sometimes I don't wonder that the gods left and of course, we wasted the gift of the guardians they left behind." He shakes his head as I listen idly, making sure to catalog each step we take in case I need to get out of here in a hurry. His mention of the gods and guardians does make an old ache flare in my heart, but I quickly focus elsewhere.

"But that's nothing for you to worry about, dear. Just some ramblings from a history lover. You'll be quite safe here with us."

He pats my hand again before we come to a stop at the bottom of the stairs. "There's an empty room just to the left at the top of the stairs. I'd escort you, but I fear we'd be climbing for nearly an hour before we got there!" He chortles at himself and I find a genuine smile slipping onto my face. "The wife and I live just here." He points to a worn wooden door next to the spiraling steps. "She's a bit spryer on her feet and will bring you some dinner while you get washed up. You get some sleep, now." He shoos me onward.

I pause with a hand resting on the stone wall. "I…thank you for the escort and your hospitality." Gratitude sits strange and stale on my tongue from disuse, but Geoffrey smiles all the same. That's the image I hold onto as I drag myself up the stairs into the room he pointed out. He's right. It's not much. There's room enough for a bed pressed against the far wall, one side table, a dresser, a vanity, a small table with two chairs for eating, and a small partition hiding a copper tub for bathing. There's even a window overlooking the paddock outside. I slip off my boots and my eyes shut as my cold toes slide onto a plush red rug. No, not much at all, but after having nothing at all, this place is better than a castle.

I sway in place for a moment as exhaustion hits me and reach for the table to the left as I fall, but miss and clatter to the ground in a heap. The rug is a soft landing place and I only have a moment to ponder getting up before sleep has taken me.

Snippets of life leak into my mind as I slip from sleep to waking and back again. The feeling of being lifted, the sound of water running, someone scrubbing my body, soft cloth fluttering around me, then the softness of being lowered onto a cloud before everything fades again. Dreams come to me then, mixed with memories. The flash of blue walls and a sprawling garden fill my mind along with green eyes a shade lighter than mine.

I jerk awake as all that vanishes in a flash of blazing light. My eyes squint at the light filling the room before I take stock of it and realize where I am. No longer am I in that dark, rank cage. Nor am I in the place I was dreaming of. I sigh, taking another moment to stretch out in the downy soft bed. It doesn't last long because my nose picks up on something delicious. There's a small tray of food on the bedside table covered by a silver dome that I practically rip off. The growl from my stomach tears through the room at the plate full of bread, meat, and fruit. Still, I pace myself. I want to keep all this food in my stomach and not throw it up all over this lovely room.

Once I've eaten my fill, I realize not all the things from last night were dreams. At long last, my skin is clean. It doesn't shine or sparkle like a pearl but remains dull like bone. Still, the lack of dirt is a major improvement. I've also been dressed in a pure white nightgown that reminds me eerily of the robes of the Enhanced. Luckily, whoever brought me breakfast, or lunch, based on the sun coming through the window, also brought clothes slung over the partition in the corner. My other clothes have also been cleaned and lay over the bench at the end of my bed along with my sword and dagger.

I reluctantly leave the comforting warmth of the bed and breathe a sigh of relief at a little bit of strength returning to my legs. The rest and food seem to have done some good. For the first time since being free, I walk over to the partition without leaning on anything to bear my weight. I cling to the partition once there, but I made it on my own. My thin fingers lift the brown fabric off the lattice. A dress. Surprise twirls through me even though it's a perfectly logical thing to bring a young woman. It's just been a long time since I've worn one. A very long time.

Even so, I pull it from the partition and over my head for it to flutter down over my slip. It's very simple. Straps reach over my shoulders leaving the scoop neck and sleeves of the white nightgown on display. Little gold buttons go down the front to my waist where green vines have been sewn into the rich brown fabric. From there it falls to my ankles where there's a bit of green embroidery as well. There are some flats on the floor underneath where the dress hung, but I opt for my boots still by the door. Since I don't have a scabbard for my dagger, I tuck it under the mattress and fasten the sword to my hips. Appropriate or not, I'm not leaving this room without a weapon.

I'm tugging the brush Henry gave me through my hair with my back to the vanity mirror when I hear a soft knock on the door. My hand grips the brush tight before the door opens to reveal a plump woman with golden hair peeking her head in. "Sorry to intrude, but I'm glad to see you up! We were worried you'd never wake!" She comes in and takes the empty food tray out to a waiting cart. I watch her every movement carefully before going back to brushing my hair. This must be Geoffrey's wife.

"Thank you for all you've done for me." The words don't come any easier than they did before, but the woman smiles brightly at me anyway. At least, until she sees me brushing my hair.

"Och, what are you doing there? Give that to me." I blink as she takes the comb and spins me around, then starts pulling it through my hair far easier than I did. My eyes look down at the desk in front of me rather than my reflection. The woman doesn't notice. "You certainly did give me a fright when I came in to find you laid out on the floor like the dead. Barely even woke when I hauled you into the tub!" My head snaps up to see her face in the mirror.

"You did that?" She certainly looks strong enough to do it, but something in me thought Geoffrey's wife would be as feeble as him. Her biceps flex with each stroke of my hair and I consider myself corrected.

She nods. "Aye, I did. Practically had to scrub your skin raw to get all the dirt off." She clicks her tongue with disapproval, golden hair interspersed with braids falling over her shoulder as her head tilts to examine her work. "You need some sun, lady. And this hair." Her tongue clicks as she trades my comb for a small container in her apron pocket. "I thought you might be needing this, so I brought it along this morning. A lot of the girls use it for their hair." She gathers a bit of what looks like salve into her hands before passing me the small circle. "You can call me Mrs. Geoffrey, but my name is Lisbet. I'll answer to either and tell anyone you need something and I'll come running."

I nod along to her words, but I'm preoccupied with whatever she's given me. My nose twitches as I sniff it and the strong scent of pine drifts up as Mrs. Geoffrey runs gentle, practiced hands over my hair. "What is it?"

"It's a special mix from pine resin. Makes your hair silky and shiny after a few uses." She gathers my half-hearted waves behind my head and I sigh at the memory of my wild curls. "You might need to apply it every day for two weeks to get some shine back, lady. If you pardon my saying so."

I snort. "Certainly not. It's the truth."

She smiles at me in the mirror and I get a glimpse of warm brown eyes in a charming, round face. "I brought this as well. The girls dip their toothbrushes in it or swirl it around in their mouths. Makes the teeth white and the breath fresh." I sincerely doubt that since a brief whiff of the stuff tells me it's a teeth corrector potion. One swish and my yellowed smile would turn white as snow without a trace of cavities or rot. Kind of her to say it's a simple beauty enhancer to spare my feelings. All the same, I slurp up a mouthful and swish three times before the liquid vanishes of its own accord, leaving perfect teeth behind.

Mrs. Geoffrey nods approvingly. "Now, how do you want your hair done? All up?"

My head shakes slightly with my eyes locked onto her face. "That's not necessary."

Her big hands remain heavy on my shoulders. "Nonsense. You're the Master's guest." Apparently, no isn't an option. "Either tell me your preference or I'll choose for you." I almost laugh at the sternness lurking behind her sunny tone, but wave her on to choose for herself.

"Has he come by? Master Silvanus." It's tempting to roll my eyes at his title, but I doubt Mrs. Geoffrey would appreciate it very much.

It takes her a few moments to answer since all her concentration is taken by my hair. "He has, but you slept a long while, lady. Two nights and half this day." My gaze drifts to the window. Kind of Silva not to wake me even though he should have. We have a mission to complete. This isn't a vacation. "I'm sure he'll stop by again today. Master Henry is outside with the horses now, if you'd like to see him." I nod slightly. We need to settle on a story and stick to it, especially now that the servants know about me.

"There. You look proper now." Her silence is clearly her waiting for me to look at my reflection, so I lift my head to gaze into my own eyes. Gods. I look like one of the many dead I've sent Under. She did my hair beautifully. The almost black strands have been corralled into a swirling bun on the back of my head with little braids interspersed. A few waves frame my face nicely but do nothing to hide the gauntness.

There are light purple shadows still under my eyes and my lovely freckles have all but vanished into ghostly splotches. Even with the weight potion, my cheeks are sunken, and my head looks like a skull. "It wasn't hard lifting you since you're all but skin and bones. What kind of trouble did the Master save you from?" Mrs. Geoffrey's voice is soft and gentle without a trace of judgment.

My lips part as I try to quickly think of a story that makes sense. Geoffrey said I had the speech of a lady, so why not adopt what they already think I am? I sit up a little straighter as I look back at her. "My parents passed away a few years ago and my uncle took over our house and land. He didn't take kindly to me, whether because I was to inherit or for another reason, I don't know. He locked me in a room and left me there for…a long time."

I let the bits of truth in the words leak through and her hands on my shoulders squeeze with sympathy. "I managed to get away and was on the run when Silva and Henry found me." My head dips slightly with the weight of sadness from such a story.

Mrs. Geoffrey moves to the side and crouches next to me. It occurs to me that while Mr. Geoffrey seems to be close to fifty, his wife looks almost ten years younger. He must've been quite the man in his day to catch such a woman. Her brown eyes swirl with warmth and empathy and she takes my hand. "Don't you worry about a thing anymore, child. You'll be taken good care of here." She smiles brightly when my head lifts a bit. "Who knows? Perhaps you'll find a life here that you never could have dreamed of." She squeezes my hand with a conspiring twinkle in her eye. "I've never heard a lady call our Master by a nickname before." I hold back a snort at the insinuation that Silva and I are close, even friends, as she stands to move to the door.

"I'm glad to know more of you, lady. What you've said…well, it explains a bit about the scars all over you." My back goes stiff at the reminder while she rests her hand on the door handle. Her bright smile takes away a bit of the sting, but the memories still sting. Even so, I see an opportunity here and I have to take it.

"Mrs. Geoffrey, I have a few questions, if you don't mind. It has been a while since I've been able to know about the world." She pauses and nods. "Well, I'm a bit embarrassed to say. Would you mind simply telling me a handful of things that everyone would know? So I don't have to reveal my ignorance?" Hopefully, she'll tell me what I need without me having to reveal how little I know. Silva and Henry know who I am, so they may lie, but Mrs. Geoffrey has no reason not to tell the truth.

Her brows furrow, but she nods. "Of course." She takes a moment to think while I wait patiently. "Well…we're in Cameria right now, northeast of Dulsia. Queen Letitia still rules despite the death of her husband a few years back." Mrs. Geoffrey's face falls. "And you'll know about the princess, of course."

I stiffen and look down at my hands as they curl into fists. "Still missing, then?" My eyes raise to catch her sad nod. "And her betrothed? The prince of Belterra?" A knot forms in my chest at merely bringing him up, but Mrs. Geoffrey's brows pull together once again as she sets a hand on her hip.

"Never knew about any betrothal, but the prince was sent back to his country to the west just before the princess went missing." She leans towards me a little. "Rumor has it that he took the princess back to his country. Locked her up as punishment for not wanting to marry him. He's barely been seen around his country since."

"He'd never do that." The words slip out before I can choke them back and I try to soften them with a weak smile.

Lisbet Geoffrey raises a brow at me. "Did you know the royals?"

I let the question sink into me before meeting her curious gaze. "You could say that." The memory of sweeping ballrooms, glittering dresses, and secret kisses comes back to me in a rush so potent that I nearly fall off my stool. My throat clears as I shrug. "You know how ladies love to gossip, Mrs. Geoffrey."

She considers me another moment before smiling. "Of course. Make sure you spend some time outside today. Henry is in the paddock with the horses should you care to see him." She nods to me then opens the door to go on with her work, one of the wheels squeaking on the cart she rolls.

I don't look back at my reflection as I get up and walk to the door, leaning against the frame once there. The view is better now that it's daylight. A rail surrounds the lines of rooms around the rectangular building with a sort of public square in the middle. I take a deep breath of the fresh air tinted with the scent of horses and hay. It'll take me some time to get used to the world again, but I don't mind. It wouldn't upset me if I had a lifetime to simply run my hands over wheat fields, bathe in streams, and run with horses. But of course, that isn't the case.

The information gleaned from Mrs. Geoffrey doesn't change my plans for after I leave this beautiful place. It doesn't make them any easier, but I've long since stopped expecting the world to be kind to me.

I grab the fur wrap hanging on the screen before moving to the spiral stairs and walking down with a hand braced on the stone wall. Speaking of horses, I should find out where Banshee is in case I need to make a quick escape. Mr. Geoffrey stands in the opening towards the paddock shouting at some poor stable boy. Slowly, I make my way towards him. "That's why you don't let them off lead until they're in their stall, you dolt! You're lucky Katrine was already on her horse and could run her down. You best hope she comes back with her or I'll sit on your back so you can carry me around the stables! Get out of here!"

I press my lips together to keep from laughing at the sheer terror on the boy's face as he scampers away. Geoffrey's milky blue eyes lift to spy me and his cheeks tint red. "Sorry about that, lady."

A smile tugs on my lips as I wave away his apology. "Are you the stable master, then?"

His eyes get big and he slaps his thin leg as he laughs. "Ah, no. The stable master would be my wife, lady. I just do the yelling when she's busy doing the hard work." It's hard to keep a smile off my face, especially when he tries to gift me a shallow bow. "When we were first brought here by Master Silvanus, we were struggling. My wife had to manage the family farm through the busiest months while I was…kept away." He adjusts his hat and I note he has dark marks around his wrists. Almost like metal cuffs. "Afterward he brought us here and Mrs. Geoffrey finally got to shine like she deserves." His bowed legs shuffle around me to spy his curvy wife's frame on the opposite side of the stables whispering to a horse as she brushes its neck. A soft smile tugs on my lips as she shoots her husband a tender smile.

Mr. Geoffrey clears his throat and claps his hands together before facing me again. "But I'm going on and on! Can I help you in any way?"

I take a step closer with a nod. "Yes, actually. Do you know where Banshee is kept? My horse?" I specify when his face goes a little pale.

He laughs a little nervously at the name even as he nods and waves down the stable hall. "Aye, she's just there. At the end of the hall." Geoffrey pauses a moment as he looks me over. "Banshee is quite a name for the horse of a lady." I smirk slightly. For a lady, perhaps, but it's perfect for an assassin. "But I won't say it ain't apt. Heard her whinny this morning and thought sweet Death had come to claim me."

I hum a soft laugh along with him while thinking it probably wouldn't reassure him to know I'd met a few banshees in my time. One meets a few when surrounded by death. Unfortunately, they're quite misunderstood creatures. After all, they don't cause the death themselves, they merely announce it so people aren't taken completely by surprise. It's a kindness if one really thinks about it. "Thank you. I'll make it that way on my own." He nods and fixes his eyes on the entrance, no doubt hoping for Katrine to return with their lost horse.

I move to the side and look longingly down the hall before moving outside toward the paddock. Now that I know where Banshee is, it's more important that I speak to Henry. My hand slides over the stone before I exit the cover in exchange for the sunny paddock. I cling to the fence as I walk, especially since the sun is nearly blinding as it beats down. The heat feels good compared to the cool winter air. My eyes adjust and I manage to see the glimmer of light glinting off metal.

Moving closer, I see Henry isn't alone. His shirt is half unbuttoned and billowing, the sweat covering his muscled chest sparkling in the sun, while Silva still manages to look coiffed. I'm shocked I didn't see his blazing red hair a mile away as it dances like flames while he and Henry spar with longswords. Neither seems to notice my approach, so I reach the last fence before the open field and sit on the soft grass.

Then I simply watch.

They're both good, but I was expecting that. The fun bit is seeing the difference in styles. Henry fights like a soldier; firm, but light on his feet with excellent footwork. Silva was taught swordsmanship, not just how to fight. Each move is a step in a dance, each strike ends with a flourish, and every dodge is laced with flair. He's the one my eye is drawn to. At least, until something dark lurking nearby catches my attention.

Chapter Five

Fears

Silva

Sweat is dripping down my neck and sliding down my spine in the afternoon sun, but my focus remains on Henry. His sword and mine meeting again and again is the only thing that exists; the clanging of metal, the feeling in my arm of pressing forward, the quick sliding of my feet as we dance. I love the ballroom, but this kind of dancing feels purer. It certainly lacks the politics of court.

Henry's brows furrow and my smile widens at the tell. I reel back about to strike the killing blow when a laugh echoes over the field. My head whips to the left and I'm shocked still by the sight of a woman holding a solid black cat in her lap that seems to be licking her nose. "Touché." Henry pants as his sword tip rests over my jugular. I sigh, flicking my wrist to toss the steel out of my way as I sheathe my sword.

"A bit unfair."

He chuckles, sheathing his sword as well. "You'd still be dead, unfair or not." My eyes return to the woman who I realize is Roux. I hadn't recognized her before. She's in a dress and that moonlight skin is finally clean and practically reflecting the sun at us. Even her hair looks better, healthier, and is tied up on the back of her head. For the first time, I realize she must be beautiful without the vestiges of death still clinging to her. "Of course, the cat that means bad luck would find her," Henry grumbles as we head over.

I shove his shoulder lightly. "Don't be superstitious." I scold and smile at the light shining out of Roux's eyes as the feline curls up in her lap with paws playfully swatting at the waves escaping her bun. "You look well." Those sharp green eyes flick up to me as she tames the first genuine smile I've seen on her face.

"It's a miracle what a few baths and a tough scrub brush will do."

I hum and settle beside her while Henry follows suit a bit reluctantly. "You know, black cats are bad luck." He just can't resist and I sigh as her eyes cut to him.

"And I'm just a murderer with no morals or thoughts except kill, kill, kill." The words are said so sweetly I have to repeat them in my head to realize what she really stated.

Henry grimaces at the scold, but can't hold back another grumbled sentence. "Ill omen comes for ill omen. Fitting."

"Oh please." Roux snorts. She lifts the cat tenderly, then holds it out towards Hen. "Say you're sorry or I'll make sure bad luck befalls you." It's a clear command and my head swings to him to see if he'll obey or not. His eyes burn into the pale green of the cat's and my lips press together to keep in a laugh as he mumbles a soft apology. The cat melts back into her lap purring loudly as if satisfied with the sudden high treatment. She glances between us. "I am here for a reason."

"Really? Not just for the show?" I tease and my heart beats a bit faster when her head snaps to the side.

"If I wanted to watch monkeys dance, then I'd watch the stable boys."

"Think you could do better?"

She's silent for a moment as irritation simmers behind her eyes. I'm sure she could, but we both know she can barely stand at the moment. "Not today." She relents and I grin at winning while Henry looks ready to jump between us. After a steadying breath, she goes on. "This is the story that we tell those who ask and, when it's time and if it's necessary, this is what we will tell your parents."

It's a good cover. Everything has its place and it's short enough to remember. Henry and I can make excuses for not knowing the details since we haven't known her long. The rest we'll trust Roux to make up on her own. The irony of trusting her isn't lost on me, especially given she said she didn't trust me when we arrived. But she hasn't killed any of my servants, so I'll trust her to do her job.

"Do you keep these lies tucked in your back pocket for special occasions?" I ask while stretching out a bit more on the soft grass.

Her head is tipped back to take in the sun while her hand hasn't paused its ministrations on the cat's tummy. "Just as you keep compliments stored in your back pocket for court, lord's son." A smile cuts across my face at the same time her lips stretch.

"Might want to keep some yourself, Roux. You'll be staying here a bit longer than you might have desired." I tease, but the light has shuttered from her eyes.

Henry fills in the blanks for her from his place a few feet away. "Lurec arrived here, then immediately set off again. He shouldn't be gone more than a month at the very most, but…" He trails off. It prolongs Roux's stay far longer than Henry wanted, but then again, a day more is too much for him. I'm more interested in Roux's reaction because I've no clue what she plans to do after all this. I told Henry it wasn't my problem, but that doesn't mean I'm not curious.

Her eyes narrow, the only sign she heard him, before her head swivels towards me. "Why?"

My shoulders lift and fall. "Not a clue. It's not abnormal for him to leave all of a sudden, not even after a trip, but the servants say he was in a rush. Sweating like a rutting hog, were the exact words spoken to me." Thoughts fill her green eyes, her focus wavering only when the cat rises and trots over to the fence to hop on top. She looks back towards the stables only to freeze. I follow her gaze and grin at the pack of dogs rushing out towards us. Henry smiles too and we all move onto our feet to avoid being run over by the barking beasts, but Roux doesn't only stand.

My lips part as I watch her sprint to the fence and vault over it right before the dogs crash into us. Henry greets them joyously, letting them tackle him to the ground to cover him in slobber. My nose wrinkles as I let my hands run over their heads with my eyes on Roux. I can't help but draw a comparison between her and the cat. The black mass grows as its hair stands on end and hisses at the dogs daring enough to come close. I've no doubt that if Roux's hair could stand on end, it would. It takes me almost a minute to identify the feeling on her face, well-disguised as her emotions usually are. I'm surprised to name it. Fear. Terror, more like.

I look between her and the dogs with a raised brow. "Don't like dogs?"

She bares her teeth at me. "*Keep the mutts away from me.*" Her eyes snap back to them as they bark and my easy smile vanishes as she starts trembling.

I meet Henry's scanning eyes before waving him on. "Take them for a run, would you?" He looks her over one more time before nodding and running away from us with every hound on his heels. When I turn back to Roux, she's gone. Warily, I look at the cat. It stops bathing itself to stare unblinkingly at me, then looks idly down to the side. I step closer and peek over the side of the fence to find my assassin folded in on herself with hands fixed over her ears.

I'm jumping over the fence without a thought and frown before crouching next to her. "Roux." She makes no move to signal she heard me. Carefully, I reach out a hand and it's barely touched her shoulder when her hand snaps up to grab my wrist in a vice.

"Lay a hand on me and you'll lose it." She spits while squeezing my hand with more strength than I thought she had.

I scan her for another moment before letting the corner of my mouth lift. "I didn't know assassins were afraid of anything." She tosses my hand away as if she can't stand to touch me, but those blazing green eyes stay focused on mine. "What exactly is it about them that you fear so much? The floppy ears? The wagging tongues? Oh, it's the wiggly tails, isn't it?"

"I still have a sword at my side."

"Only if you can stand, Red Death."

Her hand moves to my shirt as she draws me close. I can see those gold flecks swimming in her emerald eyes as they burn into mine. "I don't need to stand to kill you."

I give her a fox's grin as I pull back, moving across the ring as she catches herself before she falls flat on her face. "Then let's see it." I dare, a thrill trilling down my spine when she uses the fence to rise to her feet. Steel sings as she draws the blade with a completely steady hand and sets her fur wrap on the fence. The frantic darting of her pupils calms as she focuses on one goal; killing me. My fingers drum at my sides as if on a piano as I wait for her to strike.

I don't have to wait long.

The sun catches on the sword as she brings it up in a neat slice and I dodge it easily, but what I don't expect is her to keep going. The sword swipes up and down like the spinning arms of a windmill. Each move is practiced and fluid as she comes after me while I stumble over myself getting out of the way. When I'm stable and on my feet again, her sword slices straight down through my shirt. I huff, "That's silk!" She smirks and swipes the sword towards my neck next.

I roll out of the way and thank the gods when she places a hand on the fence as her knees wobble. She may be able to walk a bit better, but footwork and remaining in the same position for too long is too much stress for her legs. I'm about to call it when she looks over my shoulder. "Gods." She breathes as all emotion leaks from her face. My head whirls around in the direction, thinking my father may have returned, maybe a creature found Henry—

But all I get for my worry is a blade pressed to my throat. Roux's quiet laugh is soft music as I turn back to her with my hands held out to my sides. "On your knees," She commands and a crooked smile blooms on my lips.

My head shakes. "It'll take a lot more than that to put me on my knees, Roux."

She steps forward with the long blade now pressed horizontally against my jugular. "I didn't take you as gullible." She's out of breath from the small flurry of activity, but victory is scrawled over her face as sparkling eyes and a wicked smile. She even has little dimples dotting her sunken cheeks. This expression…this is Roux's true face. Or whatever her real name is.

I swallow, my throat suddenly dry, before I answer. "I didn't take you as a cheater."

She snorts and tempts a smile onto my lips. "A small tip, lord's son." The edge of her blade stings as it dips into the fragile skin of my neck. A trill of warning shoots down my spine, but my eyes don't leave hers. "Everyone cheats when it comes to life or death." Roux backs up, but keeps the sword pointed at me until she's on the other side of the ring. "I won't count this as a win against you. You never drew your weapon. I'll beat you in combat another time since I'll apparently be here for a while." She sheaths what used to be my sword with eyes drifting to the cat still sitting serenely on the post. It seems like an afterthought as she rewraps the fur around her shoulders and I wonder how used to the cold she must be after so long on the mount, if the cold wind is merely a breath for her, or if its touch burns.

I take a step towards her with a hand wiping away the drops of blood trailing down my throat. "Since you're back to your normal self and like you said, you'll be here a while, I thought I could give you a tour." She'll need to know where my father goes when he's here anyway, so this is as good a guise as any.

Her hand slides over the cat while her gaze flits over me with surprise tinting those brilliant eyes. "You'll need a new shirt." I look down and grimace at the state of what was a perfectly good shirt. "But fine. Let's go." When I look back at her, the cat is snuggled up in her arms. Shaking my head, I unlock the gate and she tentatively peeks around for any stray dogs before following me to the stables.

"Master Silvanus!" Geoffrey's voice drifts over the instant I spot the older man in the wide doorway. A smile instinctively tugs at my lips as my strides quicken so he doesn't need to walk any further. "What you asked for." He says, offering me a sturdy-looking cane.

I nod as I look it over. "Perfect, Mr. Geoffrey, thank you." He grins at me before looking to Roux and doing his best to bow, nearly losing his large straw hat in the process.

"Course, sir. You both have a good day now." He scuttles back towards his room while I turn to the assassin and offer her the cane. Her brows raise.

"You're walking better, but you need it for when you're stationary. At least for a while." She still doesn't take it, so I let the bottom hit the ground before offering her the knot at the top. "Come now. Surely you could turn this into another sort of weapon. It has its merits."

Her eyes roll, but she lets the cat jump to the ground to claim the cane. "Save me from the day you start thinking like an assassin." She stomps towards the entrance while I frown at her back.

"I thought that was perfectly logical." I object, dodging the cat as it darts after her. We're quiet for a bit as we move onto the road guarded by tall trees littered with unfurling leaves leading to the house. "Why dogs then?"

Her eyes flick over to me, then she focuses back on the road ahead of us. "Everyone is afraid of something."

"But dogs?"

"Give something to get something, lord's son."

"Then give something, assassin." I dare, refusing to be scared off.

Her hand squeezes the cane until her knuckles go white, then she tilts her head back to look at the trees for a moment. I move to her side rather than walking behind her and our eyes meet. She scans mine, searching for something, before she finally speaks again. "You learn to fear dogs when they're sent after you in the dead of night." Cold drifts over the back of my neck even though she says it as if it happened every other day. "You learn to fear the barking, the growling, the louder it is the closer they are, and the closer they are, the more likely it is you'll get caught." Ice leaks into her voice. Ice and fury. "You hear the snapping of their teeth in every broken twig, hear their breath in every puff of wind, feel their claws in every bramble tearing at your clothes and skin. And if they do catch you, well…" She chuckles without an ounce of humor as her glassy eyes roll to me. "You hope they kill you before they begin ripping you apart limb from limb."

I swallow, rolling my shoulders as my mind showcases the imagined scenarios. But they weren't imagined for Roux. I turn back to her with my hands sliding into my pockets. "Is that how they caught you?" She raises a brow. Right, I haven't given anything in return for her information. "Well," I sigh. "I'm afraid of losing all that I love and hold dear—"

"Everyone is afraid of that." She interrupts and spins on her heel to stop our progress. Her eyes burn bright like green fire. "Ask a man who only loves himself what he fears and he'll tell you he's afraid of death. Everyone is afraid of losing what they love. What do you fear? Viscerally? In your gut?"

I stare at her a moment, weighing the pros and cons of telling her before simply giving in to the deal we made. A tryst, of sorts. "My father."

Interest enters her eyes now. "Is that why you want him dead?"

My head shakes as I look around to make sure we're alone. My hand cards through my hair as I think through the logic behind the fear. Or at least what seems like logic. "No. I want him gone so that I can be lord and take care of this estate and its people the way they should be taken care of. I fear him because of the power he has over me." We start walking again and I take in every inch of the tall house ahead of us. My home and the house of my jailer all in one.

"He can disinherit me, toss me out on the street with nothing, banish me from my home, even kill me without recourse or resistance. He can take away the very essence of who I am without batting an eye. I fear that almost as much as I fear what he'd do to this place if I wasn't here." The ruin he's wreaked is already too much. Tenants left with rotting cottages, left to starve with no help, no employment, and whole settlements dashed because they weren't producing. Who knows what he did before I was old enough to notice. It's a miracle I've saved what I have so far.

Roux is silent for a few steps as I shake away the memories and look at her with a pointed expression. She huffs, but I believe the corner of her lips has turned up. "I've been chased by dogs a few times, but the memory I referenced was when I was being moved to the Prison on the Mount."

"You got out?"

She doesn't seem to mind that I interrupted her this time since a slow smile creeps onto her face. The hair on my arms rises at the sight. "The moves were always sudden so I wouldn't have time to plan if I managed to find out when one was going to happen. This time, it seems it was also a surprise to the guards managing me. I behaved well. Hung my head, acted tired, sad, and defeated to lull them into a false sense of security. Until we got outside." Her smile grows and I find myself leaning closer to hear her every word.

"They were fools. Simple rope ties were all that held me and after knocking out two guards close to me with a few easy moves, it was child's play to cut the ties with their weapons. After that, I took to the woods. For a while, I was free." Her smile vanishes. "Then I heard the dogs and…well."

"They didn't tear you apart." I end for her and her teeth flash in something very unlike a smile.

"They tried." Her hand smooths over her right thigh in a slight curve. I'd glimpsed her naked body, but didn't study it and wasn't close enough to discern any true details of her scars. Only that there were many. I'd noticed today that she walks with a slight limp, perhaps the product of the tale she just told, but I know nothing more. It's clear that this topic has run its course, so I let the soft sound of nature wash over us the last little bit of our walk.

We arrive at the front doors with columns standing on either side of the few steps leading inside and she pauses. "Your mother…?"

I wave her forward. "She's painting today. It'll be past dinner when she leaves that room." Roux's steps are a bit more tentative now, but she follows me to the doors that automatically open thanks to the servants waiting just inside. Idly, I notice her grip tightens on her cane once again. From nerves, or because it's an inconspicuous and unexpected weapon? Maybe giving it to her wasn't the best idea. A passing thought flits through my head so suddenly that I nearly trip.

I've just invited the snake into the chicken coop.

Chapter Six

Love and Anger

Roux

Walking into a tall, imposing building isn't exactly something I want to be doing again so soon after escaping another, but I find myself following Silva anyway. He risked his life by distracting me from my panic earlier, so the least I can do is accept a tour of the home that clearly means so much to him. There was no guarantee that I wouldn't be so unhinged in my fear that I'd be cognizant enough to avoid killing him, yet he did it anyway. Couldn't risk the sanity of his assassin, more than likely. Still. I'll need to know the layout of the place anyway.

My eyes appraise Silva as he speaks to the servants just inside the doors while I stall on what could be considered a front porch. Not many have towering stone columns, but to each their own. I watch and note how Silva's workers listen intently to him, smile easily, and carry out his orders to the letter. It's a rare man who inspires that kind of loyalty and diligence.

"Nestra," He calls and my teeth grit at the fake name before I step through the tall doors. The servant's eyes burn into my back, but I'm distracted by the grandeur of the house. Being tall and imposing from the outside is the only thing it has in common with the prison. Everything inside is light, bright, and wide open. Long halls stretch to my right, left, and dead ahead showing how vast this place truly is. The walls of the entry almost glow from the way the sun pours in from the grand, arched windows onto the subtle gold wallpaper. Tiny details like small flowers and swirling vines are etched onto corners and the stone half columns lining the walls. I regret not switching to the flats as my boots stamp over a richly colored carpet onto the gleaming herringbone floor. It reminds me of arrows pointing further inside. *Keep going*, they seem to say. *Explore me.*

I slip off the boots and leave them by the door with my small cloak. "Keep these nearby for me," I tell the appalled servant before walking back to an amused Silva with my cane clicking against the floor. The look on my face tells him that he'll lose more than a shirt if he makes a comment.

He grins. "The place was commissioned more than a hundred years ago. As the story goes, a royal took a certain liking to an ancestor of mine and bestowed mounds of gifts upon him, including this manor." I continue looking around while Silva talks, marveling at the high, arched ceiling dripping with gold detailing and crystal chandeliers. Sure, I've been in plenty of fine houses and palaces, but rarely as a visitor. As an assassin, there's no time to admire the paintings or stone carvings. "The royal then named him a lord so they could be seen in public without disgrace to either family. Well. Minimal disgrace anyway."

"Born of love then," I murmur as I walk between the two wide, curved staircases. My fingers skim the swirling bottom of the carved banister that reminds me very much of a woman's skirt as it gathers at her feet when she turns. I peek up at the balcony lining the upper half of the second floor ahead as Silva hums and moves to my side.

"I suppose so. Never thought of it that way."

I snort, watching as the sound brings a smile to his face. "Is the lord's son a cynic on love?"

He raises a brow. "Are you not?"

My eyes roll, but my chest is suddenly tight. "Right, what would someone like me know about love?" An assassin, a killer.

"I didn't say that."

"You didn't have to." I look into his eyes as the magic of this place fades. "Tell me this, lord's son. Do you doubt the love you have for Henry? He's close as a limb to you, isn't he? Do you spend nights lying awake wondering about his loyalty or trueness?"

Silva's jaw locks, but he shakes his head. "No, of course not—"

"And your mother?" His gaze turns sharp now, but I have no intention of stopping. "Do you doubt the love you have for her? The love she has for you?"

"*No*—"

"Then you believe in love wholeheartedly." I end, picking up the cat still twining around my feet to hold it close to my heart to stave off the ice growing in my chest. His eyes lose the light of building anger as he stares at me, considering my words. "There are a countless number of different types of love in this world and many of them run deeper than romantic love. Now," I heave in a deep breath. "Show me your father's room." I have no desire to see the rest of this great, fine house anymore.

Silva doesn't move and instead crosses his arms over his still half-bare chest. "You strike for the heart, don't you?"

I give him a sharp smile while my hand tightens around the knot of my cane. "It's my specialty."

He scoffs and lowers his voice. "Just because I'm a cynic doesn't mean I haven't loved or don't believe in love. But the way you speak about it makes me surprised you still do." My eyes narrow at him, not giving in a step when he moves closer. "You must have had a family before. A life. Love." His voice is gentle even as his eyes simmer. "You're no older than twenty-five and the killings only became prolific a handful of years ago. What were you before? What made you into this?"

The only thing that keeps me from reaching for his throat is the purring cat in my arms. I level him with my gaze, letting my cold smile widen when he doesn't back away. "Give me all you want, Silvanus." He shuffles just slightly when I say his full name. "That's information you'll never get from me."

"Why not?" His response is so quick that I almost blink with surprise.

I pull away and shake my head. "What do you think this is? Who do you think I am?" It takes a moment for the questions to sink in, then he pulls back too with his body softening. For once, I find myself looking forward to his answer.

"I...I thought we were—" He raises a hand and runs long fingers over his eyes. "Forget it. Come with me." He leads the charge up the stairs while the cat and I stare at him for a few seconds before following.

*　*　*

Once we reach the top of the stairs, we walk through a grand archway into another long hall. Something about this space seems darker even though the floors and walls are the same. More paintings are scattered throughout and all of them reek of propriety and are done well, but without any lightness or joy. Something in me doubts that any belong to Silva's mother. Directly forward lies his father's room while he tells me his mother sleeps down to the right. "They rarely ever stay in the same quarters as she likes to stay in the round rooms. More windows and more light for her paintings, she says." A bit of levity returns to his voice when he talks about her. I wonder if the delay in meeting her is truly to keep my identity under wraps or because he's waiting to see if I'm worthy. After our tiff today, the introduction might be farther off than I thought.

"Tell me more about your father." I probe a bit as I stare at the double doors straight ahead. "Is he loyal to your mother?"

Silence fills the hall before I glance back at Silva who is staring at me with his back held straight as a rod.

"I don't exactly keep track of my parent's activities in that arena."

"But in your best estimation?"

He looks away, scanning the intricate details on the sconces. "I doubt it."

"Hm." That could certainly be helpful information.

Silva's eyes snap back to mine at the sound. "No."

I raise a brow. "No, what?"

He pauses a moment with his lips parted as if searching for a reason. Instead, he asks a question. "Do you really want that? For him to look at you like a scrap of meat?" His distaste is clear and endlessly amuses me.

"It's less about what I want and more about how I'd like to get the job done. If letting him look at me in a certain way, letting him assume something about me, makes it easier to get him alone, then I'll allow it." His frown deepens as the corner of my mouth lifts. "Why does the thought bother you so much?"

His jaw ticks. "That's not how you deserve to be looked at."

"And how do I deserve to be looked at, lord's son?"

"Like a predator. Like fire. Something that has beauty, but can easily rip you apart if given the inclination."

For a moment, I'm shocked silent. Then I'm fighting a smile as I turn to continue walking down the hall. My little feline friend has elected to walk with us, twirling around my ankles and cane. "This might shock you, lord's son, but what people think does not affect me. Who I am, my worth, is only affected by what I think of myself and what I do." Which, granted, might not mean much to him since I've killed people for money. I had my reasons. Worthy or not, I've never done anything without purpose. I glance at him out of the corner of my eye. "I have the monopoly on deciding what is and isn't worthy of me."

His lips purse. "I only meant that—"

"Yes, and that's very sweet, and absolutely none of your concern. I will do whatever I think necessary for the job you have tasked me with. I will use every tool at my disposal without remorse and you will not question what tools I deem appropriate." A bit of a smile manages to break through my defenses. "Just like I won't tell you how to rule your lands once my job is complete." Because I'll be long gone, but that's beside the point.

Silva seems to be struggling with the decision to say something or stay silent, so I help him out by stepping close and letting my fingers glide down his ripped, silk shirt. Taut muscle lies under his freckled skin and I try not to let myself get too distracted as I hold his gaze. "Now is when you say, 'yes ma'am.'"

Indecision vanishes from his eyes as they refocus on mine, a soft burning in their depths still simmering from leftover frustration. After a moment, he sighs and lets a small, sardonic smile leak onto his lips. "Yes, ma'am." My toes curl on the dark carpet before I nod once in satisfaction and take a step back.

"Good. Now, are you going to show me my room or not?" I take a few more steps to the right as he shakes his head as if to clear the fog before flicking his chin the opposite way.

"Our rooms are actually in the west wing." He moves backward in that direction while my brows furrow.

"*Our* rooms?" I repeat and the grin he tosses back at me is absolutely wolfish.

"If you had to stay here longer than anticipated, your cover was going to be a consort. That's no longer appropriate with the spurious lies you came up with, so now I'm going to be courting you." Somehow, he makes the word spurious seem like a compliment.

I blink, automatically going through all that entails before shaking my head. "You should have told me before doing that."

His eyes roll as I speed up to limp by his side. "Like you consult me?"

"I'm the professional, Silva. You're the virgin." Irritation flashes through those clear eyes while I smirk.

Silva only shrugs and my teeth grit at the nonchalance. "Then I suppose you should ready some of those lies you keep in your back pocket, Roux." I don't dignify that with an answer. Idly, I notice the carpet changes to red down this hallway and make a mental note that blood wouldn't be immediately detected here. Let's hope the carpet is red in the lord's room as well. "In polite society, you wouldn't stay near a man's room, but in the women's wing. I figured you wouldn't care and wouldn't tell."

The cat following me darts ahead, which Silva frowns at, following the feline as it flounces down the hall. "What have I said about tempting danger, lord's son?"

His eyes cut over to me and when he sees I haven't drawn a weapon, he looks ahead again. "Teasing you could hardly be considered treacherous—" He eats his words and a little bit of the carpet as I stick out the leg of my cane to send him tumbling forward face first. He sprawls out over the floor and I press my lips together while continuing to walk ahead.

"What was that again?" I call back and chuckle at the shuffling, clumsy sounds of him standing. My eyes look him over as his hands brush through that copper hair. There's no anger on his face. In fact, the corner of his lips has tilted up and his eyes are sparkling.

We stop at the end of the hall where it veers off to the left. His head tilts slightly. "I didn't expect you to be so..." He struggles and I cross my arms as I lean against a wooden door gilded with gold.

"So what?"

"So human." He admits and once again I almost laugh.

"Legends often are, despite the stories told about them." Gods, I have stories. So many that sometimes I wish I could pour them out of me like water, and then watch them float away. I meet Silva's eyes and hold his gaze sternly. "With you, I can be human.

We're allies," for now, "and with that comes a slight lack of enmity."

"Slight." He repeats with a charming smile that I don't return.

It fades as I go on. "One day you'll see the legend. You'll see the monster everyone talks about and I'm telling you now, Silvanus, the best thing you can do then is get out of my way." Targets I've yet to catch float through my eyes, missions left uncompleted, traitors still alive, but all that in good time.

Silva takes this in slowly and I find myself checking the halls to either side of us a few times just in case. "Every dragon needs their lair, then." My eyes snap to his and while the words sound like a tease, the edge in his eyes lets me know he hasn't taken my warning lightly. Good. He moves around me to the slightly arched doors with onyx handles. Nerves creep up on me as I remember a particularly fiendish young guard in the same position as he flung open the doors to reveal my cell on the Mount.

"Just open them, Silva." He's hesitating as he struggles to read the look on my face. Unlike that guard, he swings the ornate doors open gently to reveal the room. It's not dark or dank, nor does it smell like putrid flesh and mold. This must be the twin tower to his mother's beloved rooms because the circular space is practically made from windows. Rows of glass line the curved emerald wall decorated with picture frame molding, but here pieces have been painted. Small roses at the peak of the panels are blush pink as they bloom from the deep green of the walls.

I step further into the room and can see rolling hills for miles around as well as a slice of both the gardens in the back and the road in the front. "Thought the view would help you keep abreast of people coming and going." I run a hand over the creamy white down comforter on the four-poster bed, then let my fingers twirl through the gauzy meadow-green curtains meant to be drawn if one wants to sleep more. "A bit more comfortable than what you're used to, I hope." My eyes cut over to him and he smirks at the warning on my face. However, there is a sliver of true desire for my comfort in his eyes. I dismiss it and continue my evaluation of the room.

The floor is a dark wood with a soft, subtly patterned carpet under the bed. My fingers glide over the ornate furniture, all without a trace of dust of course, and decorated with more carved wooden roses. There are even two chaises covered in decadent pink velvet that's soft as a tuft of cotton sitting to either side of the bed. "Just a tad," I reply and turn around to find Silva leaning against one of the twin dressers to the right of the door.

He flicks his chin to the left bedside table. "There's another gift in the drawer."

I raise a brow while stepping backward towards it. "Another?"

Silva shrugs and waves a hand through the air, gesturing to the room. "This room is yours." I pause with my hand on the drawer. "We don't use it except for guests and those we rarely have. No one will miss it. Besides," He grins at me. "It suits you."

My head shakes. "Think about what you're offering, lord's son. A lord, as you'll soon be, is offering assistance to a known assassin, thief, and malingerer." He stands there staring at me for a moment before he turns around and quietly shuts the doors, enclosing us in the room together. The next moment, I stride over to a window and push it open wide, letting a cool breeze swirl through the room.

I take a deep breath of the fresh air as Silva moves to my side with hands in his pockets. "I realize there could be consequences, but you're not going to be caught. And even if you were, you'd never give me up."

I glance over at him and barely have the cognizance to make my eyes sharp. "What makes you think that?"

The corner of his mouth lifts as he turns to face me. "Because, no matter what I don't know about you, I know you're angry. If they somehow took you alive again, locked you up, and threw away the key, I know you'd never tell them a thing because that would be your last act of defiance. The last punch thrown." My hands curl into fists as he talks and I feel that anger boiling inside me, pure rage that I'll one day find an outlet for. One day soon.

I take a deep breath, two, actually, before letting my hands relax again. "So, you trust my anger, not me." My tone is a little lighter than before and he smiles.

"Right now, your anger is you." Silva turns again to face the sun lowering over his land. "But I also offer this room because I'd like to see what you're like without it. And I'm willing to wait." I don't give him an answer. He already knows the words I'm not saying.

He'll be waiting a long, long time.

We're silent for a few beats before a soft meow shatters the quiet. Silva turns first and frowns. "He cannot stay in here." I turn and smile at the sight of the black kitty sitting primly on the end of the bed.

After walking over, I wiggle my finger under the cat's chin before looking back at Silva. "My room, my rules. He stays."

His nose wrinkles, but he doesn't fight me on it. "At least give him a name then so I don't have to call for 'rat bastard' when I'm yelling at him."

I shoot him a disapproving expression while my hand moves to the cat's ear. "He wouldn't do anything worth yelling at him for." His pale green eyes shut and the corner of my mouth lifts as he purrs.

"Henry would remind you that black cats wonder around graveyards looking for tortured souls to swallow." A half-smile leaks onto Silva's face as he settles down on the chaise with the golden sun highlighting the freckles across his chest. He'd never replaced his shirt that I ripped. It also makes that copper hair shimmer like fire.

I look away and take a breath before smirking. "I have the perfect name for him then. Graves." There's a beat, then Silva is laughing and my head snaps over to catch the sight. His pink lips stretch wide over pristine white teeth as he slides a hand over his stomach to try to control the feeling. I note that his eyes shut and crinkle a bit at the sides when he truly laughs. Sweet.

Marginally, a real smile inches onto my face. When Silva's eyes open, he blinks as he looks at me before returning the grin. "You'll give Henry a heart attack when he hears that. You have a morbid fascination with death."

I hum. "So do you." His smile slants as he gives me a shrug. The similarity is part of why he's curious about me. Part of why he hangs around me more than he probably should. Silva makes no move to leave, so I heave myself up onto the cloudlike softness of the bed beside Graves. "Do you plan on staying here since you're now vying for my affections?"

Silva raises a brow as his head turns in my direction. "That isn't exactly how courting works in high society."

I smirk. "It does if you're good at hiding it."

"Visited a few lord's beds in your time, then?" The question is light and nonjudgmental.

"Lords, barons. A prince or two."

Silva sits up at that and glances over at me. I wave a hand at him, dismissing his question before he asks it. "I've been to many places and have seen many people. The stories can wait for another time." Maybe.

He hums and swings his legs down to the floor. "I eagerly await the day, then." And I can tell that he truly will. "But to answer your question, I'm still here because you haven't seen your other gift yet." We both look at the drawer. Rolling my eyes, I reach out with my foot and pull it open to reveal rows of bottles. "Weight potions that vary from ten to thirty. Figured a fifty or hundred was pushing it." I nod along slowly, taking in the colored bottles set up in neat little lines clearly organized by Silvanus.

"Thank you," I murmur and take in the clear blue of his eyes. It's been a long time since someone has tried to take care of me. Even if I'm just using Silva's hospitality for my own ends, his effort is sweet. If he thinks it'll make me care or make any difference at all he's a fool, but it's sweet all the same.

He smiles and this one has a more genuine tint than the last few. "My pleasure. It's the least I can do for my assassin."

I roll my eyes again. "If you're keen on gifting me things, then I'd like a gown dripping with the blood of my enemies, emerald hair pins sharp enough to gouge eyes from the socket, and shoes with a blade along the heel."

He huffs a soft laugh with eyes shining like starlight. "I'll keep that in mind." My gaze returns to the drawer and I pluck a bottle from the neat lines. I consider it a moment. It'll take a lot of work to get me and my body back to where they used to be, but this potion is the first step in a long road. I down it in a few gulps.

Let's get started.

Chapter Seven

Dark and Light

Silva

Roux starts the next day with a hearty meal, then goes out for a run. Well, it's not really a run since she can barely jog, but she tries with that little black cat on her heels. The next day she tries again, and again the next day, repeating the attempt until a week has passed and she can actually run. The potions I gave her are doing their job since every day I see her put on a little more weight. A good thing too since she probably weighed seventy pounds soaking wet. If that. I thought about getting her the maximum hundred potion, but gaining that much all at once puts too much stress on the body. One has to eat the proper amount to keep up with the potions and even fifty is a little too risky.

Every day she eats more and more, sometimes ordering multiple trays from the kitchen. I have the servants reporting to me simply out of curiosity and a desire to see her better. Healthy. After another week, she can run and walk without her cane, even if it isn't for long periods. She still has a limp, but it's barely noticeable and doesn't slow her in the slightest.

She'd been so busy with herself that I'd barely gotten to speak to her. Hen has kept me company, my mother too when she isn't enjoying her independence with the absence of my father, but

I'm distracted by thoughts of my assassin nearly all the time. Which is why I'm currently waiting for her out in the cool chill of the morning before she leaves for her run.

Fog drags itself over the hedges and plants behind me, seemingly creeping out of the lake just beyond the garden. I'm watching it coast over the dew-covered grass when sharp steel prods the small of my back. "Here's hoping you're just happy to see me," I comment and smile at the sound of her surprised chuckle.

"You need to work on your vigilance." The dagger tip vanishes as she turns in front of me with a smirk. I'm glad to see the blade is the one I left on her pillow the other night. The guard's dagger that she'd been carrying would have been a giveaway, so she needed a new one. My eyes return to her face as I take stock of what's changed.

Her cheeks have gotten fuller, losing the skull-like hollowness, and are brushed pink with the chill of the morning. Those sharp eyes are unchanged, but no longer sink back into her head. Soft curves are returning to her body and are more pronounced than I would have guessed. Each mark of improvement satisfies something in me. Like seeing a species return after it was thought lost. Although her skin remains pale like bone and her half-hearted waves stay dull. Even so, she's a beautiful sight.

"Have you finished your appraisal?" Her gaze is pointed as my eyes return to hers.

I let a half-smile stretch across my mouth. "Nearly. How are the ribs?"

"I'm not a prized pig you're feeding to auction off." She snaps, but my smile only widens at the challenge. Ever since she told me that I'd see the monster, see the legend, I'd been waiting for it with bated breath. I want her at her best because I want to see it, see *her*. "Stay out of my business."

"Then I suppose you don't want any of the lovely breakfast I had planned?" I wave my hand to the tea room just inside the windows, but she doesn't even glance at it before shaking her head.

"No. I have work to do." I'm about to argue with her when Henry exits the house looking slightly shaggy as if he got dressed in a hurry. Roux smirks. "Good. Henry can dine with you so you don't get lonely."

"And if you get lonely?"

She points down to her ankles. "That's what he's for." I sigh as I glance down to find Graves twirling around her feet. Roux commences her stretches while Henry moves to my side with eyes trained on her.

I raise a brow at him. "Why are you up so early?" His mouth opens, but Roux is faster.

She chuckles and reaches for her feet. "He likes to follow me to make sure I'm not causing too much havoc." Her spine straightens and she spares my friend a wink. "I'm flattered, really, but feel free to take a break this morning." She turns on her heel and the frozen dew on the grass crunches as she starts running towards the stables with Graves on her heels.

I watch her go, taking in her lithe body, how straight her spine stays as she jogs, the way her hair sways with each step. At least until Henry swats my chest. "As for you, I rarely see you up before ten. What are you doing? Or, more specifically, what are you thinking?"

I sigh and wrap my arm around his as we head inside. "She's interesting."

"There are plenty of interesting things that won't kill you."

A grin blooms on my face as I glance at the warm brown eyes of my friend. "But those things aren't half as interesting." He huffs at me and pushes my arm off as we come to the tea room. I dismiss all the servants so we can be alone and only speak again when the doors shut. "What? She hasn't done away with us yet. I take that as a good sign."

Henry shakes his head as we settle across from one another at the breakfast table. "*Yet*. Don't you realize the stronger she gets, the more of a danger she becomes?"

"That is rather the point, isn't it?"

He grits his teeth together while tossing food onto his plate. "We want her to be a danger to your father, not to us." His voice lowers so we're not overheard, but I just shrug.

"And you think the best way to do that is to give her a wide berth rather than befriending her?" He drops the egg spoon into the porcelain dish with a soft *plop*! My nose wrinkled—I wipe a bit off my cheek before looking over my clothes to make sure none will stain the dark turquoise of my pants. Henry, of course, has other concerns.

"You can't befriend assassins!" He hisses across the table and half-stands in opposition.

I resituate my napkin in my lap. "Careful, Henry dear, you'll spit on the food." He sighs, crashing back down into his chair and rubbing big fingers over tired eyes. "Hen, I know she's dangerous. I know she's a killer." He looks up at me again with half-hope in his shaded eyes. "But she's also a person." He deflates as I take his hope away. "She has reasons for what she does and led a life long before she became the Red Death. Doesn't she deserve to be known?"

He rolls his eyes, the corner of his mouth lifting in reluctant amusement. "She chose to be unknown when she became Roux. But let's say yes for the sake of argument. Why does it have to be *you*?"

I think about his question a moment before answering. "I want it to be me." In all honesty, it isn't my choice at all, but hers. She gets to choose whether to be known or not and I want her to choose to be known by me.

Henry groans but seems to give in as he starts eating. "This is Bal all over again."

The corner of my lips turns up. "Ah, Bal. We had fun on that trip." He harrumphs in clear dissent while I idly spoon honey into my tea. "You had just as much fun as me if I remember correctly. More, perhaps."

His cheeks brush darker. "We never should have taken whatever that crazy witch gave us." But there's a little smile trying to sneak its way onto his face.

I hum. "It was in a red bottle. We had to drink it." Red, the color of luck and passion, not to mention life's blood. "A very pretty bottle, I think it was. Glass with little ridges on the sides. I think I still have it rattling around somewhere."

"It wasn't the bottle that made my memory almost disappear."

I smirk. "You did take quite a long swig."

He throws his hands up. "The witch was staring at me! I was afraid if I didn't drink enough, she'd stuff the thing down my throat!"

I laugh softly, thinking back to the red-tinted memories of that night. Part of whatever potion she gave us turned our vision red. Everything was suddenly in shades of the color for a few hours. Or at least until we woke up after passing out in the booth of a disreputable club. "I gave you an accurate report. Through red-tinted memories, of course, but I'd have to be blind to have missed the two ladies perched on your thighs." Henry's cheeks darken further and I wonder as I have a few times whether he remembers a bit more from that night than he'll let on.

"But we weren't supposed to be there in the first place." He reminds me of his point.

I only shrug. "And look how well that turned out." He's smiling now even as he shakes his head and I grin back. "You might try talking to her rather than judging her so harshly." He tugs in a deep breath as he looks at me and I know he's pondering my words. His mouth opens to go on, but my eye is caught by a growing dust cloud outside on the road leading to the front doors. I rise from the table and head towards the mystery with Henry at my side.

"Your father?" He questions as we step out of the front doors.

I squint in the early morning sun to try and see better before shaking my head. "The carriage is black." My father prides himself on a mostly gold carriage. Gold that could have been used to feed our tenants. No, he'd never ride in such modest transport. We walk out onto the front porch to see things a bit better. A recent memory comes back to me, one of the Prison on the Mount, appearing before my eyes like a sudden crack of lightning. "Gods." I breathe before grabbing Henry's arm and pushing him forward down the three steps into the gravel. "It's the warden. You have to go find her. Do whatever you have to in order to keep her away. *Go*." He sprints off in the direction Roux ran and I pray to the goddess of mercy that he reaches her in time.

Meanwhile, I clasp my hands in front of me and stand up straight to greet the warden. She's brought a small group with her and the six ride alongside the coach on dark horses. The soft thunder of hooves echoes my beating heart as I hope she's here to see my father. If that's the case, I can simply tell her he isn't here and she can be on her way. If she's here for another reason...I doubt things will end well for any of us.

The carriage rounds the drive before coming to a stop and my servants are quick to step forward. Annaliese Warren steps from the carriage looking every bit like a shadow disgruntled to be pulled out of the dark. She's clad in tight-fitting black with belts and weapons strapped to her as if she carrying her own personal armory. Her boots hit the gravel and she swipes her cape from the carriage as her second-in-command steps out clad in a looser outfit colored a dark grey.

"Warden. Deckree. Good to see you both alive and well after the unfortunate events at the prison." Anna's eyes sharpen and I bite back a laugh at how easy it is to get under her skin. She's known my family for a long time, before I was born. I believe she knew my father first since they're similar in age. She has visited this house many times at my father's invitation, he'd much rather invite her here for a day or two than visit the prison. We avoided her as much as we could when we were children, but it wasn't always possible.

Henry was just a soldier's son back then, waiting for his father to come home. His mother worked here, so we became friends. One day, we were playing in the gardens as the warden passed by and I made some snide remark. He laughed and the warden appeared in front of us in an instant. I tried confessing, but she couldn't lay a hand on 'the lord's son'. Henry, however, had no such protection. She beat him within an inch of his life before my father sent him away with his mother. I didn't see him again until a year later.

From that day on, I swore to hate Annaliese Warren and use every tool at my disposal to undermine her. And certainly laugh at her as much as possible. If she's still living by the time the Prison on the Mount comes into my hands, getting rid of her will be top of my list. I'm under no illusion that she doesn't realize this herself and that's more than likely why she also hates me. Now, that hatred had smoothed into casual enmity, but damned I'll be if I go back on my oath.

"Good to see you also escaped unscathed." She doesn't sound particularly happy about the fact, but I smile at her anyway. Deckree gives me a weak, apologetic grimace in lieu of her leader's sour face. As if I'm not used to it.

"I'm afraid my father is away. If you've come to see him, then you've had a wasted trip." Her soldiers dismount their horses and I have a sneaking suspicion that her reason for being here isn't to see dear old dad.

She shakes her head. "I'm here to watch over the lord's family until more suitable arrangements can be made." She pauses a step below me with dark eyes shimmering. "Lovely to be a guest at this estate once again. It has been so long."

"Too long, certainly!" My mother's voice leaks from the house and I turn with softening posture to face her. She's pure grace walking, even in an apron and dusty blue day dress with the sleeves pushed up past her elbows. A smile tugs at my lips as I note the blue paint splattered over her hands and the green smeared over her cheekbone. Our skin is a stark difference from one another's, mine having the lightness of my father's while hers is a rich brown, naming her a native of the south. Her wild curls have been temporarily tamed into a knot on the back of her head and the sun tints the dark mass copper.

She stops beside me, her wide smile pushing up round cheeks to nearly shut her clear eyes, almost the only thing we have in common. "Come inside, then. Silvanus has a few things that need tending to, but I'm free to entertain."

Anna dips her head respectfully before waving her soldiers in. "You're always so welcoming, Meira, thank you." The warden pauses, last in the line, and turns back to me. "I believe this is yours, by the way." She holds out a bolt of fabric and drops it at my feet. It's so soiled and covered in filth that I nearly don't recognize it, then I see the missing clasp. This is the cloak I'd given Roux at the prison. The one that led to her escape. Shock shoots through me first, then I shove all emotion down as I look back to Anna's face.

"How kind." My tone is no longer light and accommodating, but the fact only brings a sharp smile to the warden's face. She heads in at last as we watch the line of soldiers march in unison.

My mother leans towards me. "Run while you still can." She winks at me before I stoop to press a kiss on her cheek.

"Might want to temper that smile, mom. The warden might take offense."

"Och." She scolds and pinches my arm. "Behave yourself, Silvanus. Or are you still here because you want to come in?" I'm off the porch in an instant, leaving the cloak behind. I glance back to catch my mother's wide smile before she steps back inside the house. She's always so light when my father is gone. After he's dead and the mourning is over, I hope she can be like this all the time.

My smile fades as I'm reminded of the person who is supposed to make that happen and hope Henry made it to her in time. Although I'm not sure what he could do to stop her if she already saw the warden.

I walk through the stables and the paddock without finding either of them, but hear a shout coming from the edge of the woods. My eyes scan the wood line until Henry comes out panting but without Roux. His head shakes and my stomach drops before he comes close enough to tell me the news. "I can't find her."

Panic, strong and sure, swirls in my stomach as I look around and try to think about where she'd go. My wide eyes turn to Henry, then in the direction of the grand house. If she already saw the carriage and the occupants, there's only one place she'd be. "Gods, she's going after the warden." People stare at Henry and me as we rush back through the stables, dodging the servants bringing in the horses and carriage to get out. We skid to a stop as I look down the road to find exactly what I dreaded. Roux stalks towards the front door, dagger drawn and glinting in the sun with her every step.

"Shit." Henry breathes before we race towards her. Every step she takes is deliberate, slow, and firm. A predator unafraid that her prey will run or that she can be stopped. Still, we have to try.

Pebbles fly as we coast to a stop just behind her and I'm not surprised when she spins around to press that dagger to my throat. "Roux, you can't do this." Her wicked eyes burn into me and I swear I see flames flickering deep within stoked with pure, unadulterated rage. "There are six soldiers in there. Not to mention the warden and second. None will go without a fight."

"Good." She states without a moment of hesitation or doubt. She turns back to the door and I slide in front of her, swallowing when I see her jaw lock.

Henry takes a stab at convincing her. "You do this and you're outed. Everyone here will know who you are. People will come for you; Enhanced, guards. You'll be pursued like a fox in the hunt!"

Her expression doesn't budge. She only levels her burning eyes with mine and even with the blade between us, I want to lean in. "She put me in a cage."

I hesitate, weighing her words and pondering how to state the truth in order to turn her around. All the while, I'm ignoring the pang in my heart at the hurt stirring the embers of her fury. "My father put you in those prisons—"

"You know *nothing*!" She finally bursts and holds the tip of her dagger to my chest, pushing me back into the door. Henry steps forward to pull her off, but I shake my head with eyes locked on hers. "The warden captured me! *Tortured me*!" The revelation steals my breath away, but she's not done as words spill from her like water from a broken dam. "Your father is in charge of the Prison on the Mount, that is all. She followed me from prison to prison as if I were her pet, all the while offering me freedom on a leash. Your father might have known, might be aware, but he's his own master. Annaliese Warren is a dog owned by the person seeking that damned book!"

My eyes narrow. "Who?" There aren't many people above Anna. If Roux says she's under someone's thumb, that someone would be extraordinarily powerful indeed. And this book would have to be something special for someone like that to be after it.

Roux gives me no answers. She only presses her blade down harder until a bead of blood gathers on the tip. "Move."

It isn't a request, yet I wait another moment as we stare off, daring one another to make a move. "Sil." Henry's anxious voice calls me away and I see the servants returning from caring for the horses. Sighing, I slide to the side to let Roux pass. She steps forward and wraps her fingers around the ornate handle as if touching a lover.

I take a breath. "Do this and you betray me." Her head snaps towards me as if I uttered her deepest secret. For a moment, the rage and murderous intent in her eyes is pushed back to give way to deep, heart-wrenching grief. Then it's gone in the blink of an eye.

She turns back to the door and her knuckles turn white as she clings to it. "You betrayed me the moment you forbid me."

"I didn't forbid you." I take a step closer to her side, but make sure not to touch her. "I'm just saying not now. Not like this." The words hover in the air and she doesn't open the door but shoves me to the side. The dagger slides home into its sheath before she jumps off the porch and slinks off towards the forest.

Relief courses through me so potently that I nearly fall to my knees. She's safe. Disaster averted. Henry clears his throat and I turn back to him along with the curious servants. I plaster a smile on my face and explain that it was a minor disagreement, but my mind is still on the things Roux revealed.

It wouldn't surprise me if the warden was working for someone. She's a principled woman but doesn't mind aligning herself with those similarly minded. But what about a book would make someone seek out a warden to hunt it down? And what does any of it have to do with Roux? My head shakes as the servants go on with their business and Henry claps my back as we face the forest where she vanished.

"Still keen on befriending her?" I see him raise a brow in my peripheral vision, but only pat his shoulder in return. I doubt it would reassure him that this has only made me want to know her more.

* * *

I make my way to my room after having wasted the rest of the day avoiding Annaliese and pondering my many questions. To my knowledge, Roux hasn't returned from the woods. Although I doubt coming to see me after today is high on her list of things to do.

"Thank you, Mary." The maid who brings around the food nods to me before I note the red mark on her face. "Wait, what happened there?" My brows furrow as her cheeks turn red at my appraisal.

"Nothing." She squeaks, her blonde ponytail waving like a flag as she shakes her head. "Just an accident."

My lips press flat. "Accidents don't leave fingers on your face. Who did that?" She curls in on herself at my harsher tone, so I take a step away from her towards my room. "That isn't permitted in this house, Mary. You know that." It was more than enough trouble to deal with when my father was hitting the servants. I certainly won't allow some visitors to do so.

She shakes her head again, brown eyes widening in her heart-shaped face. "It won't be a problem anymore, sir. Thank you." Her smile is weak, but genuine as she hurries away down the hall. Sighing, I make a mental note to check on her in the morning as I push open my door only to find Roux laid out on the bed.

At first, I'm shocked still. She's wearing nothing but one of my shirts, a forest green one that matches her brilliant eyes. It only comes down to the tops of her thighs and has small ties at the top that she's left open down past her collar bone just above the swell of her breasts. "You rented out my room." She states.

I move into the space and shut the door, locking it behind me. "So you've taken mine?" I finally manage to speak as she looks around at the navy walls detailed with gold and the constellations painstakingly painted on the ceiling.

"I like it." Her hand reaches up to skim the gauzy white curtains that drape around my bed. "Although it's not what I expected."

I hum. "My mother painted the ceiling. It's the sky on the night of my birth." My eyes take in the swirling colors mixed with glittering stars and the crescent moon gleaming in the corner. Something in me eases at the sight even with the predator in my bed. I move further into the room past the crackling fireplace, starting my normal routine of disrobing as she watches my every movement.

"Do you know why I was put into solitary?" Her ankles cross as she spins her dagger swiftly in her hands while Graves twitches his tail at the end of the bed.

"Because you can't play nice with others?"

"I was put in a group cell when I was first taken." She starts and I turn without a shred of modesty even as I shed my clothes. Roux pauses, gauging whether she should turn away, but when I make no signal, she goes on with eyes on mine. "Some random, filthy place covered in grime. You'd have probably died on sight."

My eyes roll, but she's probably right. "But they simply needed somewhere to hold me and they weren't particularly picky. I woke up covered in piss and shit with three men feeling themselves next to my prostrate body." Bile pushes at the back of my throat as a flicker of that fire I saw earlier today makes an appearance in her eyes. Still, I don't dare interrupt her. "Whatever guards handled me were novices or too afraid to properly check that they'd taken all my weapons, so I had two small knives still tucked away on my person. When I woke up to *that*..." She sneers. "My vision went red and after cutting off their favored appendages, I slit their throats."

My steps falter on the way to the bed now in only a shirt and loose-fitting pants. I swallow, the sharp grin she gives me not exactly doing much to reassure me. Her hand pats the other side of the bed and I slide onto the end so I can face her. "Quite an entrance."

She shrugs, her smile gaining a sincere edge. "I do like to leave an impression." I chuckle, then quiet in hopes that she'll continue. She does. "I killed every vile soul in that cell. Murderers, rapists, thieves, anyone in my path. There must have been at least thirty and I lost my knives halfway through, but that wasn't an issue. I killed with broken stones, bits of rusted metal, my bare hands, anything at all available to me. Gods, the rage I felt. It was…intoxicating. Better than any drink, drugs, even sex." Roux sighs as she leans back against the black headboard, and then her eyes flick to me.

"Then the warden came. She saw the carnage I wrought and ordered that I be drugged before being taken out. I evaded the darts for a while, but not even I can dodge something indefinitely." Her hands make fists in her lap alongside her blade, the knuckles so pale as they bulge out of her skin, I almost think bone has broken through. "The next time I woke up, I was strung up naked with my limbs stretched out to the sides. To make sure I had no weapons, of course." She looks down at her hands and I see her brilliant eyes go glassy. I wonder, if I looked hard enough, if I'd see the memory reflected in the pools of emerald green.

"There are many kinds of sweet, lovely intimacy, but there are also many that are sinister. I never saw the truth of that more than when my eyes opened to find Annaliese Warren waiting for me." Her throat bobs as she swallows even though her face remains perfectly smooth, as if she once again is staring down the warden. "There's intimacy between enemies. A purity in knowing that someone thinks of you, and thinks of you often, even if their only thought is the desire to feel your blood on their hands. It's a connection, even if you want to fight it." Her eyes flash back to mine and only the bedpost behind me keeps me from tumbling to the floor.

"She tortured me for a long while. Trying to figure out who I was, where I came from, what made me." The corner of her mouth lifts coldly. "I never told her, of course, and the torture stopped when she was called away to the feet of her employer. That's when I was moved from prison to prison as she dangled that stale carrot in front of my face. And that isn't even the worst of what the warden and her ilk have done to me." She rolls her eyes as if she'd simply been talking about the weather.

I pull in a deep breath and move more of my body onto the bed, crossing a leg under me. "Why are you telling me this?" My thoughts go on without my permission. *I'm glad you told me. In fact, I'd gladly listen to you talk for days without uttering a single complaint.*

She picks up her dagger again and runs her thumb over the inscription I had carved down the blade. "Because we're allies. Because, as irritating as it was, you made the right call stopping me today. And because I wanted you to understand why I am going to slowly kill each of her guards, then her." Shock shoots through me and I run a hand over my hair as I absorb her words. "I'll do it well. She won't know what's going on until it's too late and I won't scare off your father from coming home."

I'm silent for a minute or two as I think it through. "That's well said, but how can you know?"

Her lips purse. "I know I've been out of the game for a while, but I am still a professional. I've killed a lot of people for money and many more simply for my own ends."

"Two weeks ago, you could barely lift a fork."

Her nostrils flare, but she doesn't combat me. "Fine. You'll have your proof in the morning when the man staying in my room is found dead and they rule it an accident."

"*What*?" I sit straight up and her eyes narrow at my tone.

She shrugs. "I went in to collect the guard's dagger I hid and my potions since they would be a bit of a giveaway. He came in trailing a maid with a tray of food, so I slipped out the window. I was going to just climb into your room, but realized it was the perfect opportunity."

I raise a brow as the mark on Mary's face comes back to me. "He hit her." She freezes, lips thinning as she presses them together. "The maid trailing behind him." I specify and believe her mouth tilts upward slightly. It may have been her plan to kill off the guards from the beginning, but this kill wasn't planned. Or undeserved.

"He may have. Whatever happened, he found himself tumbling from a high window the next instant." Her tone is so blasé that I can't help but laugh, disturbing a napping Graves beside me. When my eyes open, her smile is softer than before and lacks the cold edge.

"And Mary saw you do this." That would explain why she said that the beatings weren't going to be a problem anymore. I should have known.

Roux shrugs again. "She saw someone do it. It was too dark for her to see my face. Although, she did ask if I needed any help with the body, so rest assured you have an excellent staff." Amusement shoots through me at the fact, but I'm not reassured. If sweet Mary was pushed that far, then I wonder what else the deceased had put her through. "I came here afterward since I thought it wouldn't do well if I were found in a dead man's bed. Even if it was mine first. I also have no desire to be awoken by Annaliese Warren's room checks in the morning, so I'll be staying here."

I smother my smile as I shake my head. "Am I to take the chaise while you commandeer my bed, then?"

The grin she now gives me is feline as she swipes a hand over the empty pillow beside her. "No, I don't see why we can't share your massive bed. It is big enough for five grown men. But also consider the story I told you a warning." The dagger moves so quickly that I only see a flash of silver before it's embedded in the bedpost above my head. I look from the blade back to her gleaming eyes. "Don't get in my way again, Silvanus." The hair on the back of my neck stands at the sound of my name and I've yanked the blade free to give back to her before I've contemplated the wisdom of the decision.

"My problem was never with you killing the warden. It was the way you were going to do it." I drag myself up to sit beside her, sliding under the blankets with more than a little trepidation. "You'd have had us all shoved through the doors of Under without a second of hesitation."

"So long as you didn't get in the way or pick up a weapon, I would have gotten all the blame."

"I'm relatively sure Anna would be rather upset if she saw me standing idly by while her guards were murdered."

"That's why you kill her before she can get angry."

"Is that your solution to everything?"

"Pretty much."

There's a grin on my face as I glance over at her and find her fighting a smile of her own. This is nice, in a slightly terrifying way. Perhaps killing puts her in a good mood. "I trust that your plan will go right and look forward to the show tomorrow morning." Some of the light fades from her eyes.

"Trust." She repeats and I'm unsure if she realizes it. My mouth opens to ask about her reaction today, and why my words affected her so much, but I swallow my questions when she looks back over at me. "You don't have to wear all that to sleep."

I glance down at my shirt and pants. "Would you rather I only wear pants since you're only wearing a shirt? My shirt, by the way?" She doesn't answer, instead wriggling under the blankets and turning her back to me. Apparently, she's done with talking for the night. I shed my shirt and lay it out at the end of the bed before blowing out the candle on my bedside table. Darkness engulfs the room until my eyes adjust to find a shaft of moonlight cutting across the bed from between the curtains. I move to shut them, but freeze when Roux's hand shoots out to catch my arm.

"Leave it."

I glance between her hand, the first time she's intentionally touched me without anger, and the curtain. "Sunlight will come bursting through that window come morning—"

"Leave it." She repeats simply and only releases me when I relax back into the bed beside her. A few minutes pass with me staring at the night sky outside before I realize why she wants it open. The same reason I gave her a room full of windows. After being trapped in the dark for so long, light is the one thing that tells her she isn't there anymore.

Chapter Eight

Remorse

Roux

I stare at the moonlight streaming in the window so clear and strong it could be white paint thrown across the room. When I was young and learning magic, I'd enchant the light to dance across the room in little shapes. Stars, moons, comets, all of them would shoot across the space as if I were in my own sky. Perhaps that's why I find it so easy to be at ease in Silva's room decorated with the same. Too at ease, perhaps.

Silva's breathing is even but has yet to turn deep. We're both still awake then. The moonlight has shifted a few inches closer by the time I speak. "Why the inscription?" My voice is hushed in the large room, but I know he hears me by the way he stills. The blade he gave me, the first thing I have come to own since being free, lays on the bedside table. The handle is supple leather with small onyx gems in the hilt and the cross-guard. I can read the swirling script written across the gleaming steel from my place in bed.

Never Break.

"It's something that I've had to say to myself over the years. Whenever my father would do something particularly dastardly or cruel." He sighs and I slowly turn over so I can see his face. The moonlight fills his clear eyes to the brim, the soft blue reflecting the light like water. "At first I said 'don't bend.' I was so against everything he stood for that I wanted to shut out all that he was trying to teach me. As I got older, I learned that bending is necessary. I could take what he taught me and use it for my own ends. A little give and take is good, better even, because if you're too stiff then you'll break under the slightest pressure." He pulls in a deep breath while staring up at the ceiling.

"There was a time when my father still wanted to win me over. Times I thought he loved me and he used that to his advantage." Silva crosses his arms over his chest and his freckles look very much like stars dotted on the light expanse of his skin. Little constellations waiting to be connected. "There was an instance where we were riding around the property to look at our land and tend the tenants on it. We came to a house, a simple one, but clean and well-kept. He lit a torch and handed it to me with the command to burn it down with the tenants inside."

I'd be lying if I didn't picture the towering flames eating up the building, the screams from the people inside, the musky smell of smoke. But my expression doesn't change as he glances over at me. I'm only a nonjudgmental listener; impartial, unbiased. The corner of Silva's mouth lifts, but the near-smile doesn't reach his eyes which have gone cold as the moonlight. "They hadn't been paying their rent for a few months. I argued with him. The house was built well, with no wear, and what if the fire would spread to those nearby? Not to mention the rich land barely a mile away or the crops that lay on it. When he smiled...that's when I realized I'd bent too far. I'd been arguing for the house, the land, the crops, all things we could profit from. Not one word I uttered was in defense of the family inside."

He chuckles dryly as if trying to shake free the guilt still in his voice. "He told me he didn't care how I did it, but to turn them out of the house. Then he rode away to leave me to clean up. It was a victory and we both knew it. I wanted to run. More than ever before, I wanted to escape him and our dance." There's still a trace of longing on his face and it calls to something in me. Haven't I wished for the same thing? "Clearly, I didn't run. I went into that house and told them the issue. Heard that they'd barely had money to spare for food, much less rent because of the taxes my father had forced on them." His head shakes as his lip curls with disgust.

"Right then and there I gave them all I had. Gold rings with precious stones, an engraved pocket watch, even the silk shirt off my back. The next day they arrived at the house and paid my father in full for all that they owed along with the rest of the year. They even had some money left over to buy food." He smiles now, bright and full. "The look on my father's face—he knew that I'd had a hand in it. There was no other way they could have afforded it. It was then that I told myself that I could never break. Never run. I'd defy him at every turn and provide for my people while he gorged himself on pleasure and coin."

"You seem to be accomplishing that well enough," I murmur, breaking my silence. He smiles, shrugging a shoulder. Suddenly, I wonder what he'll do when he's free. When his tenants are cared for and his land flourishing, will he lay back in his fine house surrounded by his fine things? Or will he want more? "What do you want?" My curiosity wins over and his head turns to face me. "You've said what you want for your tenants, but not for yourself."

Surprise lifts his brows, but he takes a minute to think the question over. "Well...I suppose that what I want is freedom." The word clangs through me like a name I forgot long ago. *Freedom.* Silva hesitates slightly and my brows pinch at the vulnerability creeping onto his face. "I told you I was afraid of my father. Afraid of all that he could do to me, and that was true. But perhaps above all, I'm afraid that I'll be just like him. Just as cruel, as callous, as terribly ruthless in the pursuit of profit or coin."

My head shakes as I let my fingers graze his arm so he'll look at me. It's a light touch, just from one freckle to another. "Take this to heart. People who are truly cruel and callous don't

care about being cruel or callous. They just are. Without regret."
He stares at me a moment as if to see whether I'm lying or not, so I
go on. "You care, Silva. About Henry, your mother, your tenants—
"

"You." He finishes and grins as my eyes widen. "My
assassin. My ally." He turns his body toward me so we're fully
facing one another and I stare at the space between us. This is
dangerous territory. We're too close, not just physically, but...in a
deeper way. My inner instinct to defend and hide fights with this
new, soft, comfort this man offers.

My chin juts out. "Don't get attached, lord's son. I have
many things to attend to once our business here is done."

Undaunted, he shrugs a shoulder. "Perhaps you'll take me
with you."

My gaze snaps to his and his smile brightens at the contact
before I shake my head again. "I'll be a leaf in the wind for a
while. I doubt you'd enjoy sleeping in the dirt every night and
stopping at disreputable inns when I can afford it."

"Ah, that's where I'd come in as your benefactor. We'd
stay in the finest room in the finest place every night."

"And when I stepped out to murder someone?"

"I'd go shopping in town. Henry would come too, of
course, he needs more adventure in his life. I'd drag him with me
wherever I went."

"And we'd all sleep in the same grand bed at night while
snuggling like a group of kittens?"

He grins. "If you like."

I hum with amusement at the picture he paints, but along
with it comes steel-toothed melancholy that rips into my heart.
Having allies can be handy on the road, but they can also be
liabilities. Especially if they're inexperienced and...friend-like.
"My life isn't a rosy one. My story was written a long time ago
with blood instead of ink. Much harder to wash away." The light
on his face fades a bit as I go on. "When I leave this place, I won't

be still for more than a few days at a time. I'll be sleeping under the stars, in trees, inside caves if I can manage it." Maybe even see a few old contacts. I'll have to take on quite a few jobs to build up a supply of cash to live on. Probably search a few hidden caches of mine to see if they're still intact. "The day I leave this place, I'll be on the hunt."

"For?"

The corner of my lips lift. "Something of mine." His mouth opens, but I go on before he can speak. "For now, the both of us should be pursuing sleep." We stare off, daring the other to turn away first when Graves comes up and happily lays between us as if irritated with our chatter.

Silva frowns at the cat. "He should not be in the bed." I do nothing to indicate I heard him and instead rub Graves' ear to coax out that deep purr. Silva rolls his eyes but lays his head down on his pillow. I smirk as I look at the cat's cute little face before I get an idea. I hadn't simply taken a walk in the woods today. I'd been scouting and found some very interesting things.

"Take the warden and her soldiers on a hunt tomorrow. South, into the woods." I think for a moment and add one more thing. "And at my signal, run."

Silva's brows furrow. "Well, that's reassuring."

I give him a sharp smile. "Trust me." Only then do I turn over and snuggle down into the blankets with Silva's scent drifting up from them. My eyes shut and a minute passes before I hear Silva speak again.

"I do."

I stare ahead of me at the inscription on my blade for a long time before finally falling asleep with Graves' warmth at my back.

* * *

It isn't a surprise that I wake before Silva in the morning, but it is a surprise how much time I spend staring at his sleeping face. Not only do those vivid red waves catch the light and glimmer like polished copper, but also stick out in all sorts of directions as if anxious to see the world. It's such a difference to the perfectly quaffed Silva that I'm used to. His face is smooth, with no bravado, interest, or snark, but clear and soft. There's still a half-smile on his lips, but it seems more innocent than usual. There are darker patches of red hair over his chest to go along with a crazed cluster of freckles dotting slightly dark skin from the sun.

Looking at him, peaceful in sleep, it's hard to believe I ever slept so well. I'd been having bad dreams long before going to the prisons, but in them and afterward, the nightmares only got worse. The smell of smoke and the blinding heat of flames lingers in my nose and on my skin, but it does no good to dwell. At least I've managed to stop screaming in my sleep. I shove the thought down and shove on my pants, and boots, then slip out the doors with Graves on my heels. If the body wasn't found last night, then it'll be sure to be found this morning. It's easy to slip through the servant's passageways out into the morning where I make it to the barn at a sprint.

Graves splits off from me as if knowing the task I have today isn't one he should join me on. "I wish you luck with the mice." I bid, praying for luck myself as I sweep by Banshee's stall to deposit an apple from the kitchens and brush her down. Then head towards the woods with some leftover meat. Still in Silva's forest green shirt and my brown pants, I blend in relatively well.

Taking into consideration everything that will happen this morning, the earliest Silva will get the warden here is late afternoon. All will have to be in place by then.

I'm kneeling in the dirt looking for tracks when I finally sigh. "You breathe harder than a woman in labor." I stand and look over to a tree a few meters away. "If you wanted to go on a walk with me, then you could have just asked." My sugar-sweet tone brings a sigh out of the man as Henry steps around the tree and crosses his bulky arms.

"What are you doing?"

I shrug. "A bit of tracking." I gesture to the ground. Henry's lips screw up, but he walks to my side to examine the footprint. "There's going to be a hunt today."

"Today?" He repeats with brows furrowing. "After the events of this morning, I doubt anyone will feel up to the task." Either he pauses in expectation of a reaction or to call one out of me, but I don't give him either. His hands squeeze his biceps and I nearly grin at so easily slipping under his skin. "Events I know you had a hand in."

My face is smooth and innocent despite the correct accusation. "Events? I'm afraid I left the house too early to hear any news."

He rolls his eyes. "How do you think it looks for the Head of Security when a death occurs on their watch?"

"If it was a murder, it certainly would look very bad."

"We both know that it was."

I level Henry with my gaze and give him credit for not balking as he would have the first day we met. "Prove it then." He blinks. "If it was a murder, then surely there will be evidence. Or, has evidence already been found to prove it was an accident?" Henry's jaw locks as a smile spreads over my lips. "If it makes you feel better, treat it like any other case. Follow the evidence. Accept the results."

"But I'll know it's a lie." He stubbornly remains in his position while I walk deeper into the woods.

"It's terribly boring to be an honest soldier." I've met plenty on both sides.

Henry reluctantly follows behind with a pout on his lips and tightly held fists. "My father was a soldier. He taught me duty and honor while my mother taught me honesty and hard work."

"And did he eventually come home?" I pause to look back at him to see whether he'll lie.

He hesitates but nods once. "He did. It was with one less eye and no right hand, but he came home." I nod along and keep walking while he keeps pace. "He lost them in a firefight with rebels on the border who didn't like that the queen took over when the king died. It was a small skirmish and the rebellion was put to rest, but it cost many men their lives and him a few body parts. After he came home, I watched him struggle every day to work and provide for us until I could take the responsibility from him."

"Hardly an endorsement to become a soldier. Other professions would have offered you more money and less danger." My work isn't exactly a good example of that, but I certainly used to get paid a handsome sum.

Henry's eyes sharpen. "I'm a soldier—*was* a soldier, because I want to be one. I respected my father for it and wanted to earn the same respect."

"Did you even fight? Before your lord called you back to watch over his precious heir, I mean." I counter with a raised brow and watch his jaw go tight while his fingers flex. Hit a nerve there.

"I fought. Not in grand battles with no war and since the rebels went underground, but there was still work to be done." The words have an echo to them, as if someone else's voice is behind them. Still. I recognize the look in his eyes. He's felt what it's like to have blood on his hands and feel it drip between his fingers. "I would have carried on serving if I hadn't been called back. Silva had…caused a bit of a ruckus in my absence." Henry can't fight the small smile that rises and I wonder what kind of mess the lordling caused without his friend. He clears his throat and focuses back on me. "What about you? Did your parents teach you to pillage and murder?"

My eyes roll, but my hand does graze my dagger just to make him second guess his tone. "Course not. They sent me to a school for it."

"A school?" The soldier nearly trips over a root at the revelation. "There's a school for such a thing?"

I hum in affirmation while ducking under a low tree branch. "There's a school for everything if you know the right people. And I suppose pillaging wasn't exactly a class, but pickpocketing was." Henry frowns when I wink at him. "There's an academy for soldiers which is the same thing, I suppose. Although my schooling was a bit more...advanced." The outrage that flashes across his face nearly makes me laugh as we turn to the left. We trek up an incline where there are more tracks dried in the mud after a past rainy day.

"They taught you to kill without reason or remorse?" Henry finally gets his words back as we crest the top of the hill where the trees clear just enough to see a wide, nature-made path down the other side.

I lean back against a tree facing Henry, taking out my dagger to spin it in my hands. "Why do you think I have no reason and no remorse?" There's no playfulness in my tone this time, only cold calculation.

Henry's gaze never leaves me as he moves to the other side of the path. Although, he stays standing straight as a rod. "I mean a reason more than because you want to and you show no remorse."

"Oh, so because you don't see it, then it must not exist?" His mouth opens at my question, then shuts. "And a correction; I *really* want to kill them." I chuckle softly at his disgusted face before heaving a sigh. The tree branches sway above us as a cool breeze snakes between pine needles and leaves to make them whisper against one another. "How long have you known the warden and her ilk? How much time, in all those years, would you estimate you'd spent with them?"

His eyes narrow at me and his feet shuffle in the dirt. "I've known them since I was a child. Ten or so years." I wave my hand at him to answer my next question. Irritation flashes in those brown eyes, but he obeys. "In all that time, I probably spent an accumulated year with them. Possibly a touch more."

I hum, considering. "I spent two straight years with them and knew them long before." Memories dance before my eyes like mist in the morning. "Did you know that Annaliese Warren once vied for a place in the royal guard? She was on the fast track until she killed a young girl during a training mission. Accident or not, from then on, she was ousted." Soldiers need to be hard and firm, but not reckless or messy. A warden or prison guard, however, need only be loyal.

Henry's eyes widen and his stance slackens. "How do you know that?"

"It's my job to know." My voice is ice with a dagger-sharp edge. "The man who died last night took his pleasure where he liked, including the prisoners he caught. Delaney, her third, broke a young man's legs to cripple him after he tortured information out of him. Creed likes to cut out the tongues of her opposers to hang on her wall. Banks prefers to keep her hands clean by framing innocents to claim their possessions, land, or spouse." I take a breath, relaxing back against the tree once again. "I could tell you plenty more."

Henry takes this in slowly with eyes on the spinning steel in my hands. "You could be lying."

I shrug a shoulder while holding his gaze. "Am I?" His jaw locks and we both know I've spoken nothing but the truth. There's a weight to my words that no lie can fake. "I told you before we arrived here that I would need to learn Lord Lurec to see how he deserves to die. Did you think it was simply for your benefit? After all, why would I take such delight in how I kill people if I didn't first decide *why* they deserved death?" Henry shuts his eyes and wipes a hand over his face. He looks a bit at sea, struggling to keep his head above the water.

It's a practice I've always employed, even when I was a killer for hire. Any client who wanted someone dead would have to completely hand the reins over to me. No specific requests, no timeline, no limits. It's part of why my name became so well known. I got to be creative.

My eyes lift to the sky where the sun inches towards its zenith. It'll be time soon. "Time you got back to get ready for the hunt, Henry." He looks me over a few times, then starts walking down the path without another word. "There is one thing you got right," I call and he glances back over his shoulder to see me smirking. "I don't feel any remorse." I don't bother waiting to see his reaction as I slide down the decline on the other side toward my target.

Chapter Nine

The Hunt

Silva

She's gone when I wake up.

It's not surprising, but something in me questions if I dreamt the whole thing. Maybe the things she said, all that she told and revealed to me, weren't real. Yet as someone knocks on the door and I rise, I notice a patch of short black hair left on the blankets at the end of the bed. Graves. I grin despite my displeasure at having cat hair on the bed and slip on some appropriate clothes to open the door.

Sweet Mary stands there with near-white lips and darting eyes. "Sorry to disturb you, sir, but the warden is waiting outside for you. There's been an…incident. A death." The words wind their way through my groggy head slowly before I remember what incident she's talking about.

"Thank you, Mary. Is my mother alright? The servants too?" No doubt this'll be quite the shock.

She nods. "All fine and accounted for. We…" Her voice wavers slightly as I step out into the hall with her and shut my door behind me. When I look back at her, the words pour out. "We're so sorry about the soldier being in Lady Nestra's room. Your mother placed each soldier herself and with her not knowing about the Lady yet—"

"It's fine, Mary, thank you. Go back to your work and I'll take care of the rest." I keep my voice gentle and soft as we move through the house not only to keep from waking anyone else, but to calm Mary as well. She breathes a sigh of relief and curtsies, then all but sprints to the nearest servant's staircase. Lady Nestra will have to make a formal coming out soon. Warden or no. I take a deep breath, then head out into the soft light of morning to meet Annaliese.

Under the still-open window to the left lies the dead body of the soldier with the warden leaning over him like a vulture. My mother is beyond the edge of the house facing away from the sight where the sun gilds her baby blue robe with golden light. As far as I can tell, she has a hand held over her mouth with the other over her heart. Henry is pacing around, peering at the window, at the body, and then frowning. None look up as I approach and come to a stop on the opposite side of the warden. "A pleasant way to wake up, isn't it, Silvanus Lurec?"

I stiffen at the sound of my father's last name. By the gleam in her eyes, she let it slip on purpose. "It's a pleasure to wake up at all, considering this man's fate. What happened?" To Roux's credit, there's no sign of her here. Only the open window above and a dark stain in the soil around his head tell that he isn't sleeping. Well, that and the strange choice of resting place. I've seen dead bodies before, but the cause of death was usually starvation or sickness. Nor have I ever known the murderer responsible and held them in some esteem.

I don't regret his passing, but there is always a weight that comes with death. Especially since I had a small part in this one.

Henry is the one who answers me. "There's alcohol on his breath and a stain on his shirt from the same. Mary already said that he was getting into it when she brought him dinner. His neck is broken. All signs point to a fall." His eyes roll to mine and I know what he's thinking. My head shakes slightly and his jaw locks with irritation before he turns on his heel to head around the house. More than likely to find our relatively friendly assassin.

"I told the fool that drink would kill him one day." The warden murmurs, crouching over him with a claw-like hand reaching out towards his heart only to smooth down his chest. "He should've listened." She actually sounds sad about one of her soldier's deaths. Perhaps she has a heart after all.

"I'm sorry for your loss," I whisper and her head jerks up as if she forgot I was here.

She springs to her feet and leans over his body to leer at me. "When I write to his family, I'll be sure to mention whose house he died in and whose maid supplied him with alcohol."

My fingers clasp in front of me as whatever sympathy I feel for her vanishes. "The same house providing your food and shelter, I believe. If you think it unsafe, please feel free to leave." My voice is bored and I've no doubt my expression reflects the same. Anna fumes. "I don't believe you were invited, anyway."

Her jaw flexes and the sight of her anger keeps my instincts on edge. "I'm here to protect you, your mother, and your poor excuse of a household."

Ice shoots through my veins as I straighten to my full height. "Be very careful about what you say about me and mine. I may put up with the slights towards myself, but you won't disrespect them." They've had more than enough of that from my father. She steps over the body as if it were a log in her way and I hear the sickening crunch of a stiff finger cracking under her heel. We're almost nose to nose, now. I'm taller than her and I know the fact grates on her even if it's barely an inch.

"Or what, Lurec? You'll sick your dog on me?" She dares.

My hands curl into fists, but I only give her a charming smile. She doesn't know what's coming for her. Not yet. "Wait and see, Anna."

"Please, both of you." My mother's voice drifts over as she joins us without looking down at the dead body. "Anna, you said you'd write to the families?" Reluctantly, she nods as we turn to face my kind mother. "Good. I'll send a letter of condolence as well. In the meantime, we'll have his body taken care of properly to send back to the family." She reaches for my hand and I instantly give it, escorting her to the door as the warden bends her head. "Such a terrible business." My mother clings tight to me as we move indoors, then I remember Roux's instructions.

Grimacing, I squeeze my mother's hand. "One second. Stay here and I'll escort you to your room." Her brows furrow over clear eyes as I back towards the door. "I'll just be a moment." I turn around and head back into the daylight towards Anna. She glances at me with thinly veiled irritation but lets me speak first. "There's going to be a hunt today. It's been scheduled to honor your unexpected arrival and instead of canceling it in light of recent events, I thought it might be better to honor him with it. Bring home a fat elk to toast over in your soldier's honor."

She stares at me with those unblinking, black eyes for a minute. Maybe even two. Then she nods once. "We leave as soon as my soldiers can be ready."

"Of course." I tilt my head towards her and don't bother looking back as I hurry to my mother waiting for me.

Her quizzical eyes are set on my face as we walk through the house and up the spiral stairs closer to her rooms. "What was that about?" She asks finally.

I shrug. "I thought it would be nice."

"Mm. Being nice to the woman who almost bit your head off?" She tugs on my arm so we sway from side to side. "You act like I don't know you, Silva." I can't help but grin as we come to her door and she turns to me with sparkling eyes. Her smile is dim and there are remnants of tears on her cheeks, but at least the events of this morning haven't shaken her too badly. "For example, I've known you've been hiding something or…someone here for at least a week." My throat goes dry and she chuckles at my wide eyes.

"I, uh...how?"

She pats my chest. "Servants talk. Whispers of a girl float around and while that's not out of the ordinary, she seems to have caused quite a bit of interest among the staff." Her hands go to her hips while I struggle to get my feet back under me. "What I want to know is why you've been hiding her and why haven't I met her yet?" The scold is lighthearted, but I know she'll want answers.

I tug in a deep breath and set my shoulders. "Well...it wasn't exactly my choice." Truth. "Henry and I helped her out of some trouble on the road, so we brought her here. She needed to rest her first couple days, then when the warden came, she didn't want to interfere in our business." Mostly truth, partly lies. I proudly think that Roux would approve.

My mother swats at my arm with pouty lips and a wrinkled nose. "So when can I meet her? I've never known you to keep a girl around for more than a couple of days."

"Mom," I complain, feeling my cheeks tint red. She laughs, but her gaze is still pointed. "Soon. I promise you'll meet her soon." And goddess help us when they do.

She looks me over while leaning back against her doors, hands latched onto the knobs. "A horrible time to bring someone into the house, but that obviously can't be helped. She must be special if I can get you this flustered over barely mentioning her."

I pause in the middle of turning down the hall and smile. "She could rip my heart out."

*   *   *

By late afternoon we're on the trail into the southern woods as Roux instructed. Part of me is afraid of what she has planned, but a far bigger part is excited.

Henry seems a bit rumpled from his spot at my side, but that isn't surprising considering this morning. He takes a death on his watch very seriously and it's the only thing I'm sorry for during all this. Even if the death is being treated as an accident and he'll have none of the blame, he knows who is truly responsible. "It's not on you, Hen," I murmur, temporarily out of earshot of the warden leading her pack of two guards. The rest are staying behind to tend to the fallen and protect my mother from the assassin waiting for us in these woods. I hope the gods are laughing.

He sighs. "I know who did it and I'm not bringing her in. That's on me."

"No, it's on me. I'm telling you not to and I brought her here. Blame me."

His eyes jump to mine. "Oh, don't worry, I do." I grin at his slight lift in spirits before his near smile fades again. "I'll just be glad when she's gone. For many reasons." My brows furrow as I see something on my friend's face that I rarely find; doubt.

"What did she say to you?" Curiosity gets the best of me. He told me he'd spoken to her this morning, but wouldn't say what they spoke of. Even now, he shakes his head.

"Too much." He clicks his tongue and both our horses move forward to bring up the back of the group.

We're a few miles in when the warden stops and points to the ground. "Elk tracks. No more than a day old." She turns to me, dark eyes flashing. "Hopefully, they haven't moved too far for this trip of yours to be fruitful."

I give her a charming smile. "Come now, Anna. Let's not pretend you don't enjoy the hunt." Her history with Roux is still fresh in my mind and certainly hasn't ingratiated the warden to me. She huffs in annoyance and pulls ahead. It's just as well because as we slide under the towering trees, a slice of light cuts over my eyes before vanishing. My eyes snap up to find a grinning Roux high up in a pine. She's mouthing words and it takes me a moment to make it out.

"Get ready to run."

I hold a hand out to Henry for him to slow while the others move on at a soft trot. His brows furrow, but he follows my lead.

When I look back up to the trees, Roux is gone and there's a sudden jerk in my gut. The hair on the back of my neck stands on end and the horses begin to shuffle uneasily. "Silva," Henry calls and I nod, acknowledging that something is wrong.

The warden glances over her shoulder at us. "We'll not catch them if you—" She doesn't get the chance to finish her sentence before a tan blur leaps from the bushes and tackles her into the brush on the other side of the path.

"Shit!" Henry shouts as we both struggle to stay on our horses as they rear onto their back legs. I manage to stay on as Henry falls, but dismount my horse in favor of staying at his side. I heave him back onto his feet and go for my weapon only to find it's vanished. It's long gone, sitting comfortably in my saddlebag galloping back towards home.

The guards yell after their leader and slip off their horses who instantly sprint off to save themselves. Before either can draw their weapons, another blur pounces from the opposite direction. The mountain lion, for that's surely what it is, sinks its teeth into the back of a guard's neck as she screams. The sound cuts off with a sickening crack as it breaks her neck, then turns to the other struggling to scramble away. The two cats hiss at each other and I get the distinct feeling that they're arguing over the kill.

One plants its paw on his thigh and I wince at the claws tearing into the soft flesh. The soldier's lips are white as he traps a scream inside his mouth lest the noise start a frenzy. The other creature hisses and latches onto his wrist. Bile churns in my stomach. If they fight over him, they'll tear him limb from limb.

There's no sign of the warden, but she isn't my main concern. Henry and I have been slowly moving backward without turning our backs on the scene, but I misstep. A twig cracks under my foot and the two massive creatures swing their heads towards us. Prize forgotten, they release the man who desperately starts to crawl away. "Goddess save us," Henry murmurs and I only now notice that he's drawn his crossbow. His hand is shaking as he loads it, and aims, then Roux's head drops from the canopy right in front of the bolt with a frown on her face.

Her dark waves sway like a flag as she stares him down while clinging to a branch above her. "Don't you dare." She barely moves in time for the arrow to fly by her head and embed itself in a tree. Roux scowls at him but drops down to the ground and faces the cats.

"Roux, no—" She holds out a hand towards me and I fall silent even though every muscle in my body is held taut. The mountain lions advance towards us with maws caked with blood, some dripping down onto the green grass beneath them. A growl echoes through the wood and sends a chill dancing down my spine. It's only when the cats pause that I realize it came from Roux.

I can't break my eyes away from the predators to look at her. My body is locked with a hand latched onto Henry's arm and my other reaching towards Roux should she need it. All I can see is the flash of teeth as she bares them and the dappling of sunlight on her arms stretched out to keep us behind her. She hisses as their lips peel back while those big paws stand firm over the two dead guards. One rushes towards us and only my hand on Henry's arm keeps me standing as Roux roars.

"You have your meal. Leave now." Her voice is deep and guttural, as animal as I've ever heard it, but the animals seem to understand. They hiss at her again before retreating to the dead soldier and sink their teeth into the flesh, then slink off into the brush with barely a sound. A minute passes, but it feels like an hour before Roux relaxes out of her stance. I release Henry and he falls to his knees while I barely catch myself on a nearby branch. My breath comes fast as adrenaline pulses through my body with each heartbeat.

Only Roux's glancing touch on my side has me looking up to wicked green eyes that may hold a little concern. "At least you didn't throw up this time." She gifts me a crooked smile and I manage a weak laugh.

"Jokes?" Henry scoffs as we turn to him still on the forest floor. "You're joking at a time like this?"

Roux shrugs. "I've learned the best time for them is after near-death experiences. But we should move. The warden should be taken back to the house to have her wounds taken care of." She turns her dagger over in her hands before pointing to the left.

My brows furrow. "Why not kill her here? Or simply leave her to die?"

Those vibrant eyes burn into mine as Henry drags himself back onto his feet with the same question on his face. "This is not how she deserves to die. It's too easy. Too quick." There's a death promise in her eyes and I wonder what specific death she has planned for the warden. "Take Annaliese back to the house." She tosses these words over her shoulder while heading deeper into the woods.

I take a step after her. "What about you?"

Her blade glints in the sparing sunlight along with her sharp-toothed smile. "We're missing a guard." I look over the site, remembering the unaccounted soul. He won't get far with his wounds. Roux pauses on the edge of a patch of shadows to glance back at us. "Time for me to hunt." Then she vanishes just as the mountain lions did without a sound.

I stare after her for a bit then shake my head and wave Henry with me to find the warden. "How did she do it?" He asks over and over again as we look. "She had to have lured them here. That's the only explanation for why she was in the woods this morning. She couldn't have outrun them in a chase, so she didn't do it that way. They seemed to understand her, somehow. That isn't normal."

"You could just ask her." I interrupt finally and he blinks as if the thought never occurred to him. He doesn't respond but does make a strange choking sound that brings me to his side immediately. "By Under." I breathe as we take in the state of Annaliese. It could have been worse. Clearly. She could be being gnawed on like her guards, but the look of her isn't good either. The entire right side of her face is colored red from the blood pouring from the claw marks gouged into her skull. She looks relatively unscathed other than that, but the hit from that massive beast could have crushed a few ribs. Possibly punctured a lung.

"Here." Henry hands me the loaded crossbow before stooping and lifting the warden into his arms with a grunt. With all the blood still littered around the sight no doubt attracting more predators, we waste no time getting back to the path.

"Is she even breathing?" I peek over at her mangled face.

Henry shifts, heaving her a bit higher in his arms. Briefly, I wonder how he feels about carrying a woman who beat him back to the house to receive medical help. Something she didn't afford him when he was a child. "Yes, she's breathing. Barely." And he doesn't sound at all bothered by it.

"Would you mind?" My free hand slides into my pocket while the other holds tight to the crossbow. "If she dies." Our eyes flick to her as if she can hear even in her unconscious state, but she remains still.

He looks straight ahead as he answers. "No, I don't think I would. But I won't render her that way myself and won't say I approve of anyone else doing so."

"Won't say it?" The tease is a relief after the panic and mayhem of earlier, but Henry barely smiles.

"It's quite a thing to kill someone. To take them from life, a temporary state, to death, a permanent one." His brown eyes glance over at me. It's rare for me to see the impact the short time we were apart had on him, but he did things in that time that he doesn't like to speak about. He is a soldier, after all. He trained, went on missions, and killed. Maybe he and Roux are more alike than they think. Maybe it's that fact that makes him wish her gone. "It takes its toll on a person. Even if the killing is done for a good reason, for a good cause, even if the person deserves it. Some go mad with it. They're crushed under the weight. Some turn cruel, their kindness the first thing they murder. Some hold it inside and carry that weight down to Under or up Above to make a gift of it to the gods and goddesses who might remain there."

I know there's a point to all this, but I can't help hurrying him towards it. "And her?" We both know I'm not talking about the woman in his arms. His mouth opens and before he can speak, a bloodcurdling scream rips through the woods. It seems Roux found her prey. Goosebumps rise all over my body as we continue at a slightly faster pace.

Henry's head shakes. "I don't know. That's part of why I don't trust her." His gaze sharpens and I prepare myself to roll my eyes. "And why you shouldn't either, Sil."

I don't have the heart to tell him it's too late.

Chapter Ten

Claws

Roux

I'm exhausted by the time I drag myself into Silva's room. It's all I can do to tug myself towards his tub in the corner and sit in it with my filth. At least it's close to the fireplace and the metal is already faintly warm from the softly whispering flames. I hiss as I peel off my pants to find four long claw marks slicing down my left thigh. The dangers of enticing mountain lions. My lips press together as I survey the damage and luckily the wounds are shallow. A hot bath, alcohol, and some stitches will make me as good as new. "Just another scar." I sigh and sit on the rim of the tub as I start the water.

My teeth grit as I limp over to the small cabinet in the corner and pick out a few things. There are navy towels of varying sizes and bottles clink softly as I examine the bubble potion, lotions, bath salts, soaps, and plenty more. As much as I'd like to experiment with all the pretty bottles, I doubt my cuts would appreciate it. For now, I just grab a large towel, a small cloth, and sage soap.

The bath is far quicker than I would like. Just a quick dip in the steaming water to rid myself of dirt and clean the wound. After grabbing whiskey from Silva's bedside table, a needle, and some thread from a bag I'd been collecting various things in, I'm ready for stitches. The searing pain of cleaning the wounds with the whiskey makes me hiss a string of curses to make a sailor blush, but the last thing I need is infection. I have to clean it deep and don't allow myself breaks in between, choosing ongoing pain to get it over with sooner. Once that's done and there's a small puddle of whiskey mixed with blood in the tub, I ease out onto a stool to just breathe for a few seconds. It's been a while since I've run myself hard like this and I can't help smirking with a little masochistic pleasure. This is pain earned from hard work done well. Despite a few hiccups. I'll take this pain over sitting in that prison cell any day.

Groaning, I pat the wound as dry as I can with a towel, pleased to see that the bleeding has stopped. I settle in a chair after shrugging on another one of Silva's shirts, a dark grey this time, and prop my leg up on the edge of the tub to start sewing. Barely into my first stitch, I hear a visitor.

A soft meow calls my eyes to the perpetrator and I find Graves sitting nicely on the floor beside me as if asking permission to hop in my lap. "Too busy for a snuggle at the moment," I tell him and he looks over me once, then flounces over to lay out over one of the chaises. I'm contemplating the same thing when the door clicks. My body tightens, ready in case I need to fight or run, but I relax as that bright red head of hair slips in with a mop of brown right behind him.

I note that Silva's eyes coast over the room before a smile curls onto his lips at the sight of Graves. My body is hidden behind the screen blocking the bathing tub from the rest of the room. I'm also close enough to the window that I can climb out without being seen. If it were necessary. "I would tell you it's rude to hide in people's rooms, but I doubt you'd listen."

A smirk tugs on my lips. "Maybe I'm not hiding, you're just terrible at seeking," I reply and nearly giggle when his waves bounce as he turns towards where my voice came from. The screen is only paper, so I'm nearly visible in the right light. There are also tiny slivers where the paper doesn't quite go all the way to the edges of the wood. Henry sighs and rolls his eyes as Silva walks over, then pulls the screen to the side. Amusement alights his eyes at me once again stealing his shirt before his gaze darts down to the angry red marks.

"What is that?" His voice is flat. No trace of playfulness or teasing.

I turn my leg slightly to showcase the marks and shrug a shoulder. "Graves got rather nasty today." The cat meows in protest for the wrongful accusation, but my eyes stay on Silva. He doesn't return my banter and it takes me an embarrassingly long time to name the emotion in his eyes; worry. It's been so long since I've seen that feeling and far longer since one has felt it for me instead of towards me.

He reaches a hand out for his friend across the room. "Hen, take a look at this." The guard is there in a moment and grimacing at the sight.

"Serves you right for messing with nature."

My eyes roll as I ignore him. "It's fine. I've cleaned it with hot water and alcohol. A few stitches and it'll be fine." The reassurance sits strangely on my tongue as Henry glances at his friend, realizing he needs it.

Silva remains standing still as stone staring at the scratches. "I could get you a healing potion instead."

"Not necessary," I insist. "Someone could get suspicious if they saw you take one when you're both well. Just sit down and watch a master at work." The needle dives towards my skin once again, but veers when Silva takes a step towards me.

"Wait, let Henry do that." His light copper eyebrows are furrowed in an expression I would almost call cute if he wasn't being irritating.

I pause and look up at him in disbelief. "You think I'm going to let him near me with anything sharp? Even a needle? Not a chance."

"Henry has the steadiest hands in this house. He's stitched up plenty of wounds."

"So have I. More than him, I dare say." I glance over at Henry, waiting for the counter, but it doesn't come. He simply lays a hand on Silva's shoulder and steers him to the table nearby.

"If she needs assistance, then I'll step in." I keep in my snort when Henry glances at me pointedly. He knows I'm skilled enough to do it on my own, but Silva needs this right now. For some reason, this has affected him enough to keep him from playing our fun verbal games. My head inclines towards Henry, agreeing to the temporary truce and turning back to my leg.

Stitches aren't the most fun thing in the world, but I'll take the uncomfortable sensation of tugging skin over losing a limb to infection any day. It's strangely quiet as I work and I'm halfway finished with the first gash when Silva speaks.

"My father hit my mother." Everything in the room stills, even Henry's breath pauses for a moment as if surprised he'd share this with me. My gaze lifts from my progress to rest on Silva. "It was many years ago when I was still a boy. I heard yelling late in the evening, so I got out of bed to go see what it was." He heaves a sigh with eyes fixed on the floor between us spotted with light from the windows. Dust motes dance with his long breath, but my focus is on his clenched hands. "They were in their room and once I was just outside it, they were screaming. I don't remember what it was about. More than likely something I couldn't have understood at the time."

"But I understood what happened when the back of his hand sliced across her face and she fell. Her head slammed into the bed and she just lay on the floor afterward. Not moving." His eyes go glassy, seeing the memory play out in front of him. "Lurec didn't wait to see her hit the ground. He stormed out with his coat and hit the road while I hid behind the bedroom door. Once he was gone, I ran to her. There was blood on the floor from a cut on her head, just above her hairline, so I grabbed a blanket and pressed it there to stop the flow. Gods, it felt like hours I laid there waiting for her to die or wake up."

He swallows and I find myself unable to look away from him as he goes on, not even to continue my stitches. "Her eyes did open and I helped her to sit up after a while. But the cut…" He winces as he glances at mine. "It needed stitches. I…I wanted to do it. Wanted to help her. But after I went to get the needle and thread, I realized I was covered in blood. Her blood." He wipes his palms on his pants as if still trying to get it off. "It had dried on my clothes, my hands, all over my legs from where we'd been kneeling, and I couldn't bring myself to do the stitches. I couldn't have more of her blood on me. Even to help. So she did it herself in the vanity mirror. She still has a curved scar from it just here." He traces a crescent moon shape to the right of his widow's arch.

The story explains a lot, actually. Part of his aversion to any filth, how he reacted when he saw me stitching my wound, but not why he cares so much. And that's perhaps the most dangerous part.

"Henry does all the sewing now. Best needlework in Ayncuarst." A tiny sliver of light returns to his eyes as his friend shakes his head.

"I sew wounds, not your shirts."

"Course not. If my clothes rip, I just buy new ones."

The corner of my mouth lifts as I look back down and finish closing three of the gashes. My hand hesitates with the needle an inch from the last. It's the smallest of the bunch, only an inch or two. "Bandages," I murmur and glance up to find Henry rounding the small table, pressing Silva gently back into his seat as he passes. I fight against the rising idea in my mind before it wins over and I offer Silva the needle. "Care to try your hand?" His mouth pops open and Henry stalls while gathering bandages from a cabinet by the door. "Bring a chair over," I instruct when he doesn't move. Another beat passes, then he rises and walks over with the chair he was sitting in.

He barely makes a sound as he sets it back down in front of my knees, then slowly sits. Glimmering eyes stare at the ugly wounds covering my thigh now interlaced with dark thread. Not pretty, but better than gaping wounds. "It's the same as sewing. Stay as close to the edges as you can, then tie off at the end." My hand takes his and I situate the needle in his fingers, then lift his chin so he meets my gaze. "Try your best not to give me an ugly scar, Silvanus."

He swallows but gives me a slight smile. "Only you would name a scar pretty." The corner of my lips rises at the half-hearted attempt at humor.

"They're remnants of an interesting past and make for good stories around a camp fire." My eyes lift to Henry tip-toeing across the room as if afraid of disturbing Silva who has yet to pierce my skin. "Your soldier might even agree with me." He harrumphs in disgruntled agreement and more tension leaks from Silva's tight shoulders. My fingers release his face and rub together, thinking that I haven't touched a male gently in…well, before I was taken in. I dismiss the thought immediately. There's no time to think about the time before.

I fold my leg, pushing it into his lap and taking his other hand to lay on my knee to keep him steady. His hands tremble slightly. "I'll start." Our eyes meet as I guide his hand to the gash and easily slide the needle through my flesh before pulling it taut.

"Doesn't it hurt?" The trepidation fades from his eyes as curiosity takes its place.

My head shakes. "There are things that hurt more." Levity fades slightly as he dips the needle into my flesh and tightens the string as he should. Henry sits once again at the table with the bandages, watching his progress silently.

"I'd listen if you wanted to tell me." He glances at me before moving to the next stitch. "Your war stories."

I stare at him a moment, those vivid red waves atop his head gleaming in the fading light coming through the windows.

The urge to run my hand through them strikes me so strongly that it takes me longer to answer. "I believe I've told you a few."

His smile widens as he nods, his hands no longer shaking as he hits his stride. "As I've told you a few of mine. Maybe we'll take a break from war stories." The wound is almost closed as he tugs the two sides towards one another like folds in a cloth. "Tell me something you love."

I go still at the question as a million things dance through my head. It's been a long time since I loved anyone and the things that I love...they've changed. The finery I once treasured, I still enjoy, but those things are no longer precious. Breath is precious. Light. The ability to stand under the sky unmarred by chains or ropes. Yes, the list of what I love has grown short, but the list of people I love has grown shorter still. Even if the people on that list don't exist anymore.

My attention returns to Silva as he finishes the last stitch and ties it off like a professional. Henry comes over with the bandages, but Silva takes them into his lap to finish the work himself. His friend stands beside us, as a chaperone or to hear what I have to say. Silva has told me plenty of things that he loves even if it wasn't outright; Henry, his tenants, his servants, his mother. Maybe finery, but that's a surface love that I believe he would give up if needed. One he has given up to help others.

I watch as he gently tapes a bandage over the ugly stitches, careful not to touch above my knee despite my not caring much about decorum. He shows me so much respect. Always has. "Rain." My voice is quiet. "I love the rain. Storms. The thunder that you feel in your chest and lightning that slices through the night like a silver blade through the air." Silva pauses to look at me as I talk, those clear eyes so like the sky just over the horizon. The lightest color of blue. Henry makes no move or scoff at my simple choice and for that sign of civility, I go on.

"It was the one thing I could have in the prison on the mount. Lightning would flash outside and illuminate my cell even through that slit of a window. Thunder would shake the stones. Rain would soak the walls outside and drip through the window down the wall. I'd lick it from the stones just to get a taste of outside." Henry's nose wrinkles and I laugh softly. "You learn not to be picky in such a place, soldier." Even now, I can feel the cold stones biting into my bony knees even as Silva's tender hands wrap white bandages around my thigh. What a difference a few weeks can make.

"How did you survive it?" Henry asks as his friend finishes his task and seems content to keep my leg in his lap. I lean back in my chair, adding my other to rest on his other leg while he smirks.

I level Henry with my eyes and there's nothing soft in my gaze. "Anger unsated and business unfinished makes for a decent ward against death." Silva's finger taps on my bare legs.

"Willpower then." He shortens and simplifies my answer, but it's true nonetheless. I nod.

"And Death grants the wishes of their handmaiden." My eyes roll to Henry when he speaks, but his face isn't judging even if his tone is disdainful.

"Careful how you speak of her. She spared your father, didn't she?" Surprise echoes across the men's faces for different reasons. I'm sure Silva is shocked Henry shared anything personal with me.

He glances back at his friend as he shakes his head. "Death doesn't choose, people do. Death merely collects." Henry's dark eyes look over my face and he frowns when my lips purse.

Humor tickles the back of my mouth. "I've introduced others and have been close to meeting Death myself too many times to think she doesn't sometimes favor some."

"And you?" Silva leans forward with his hands resting comfortably on my legs. "Does she favor you?"

I smirk. "I'm not going to risk losing it by saying she does or she doesn't." His mouth opens again but is interrupted by a soft knock on the door.

My feet are instantly on the cool floor before Silva holds out a hand to prevent me from leaping from the window. "It's just Mary with dinner." He assures me but waits until I've lowered myself into the empty bathtub behind the screen to see to the door. Henry kicks the unused bandages under a dresser as the door opens with a creak.

The distinct patter of her soft footsteps soothe me as she enters the room with the near-soundless cart. "Good evening, Master Silva. Master Henry." Both greet her in the same gentle tone and I keep quiet and still to listen.

"How's the morale among the servants?" Henry asks as I hear the distinct clink of trays being set on the table. Through the slits in the screen, I see the swish of baby pink skirts as she takes a step back and folds her hands in front of her. She's the picture of a demure woman, but I know she's more than meets the eye. I hadn't lied to Silva about what happened when she saw me kill the soldier, but I didn't tell him the whole truth either.

Sweet Mary indeed saw me swing in and wrap my legs around his head, then use all my body weight to swing down, breaking his neck. After I smeared alcohol over his mouth and rubbed it into his skin, she did offer to help. I used her cart to wheel his body to the window and shoved him out before turning back to the maid who was still suffering from the shock of the encounter. I told Silva that she never saw my face and technically she didn't see it as I killed that man.

She did see under my hood when I pulled it down and walked over to squeeze some feeling back into her hands. I couldn't leave her trembling in front of the closed door with that red handprint still on her face. "I thought Death was cold." She whispered and the words clanged through me, yanking me back into that damned cell on the mount.

My head shook as I rubbed my hands over hers, letting the heat of my body seep into her. "In my experience, it is sometimes cold when we leave Life's embrace," I told her, letting her read the truth of the words in my eyes. "But when Death takes hold…her arms are warm." She nodded and eventually the shaking ceased. It was when I went to the window to sneak into Silva's room when she surprised me. She took out a little half-empty vial with dark green liquid inside and held it to the light.

"I'm glad I didn't have to kill him." She murmured with her normally light voice deepening. "But I am glad that he's dead."

Then I left and made myself comfortable in Silva's room. She hasn't said a word against me and even smiles at me in the halls when we pass. She wouldn't have been a bad assassin with the proper training. Only now does it occur to me to wonder why the vial was only half-full.

Her voice calls my attention back to her as I peek over the edge of the tub to see them through the slits in the screen. "They're faring well enough. A few are nervous about moving around in the night or dawn and dusk, but we're managing things alright." She shifts from foot to foot for a moment. "We are sorry that it happened when there's a guest at the house and…regret to say we're not sure where she is." It takes everything in me to keep in my laugh and stay very still so she doesn't hear me.

Silva smirks while Henry glances over at the screen separating us. "Not to worry. She was upset by recent events and went to stay in town. Lady Nestra should return early tomorrow and I hope what I requested will be ready by then?" My ears perk up at the sound of that even as I make myself stay stone-still.

Mary nods, blonde ponytail bobbing. "Oh, yes, it's ready. Shall I set it up in a room for her?" Silva's smile widens and I curse him for glancing over at the screen, knowing I can hear every word.

"The green tower, yes."

"The...tower?" Mary repeats. "Excuse me, sir, but isn't that in poor taste? And in the men's wing—"

Silva shrugs a shoulder. "She won't be bothered. The Lady is a...peculiar sort." My jaw locks as I vow to get him back for that later even as I fight a smile.

"Thank you, Mary." Henry dismisses her and the moment she slips out, I yank the screen to the side.

"You requested something for me?"

He nods and takes his sweet time unveiling his food before answering me. "A few things actually. Normal items that any lady would have on hand."

I squash down my excitement at the mere thought of having fine things again and frown instead. "Remember the story. I'm not supposed to have anything. I'm on the run from a cruel uncle." The reminder is for them both and Henry huffs in irritation as he tosses his dinner back onto the plate.

"That's why he ordered them. It works in our favor that you do in fact, have nothing, so Silva is kindly supplying them for you. Like a good host." His last sentence is mocking and makes it clear he wishes he wasn't being such a good host, but I'm grateful. Henry's slight participation is also more than he's given since we'd met. It's an improvement, no matter how slight. His eyes narrow at me. "The real question is if you can act like a lady." He gestures to me in the tub illustrating very un-ladylike behavior since no respectable woman should be alone with a man who isn't her husband. Much less have one stitch and bandage her wounds without being a healer. If only that were my greatest offense.

I fix sharp eyes on Henry who gulps but doesn't turn away. "I may not be ladylike, but I can act the part."

Silva nudges the chair between him and Henry out a bit with his foot. "Prove it. Eat dinner with us."

His friend shoots him a disapproving look, but it's half-hearted. "Yes, please invite the assassin over within reach of the butter knives," He grumbles and Silva smiles at him.

"I already have, dear Henry." Henry rolls his eyes while Silva turns back to me. "You'll need the practice. My mother knows you're here and wants to meet you. Anna will be unconscious for a while and well-tended by her remaining guards, so now is probably the best time."

I go still inside the tub. Meeting his mother was something I knew was going to happen, but somehow, I'm still surprised. It's clear that he treasures her and meeting her means he trusts me. At least a bit. "Okay. Tomorrow at breakfast then." Both men seem shocked at the lack of a sarcastic answer, but Silva's smile softens.

My arms lift me out of the tub and I take a moment to appreciate that I can. I've gained a slight amount of muscle back from my days before being locked away, but there's still a long way to go. I sit on the edge for a moment as I look over the bandaging. It's decent. Well enough to keep the wounds safe and clean for a while. "My Lady?" Silva calls and I glance over to his gesturing to the seat between them. A dare lies in his eyes like bait on a hook, waiting to see if he'll get a bite or lose his bait. I stare out the window for a moment. It's been a long while since I had to play a role. My eyes shut and I take a few deep breaths as I remember how it feels to be a lady, the manners, the way they walk, stand, speak. Then I turn and walk towards the gentlemen.

They both blink as if I donned a mask and don't look away as I glide over to them. I pause next to my chair and Silva smoothly stands with Henry clumsily following suit. The moment I offer my hand, he's taking it and I struggle to hold back my shiver as his long fingers skate over my palm, then claim it to take to his lips. They're soft and pink as he presses them lightly to my knuckles. The moment could have been less than a second or gone on for years. Either way, neither of us would have noticed. Or cared.

"My Lady, you look ravishing this evening." There's a tease in his eyes, but the words are said without a trace of insincerity. A thrill trills down my spine at playing the game as well as the title.

I dip in a small curtsy that's slightly off-kilter because of my injury. "I should hope I look ravishing every evening, Silvanus. Not just this one." Light dances in his eyes as he finally releases my hand and we turn to Henry. He's staring at me like he's never seen me before and I brighten my smile just to get under his skin. He mumbles a half-hearted greeting before plopping down in his chair.

Silva sighs. "You will have to treat her like a lady, Hen." We both sit down and he passes me a plate along with most of his food. The soldier stares at Silva as the lord's son pops a few grapes into his mouth and I swivel to Henry.

"This does give you a chance to ask me your burning questions." I raise a brow while disbelief echoes across his face before he looks accusingly at his friend.

"How does she know that? *How could she know that?*"

I laugh softly while Silva raises his arms in mock surrender. "You were practically yelling your questions in the woods. Sorry that I listen." He huffs, settling back against the arched back of his chair.

Silva grins, tossing a grape at his head. "Go on then, ask your questions. Ladies don't usually bite." He turns to me with eyes glowing with humor.

A smile cuts across my face in return. "Then you haven't met the right ones."

Silva leans in and I feel my instincts perk up like a cat spotting a mouse. "I did say usually, Lady. Do you count yourself among the few I neglected?" It's hard to keep my smile under control as our postures bend until our noses are inches away from each other.

"Well then," Henry states and we both turn to face him looking between us. "So you two are practically domestic, now?"

I snort. "Please. You two are practically married, so don't start talking to me about domestic." Silva laughs, filling the room with the sunny noise as I watch the joy ripple across his face. Gods, if I could bottle the sound, I would. Henry seems to be fighting a smile himself before I flick my chin in his direction. "Go on. Ask."

He clears his throat as he debates voicing them once again, then finally says, "How did you get those beasts there today? How did they know who to attack and who to only injure?"

I delicately cut into the meat Silva served me, every bit a lady as I answer, "I had one of the servants I gained a rapport with rub blood on their packs as she supplied them." That brilliant Mary, of course. "In the woods, I laid out a trail of leftover meat to the path where they'd scent the blood and instinct would take over. As for how they knew who to wound and who to kill…" My teeth flash. "I told them."

Both men go still. "Told them," Silva repeats before stretching out in his spot facing me with intrigue scrawled over his face.

"Yes. Lucky they understood." It took a little sprinkling of magic, enough to make my reflexes too slow to miss a swipe of a paw, but it worked well enough. Some magic is slower to wake, but a skill like that, once earned, never leaves the blood.

Henry sighs and sinks in his chair. "Why do I put up with either of you?" We both gift him winning smiles before he narrows his eyes at me. "Tell me one thing that's true about you." I blink, nearly letting my posture slump. His eyes are bright and determined as I've ever seen them as he looks at me. "Just one fact."

"She already has," Silva defends, but I raise my hand.

"I understand what he's asking." As a soldier, he was trained to take things as they are and face them head-on. It's clear he doesn't know what to think of me because he knows nothing about me. Well, nothing he deems important. I ponder the question and the possible ramifications of my answer before giving him one carefully chosen. "My parents are both dead. Many years past." It's a fight to keep my tone and expression neutral. Years past or not, the memories still hurt. I could wrap my heart in ice, in stone, and the mere thought of their faces would shatter the shell into bits.

Henry swallows. "Did...did you—"

"Kill them?" I finish for him with my voice sharp as a blade. The assumption hurts far more than it should. Gods, I'm being an idiot. We're friendly, yes, but not friends. Never friends. Temper shoots through me like an arrow, hot as fire, but what sends me over the edge is the hurt. And they can only hurt me if I care. Damn it. "Because murder is simply in my nature? You think me a heartless spider waiting to poison any near me for an easy score, is that not true?" My hands slap onto the table, rattling all that's on it as I shove myself to my feet. Henry's face is firm and as unyielding as his opinion of me. "Think on this, soldier. I could have killed you a hundred times over on this day alone. I could have killed Silva as he slept beside me in his bed." Henry's eyes go wide as saucers as he looks accusingly at his friend who sighs. "If I'm nothing but a heartless killer, why don't I?"

I leave them with the question, grabbing sweatpants and swinging out the window after making sure there are none but them to see me go.

Chapter Eleven

Allies or Friends?

Silva

"Why would you do that?" I ask Henry as I walk over to peek out the window but find no trace of Roux. A sigh slips from my lips and I pull back to find Graves scurrying out after the incensed assassin like a shadow.

He huffs and throws his arms out to the sides. "I had to ask! We've no clue who she is and I for one, would like to know!"

"Henry, you oaf, that's because you look at her and see only an assassin."

"Well, that's what she is, isn't she?"

"Yes, but not all she is." A frown tugs at my lips as I walk back over to sit across from him once again. "People are not pieces of paper laid on a table. They're grand houses with many rooms containing many things. She's an assassin, but she's also a human. A woman. A prisoner. A survivor." I toss a grape at his head and it bounces off his big forehead. "And now a very angry one at that." He deflates in his seat and puts his arm over his head. We sit in silence for a few minutes and I manage to nearly finish my dinner by the time his arm falls.

"Should I apologize?" The comment is sarcastic, but I grin. He shakes his head. "No, no, no. I didn't mean that."

I shrug a shoulder. "I think she'd appreciate it." The end of my fork points at him accusingly as his mouth opens. "And you were in the wrong."

He sighs and pushes himself up into a sitting position. "And you're not influenced by her sharing your bed?" I heave a breath. This was coming sooner or later. "I'm rarely one to critique your bedfellows, but her? Really?"

"It's not like that. She wanted a place to stay that was safe and free from the warden's daily room checks. She'll return to her room tomorrow." Even if the thought of not having another nightly chat with her doesn't make me overwhelmingly happy.

Henry's eyes burn into mine before he finally begins eating again. "I wish the thought of you both sleeping soundly in bed beside each other made me feel better, but it doesn't. I'd be less concerned if you were simply chasing her skirts." My eyes roll. "I doubt I need to warn you of the perils of caring for her, Silva, but I'll make you a list to keep at your bedside if I have to."

I smile at my friend's care and concern. "Ah, I'm afraid your efforts would be wasted. I'd only use it for kindling."

* * *

Henry leaves as night falls and I slide into bed staring at the window Roux left from. I blow all the candles out but for the one at my bedside and read. Some book about the gods and goddesses and where they came from. The Archer, a goddess of storms and sea, draped in blue with golden arrows that never miss their mark. The Huntress, who they say favors the Enhanced with her violet eyes, shifts forms between a dark-skinned woman and a wild dog. Finally, there's the goddess of life and death. With one hand she wields a blade emitting green light and in the other a blade covered in dark flames. At her side is the god of devotion, a warrior in his own right, who is perhaps best known for his deep love for her.

All of this sinks into my mind, then promptly slides out my other ear like a slippery fish. Everyone learns the legends and histories in school whether we believe them or not. Right now, I was simply hoping for a distraction. My gaze keeps returning to the window before I just give up. I snuff out the candle and slide down into bed staring at the curtains skimming the floor in the breeze from outside.

I'm not sure how long I lay there waiting for her. Hours maybe. Long enough for my eyes to nearly shut before I hear a click as the door opens. I sit up a bit, mouth open to greet her before I realize the figure slipping in isn't Roux. The figure is too bulky and the footsteps are a bit too heavy. They turn to lock the door while I feel for something to defend myself. I settle for the candle holder, noting enough time has passed for the wax to dry and harden. Where is Roux?

My hand slides under the blankets with my weapon as the figure locks the door before turning back to me. They let their hood fall while my heartbeat speeds up. It's one of the warden's guards, but if she means to let me see her face then I'm not meant to survive this. The light from the moon outside isn't as bright as the night before, but it's still bright enough to see by. Certainly bright enough to see the glint of steel as she unsheathes a curved dagger. She takes a few steps forward and my eyes close to slits until she stops beside my bed. The blade raises into the air. "For my leader," She whispers and that's when I strike.

There's a sharp crunch as her nose breaks under the hard metal and my legs swing out from under the blankets as I throw them over her. She tumbles to the ground and I jump over her, but not quick enough to escape her hand. Fingers wrap tight around my ankle and I trip to splay out over the floor as well. The candlestick rolls out of my reach and I drag myself toward it only to be stopped as she climbs on top of me. Her hand finds my hair and I grunt as she pulls my head back to plant her steel on my throat.

"You left my comrades and Anna in the woods to *die*. You and that cowardly guard of yours." She hisses in my ear, already drawing blood with her blade. I shove down the panic building in my chest as I think of what to do, how to act, how to save myself— "Tonight, you'll both pay for it."

It's as if she dunked me in ice. Henry. "What have you done to—"

Her grip on my hair tightens and I scarce breathe or swallow lest she puncture my throat. "I think you should be concerned with other things. I'm sure he is." Panic slices through me without resistance and my lips part before I see a shadow slink around the corner of the room. It slides through the room like a ghost, small and lithe, then blinks at me with pale green eyes. Graves. The corner of my mouth has barely turned up before the guard's weight on me vanishes. I whirl around to find her and Roux rolling across the floor in a mess of limbs and steel before the assassin slams the steel down into the guard's hand.

She tugs in a breath to scream, but Roux rams a hand into her throat so the soldier can barely breathe, much less shout. The inscription on her dagger gleams even in the dark as she yanks it up out of her hand as the guard whimpers, then holds it to the woman's throat. Her knees take the place of her hands and I wince as one digs into the bloodied palm. Tears stream down the guard's cheeks before her eyes shut and I almost think it would be a mercy if she passed out. At least before I remember she tried to kill me.

"Look at me, Creed," Roux growls, and her voice sounds more animal than human. Wide eyes scan Roux's face as she bares her teeth in a semblance of a smile. It is indeed Anna's guard Creed. She's easily recognizable now that the fear has started to fade from my eyes. "That's right, it's your old friend. Did you miss me?" Her mouth opens to scream now that she has her breath back and Roux shoves her hand in her mouth, pulling her tongue out while drawing a bit of blood from her neck with her blade.

"Remember what I said to you when you found me? When you brought me in?" The guard pales, but Roux only grins wider. "Good. Tell them hello for me." In one movement almost too fast for my eyes, her knee comes up and slams the guard's mouth closed so her teeth sever her tongue. There's no time for Creed to do anything to retaliate, however, because the next moment her throat is slashed and she's choking on her own blood.

I stare at the two in disbelief as gurgles fill the silent room. Roux tossing the tongue to the side makes bile swirl in my stomach, but I shove myself to my feet. Her bright eyes flick to mine and I note the blood splattered all over her. There's even a little nick over her collarbone where Creed must have slashed. "Henry."

She's on her feet in a moment. "Where?"

"End of the hall on the right." She shoots out the window again while I take to the door, throwing it open and tearing down the hall without a care for the noise I make. It only takes me a few seconds, a minute at most, before I'm yanking on Henry's doors. Locked. "Shit. *Shit*." I look around for something to break the door down, anything at all that I can use, but come away with nothing but gilded candlesticks affixed to the walls. There's wild thumping coming from the next room and I throw myself against the door. "Henry? Henry!" I shout, not caring if I wake the entire house with the racket.

I pause to listen for his voice. Nothing. My feet carry me to the other side of the hall as I ready myself for another charge, but then I hear someone fiddling with the lock. Hope and terror mix bitterly in my stomach as the lock slides to the side, then the door opens. Henry stands there looking like a mess. His hair is wild, his clothes ripped, and his knuckles are shredded. Still, he's alive. "Silva. By Under, what is going on—" He's cut off as I tug him close, arms locking around his body. He returns the embrace as I spy Roux crouching over a body as she retrieves her dagger from their ribcage.

"It seems as if we were both to be assassinated tonight. And surprisingly not by the resident assassin." We part as Roux snorts and I grin over at her. Everyone is safe. For tonight, anyway. Footsteps sound down the hallway and two guards from my security, Deckree, and my mother round the corner. Henry and I both look at Roux, but she's already gone.

"What is going on? The only time I heard such a racket was when you two were boys!" My mother's scold is light-hearted, but the humor fades from her face when she sees the state of us. "Goddess spare me. What happened?" Her thumb swipes across my neck and has a streak of blood across it when she pulls away.

Henry and I glance at one another. This will take quite a bit of explaining, but one thing is crystal clear. "It appears the warden's soldiers went rogue because they thought we left their comrades in the woods to die. They thought to return the favor." Fury flashes through my mother's eyes, instantly belied by gathering tears. Deckree, the warden's second, only purses her lips.

Henry's jaw locks. "You may want to look into securing better employees, ma'am."

The soldier nods once. "These events certainly are disturbing. You have my apologies." She turns on her heel and walks back down the hall with her fingers sliding over the bottom of her face. Concern was definitely in her voice, but shock certainly wasn't. With nearly all her guards dead, there's only her, Banks, and the warden left. I'd be concerned too if I didn't already know who was behind things.

Henry steps forward. "If I may address security, Lady Dinnsesk?" Meira steps forward and slides her hands over his arms, then nods.

"Of course, of course. Take care of yourself too, you hear me? And write to your parents about this." My friend shoots me a look saying he absolutely will not be doing that, but he accepts the kiss my mother gives his cheek without a fight before flicking his chin down the hall. He walks with his soldiers, back straight and head held high despite more than likely being saved by an assassin.

I take my mother under my arm and lead her away from Henry's room. "I'll make sure he assigns guards to your door if he hasn't already." Henry and I have a protector now, but my mother doesn't. The thought puts a frown on my face.

Her arm around my waist tugs me close. "And you? Henry? What will both of you do?" Well, one of us has an assassin in their bed who is more than ferocious in a fight. I'm not sure that would reassure her, so I try a different tactic.

My hand smooths over her back. "We'll manage. We fared well enough tonight." Worry still creases her brow as I hurry her past my still-open doors towards the women's wing. Thankfully, the warden lies in the sickroom on the first floor and her soldiers will remain at her side. Two of my family's guards already stand in front of my mother's bedroom doors and I smile at Henry's forethought. When we stop, my mother is wringing her hands as if they were waterlogged towels.

"I just don't know what's happening. So much death." She stares down the hall in the direction of my room before I step in front of her.

"If it makes you feel better, I'll drag Henry to my room to spend the night. Nothing has stood against us and prevailed yet." I give her a charming smile which coaxes a bit of levity back into her eyes.

She pinches my arm. "Except stupidity and recklessness, but fine. That does make me feel better." I nod and try not to think about what Roux will say about the sleeping arrangements, but turn back when my mother catches my hand. Her clear eyes shine brighter than the moon even in the dim candlelight. "If there is a single clue that this was not the act of rogue soldiers, but a deliberate attack from Anna, then you will tell me. Do you hear me, Silvanus?" Her stern voice echoes through the hall as commanding as any general.

I nod. "Yes, mom." She smiles and her stern expression vanishes as she pulls me into her embrace again.

"I love you," She whispers and I hold her tighter.

"I love you. More than the lights in the sky." Her laughter is a salve to my ears after the events of tonight and I hadn't realized how much I needed her embrace. Her comfort.

She pulls away and taps my nose. "You haven't said that since you were a boy."

I shrug. "Didn't think I ever needed to. Tonight I wanted to." My mother nods and looks me over one more time before opening the doors to her room.

"Henry sleeps in your room tonight. Remember."

"Got it, mom." I toss the words over my shoulder before hearing her doors shut softly behind her. The walk to my room is short, but I find every step heavier than the last. When I finally reach it and peak inside the doors, I'm shocked to find the body already rolled up and on the way out.

Two servants march down the stairs with it before a soft voice leaks out from my room. "To the cellar. It must stay cold before the burying."

I blink as I lean in to see Mary cleaning up the mess of blood as if used to it. "You needn't do that now."

She flinches at my voice, hand flying to her heart as she mops up the blood. "Ah, Master Silvanus! You gave me such a fright!"

I smile apologetically. "Not a surprise given the events of tonight. Best get some sleep and attend this in the morning."

Her head shakes vehemently. "Nay. We don't want it to dry and stick to the floor. I'm nearly done, anyway." After a few more passes with the mop, the floor gleams anew and she marches out the door with her tools in a bucket.

A thought occurs to me and I call after her, not wanting to grab her arm in case I frighten her. "How did you know to come here?" I have a sneaking suspicion and when her cheeks alight with red deep as rose petals, I know I'm right. "No matter, Mary, thank you. Tell Henry he's sleeping in my room tonight if you see him." She curtsies and all but sprints away from me to tend to Henry's room while I head back to mine.

No sooner have the doors shut than she reveals herself. "I hear we're adding a third party to this sleepover." I whirl around, spotting the assassin sitting on top of a seven-foot-tall dresser as if it were a lounge chair. She smiles at surprising me and I'm glad to note she'd already wiped the blood off herself as well as changed. I wonder where she hides her clothes soaked in blood.

"Surprises aren't the best idea right now." I move over to my bed and put a hand over my side. My chest burns like my heart is trying to break through it.

Roux barely makes a sound as she dismounts the dresser and walks over to me in that lovely green shirt of mine that looks so good on her. "What did you do?" Her hands are shockingly gentle as she pushes me onto the bed, lights a candle, and peels my hand away to reveal a slash of blood.

"Ah, she must have nicked me during the struggle." I look up at her as she all but straddles me with her eyes pinned to the scratch. "Your turn to stitch me up." The thought of her sitting in my lap, keeping close as she closes the wound, doesn't sound bad at all.

She snorts, barely glancing at my eyes. "Nonsense. I've hidden at least five healing potions around your house in case of emergencies. We'll use one of those for this."

I frown. "Why should I get to use a healing potion when you wouldn't?" Now she does meet my eyes and I'm glad to find some humor swimming in the emerald depths.

"You're nearly a lord. If you use a healing potion everyone will understand and expect it. If one goes missing without a reason, it would be suspicious. I hid the surplus for myself in case I got into unforeseen trouble."

"You're trouble." Her eyes widen, surprise and laughter dancing in the wild green. "But I like you. I still like you even after seeing that woman chomp her tongue out because of you." My hand raises to make a chomping motion as she smiles brilliantly for a single moment, and then it fades.

I feel her hands on my face and I open my eyes again even though it feels like it takes hours to do so. I don't remember closing them, anyway. "Silva? Gods, Silva, what is wrong with you?" She rips my shirt open and that wakes me up a bit.

"You could have just asked and I would have taken it off." My words slur and mash together on the way out as she bends down to look more closely at the wound over my ribs.

"Above and Under. It's poison. You're poisoned. Creed must've covered the blade in some toxin—*shit.*" Her weight leaves me and I feel bereft at the loss, my eyes closing once again. "Don't you dare shut your eyes, Silvanus. Keep your eyes on me." It's a struggle to obey and the image of her, once so crisp and clean, shimmers and waves like heat off dark rocks.

"What about you?" My hand lifts and my thumb coasts over the small slash over her collarbone.

She winces slightly as I touch the wound, but her eyes glow brighter and wilder at the pain. "I can tolerate many poisons. It's called mithridatism. Even though I've been out of practice for a long while." I want to ask her more about it, learn more about her, but my thoughts seem slippery as eels. All I can focus on is her before me.

"Your eyes...you have the prettiest eyes. Like snake scales. Like the forest."

"Mmhmm, keep going," She insists before there's a sharp pain that wakes me up. My hand lifts to find the cause, but Roux slaps it away. "This is to help, you dolt. Henry, get me the purple vial in the bag under the bed. Now." Henry is here? I hadn't even heard him come in. "Drink this." Something is pressed to my lips and I turn my head away only to have Roux turn it back while pinching my nose. I swallow and glare at her while she gives me a strained grin. "Act like a child and you're treated like a child."

"If…if that was true…then Henry would…get the rod every hour." She glances at something out of my sight and I feel a sharp pinch on my thigh.

"I'll remember that, Sil."

"Keep talking. I need you to stay awake as long as possible," Roux says, and I want to obey, but keeping my eyes open has become a monumental effort. A hand claims my face, and I feel her weight settle onto me once again. "Awake, Silva. Stay awake." Her nails dig into my face hard enough to sting, but not hard enough to draw blood. I find I don't mind.

"Stay on me and I doubt I'll fall asleep."

She hums, dry and lilting. "I suppose I'll take that as a compliment."

I strain against the darkness now, the shadows lapping at the edges of my sight like dark waves. "Didn't mean…to be rude." Gods, what am I saying?

"If you think that's rude, then we haven't spoken enough." Her voice is tinted with humor and I once again wish I could see it shining in her eyes, but this time my eyes are too heavy to force open. Henry humphs in agreement off to the side.

A blur that I guess is Henry shuffles back and forth behind her. "His fingers…they're turning blue."

A string of curses leaves Roux's lips as her hands fly in a flurry of movement my eyes can't follow. I only catch snippets of her whispers. "No choice…last resort…he's dying." Black spots now dance in front of my eyes even while open and I desperately search for something to hold onto. My fingers catch on bare skin and her fingers tighten on mine before her other hand rests over the wound. Light filters through my shuttered lids, but it seems wrong somehow. It's not the cold light of the moon or the warm light of a candle but gleams with its own power.

"What are you doing?" Henry's awed voice leaks into my ears.

Roux sounds strained when she answers. "Transferring the wound." Her hand is still in mine and I hold it tight as if it's my anchor and I'm in a stormy sea. Her other hand, the one glowing with a soft, green light, switches between my side and hers as my head slowly clears.

"Wait, the poison—"

"Will not kill me." Her voice is firm and leaves no room for argument. It's too late anyway. My wound seals and she lifts her shirt as the same gash blooms over her right side. The glowing fades and the room seems suddenly bereft without the light. Without magic.

She sways in place, hand going to her head, and I lean forward to slide a hand onto her arm to steady her. She slaps it off and grabs hold of the bedpost instead. "Don't touch me." Venom is laced into every word. I hadn't heard that tone since we'd met and it stings more than I'd like.

"We just want to help. You should lay down." Henry says as I try to clear my head. The cloud muddling my brain is fading even though the tiredness limning my limbs feels as if I've been pummeled all over.

"I don't want your help." She hisses, teeth bared. "I am *furious*."

Henry and I glance at one another dubiously. "With us?"

She sighs and suddenly the anger slakes from her face. Silver lines her eyes before she puts her face into her palms and slowly lets curved fingers drift into her hair. The reaction is answer enough. She's furious with herself. The why can wait until she settles and I know she's safe. I reach for her again and tentatively let my fingers glide over her arms. When she doesn't move away, I nod to Henry and he moves to the opposite side of the bed as we maneuver her together so she's laying on her good side beside me.

"Get a healing potion from the stores—" I tell Henry before her hand shoots out and latches onto my wrist with a surprising amount of strength.

"Healing potions don't work on poisons. They fight infection and fix gashes." She tells me, her usually sharp eyes strangely unfocused. "I need the herbs from the side table." Her hand releases me to point and I swallow a groan of pain as I lean over to grab the bunch of dried sprigs.

I show her the bundle. "Now what?"

Her hand hovers between us, palm up. "Give them to me."

My grip tightens on the herbs as my eyes narrow. "What needs to be done?"

She huffs, shaking her hand for emphasis. "They need to be chewed and spread over the cuts like a salve." I ruminate on this for a moment before shoving the bunch in my mouth. A pungent, bitter taste fills my mouth and I nearly cough it up but manage to keep chewing. "Ugh." Roux lets her hand drop and the fact that she isn't scolding me speaks to how ill she's becoming. For me. She's ill because of me.

My head tilts to a cabinet and Henry immediately walks over and plucks a glass, then hands it to me. I spit out the vile concoction and don't look at it as I spread it over the cut on her collarbone. She winces at first contact, then laxes. "I wouldn't have thought you'd be one to spread spit and leaves over my wounds."

My nose wrinkles with disgust, but I continue my work. "Friends do what's required, not always what's desired." I pull back and wait for her to pull up her shirt or for her permission to do it myself. When she does nothing, I glance at her only to find that she's frozen. The only thing moving are her eyes scanning my face. Slowly, she pulls her shirt up and bunches the fabric over her breasts. I swallow at the large expanse of her skin now on display before Henry flicks a lightweight blanket over her lower body and I'm not sure whether I should be disappointed or grateful.

"We aren't friends." She whispers and my eyes flick to hers before I start slathering the salve over the wound that should be mine. Her voice is no longer sharp and venomous, but desperately soft. It's almost a plea.

"I'm afraid taking care of one another, sharing secrets, and not murdering us makes us friends."

Her lips press together a moment. "I don't have friends." Henry huffs off to the side and marches over to lay out on the chaise under the window closest to us, apparently done with today. I only smile.

"Well, congratulations. You now have two." I set the glass on the bedside table before shrugging off my shirt and using it to wipe off my hands. The cloth is thrown across the room before I face Roux again.

Her face is hard and she reaches out to latch onto my leg with nails digging into my skin like claws despite the cloth of my pants. "I don't want any."

I shrug. "Condolences, you have two." She makes a noise of disgust and pulls away from me. Confusion swirls in my gut as I turn my body to face her. "Why is it so bad? You haven't minded being allies."

"Allies are useful and disposable. Friends betray you because you trust them, they're a weakness to exploit, and when they die their blood is on your hands. Especially if you have to kill them." Her hands curl into fists even though she can't hold the tension for long. Her eyes have regained some of their sharpness and I'm glad to see it even if the iciness is aimed at me. My mouth opens, but she only rolls over on her side with her shoulders bunched from the pain.

Irritation flashes through me, hot and fast, so I turn my back to her as I lay down as well. The feeling barely lasts a minute before I'm turning onto my back. "If allies are disposable, why save me?" Why take away the wound, why let me dress it, why expose her magic?

The room is silent as she gives me no answer.

Chapter Twelve

Act like a Lady

Roux

I don't fall asleep when Silva does. It's just simpler to pretend I have.

When his breathing deepens, my eyes open and I turn back over with a relieved sigh. My side hurts, but I'd rather face the bit of pain instead of Silva's questions and penetrating eyes. I take a few moments just to look at him. He has that innocent look about him once again and a small smile on his lips despite everything that happened. His hair isn't too crazed yet but lays starkly over his pillow like blood on snow.

For a moment, I wonder if the burnished bronze would be soft as downy feathers between my fingers.

My head shakes as I tug my hands closer to my chest as if they might mutiny. I've been a fool. It wasn't my intention to reveal my ability to do magic, I'd intended not to tell them that bit of me at all, but here I am. There was no guarantee that my herbs would have saved him as I know they'll save me. I've had a go-bag packed and hidden since my first week here with various things that would help me on the road. It's a good thing I hoard useful things.

The corner of Silva's lips tips up and mine copy the movement. After killing so many, it's a surprise that I balked at the idea of Silva's death. There's a difference, of course. All those I've killed deserved death in one way or another. Silva doesn't. The thought of seeing that shock of red hair vanish as he was lowered into the ground chills me to the bone. Part of me knows that this is a failure. I've revealed vital information that can be used against me for other's advantage and stopping his death, even rightly so, has weakened me. It also names a weakness; him. Both of them. My…friends. Or as close to friends as I can get.

I've avoided having friends for years, long before I was locked away. Allies, lovers, and enemies, that was all I could have. All that was safe. Friends, any kind of love, they're dangerous. They cause people to throw aside their cause to follow another without thought, without reason. And that's without adding the complication of betrayal and treachery.

Biting back a groan, I push myself up and back so I'm sitting up against the headboard. My body aches like I've been running for days, but it'll fade. A glance out the windows reveals the moon is high in the sky and I'd guess we have a few hours until morning. I rest my head back and let my eyes shut for just a minute. Graves is happily snuggled at the end of the bed because Silva is unconscious and can't stop him. The fact has a ghost of a smile drifting over my lips.

"I appreciate it, you know." My head snaps over to face Henry who has tucked a muscular arm behind his head. "All you did for him tonight. For me too." There's a shocking lack of judgment in his voice even if the words sound a bit gruff. "I'm sorry for earlier. It was callous and rude for me to assume such a thing about you and your parents." Pure shock ripples through me and makes me slow to respond.

"I…" I hesitate, glancing at Silva before staring into Henry's hooded eyes. I'm not sure if it's the surprise of Henry's civility, the poison coursing through me, or if Silva's state has shaken me so much that I've temporarily lost my sanity. Whatever the reason, I answer him in a hushed tone. "I wasn't always this. I was just a young woman with a thousand paths laid out before her. Ripe for the choosing." Gods, that was such a long time ago. I could have done anything, been anything. The future was so bright it was almost blinding. Never would I have guessed I'd end up down this path. Never.

Henry presses his lips together, wiggling a bit to settle further into his place laid out on the cushiony chaise. "What changed?"

I heave a breath. "Absolutely everything." My entire life was torn apart into pieces so small they barely existed anymore. "Afterward, I only saw two paths. Kill myself or kill those responsible." Flashes of memory dance through my eyes; towering flames, hundreds of screams, people choking on smoke, the smell of sizzling flesh, the darkness of the woods, and my lungs burning as I ran.

"And now?" Henry interrupts my thoughts and my eyes snap back to his. "Are those still the only paths that you see?" My lips part, but my attention is snagged as Silva slides closer. I'm immobile as he wraps an arm around my leg and his head of wild waves lays on my uninjured thigh. Graves settles between my legs but I dare not lift my eyes to meet Henry's for a solid minute. This is what happens with friends. You care about them, what they think, what they do, and all it does is hinder your goals.

Emotionless, I look back to the soldier. "There's only one path now." He takes the hint that this conversation is done and closes his eyes. I wait a while. At least until Henry is snoring softly, then look down at Silva once again. Anger slices through me, anger so potent that it brings tears to my eyes, but I can't bring myself to shove him off.

A drop appears on his cheek and my brows furrow as I wipe it away only for two more to appear on my hand. I lift a hand to my eye and realize they're tears. I pull in a deep breath and tilt my head back to keep in the torrent. No. Absolutely not. Caring isn't something I can do anymore. Him—them—they aren't a choice that I can make. I chose my path long ago. They are a weakness I must purge.

Graves purrs in my lap and I look back down as he turns onto his back, his long hair sticking to every surface possible. "You do not count," I whisper, tickling his belly. "You can take care of yourself. These men…they're soft." He nips at my fingers and I tap his nose in recompense. Soft enough to take in an assassin on her last legs and feed her, clothe her, and gift her things. It's lucky they haven't killed themselves by inviting a bear inside simply because they have cute ears. "I can't lose anyone else." I wouldn't survive it.

My eyes wander back to Silva's face and tentatively, I brush my fingers through his waves. I was right. Soft as a goose feather.

Despite it all…I'd be lying if I said I hadn't grown a bit soft towards them as well.

*　　*　　*

"He's not dead then?"

I turn to look at Henry standing at the side of the bed and raise a brow. Dawn has come and apparently with it comes stupid questions. "Look at him. Think about what you just asked me." I see him bite his tongue as he looks Silva over again. The chest that rises and falls steadily, the color in his cheeks, and the little twitches in his fingers as if missing me as his pillow.

"I know that he isn't dead. What I meant is whether he'll be okay or not," Henry corrects as I clean the herbs from my wounds. I'm still sore and my stomach feels as if it's rioting, but I'm better. The other effects should wear off with the day.

"Why wouldn't you just ask me that in the first place?"

He sighs, running a hand over his face. "Woman, just—"

"Yes." I look over the clean wound on my chest. No trace of poison or infection. "He'll wake with no ill effects, but he'll be ravenous."

Relief slackens Henry's shoulders as I slide off the bed and walk to the window. "Why couldn't you have just said that, then?" He accuses and I hum in amusement.

"I like ruffling your feathers. You make it too easy." I tug aside the curtains a bit more and glance at the sunrise. "Breakfast should be soon. He'll be fine, so make sure he's up and dressed. You too."

His brows furrow. "Shouldn't he rest?"

My head shakes. "He needs food after the healing potion or else it'll start eating his insides. Remember I'm meeting his mother this morning, so he'll need to be there or else she'll worry." And that's one thing I'm sure Silva would like to avoid. Even if skipping it doesn't seem like a bad idea since my stomach is in knots.

"Hey." I pause at the tone of voice and glance back to find unease scrawled across his face. "I haven't forgotten what you did last night. What you wielded."

My eyes roll. "I saved both your lives and yes, I used a pinch of magic to do so. Not much else to it." With nothing else to keep me here, I spare one more glance at Silva before heaving myself onto the window ledge.

"You could use the door—!" Henry calls after me as I swing out and slide easily on the gilded décor of the house into my, thankfully unoccupied, room. Graves seems pleased as well and finds a nice spot of sunshine to lay in while I survey the bags strung up around the room like hanging bodies. A much more pleasant surprise lies inside the long garment bags, I hope.

I walk to the first and open it, gasping softly at the wispy lavender fabric that escapes the bag like smoke from a pipe. My fingers dance over the silk bodice and the ribbons that make up the straps. It's so fine. One of the finest gowns I've ever seen. I race to the other bags, ripping them open to reveal beautiful dress after dress; some for during the day, some for fancier events, all for varying seasons, all of varying colors and styles. A soft meow has me turning to Graves on the bed pawing at a large box big enough to stuff a person inside.

I rush over and toss the top aside to reveal piles of folded tunics of varying colors, pants, multiple pairs of flats, boots, and a belt of simple daggers. "Oh, he is *good*." My head shakes as I lay out the clothes in the box on top of the bed so Graves can have the container. I fight him off another moment as I reach in to pull out a green cape so dark it looks black. The clasp catches my eye, though. It's familiar. My thumb rubs over it before I realize it's a replica of the clasp from his old cloak, the one I used to escape the prison. I run my fingers over it one more time before picking up the small card on top.

Nothing but the best for my assassin. Even with these, feel free to steal my clothes anytime. I smile and run a finger over the ink before tucking the note away in the nightstand. I look around the room at the precious things and plop down on the chaise behind me. Generosity isn't something I'm used to since being passed from prison to prison. I haven't experienced it in so long. Until I came here.

There's a soft knock on the door and I shove the daggers into the bedside drawer. "Come in." The handle turns and I brace myself, then relax as Mary steps in.

Her smile is bright when she sees me even with the surprise lining her eyes. "My Lady. I wasn't aware you already returned from town." She curtsies and looks me up and down. I become aware I'm still wearing Silva's clothes and stand with my best smile.

"Yes. Being that I have few clothes of my own, Silvanus allowed me to use his for the time being." I gesture to the shirt and pants hanging loosely from my frame. I'm not sure why I lie, she has seen me murder someone before, but something about admitting I've been sharing her soon-to-be lord's bed feels…intimate. "Not particularly suited, but comfortable."

She tries in vain to keep the flabbergasted expression off her face, but she asks me no questions on the subject. "That shouldn't be a problem anymore. Have you decided on what you'll wear for the day?" Mary walks over and sets out a few things on the vanity; hair pins, rouge, lip color, multiple brushes, and varying bottles of lotion. It's a treasure trove compared to the simple brush, teeth potion, toothbrush, and hair solution Mrs. Geoffrey gave me that I had there before. I glance over my clothing selection while thinking about the role I'm about to play. My mouth screws up to the side as I step forward and let my hands glide over the dresses, then stop.

This one is jet black with boning on the outside and wisps of fabric making up the skirt. Bright red roses with deep green leaves bloom around the bottom with vines reaching up towards the waist. Some are even stitched into the corset top and vines swirl around the long sleeves. "This one, I think." I turn back to Mary who nods her approval.

"A lovely choice. Especially with the recent occurrences in this household." Her voice is careful and I can feel her eyes on me as I lay out the dress on the bed. My eyes flick to hers. I knew we'd be having this conversation eventually.

I round the bed to stand in front of her with hands clasped. "Mary, I know you owe me no loyalty but have kept your silence about what you saw the other night and the favor I asked you yesterday morning. I've no right to ask you to continue your silence—"

"Oh, lady, you needn't worry about me." She assures me, taking my hands in hers without a moment of hesitation. Our eyes meet and I'm suddenly struck by how young she must be. She can't be more than seventeen. "This is a truth I would never tell the heads of the household, but if I'm honest…" Her eyes shutter as she glances to the ground. "All the servants are relieved." Her head lifts again. "Not about what happened to Master Silva and Master Henry. We'd never wish any harm on them. To the warden and her ilk, on the other hand…" She shrugs.

"We don't bring things to the attention of our leaders because we know they have many a weight on their shoulders. But the warden treats us cruelly and has taught her guards to do the same. The servants in the house and the stables feel as if an ancestor, a ghost, or a great protector is finally taking their revenge." Mary giggles, the sound light and airy, but all I can do is blink. I'd been hailed for killing before, but never had it taken me by complete surprise.

My hands squeeze hers when I recover. "Thank you for all you've done for me."

Her eyes go wide as she shakes her head. "No, thank *you*. Tell me if there's anything else I can do. I've made myself your dresser, so you can call me up here at any time without suspicion." A smile tempts my lips. Yes, she would have made a fine assassin.

"Well, getting me presentable would be a fine start." She gives me another smile before tugging me to the podium in front of the foldable mirrors and getting to work. I'm out of Silva's clothes and into the stunning dress in minutes, then she sits me down at the vanity to do my hair. To her credit, she doesn't ask about my scars or the bandages on my leg and now my side. I suppose servants aren't supposed to notice such things.

I drag my bottom lip between my teeth as I stare at my reflection. It's a risk to let Annaliese and Deckree see me again. Hopefully, I look too different from when they last saw me to recognize me now. At least as long as I keep from straddling them with a dagger in my hand. Then they'd know me on sight.

Mary crouches in front of me to paint my lips a dark red. "Are you her, lady?" I raise a brow as a silent command to continue. She swallows and stands, twisting her hands in front of her. "The Red Death." My eyes don't leave her pensive face for a few beats.

"If I was?" My head cocks as I wait for her answer.

She takes a deep breath. "All know the stories of the Red Death, but in lower circles, they aren't feared so much as…revered. They kill many, most in terrifying ways, but all the victims I've heard of have been cruel, greedy, perverted, or worse."

"And how would you know those things?" There's just enough bite in my voice to hurry her answer so she doesn't have time to lie.

"Servants know what goes on in a house. They talk and listen while the higher born may not."

I hum, standing up and straightening my dress. She'd done a fine job with my hair and part of it is pinned up in a swirling coil while the rest tumbles down my back. The half-hearted waves are turning into large curls and I have every hope that one day I'll have my loose ringlets back. There's even a tint of lighter brown in it with all the time I'd been spending in the sun. My hand rests lightly on Mary's shoulder as I look into her eyes. "I'm only Lady Nestra here. That'll be all the questions for now." Her eyes shimmer at the fact that I didn't exactly say no.

She curtsies and leaves the room while I slip on a pair of dark green flats, then move the large box containing Graves to the floor so he doesn't knock it off the bed. "Wish me luck." I wink at him before taking one last look in the mirror. I'd filled out nearly to my old self without the mounds of muscle, but that'll take more than a potion to regain. My body no longer looks skeletal and I'm quite proud to have a bit of a tummy even if it's hidden by the dress. With the fine clothes, healthy body, and Silva on my arm, I should be unrecognizable.

Still, it's best to be cautious. I lift a hand and wave it over my face. My reflection in the mirror shimmers like a mirage before changing ever so slightly. The scars on my face and the new scratch on my collarbone seem to vanish before my eyes. It's a simple mirage, but if I run into the warden or her soldiers, I don't want a scar to give me away. Even if I'm rather fond of the marks.

The final touch is the dagger Silva gave me and I cleaned. I affix it to my hip before walking out the door with my head held high.

Time to play the lady.

*   *   *

I steady my breathing as I walk down the red hall and make sure my walk is right before moving through the archway to the balcony looking over the entry. Silva and Henry stand in the middle of the room already changed. Henry wears a champagne shirt with white pants and his normal soldier's boots. A sword remains on his hip and I'm glad I won't be the only one with a weapon. Silva wears a black shirt and blood-red pants so dark the color is barely discernible, but his coat is an emerald green along with his suede shoes. As always, his hair shines like a beacon atop his tall frame with the waves bouncing as his fingers tap against his leg.

I'm smiling slightly as Henry reaches up and messes up Silva's hair while I descend the right staircase with my fingers barely skimming the stone banister. Once at the bottom, I lean against it and let my shining nails, courtesy of Mary's scrubbing, tap on the hard surface.

Henry is facing this way, so he notices me first and his eyes nearly bug out of his head. I wiggle my fingers at him before Silva turns on his heel, and then freezes. A scathing remark rises to my lips, but when I see the way that he looks at me, I can't bring myself to say it. His eyes are the only things that move as he looks me up and down with languid ease. Goosebumps rise on my arms at the heat caged in that one look as I walk over and offer my hand. "All better, then?"

He takes my hand, his grip light as a butterfly, then dips to kiss my knuckles. "Yes. It seems Death favored me this time." He straightens with his gaze locked on mine.

"Wise to stay on her good side." His eyes glimmer and shine like stars as I turn to Henry. He bows as I give him a polite curtsey.

Henry still doesn't seem to be fully aware of who I am anymore. He looks me over a few times, then shakes his head. "You look...you look—"

"Devastating," Silva finishes and I grin at the compliment.

"So I should hope. Although you should probably stop gaping or they'll think I'm trying to catch two fish with one hook." I give Henry a pointed look. He promptly shuts his mouth and looks to the floor even though his eyes wander back to me within the minute.

Silva steps forward and lifts his hand to my face. "What happened to your scars?" His fingers come close to skimming where they're hiding, so close I can feel the heat of his hand. I'm not sure which surprises me more; the casual near-touch or the fact that he knows my face well enough to trace my scars.

"Mirage. Thought it might be prudent." My voice is soft so it doesn't echo in the grand room.

Silva's eyes shine with interest. "Ah, yes. That brings up an interesting conversation we should have."

"I'm under no obligation to tell either of you anything." The words are sharper than I mean them to be, but I can't bring myself to be sorry. All I can think of is how he helped me, his fingers on my skin, and the image of him being lowered into an early grave.

Silva takes a breath and slides his hands into his pockets. "Certainly not, but we do love hearing all you have to say." His eyes are irritatingly earnest.

"Especially on this," Henry adds.

My hands curl into fists as I shrug. "I have enough to make a difference, that's all. Nothing grand or specialized."

Silva rocks back and forth on the balls of his feet while Henry scans me. After a minute, he offers me his arm. "We should be getting on, anyway. Wouldn't want to be late." There's a bit of nervous energy in him as we walk too quickly towards the tea room. The doors to the baby blue room are wide open and relief mixes strangely with frustration in my gut when I see the warden and her soldier aren't present. There's only one person within besides the servants.

"Silva, I was starting to think you'd gotten lost." His mother rounds the table with a wide, welcoming smile on her face. I'm surprised at the stark differences between her and Silva, but there are hints of a relation; the shape of their smiles, the ears, and when her eyes scan me, I note that they're exactly the same shade as her son's.

"Hard to get lost in a house I would know blind, mother." He accepts her kiss on his cheek while Henry does the same before she turns to me. Silva takes a breath and I try not to let his nerves rattle me. "Lady Meira Dinnsesk, this is Lady Clytemnestra...Sassian." My eyes cut over to his face as he smirks. "Nestra, my mother."

I curtsey despite the slight twinge in my leg and rise with a smile. "A pleasure to meet you, Lady Dinnsesk. I've heard only good things about you from your son."

She waves my words away with a careless hand. "Oh, I'm sure that's not true. And please, Meira is fine." Her arm tugs me from Silva as she drags me over to sit beside her at the table.

I glance back at Silva and mouth, "Sassian? Really?" He chuckles and shrugs while following close behind.

"Tell me what bad things I should've told her and I'll be happy to do so," He says as he settles across from me with Henry beside him.

"Och, hush. Let her tell me about herself before we bore her with our own stories." She turns back to me, round cheeks nearly eclipsing her eyes as she smiles. She is a rather curvy woman, opposite of Silva, so I'd guess he takes more after his father. At least physically. "I know my boys helped you out of some distress, but that's about all I know."

I take a breath and keep up my smile as I prepare to lie to this woman's face. The story is short and full of as much truth as I can manage. We all came together on the road where they took me on with only a horse and rags to my name. They brought me here where I convalesced until I was well enough to see her, then put off the meeting while the warden settled in. Seeing that things only got worse, there was no sense in delaying any longer.

As for what transpired before we three met, I tell the same story that I told Mrs. Geoffrey. My parents are long dead and my estate passed into a cruel uncle's hands who kept me apart from the world. "How terrible!" Meira sympathizes. Her hand reaches for mine and I force myself not to pull away from the sudden movement. She squeezes my fingers. "You'll be safe here and are welcome as long as you like. It's rare for me to see Silva in such high spirits anyways."

I'm shocked to see Silva's cheeks brush red as his mother winks at him. Henry smirks and I have a feeling that this is a rare moment where Silva has been knocked off balance. The fact has a smile tugging at my lips. "I'm glad I could cheer him although I'm afraid we neglect Henry most egregiously." We all turn to him as he nearly chokes on a sausage link. Silva happily beats on his back until he's swallowed and Henry shoots me a firm look. I raise my glass delicately to my lips to hide my grin.

"I don't mind a release from Silva's company for a while. I've been able to get some work done." The playful jeer lands lightly on Silva's shoulders who doesn't hesitate to flick his ear.

"And no doubt have suffered from a lack of fun." Silva leans back in his chair before he jolts slightly and shoots his mother a sharp look even as he straightens again. I believe she may have kicked him under the table.

She shakes her head at their antics. "The hope was that the two of you would balance each other out, not add to each other's chaos." The scold is weightless. Whenever she looks at the two of them, there's nothing but joy in her eyes. She turns to me, her smile unfaltering. "Which are you, Nestra? A troublemaker or a hard worker?"

I glance at Silva to answer. "I like to have fun in my work, my Lady." He smirks but tames his smile when she looks between us. "I've heard you love to paint." I go on before she can ask about the kind of work that I do.

Her face lights up. "I do indeed. You're welcome to join me whenever you like."

A very unladylike snort finds its way out of me at the thought. "I'm afraid I've no talent with paints." Though there were days a long time ago when my hands were almost always smudged with charcoal from sketching.

"Who said anything about talent?" She counters and I pause a moment to listen. "I love to paint because it's fun and I enjoy doing it. Not because I'm talented." Silva's mouth screws up to the side as if he'd like to object to some part of that, but I only nod once.

Meira opens her mouth to go on, but the words die in her throat as she looks to the doorway. "Anna." Her name clangs through me and I realize I nearly forgot she was here. Nearly forgot my purpose wasn't to dazzle and impress Silva's mother, but to kill his father and kill the warden in the meantime. Meira doesn't seem too pleased that she's come either. "Shouldn't you be resting?"

"I will not be sequestered to a room like an invalid or prisoner. I'll be better soon enough." The warden's throat is raw. No doubt she's been screaming as her skin knit itself back together. I'm frozen as I stare at my lovely plate that Silva piled full of food, but I can't bring myself to eat any of it. Her presence spoils it. Rots it. Memories drift through my head of her tossing burnt, molding loaves of bread into my cage and how her eyes gleamed as I tore into it. Sometimes it was all I had for a week.

If I look at her, I'm not sure I won't kill her on sight.

"I thought it would be better considering what your soldiers did last night." Meira's voice is clear and unrelenting. Something in me twists at the fierce determination of a mother's love.

"Would you tie me to the bed, Meira?" Cold chains weigh heavy on my wrists, on my ankles. The cold steel almost burns from the chill and each link rings like a heavy bell every time I tug on my bindings. Silently, I let my silverware clink on the table to lay my trembling hands in my lap. *Come now, Roux. You're free. You are no longer under her power.* I try to soothe myself, but all I feel is rage.

My foot is nudged softly under the table and my eyes snap up to meet Silva's worried ones across the table. I take a deep breath. Right now, I'm not Roux. I'm a lady with no connection to the warden except for the space we take up in this room together. Wild rage won't do anyone any good. It has to be sharp and focused like a blade poised to strike. My eyes shut and when I open them again, memories no longer cloud my vision.

"I debated it," Meira responds to Anna's tease. "You are under investigation by this house. Your guards attempted the murder of my boys and that is more than unforgivable." Ice lingers between her words and I wonder if she learned to be cold from her husband or other sources. Henry humphs in agreement and it's clear that he's the one heading the investigation. I'll need to keep an eye out for him. Annaliese hesitates and I finally turn to see the emotion on her face. If she's stalling, then it's because she has something to lose here and I need to know about it.

My head slowly turns to take in Annaliese Warren standing resolutely between her two remaining soldiers; Deckree and Banks. Her fingers dig into her second's shoulder like talons and I realize with growing gratification that she's supporting most of her weight. Her other hand is held against her right side. I'd snuck around the other night and heard the nurse talking about her one and only patient. Three of her ribs were broken from the big cat tackling her to the hard ground. Every breath must cause her immense pain. No longer is she strapped into her usual uniform, but in black slacks, a black shirt, and a black cloak whose hood hides her face.

"Of course, I understand how upsetting it was for you. But surely I can be well watched with you, your son, and your head of security in the room." She doesn't name me and apparently has decided I'm not enough of a threat to pay attention to yet. A grave mistake, but one that works in my favor. "My remaining guards attend me as well." She emphasizes her losses since coming here. Losses caused by me. Meira huffs, but seems content enough to let Annaliese join us.

It's only when the three are fully into the room and out of the shadows of the corridor that she lifts her head. The hood falls. Satisfaction shoots through me like a shot of alcohol as I see the angry pink gashes marring the side of her face. She had to have drunk at least three healing potions right after the other to make it look this well. No doubt she feels sickly after so many, but still, magic couldn't fix everything. Her right eye is gone and has been replaced by what looks like black glass that glints just as her other eye does.

Her good eye traverses the room as none of us stand to receive her and I don't so much as flinch when her gaze lands on me. Only then do I stand and I see Silva stiffen as I do. I've schooled my smile into something polite and manage to let my hands rest easy at my sides. It's good that she sees me standing first. She scans the dress I have on, the fineness of it, and the ease with which I hold myself. She'd seen a little of me before I was that withered thing trapped in prison after prison, but never did she see me like this. She shouldn't recognize me. Funny how the image of a person can be changed so quickly. You could know someone for years, then they change and that's the only memory you have from then on. The mind is fickle, the memory vague and deceiving.

Her eye narrows at me as she staggers over with her guards. "This is Lady Nestra. She's a guest of my son's." Meira introduces, but neither of us looks away from one another. We're only a foot apart and my fingers twitch. It would be so easy to end her here and now. My dagger is only a move away. Her heart, blackened and small as it may be, is an easy target. The satisfaction I feel, the pleasure, the excitement of seeing her feeble, pales in comparison to the anger that rises in me as sure as a sunrise.

Her gaze burns into mine and I don't back down. Never will I back down. Never will I break.

She's far taller than I am and glowers down at me when I don't cower. "Have we met?"

My smile tilts. "I know your name and occupation. We've never been properly introduced, so far as I can recall." The iris in her good eye bounces around my face and I know she's cataloguing it for further study. I'm thankful I remembered the mirage this morning. She has more reason than most to know my scars on sight. She'd caused a good chunk of them. Her lips part as confusion travels across her face before settling into vague suspicion as she looks me up and down again. "Do I look familiar?" There's nothing but innocence in my tone even as Henry shifts across from us.

She leans an inch closer with her one good eye searching mine. "Perhaps. Have I arrested you before?"

My laugh fills the room. "Certainly not. If I were to enter a criminal occupation, I should hope to be good enough to evade arrest." I turn to Meira and share a conspirator's smile while knowing turning away from the warden will make her see red. I'm still aware of her every move, her every breath.

"Everyone is caught eventually." Her voice has darkened along with those black eyes when I turn back to her.

I hum politely as a noble does when someone says something vaguely interesting. "Then there's always escape." We stare off for a few moments as I see her searching for confirmation or a clue as to who I may be. I'm the one to break the stand-off. "You look quite weak, Annaliese, please sit." I gesture to the table without taking my eyes off her. Her hand trails to the sword still on her hip despite my doubt that she can wield it well at this point. She suspects me. Good. I want her drowning in suspicion and paranoia before the end.

"I go by Warden or Anna." She corrects, her voice sharper this time.

"Certainly," I affirm with nothing but an innocent blink. Deckree finally steers her to the other end of the table to sit at the head with her guards on either side of her. She's out of reach now, but there are more ways to get to a person than to touch them. We all sit and I feel Silva's eyes on me, but I'm not concerned.

This is a game I know how to play and I'm determined to win it.

Chapter Thirteen

Kill the Messenger

Silva

Watching Anna and Roux together after seeing their dynamic in the prison on the Mount is…jarring. In that dim tower, they were separated by a line of bars but Roux seemed to have all the power. She had nothing to lose and everything to gain as Anna bargained with her. Now she's free and has absolutely everything to lose while Anna has everything to gain by capturing her. If it were someone else in this situation, I might've laughed.

"What family did you say you were from, Lady Nestra?" Anna asks as she leans back in her chair in stark contrast to her usual stiff posture. She's weak. I've never seen her weak before. Even though Henry and I found Anna after the mountain lion attacked her, seeing the marks now in the bright morning light is completely different. I nearly feel bad for her before remembering what she did to Henry and Roux. Still, there is a sort of sobering effect in seeing a being of power brought low. Even if she deserves it.

"Sassian." Roux risks a pointed glance in my direction for bequeathing her the name. "My family owns a small estate in the northeast, near the border with Belterra." Either she's done her homework and there just so happens to be an exact estate or she's going to kill them before they can check. The two of them are playing chess, employing moves and countermoves to try to figure out the other's strategy. Roux would no doubt equate it to a dance. Well, if that dance was around a pit of knives and you were certain your partner was trying to push you into the hole.

There seemed to be a glimmer of recognition in Anna's eyes as they stared at one another, but she didn't command her guards to take the assassin in. I know the warden. If she suspects her, then she'll gather evidence and information before striking. The shock will wear off and then she'll start gathering the pieces together to see how it all fits. I only hope Roux puts a dagger in her chest before she realizes the whole scheme.

"Where, exactly?" The warden continues, but Roux has an answer for everything.

"Decant. It's small, I doubt you've heard of it." Anna's nose wrinkles at the quick response. Her soldiers are markedly quiet as are Henry and I as the two face off. My mother has been simmering since Anna came in, but now seems to just be listening. She can see there's something between them. I hold in a sigh. That'll take some explaining. "Have you visited the north?" Roux goes on as the warden opens her mouth to ask yet another question. Those emerald eyes shimmer with fire from that wild rage slumbering within her chest, but her tone and bearing speak of nothing but a lady. I wonder how long she can hold back the flames.

"I have traveled many places. Hunting criminals, low lives, and the like takes one everywhere." The warden answers with eyes affixed on Roux. Well, eye, I suppose.

Roux is undaunted as she speaks again. "It's lovely. In the winter months especially. All the snow covering the pines and the sunlight glinting off the frozen rivers." Anna stiffens. Something about this has hit a nerve. Frustration washes over me at not knowing more about Roux and her dealings with the warden. Even though I suppose I know far more than I ever thought I would.

"Do you prefer the winter months?" My mother tries to lighten the conversation even though the effort will more than likely be futile.

Roux glances over, her fork poking at the pastry on her plate. I'm not sure if any of us has had more than a mouthful of food since the warden sat down. "No, not particularly. Cold seeps into the stone walls and floor to chill me to the bone."

"Stone?" Anna catches onto the word and clings to it like a lifeline. Her knuckles are white as she squeezes her silverware in each hand.

Roux turns to her with an easy smile. "Yes. Like the stone steps in the entry? All great houses have some room made of stone and it's always frigid in the winter."

"I do hope a lady doesn't have to sleep on a stone floor. You'd become as filthy as a pig in its stye." Anna's eyes are trained on her, watching to see any reaction that might be incriminating. Roux makes no sign that the words bother her, but I know they do. She'd rip apart the Prison on the Mount stone by stone if she could. Once she's free from this place, perhaps she will.

My mind is suddenly full of the image of Roux trembling in the paddock as the dogs bark outside it. The surroundings change from the sunny outdoors to a cage drenched in darkness; her small body tucked away in a filthy corner. I'm speaking before I realize it. "The cold is abominable. That's why I prefer to lounge beside a wide fire surrounded by heavy blankets for most of the season." Eyes turn to me, but I only give a lazy smile.

Roux raises a brow at me. "Like a cat full of mice?" My smile widens at distracting her enough to reply.

"Exactly so. Perhaps you'd like me more if I was a cat."

"I'm sure I've never said I liked you at all."

"Don't you, though?" I dare and feel pleasure skitter down my spine as a little sharpness leaks into her grin. There's my assassin.

"Sassian is a very unusual name." The warden reclaims our attention as she struggles to sit up properly. Henry catches my eye and barely shakes his head instead of an audible scold. The name may not have been a good idea, but it certainly was funny. I shrug, helpless to my nature. His eyes roll as we tune back into the conversation. Anna takes a long swig from her glass. "Something about it sounds familiar. Like I've heard it before."

Roux takes her time pulling her jam-covered spoon from her mouth. "You know, it does sound like something. An occupation, maybe?" Henry and I hold our breath. We're skating over thin ice now.

Anna's piercing eyes sharpen. "Exactly."

Laughter makes me jump, especially when I realize it's coming from Roux. We hesitantly join in before she levels the warden with a look. "Ah, that is an entertaining thought. I wonder why you've come up with it." She raises a cloying brow. "I did hear about the unfortunate events at the prison. What a sight it must have been to witness." Anna locks her jaw. My foot pokes Roux's under the table and her eyes flash to mine. I don't dare shake my head, but the warning is clear in my eyes. It's one thing to play with Anna, but another entirely to bait her. She huffs and pins me with a look of her own.

Words she said not too long ago echo in my head. *Don't get in my way again, Silvanus.*

"Silva told me what happened. Awful business, of course." Meira smooths over the conversation somewhat. I almost wish I could tell her that the attempt is folly. These two are not to be tamed.

"Yes, well." Anna sits up a bit straighter when servants enter the room to clear everything away. "Things will be put right soon enough."

"You have a lead?" Henry speaks up, something he rarely does in Anna's presence.

Her sharp eyes land on him and, to his credit, he doesn't flinch. "That's privileged information." My teeth grit at her dismissive tone, but Henry only tugs in a breath. He's used to the treatment from her and I hate it.

"Sniveling dog." Banks sneers at Henry as my mother is distracted thanking the servants for helping her. My fists clench even as he sends me a firm look not to interfere. Turns out he needn't have stopped me.

"What was that?" Roux's voice slices through the room causing even the servants to stall before continuing their work. Her eyes blaze as Banks turns to meet them. "You said something, I believe." Shock ripples over the guard's face and she says nothing. Roux isn't satisfied with that. "Since you won't answer, I'm forced to assume you were merely addressing yourself. A strange moniker, but I won't say it's inaccurate." Banks' face flushes red with anger, especially when Henry and I try to smother our grins.

"You—"

I clear my throat to interrupt whatever insult was about to leave Banks' mouth. "I promised Lady Nestra a turn around the gardens, if you'll excuse us." It's probably best if I get us out of here before there's any bloodshed. My feet carry me around my mother as I press a kiss to her cheek, then pause beside Roux to make one last comment. "I do hope there are no hard feelings between us after the mishap with your guards." Anna's head whips towards me, but I only smile.

"Mishap?" My mother echoes at a slightly higher pitch, but the room remains focused on the warden.

She takes a breath, fighting the wince of pain from her ribs. "An unfortunate occurrence, but I do train my guards to be loyal." Her words don't even pretend to be an apology. Roux wraps her arm around mine and I tug her close to lend her some warmth. The tips of her long fingers look almost blue just as mine did from the poison. I wonder how much of her strength is an act.

"Is that an admission, warden?" Henry asks with a voice smooth and firm. "Loyal soldiers don't go against their leader's command." A smile tugs at my lips. Well done, Henry. Even Roux seems to be fighting a smile at my side.

Anna's lips part, but my mother beats her to it. "Be very careful about your next words, Anna." Her one black eye meets the clear blue of Meira's and I can see her reconsider. In a physical battle, the warden would almost assuredly win, but in court, Meira has far more power. My mother could severely damage the warden's influence with only a few words to the right people. It's that reason alone that she respects her. Or at least pretends to.

"They were too loyal. I would never approve of such an ill-conceived and sloppy attack." Henry scoffs, but it's the ladies who have locked eyes. My mother nods once in acceptance. Although, I don't believe for a moment that she believes her. Anna opens her mouth again only to be interrupted by the doors of the room slamming into the walls as they open. Fine jars and vases tremble with the impact, but my attention goes to the body my servants are dragging into the room.

"What's the meaning of this?" Anna shouts as they lay the man out just inside the doors on the carpet.

"He said to bring him to you before anything else." Someone answers while I stare at the mess of his body. All of his clothes are ripped and caked in mud, one of his arms is twisted at an unnatural angle, two of his fingers are gone, ripped or bitten off, blood soaks his left hip down his leg, and his face looks like it was smashed against a tree a few times.

"Gods, what happened to the poor creature?" My mother asks before planting a hand in front of her mouth.

"A-An-Anna." His voice gurgles out of his chest and the warden falls to her knees beside him.

"Delaney?" She names one of her guards, the one that went missing in the woods after the mountain lion attack. His mouth opens and closes as he fights to speak. "Water, give me water." Anna commands and Deckree instantly hands her a glass that she tips none too gently into the guard's mouth.

"Warn-warning. She…she's back." Anna's spine goes stiff as a board as the soldier reaches up to his shirt. Apparently, this is too slow for her because she slaps his hand aside and rips what's left of his shirt open with a tug of her hand. Gasps litter the room, including from the warden's stoic, surviving guards. Large, ugly red letters have been carved into his skin covered in dried blood and dirt. The words are surprisingly legible despite a blade being the utensil and a man's chest being the canvas. Still, I stumble forward a few steps before reading the words.

I'M COMING.

Desperately, I try to gather my wits as I take a few steps back to Roux's side as the warden starts shouting for security and healers. "I want an entire unit here now! Search the forest! Surround the house! I want a messenger in this room! NOW!" It's as close to panic as I've ever seen the warden and her eyes are wild as she looks around the room as if seeing ghosts in every corner. Henry moves to the doors and begins talking to the two soldiers from his security team in urgent, hushed tones.

I peel my gaze away from the prostrate man as he starts gasping for breath and look at the assassin beside me. A wide grin leaking wicked glee alights her face as her eyes take in the macabre sight. Those emerald eyes gleam with grim satisfaction and thinly held joy and I don't know what it says about me that I think she's breathtaking. Her eyes flick to me and she winks.

"I…I think I'm—" She puts a hand on her heart and its pure instinct to catch her as she faints.

"Nestra?" I call, lifting her into my arms easily. My mother rushes to my side and gently brushes away a few strands of hair from her face. "I'll take her outside for some fresh air. You'll handle Anna?"

She nods and lightly pushes me towards the door. "I'll deal with this. Take care of her." My mother pales as she faces the scene, then she lifts her head and pulls her shoulders back. "Anna, come away, you're still injured..." I don't hear the rest because I'm walking out. My nose wrinkles as I step around the sullied carpet with the dying man atop it and strut out the door.

Henry follows a moment later and I pause in the archway. "Keep an eye on the warden. She's becoming unhinged."

"And her?" He gestures to Roux who seems like she could be asleep in my arms.

"I'll handle our fainting lady." Her lips twitch down and it's almost enough to get me to grin. Henry claps me on the back before heading back in where the warden is still screaming commands. It's a pleasure to be able to escape as I walk out into the open air. "So, the fainting was for...?"

Roux's eyes open and she crosses her arms over her chest. "My feet hurt." A light chuckle shivers out of my chest as I take her deeper into the garden and she gives me the real answer. "Best the soldier didn't look over and see the artist that carved such lovely work into his chest. Even a miraged image." She waves her hand over her face and the visage vanishes to reveal those cute little scars again.

"How did he get back?" He must have crawled miles to get back to the estate.

Roux shakes her head. "I'm as shocked as you. I left him for the creatures of the woods to rip apart. I figured he'd eventually be found by a passing patrol who would bring along my message." A smile tugs on her mouth. "Although this certainly was a more dramatic and satisfying delivery."

I duck into an alcove covered in twisting ivy out of the view of the house before helping Roux back onto her feet. Her hand remains on my shoulder as she steadies herself and my brows furrow with worry. Maybe I should've taken her upstairs to lie down. She catches my expression and sighs. "Poison is still in my system, so I'm a bit unsteady on my feet." It's the closest she's ever been to admitting a weakness and I'm shocked still for a moment.

"Well, I'll gladly carry you wherever you'd like to go, my Lady." A charming grin blooms on my face as her eyes roll. Still, there's an edge to her eyes as she wraps her arm around mine before we start walking again. And not a hostile one. "Tell me about your magic."

She looks up at the sky and heaves in a deep breath. "I use it as a courtier uses makeup or a thief uses a cloak. It's an extra tool at my disposal."

"But you *wield* it." Everyone has a little bit of magic in them, but very few have enough to do anything with it.

She shrugs a shoulder at my incredulous tone. "I was taught as many are taught." I bite my tongue to keep from barraging her with the dozens of questions that flood my mind. Best not to push her. "I suppose you and Henry know that if you speak a word of any of what I tell or have told you, then I'll string you up in your yard by your entrails." My feet stumble over nothing at her words and when I glance over, her expression is nothing but lovely.

"Like the palace guards at Crystal Bridge?"

A smile drifts over her lips along with a flicker of surprise in her eyes. "Always flattering to find someone who keeps up with my work. But they were simply pawns in my way." I swallow at the thought of what havoc she can wreak when her sights are purposefully on you. The image of her tossing that woman's tongue aside rises to the surface of my mind and my stomach flips. Although, I'm not sure for good or bad.

"I'm hurt, my Lady." I lay my hand over my heart as she presses her lips together. "Friends always keep each other's secrets." Now it's her turn to nearly trip. She tugs her arm from me without resistance as we come to the end of the archway. Her hand clings to the lattice as she scans me and I lean against a column on the other side. "Don't think you can fight it now, Roux. We're friends. We're…fond of each other." The tease brings a grin to my face, but I mean every word.

Her eyes burn into me like hot pokers and even in her weakened state, I don't see it when she moves. Thin fingers wrap around my throat as she presses me back against the lattice. There's no pressure, not with the flimsy wall behind me, but her fingernails prick my skin in a clear promise of violence. "Let me tell you about the last man to call himself my friend." Those gold flecks swim in the wildness of her green eyes and I can't help glancing at her pink lips as she speaks. They look terribly soft. Her nails dig further into my skin and my mouth goes dry as my eyes return to hers.

"Tell me," I whisper, heat flooding my body when she glances at my mouth.

Her other hand slides up my chest while mine hover over her hips before settling on the slight curves. I'm thrilled she doesn't pull away and instead slides nearer. "There was a man, a merchant, who sold cheap knock-offs. I bought a bracelet from him for a job and left the next day without a trace." Every word she says seems to echo in my empty head while her hand keeps inching up my chest. She's a spider drawing me easily into her web. "Later, I found out that he told everyone he knew the identity of the Red Death. That he was their trusted confidant. My friend."

Her tone deepens and my instincts perk up, but every one of my senses is devoted to her. Taking in how the tip of her nose moves as she talks, how her lashes brush her cheeks with each blink, her sage and pine scent, and the feeling of her body under my hands. "It didn't take long for one of my enemies to find him and see what he actually knew. They flayed his skin from his body." She drags one nail down my chest as if it were a knife and stops at my belt. "Piece by piece. Then they dripped poison into the open cavity." One of her fingers taps on my sternum as if it were drops of toxin. "It ate away the leftover flesh still on the bone until it was clean and white like snow."

She shrugs, letting her fingers tap on each one of my ribs as it goes down. "He must have died at that point or stopped being useful because I found him like that when I came to take care of his rumors myself. His heart lay on the floor. They cut it out carefully so he could see it before he died." Her eyes burn like green flames as she squeezes my throat and I tug her closer. The corner of her lips twitch. "And he wasn't even my friend. So…" She goes up on her toes so our faces are mere inches from one another. It's incredibly tempting to lean down to taste her sharp words, but her hand on my neck keeps me still.

"Never say that you're my friend. Never say that you know me. Never, Silvanus." Yet she never says that I'm not and that I don't.

"Fine." I relish the suspicious narrowing of her eyes. "Then what are we to be? Allies again?"

Her lips purse. "Assassins can have allies, lovers, and enemies. The safest position for you would be enemy."

"Enemy?" My brows raise. I know which of that selection I would pick.

She smirks and nods. "Yes. I have plenty of those and killing you would be rather low on my list."

"Ah, so long as you don't forget about me." She shakes her head, but finally releases me from her grip and slips away from my hands. Heat floats away with her and I feel cold without her body against mine. She spins on her heel and moves out of the alcove with me trailing behind.

"Of course not. I'll think about you like the horse does the fly."

I frown. "Flattering." Her laughter fills the air as we exit the hall made by hedges to a manmade lake shaped like a long rectangle with a fountain in the middle. She walks to the edge and settles on a stone bench. She looks out over the water as a breeze teases the strings of hair that have escaped her updo. As she takes a deep breath with her eyes closed, it almost looks like she's at peace here. I settle beside her and I'm glad when she doesn't move away.

"Things will have to move quickly now." Her eyes open, but remain unfocused. "I haven't exactly been taking my time, but they'll have to die within the next two days. They can't be allowed to send word to anyone off the estate."

My brows furrow. "The warden was already calling for units—" I trail off when her head shakes.

"She was shaken." She sounds nothing but pleased at the fact. "The man will take a bit to die, less than half an hour I'd say. After she wrings all the information she can out of him, she'll only trust one of her people with a message. With only two left, she'll keep Deckree with her and send Banks." A smile begins to creep over her lips and I nod slowly as I catch on.

"You have no intention of letting her leave this estate."

That smile widens and I find myself smiling back. "She won't get five miles. I already have a pack and a change of clothes waiting in Banshee's stall. I'd say we have about an hour before Banks is packed and on horseback." I blink as pleasant surprise rolls through me.

"We?"

She rolls her eyes and I'm sure the smile on my face is embarrassingly big as she glances over. "I figured you'd beg me to come."

I reel in my grin and clear my throat with a shrug. "I was ready to plead."

She smirks, eyes shimmering with mirth. "I look forward to seeing you on your knees some other time. For now, you might want to change."

I pinch my shirt and hold it away from my chest. "You don't like my outfit?"

Her snort echoes over the water. "You wouldn't like it if you got it dirty."

"Mm, did you just think of someone else? I'm touched." I laugh as she shoves me off the bench and I stumble onto my feet.

Her hand waves me away. "Meet me in the woods in an hour." I give her an exaggerated bow, then hurry away back to the house before she can slap me. I'm struggling to contain my smile as I jog back to the house to ready for our adventure.

Chapter Fourteen

Death Comes for Us All

Roux

Banshee is ready to run when I reach the stables. I bribe her with an apple from the kitchen as I change beside her, tucking my lovely dress safely away into my pack. Graves watches while sliding back and forth through the bars of the stall, but he seems more interested in some birds that have roosted high above us. Meanwhile, Banshee has long since finished her apple and is sniffing my pockets for more. "Just the one this time, girl. Maybe we'll find some clover while we're out." My fingers slide over her velvet nose as I stare into one of her dark eyes. She whinnies and I grin before tucking the pack away under some loose straw. I squat and pull my knees up to my chest one by one to experiment with the new clothes that Silva got me.

The whole of it is black as a shadow and closefitting. The fabric is tough, like a more flexible cousin to leather, but with pockets of loose cotton around my joints for ease of movement. There are pockets everywhere and I make sure to load up on daggers just in case. Usually, I'd strap rows around my body like lines of scales, but that's a bit too conspicuous for out in the country. I have a bow and quiver hidden in the woods, so the extra weapons aren't needed. Even if they would give me comfort.

The deep green cloak is the final touch before I sling myself onto Banshee's bare back. It'll take too long to saddle her now and I don't mind going without. I almost prefer it. This way I get to feel her breathing and the way her muscles quiver with excitement. The latch has barely slid from the lock before she bursts out and I can't help my laugh as a stable boy leaps out of her way. I wave and give him a farewell before we're out of sight. The last thing I need is for him to think I've been swept away by Banshee and to tell Mr. Geoffrey that I need rescuing.

"Alright, let's see what you've got," I whisper and grip tight to her mane as I let her have control. She snorts, chest heaving as we careen into the woods at full speed. There's a wide grin on my face as the wind stings my eyes and tugs my hair from its pins. The sound of her hooves hammering into the path fills my ears along with her breath and the howl of the breeze. Gods, it's been so long since I've been able to be like this. It's been too long since I've felt free.

It's tempting not to stop. I wonder how long and far she would go if I let her. At the same time, I wonder what I would do if I freed myself from my list of responsibilities. My soul aches, restless, cursing me as I bring Banshee to heel. "One day," I soothe, running a hand down her neck as she shakes her head as if in denial. "One day we'll run free, but for now there's a job to do." I urge her to the edge of the forest where I hid my weapons and loop the quiver around me while keeping an eye out for Silva.

That thing howling for release in my chest settles at the thought of him and focuses. It's been so long since I was close to a man the way I was close to him in the garden. The feeling of his hands on my hips still lingers like the sweet sting of wind on a long journey. His lips looked so soft and he was so willing, so ready to accept anything I'd give him. I haven't been with anyone in so long…I swallow and shift on Banshee. No, not a chance. The first rule in this business is not to sleep with anyone you actually like. Things afterward always get messy and that isn't something I can afford right now. I have a job to do. A mission.

The soft clop of hooves has me turning with a dagger in my palm before I see a flash of copper hair. My head shakes. "You should wear a hood over that blazing hair or we'll be seen a mile away." He exits the wood with an undaunted grin and I fight to keep myself from returning it. "Hood." Silva huffs, but he flicks his hood up before falling into step beside me as we travel parallel to the main road. Banks will have to take it to leave the estate in the direction she wants to go.

"You look good in those." Silva's husky voice drags my attention from the road as he flicks his chin to my battle attire.

I look back to the road. "You should have seen what I used to wear."

"Was it fine?"

I choke back a laugh and glance at him with a wistful smile. "It was tough. Made for me by the selkies living near the pink beaches of Pernum." Silva's eyes go wide and I don't bother to hide the smugness on my face. It was a magnificent suit. "Deep red darker than blood, strong enough to withstand a direct hit from a blade in some places, but comfortable enough to sleep in."

It's silent for a moment as Silva no doubt sorts through the list of questions in his head. "What happened to it?"

A heavy sigh slips from my lips. "I hid it away before I was taken. It's probably been filched by now." Gods, what a waste.

"Did you know, then?" He brings his dark horse forward a bit so we're walking side by side. "When you went out that day or night. Did you know that you were going to be taken?" The question sends a chill slithering down my spine as if I'm back in that moment, snow all around, ice gilding the trees like glass, and a trap waiting for me beside a frozen river.

My shoulders roll back as I straighten. "I should have." The whispered words are carried away on the breeze as we finally stop at the crest of a small hill. It has the perfect vantage point of the road along with a lovely patch of clover that Banshee latches onto as soon as I slip off her back. My hand slides over her side before I make a few hand gestures and a soft green sparkle settles over her.

"What's that?" Silva nearly makes me jump as he appears over my shoulder.

"A no-roam spell. Keeps her within a couple of feet of me without having to tie her up."

"And the hand symbols?" I roll my eyes before he holds up his hands in surrender. "Last one for a while. Promise."

There's a smile tugging on my lips as I answer. "Spells can be said in any language, but oftentimes there's one in particular that works best for each person. My magic works best with sign language." I see him swallow a dozen questions as I inspect my bow and draw an arrow just to be ready.

"That's handy for an assassin."

I hum, trying not to show my pleasure that he takes an interest in my work. "It's definitely easier to cast in a language that uses minimal noise." Silence descends and Silva sits on a nearby stool of moss while I sit in the dirt with a clear view of the road. She shouldn't be long now. I take the time to braid my hair to keep it out of my face and keep my hands busy.

"Why did you bring me?"

My eyes snap over to him fiddling with a button on his cuff, but his eyes are focused on me. "I thought you said no more questions."

The corner of his mouth lifts. "I said for a while. It's been at least a minute." My eyes roll while I fight a smile. "I mean it though. Why me?"

"You think Henry would have come out into the woods with me alone after last time?"

Silva chuckles, wiping imaginary dirt off his black shirt that looks *very* good on him. "He is a bit busy at the moment. He barely acknowledged me when I told him I was sneaking away with you." My eyes roll at his choice of words, but he doesn't repeat his question. He leaves the question open, letting me decide whether I want to answer it or not. I swallow another heavy sigh.

"I like this place. I want it to survive the transition and the violence I've brought down on it. I want you to remember what I've done, where we've gone, in case you need to protect it in the same way." I wave him over and he instantly moves beside me. The heat of his body sears my side as I point out at the road framed by boughs of pine. "This is the best vantage point to see people coming and going without being seen. It would be a good place for a sentry once I've left." He nods and I try not to notice his breath skimming my ear as he looks out at the view. Our eyes meet and he can't be more than five inches away, but he doesn't step back.

"Will you come back?" His voice is softer than the rustling leaves above us. "Once this is all said and done, I mean. After you've conquered the world."

A breathless chuckle leaves my lips, but his expression doesn't falter. He truly believes I can do anything. "I doubt I'll survive all there is before me, Silvanus." I hadn't planned to, either. The only thing keeping me alive for years has been the thought of revenge. Without it, I wouldn't be surprised if I simply dissolved into ash and floated away in the wind. Nor am I upset about the prospect.

His brows furrow and he takes a tiny step closer so that jasmine and verbena scent embraces me. That hood frames his face in darkness, making it seem like we're in a private room all our own. "You'll survive. You…you have to."

The why is on the tip of my lips. Why does he need me to live? But then I hear the soft thunder of hooves and my head snaps to the side to see a rider fast approaching on the road. "Archer's arrows!" I curse, scrambling to nock an arrow and take aim. My heart is hammering from Silva's closeness and the adrenaline of the hunt as I steady the head on the lone hooded rider. Two deep breaths steady me and I hold the third as I ready myself to release the arrow.

"Wait!" Silva hisses and shoves his hand out to hit the bow. The arrow slips through my fingers to shoot towards the rider only slightly to the right. We watch it fly with baited breath and I'm not sure whether to feel relief or dread when it sinks into the target. They fall off the horse like a sack of potatoes before I turn and grab Silva's shirt. I'm not sure whether to shake him or run him through.

"What were you thinking?"

His clear eyes are wide as he stares down the bank at the still figure. "The rider isn't Banks. The way they sat on the horse wasn't the posture of a soldier. They were hunched over like they were barely holding on." My anger and skepticism fade as horror takes their place.

"A dummy. They sent a fake in case I was here. *Shit.*" How could I have fallen for such a simple maneuver? I'm on Banshee's back in a second and rushing down the hillside towards whoever I just shot. They haven't moved a muscle and remain frozen as my feet hit the dirt beside them. I flick their hood back and freeze at the sight of blue, milky eyes. "Mr. Geoffrey, gods." Gently, I turn the old man over as he coughs. Silva is there a second later and helps me to lay him out on his back.

"They told me to—" He coughs and I'm certain he's inhaled at least a mouthful of dirt. "ride to the border of our lands, then turn back. They wanted a better rider, but—" *Cough, cough.* "I couldn't let any of the kids take the risk."

"Of course not, you're too good a man, Geoffrey." Silva takes out a hanky and wipes it over the man's sweaty brow while I survey the damage I've wreaked. It didn't pierce his heart. Silva's hand pushed me off enough to throw off the shot, but it is lodged deep into his left shoulder.

"I'm so sorry about this." Guilt, something I don't feel often, seeps into me as I slice through the long shaft of the arrow with my dagger.

"Lady Nestra was scared about everything that's happened, so I took her to practice archery. We shouldn't have practiced so near the road." My eyes burn into Silva's for a moment, but he only shrugs a shoulder. We would have needed a cover story eventually. For him to think of a good one at a moment like this…maybe I was wrong to dismiss his benefactor idea out of pocket. But those are thoughts for another time.

I slice through the guard's cloak covering him and press the fabric to the wound while he groans. "It's alright. Just…just fine." His words are slurring and his eyes are unfocused. Everything is clearly not fine.

I meet Silva's gaze while keeping pressure on the wound. "I'll help you get him onto your horse, then you must take him back to the house. He needs a healing potion or he'll bleed out."

His brows furrow and lips flatten. "And you?"

My head shakes. "He's our main concern right now. Let's move."

It only takes us a minute to get Mr. Geoffrey onto Silva's horse, but he's losing more blood every second. I'd made a poor bandage out of the cloak they'd thrown on him and tied it tight. It should last. Then again, there's a very cruel difference between should and will. "Come back with me," Silva insists and I grit my teeth.

"Go now and go fast. No arguments." I slap his mare on the ass and she takes off down the road with Mr. Geoffrey in Silva's arms. Blood stains my hands and the dusty ground at my feet eagerly drinks up what was left behind. Perhaps that's why the world can be so cruel. We've been feeding her blood for centuries. "His won't be the only blood spilled today." I rub dust onto my hands before slinging myself onto Banshee's back and digging my heels into her sides. There's only one other way off the estate towards the east. It's thick with briars and swampland, but apparently that's preferable to the Red Death. A smile tugs at my lips.

They're going to wish they'd been granted a quick death by my arrow. Now, I'm angry and I have no intention of killing quickly. The earth will feast on a murderer's blood today and it won't be mine.

*   *   *

I leave Banshee at the edge of the muddy land with my green cloak and without an attachment spell. She'll find her way back to the estate if I take too long here. Using her as a lift, I vault myself up into the wavering trees. My hand slides over the bandages on my thigh as the wound pulses, but I have to hope Silva's stitches will hold up. Cypress branches stretch out over the long grasses hiding deceiving puddles that can engulf a man in a minute flat. A grim smile tugs at my lips. They must really be afraid of me to choose such a treacherous path.

The trees supply me enough of a path to the thin road through the mud, but it winds and twists like a snake. Not to mention the moss that hangs and sways from most branches like swaying hair. I'll be hard-pressed to get a clear shot at my target even from a high vantage point. My side and thigh ache along with my arms from hauling myself into position. My body may look nearly back to normal, but my muscles are not. A twig snaps and I nock an arrow. Even if I can't get a direct shot, dealing her a wound would only help me. My eyes flit over the worn path, dipping into the long, golden grass on either side before I lower my bow. Just an animal, I suppose—

A hand wraps around my ankle and yanks me from my perch before I can finish the thought. I barely get a glimpse of Banks' wide grin and pale face before I slam into the ground. All the breath in my lungs coasts out with a *whoosh*. Desperately, I try to push myself back up onto my feet while gasping as my lungs cry for air. My left side burns and I know I've broken at least one rib.

"You've gotten a bit slow, Roux." Banks saunters up next to me and tosses my now-broken bow into one of the muddy pits. "That old limp acting up?" Her smile is cruel and sharp as she swings her foot towards my stomach, but I lash out with a blade from my pocket and slam it down into her boot. A shocked yell leaves her lips as I roll away from her and gulp in all the air I can manage. I yank myself to my feet using a tree for leverage while she tugs my knife out of her foot.

"Now you've got a limp of your own." I chuckle as she shoots me an infuriated look. Her shout is angry now as she marches toward me with her sword drawn, ruby hilt glittering in the filtered light. She brings it down and I barely manage to dodge the blade. It bites into the bark of the tree behind me and slices across my shoulder as I lean backward against the trunk, then shove my foot against her torso. She stumbles back and leaves the sword buried in the tree. I don't bother trying to pull it out. I prefer my daggers anyway. My side hurts with every breath and I adjust my count to two broken ribs. No matter. I've fought with worse.

Banks pants like a bull about to charge, but her eyes burn into the sword behind me. She has no other weapons. "She'll catch you again. You know that."

I snort at the poor effort to buy time. Then again, Banks and I always had the same weakness; we like to play with our prey. "She won't leave this estate alive." Her smile doesn't dim and I fight to keep myself from frowning. Have I missed something? This day proves I'm not infallible. Is there a piece of vital information I haven't found yet?

"She's no fool when it comes to you anymore. A messenger bird was sent out this morning calling for who we need." A chill slides down my spine. "You know who that is, don't you, Roux?" Her voice is cloying and calls to the rage caged deep in my chest. I have small knives in each palm, blades sharp and shining. "Although…we didn't need them to catch you the last time. All we needed was that slice of bait." I remain still. She's baiting me, I know she's baiting me. The advantage lies in seeing the first move before it happens and she won't convince me to make the wrong one. "Why you believed the prince of Belterra would have anything to do with someone like you, I don't know, but you certainly came running when you thought he needed help. Didn't you?"

My blood feels so hot that I'm surprised my skin isn't bubbling off the bone. "You don't know a lot of things. Annaliese still doesn't trust you with the heavy lifting?" Fury shines bright in her eyes and I know this is my moment. Enough teasing.

I fling a knife forward and it buries itself deep in her right shoulder. Shock ripples across her face and I throw another. While she dodges, I slide two more knives into my palms and throw myself at her. Again and again, I bring my knives down on her as she stumbles backward, blocking each swipe with black gauntlets. One swipe slides my blade between the scales of her guards and she twists it out of my hand. I make a play for the knife in her shoulder, but she takes advantage of my open side and rams her fist into it. Thankfully, it wasn't the side my broken ribs are on. In retaliation, I slam my heel down on her foot I'd run through and leave a slash across her cheek. Her curse slides away on the breeze as she blocks an upward strike before slamming her elbow down onto the bandages wrapped around my thigh.

I stumble backward, reeling from the pain as she finally tugs out the dagger in her shoulder. There's also another cut on her jaw, but it's not enough. Not nearly. "Thought I saw you favoring the wrong leg." She holds a hand to her shoulder with a grimace. "The warden will leave this damned estate, but you won't, Red Death." Our pained gasps fill the small area, but we're far from done. She charges me and I slide to the side, but not fast enough to escape her grasping fingers. They tangle in my shirt and we go tumbling down the slope. We both land in a wide oval made from mud and puddles with a wet *splat*! The mud softens my fall, but my ribs feel like they've shattered into a million pieces. Black spots tease the edges of my vision while I blink rapidly.

No, I have to stay awake. I don't know where Banks is and if I don't get out of this pit, I might sink until I suffocate on the wet dirt. Already, the mud licks at my cheeks and soaks my hair. Panic swirls in my stomach at the thought of being dragged under the mud like a self-burying grave. I shove the feeling away. There's no time to panic. I take a deep breath and slowly lift my arms bit by bit. Banks is out of my sight and there's mud slathered over my ears, so I have no clue if she's already stalking this way to drown me. All I can do is work to free myself.

Long minutes pass as I fight to sit up while straining my ears for any sound that might prelude an attack. My limbs are heavy and tired, but the adrenaline keeps me conscious and relief courses through me as I finally manage to sit upright. I swipe the mud from my eyes and do my best to clean out my ears as I take stock of where I've landed. It seems like I'm in a small pocket of mud surrounded by cattails and long grass. There's still no sign of Banks, but I can hear sloshing and soft swears not too far away. My head turns to the left as I ignore the mud-caked strands of my hair sticking to my skin. There. The shore is only a few body lengths away.

I lean forward and grab hold of the cattails as close to the root as possible, then tug. They break when I'm halfway out of the mud, but I manage to keep my balance as I sink down nearly to my hip. At least I'm standing. My gaze snags on Banks still sitting in the mud, but she's sunk down to her waist. She's flailing about and I slide a hand over the daggers still in my pockets. I move to take a step toward her before a rumble shakes the air around us. We both freeze and I look to the sky to find it clear of any storm clouds. My gaze casts down to the muddy pit around us before focusing on the middle.

Bubbles the size of a human head slowly rise to the surface and pop with languid ease to spray green drops on the surrounding cattails which wither immediately. Those green drops mean only one thing. "Stop moving!" I hiss over to Banks who has resumed her flailing about like a bug in a spider's web.

"So I can make an easier target?" Spit flies out of her mouth with the words and I can see the panic reflecting out of her eyes. She only works harder, trying to scoop mud out of the way, yanking grass and plants up out of the ground in her attempt.

"There is something else in here!" My words fall on deaf ears as she ignores me. The bubbles come faster now and I forget about Banks in preference to saving myself. It seems people avoid this path for more than simply being a difficult trek. Swamps, bogs, and wetlands hold mysterious things best left to their own devices. Whole skeletons arranged perfectly on the outskirts, clean as fresh-cut marble, with strange footprints leading back into the muck have people giving places like this a wide berth. There are other more grim stories of coughed-up limbs massacred with misshapen teeth, but I'd rather not find out if any of those stories are true.

I lock my fingers under my leg and try to tug it out rather than trying to walk. After about half a minute of struggle, my leg is free and I take a step with a loud *slurp* as my foot sinks back into the mud. Gods, my rib hurt. Each breath feels like breathing flames, but adrenaline keeps the true pain at bay. Another minute passes as I yank up my other foot and toss it forward. Both of my flimsy flats have vanished into the pit so I'm walking barefoot, but I couldn't care less. A glance back to the bubbles reveals that the mud is starting to ripple like water as something huge begins to shift underneath the surface.

I'm still at least three body-lengths from shore.

Two more steps later, I check on Banks. She's managed to get to her feet, but with all the mud she swept aside she's only dug herself deeper. The slop is up to her armpits and she only sinks more as she struggles. Little waves begin pushing and pulling at me as bigger and bigger ripples echo from the middle. "Shit, shit, *shit*." I tug harder on my leg before tossing it forward. "Too slow." Whatever has been stirring now moves around the pit. All I can see are glimpses of greenish-brown scales and a head wider than the span of my arms.

"Gods, what is that?" Banks finally seems to realize that there's something else in here with us. It seems to realize the same. It pushes waves of mud in front of it as it turns towards us and I frantically unclip my dagger from my belt loops to strap it around my chest. Banks starts screaming as I undo my pants. The pit is tugging down on them every time I take a step, so I might as well let it have them. With nothing weighing me down, maybe I have a better chance. My next step is blissfully easy and puts me within two body lengths of the shore. Mud squelches between my toes, but I'm making steady progress at a much faster pace than before. Sweat drips down my body so what isn't covered in mud is dripping with perspiration. I push on.

I'm one body length from the shore when it reaches Banks.

Its maw opens wide to reveal rows upon rows of yellow teeth as long as the dagger strapped around my chest. Its eyes are bright green with black slicing down the middle, but they're so far back on its head that it can't possibly see her. A scream rips out of her chest and I wince as the creature's pale tongue unfurls from its mouth to run over her body as she struggles. As soon as it touches skin, the tongue snaps back and with a few flicks of its scaled tail in the mud, the mouth closes around her. The teeth fit together like prison doors sliding shut, but I can still see Banks inside its mouth.

"Help me! Gods, please help me!" She pleads, but all I can do is watch as the creature's throat undulates, and then dark green sludge bursts out to soak her from head to toe. The smell is wretched and I nearly spill my guts as the stench fills my nose. Banks inspects the goo as it drips off her hand before her screams start anew. Her skin starts to droop, then drip, before it begins to melt off of her. It's all I can do to drag my eyes away as I push myself forward. My body starts trembling from the effort, the pain, and the fear. I can't die like that. I won't.

Banks' screams continue until they turn into pleas for help, for the warden, for her mother, then it's quiet. The sound echoes in my ears and I doubt I'll ever get it out. But I only have one focus right now. Get out. Survive. I feel the shift when the creature dives back into the mud but don't risk looking backward.

Three steps keep me from the shore. Just three. Little waves lap at my back and tears rise to my eyes from the fear nearly choking me. I keep moving forward.

Two more steps. Tears stream down my face as I feel hot breath hit my back tinted with the fresh smell of a carcass.

One step. It's tongue slaps against my back, wet and heavy, and knocks me onto my face. My broken ribs chafe against one another and I grind my teeth to keep from crying out. I draw my dagger and push forward just enough to sink it into the soft ground of the shore. My muscles scream for rest as I haul myself forward with the last of my energy. Those long teeth loom above me just as my knees hit the ground and I roll out of the way as it takes a big bite of nothing but mud. A relieved sob leaves my lips as I lay prostrate on solid ground at last. At least, until its large body begins rocking back and forth so waves of earth splatter over me. It takes me far too long to figure out what it's doing.

It's trying to suck me back in.

Hit me with the right wave and the weight would drag me back into its waiting maw. I yank my dagger from the ground and scramble to stand but only get to my knees before I feel teeth sink into my leg. A scream shreds out of my throat and I turn with my dagger, slicing and slashing any part of it I can get to. The teeth vanish as it gurgles with pain and my fingers dig into the ground like claws as I finally haul myself back up to the path out of its reach.

The trees above me sway and blur as the adrenaline keeping my pain at bay fades. The stitches in my leg must have burst, the old slash on my side and the new one on my shoulder are now caked with mud, my ribs are broken, and my right calf is burning like it's on fire. I try to sit up, but my vision swims until I'm flat on my back once again. At least that thing is away from me. My head lolls, staring down the path that leads to the estate. Silva's question from earlier comes back to me.

"Will you come back? Once this is all said and done, I mean. After you've conquered the world."

I hadn't intended to. It would be better, and safer, for everyone if I left here and never came back again. But after everything that's happened…I'm not sure anymore. It's still very likely that I'll die on my quest for revenge. There are plenty who have wronged me other than the warden and a few things I need to collect. After all that, if I survive, would I come back? Will I even get back to them today?

"Yes," I whisper to the sky. I'll see that sweet, stupid look on Silva's face again and tease Henry until he's furious with me. Groaning, I shift so I'm on my stomach and push myself up onto my knees. I measure every breath carefully, letting the blurriness fade while my teeth grit at the pain. My body nearly gives out to leave me toppling back towards the muddy pit, but I make myself take a step forward. Then another. And another. The pain is excruciating, but it's no worse than I've had before. Just one step at a time. Silva's words run on a loop in my head to distract me.

"Right now, your anger is you. But I also offer this room because I'd like to see what you're like without it. And I'm willing to wait."

"But I like you. I still like you even after seeing that woman chomp her tongue out because of you."

"Your eyes…you have the prettiest eyes. Like snake scales. Like the forest."

"We're friends. We're…fond of each other."

"So long as you don't forget about me."
"Never break."

They become the threads of a rope I use to tug myself towards him, towards the estate, towards my unfinished business. I've no clue how long I walk or how far I get before I see a speck drawing closer and closer. I can barely make out the shape of a horse and rider before I collapse. Information slips blearily into my mind as Silva slides off Banshee and falls to his knees beside me, then I feel his arms heave me into his embrace. Mud and all.

I barely hold onto consciousness long enough to hear his final plea. "Stay with me, Roux. Just for a little while longer. Please stay with me." I don't have the energy or the heart to tell him that that was never part of our deal.

Chapter Fifteen

Hurt

Silva

She's dead.

That's my first thought as I see her fall into the dirt covered in mud and blood. She doesn't even try to stop her fall. At that moment, my only thought was that the most vital, devastating, brilliant light I've ever met has been snuffed out like the flame of a candle. The next moment I was in the dirt beside her and holding her close without a care for the filth covering her. The stench of the drying mud fills my nose so potently tears fill my eyes.

"No, no, no, no, no." I breathe as those green eyes, usually so sharp and bright, don't even focus on me. "Stay with me, Roux. Just for a little while longer." Her eyes shut as I gather her into my arms and hurry to Banshee while trying not to jostle her too much. "Please stay with me," I repeat those words over and over as we speed towards the house as fast as the mare can run. It's within sight when I turn and round the stables to enter through the back. I want to strut through the doors of my house and demand all the healing potions for her, get the best physicians to tend her, as well as lay her in my soft bed, but Anna is there. Roux is vulnerable and her cover would be blown if any saw the clothes she's wearing. Even covered in mud.

I wrap my cloak loosely around her while taking a deep breath to steady myself. "You'll be alright." My fingers brush her throat to feel a butterfly pulse before I walk into the stables. My state, as well as hers, instantly calls attention. A stableboy gapes at us and I seize the opportunity. "Call for Mary from the house and send her to the room on the right at the top of the stairs. Not a word to anyone else." He swallows and nods so hard that I'm surprised his head doesn't come off. "The Lady took a tumble off her horse, but she only needs rest. She didn't want to trouble the house." He nods again before sprinting out the front doors. I make my way to the room with purposeful strides. At least the stables are calm and quiet with one of their leaders injured.

I'd brought Mr. Geoffrey here much the same way only an hour ago. He's laid up in his room guzzling healing potions with his wife clinging to his hand feeding him soup. He'll heal in a week or so. The arrow nearly went all the way through his shoulder. My gaze drops to the assassin in my arms as I wonder what in Under she got up to while I was gone.

I arrive in her old room and place her as gently as possible into the tub before starting the water. Best to clean what I can to see what condition she's in under the caked-on mud. There's blood on her, that's clear to see, but I can also see glimpses of torn flesh under the filth. Any wounds need to be cleaned before being treated. I kneel next to the tub, grabbing a cloth off the edge to wipe some of the grime off her face while reaching for her wrist. That pulse is still there. Faint, but still there. "Friends don't leave without saying goodbye," I whisper, my hand sliding down to hold tight to hers. "Oh, but we're supposed to be enemies now. I suppose it would be rude of an enemy to die without being killed by their nemesis." I chuckle dryly as my eyes begin to sting. "So, you have to wake up either way. Wake up and never say goodbye or wake up and kill me. So long as you wake up."

Tears start falling down my cheeks as she remains perfectly still but for a shallow rise and fall of her chest. "Wake up." I shake her hand slightly. "Wake up, Roux." Yet she doesn't stir.

The crash of footsteps has me turning towards the door and there's some relief in finding Mary and Henry standing there. "Gods, Sil. What—"

I push myself to my feet and set my shoulders. "We need to clean her to ascertain her wounds. Mary?" She doesn't hesitate to rush over and grab a washcloth before starting to wipe away the muck. Her lack of surprise confirms my suspicion that she knows more about Roux than she lets on. Perhaps more than I do. "Henry, she'll need clothes—"

"Bandages, healing potions, probably a painless potion. Got it." He slides out before I can finish the sentence and I breathe a sigh of relief at having goals in place. At least, until I hear Mary gasp. I'm back to kneeling next to the tub in a moment and follow her gaze to Roux's ankle. My blood goes cold when I see what looks like a bone, or maybe a long tooth, jabbed through her right leg.

"Clean around the wounds. She doesn't have to be spotless, the wounds just need to be clean." I pick up a towel and wrap it around the wound as best I can.

"What happened, sir?" Mary's hushed question fills the room and I sigh.

"That can wait until later. For now, let's make sure she's safe." My eyes meet her wide brown ones that shimmer with determination as she nods.

We work in tandem. Mary disrobes her down to her undergarments which is thankfully easy since Roux has already shed her pants somewhere else. We both frown at the dark bruising blooming on her side, but it's only when Henry gets back that the real work starts. During her bath, we'd disposed of the mud-logged bandages on her thigh to reveal broken stitches. Her other wounds include a gash on her shoulder, obviously the tooth in her leg, and Mary thinks she has a couple of broken ribs. Banks certainly seems to have put up a fight.

"At least these have closed," Henry murmurs as he splashes a little alcohol on the scab on her side; the wound she took from me. Out of all of us, he's the one with the most experience with injuries and how to treat them. My eyes are locked on hers as he cleanses each wound, but she still doesn't stir. He sighs as he reaches her calf. "This will have to come out." I wince at the thought. He's right, of course. He already wrapped her broken ribs and a healing potion will take care of the gashes. It's the only thing left.

I rise to my feet. "Let me move her first." They both slide out of the way and I tenderly lift her into my arms to lay her out in the bed. The wet towel around her calf is exchanged for a dry one as I look her over. Roux looks more bandage than woman now and her eyes haven't twitched once. "What can we do?" Even if staring at the fang makes my stomach turn, I'm determined to do anything to help. I flick a lightweight blanket over her as Henry answers.

"This will more than likely wake her up. The pain." Henry lets a hand coast over my shoulder as I grit my teeth at the conclusion. "We'll need to hold her down."

I shake my head. "No, we won't restrain her. Not in any way."

Henry sighs and steps in front of me with heavy hands landing on my shoulders. The touch is solid, grounding, and his earnest eyes have my posture softening. "It's to keep her from injuring herself further or hurting any of us. It's necessary." His earnest eyes shine and if I've learned anything in all my years, it's that I can trust him. I nod once. "You don't have to."

An almost smile teases my lips. "The fact you think that's true is comical." I step around him and stand next to her head before looking at Mary as Henry moves to the foot of the bed. She looks between us and takes a deep breath. I suddenly realize this is the longest we've been together and she hasn't blushed or stumbled over her words. There's confidence and bravery in helping friends. I'm glad she's found hers.

"Alright, one," My hands slide onto Roux's shoulders as I stare at her unconscious face. "Two," Mary's hands rest on her knees as Henry braces a hand on her ankle and the tooth. "Three!" We all latch on as Henry tugs. A mixture of relief and dread shoots through me as I finally see the green of Roux's eyes again as they flash open. Then her scream fills the air and all my relief vanishes.

"It's me! It's me and Henry and Mary! We're helping you!" I shout through her yelling as she thrashes about on the bed. Guilt and shame rush through me as I put more of my weight on her shoulders to keep her still. "Try to be still! You're hurt!" My voice breaks as I see tears escaping her eyes from the pain. Her hands come up and her nails shred into my skin. "It's Silvanus! It's Silva, Mary, and Henry!" I lean down, letting my arms lay over hers as my hands frame her face so she'll look at me. "Look at me. Just at me." Her crazed eyes focus and barely a second passes before her body stills. I brush her hair back from her face as tears fall down her cheeks in a torrent and her hands leave my arms in exchange for squeezing my wrists.

"Got it. I'll clean this, wrap it up to help it heal, then she'll need to down a few potions. Painless potion first." Henry says, but I don't turn to look at him. Mary presses the painless vial into my hand and I hold it to Roux's pale lips, tipping it when they part.

"I could…kill you." She says tiredly.

At long last, I smile. "You're a little busy now. Another time." She hisses when I hear the slosh of alcohol on her skin. "But, merely out of curiosity, how would you do it? Kill me, I mean." My grin widens at the barest sliver of annoyance that slips into her gaze. "There's my assassin." Her grip tightens on my wrists in slight retaliation.

"I'd poison you."

I frown. "That seems rather unexciting."

Her eyes roll. "I'd poison you…so your body wouldn't be damaged. Your face… your face is too pretty for an ugly death. Afterward, I'd stuff you." She gifts me a macabre smile. "Put you in the foyer to…welcome my guests." Exhaustion has sapped her strength even for speech, but naturally, she wastes energy to finish her threat. I believe Mary releases a breathless chuckle at the end of the bed while Henry scoffs in clear disapproval.

I grin. "That's more like it." She snorts, then winces with a hand moving to her side.

Henry sidles over and places a healing potion on the bedside table. "Finish that. I'll get you some food." Their eyes meet and she swallows.

"Thank you." The words are hushed, but spoken all the same. Henry softens as he nods, then walks out after washing her blood off his hands. "You too, Mary. For everything." The young woman turns a bit pink at the show of gratitude as she picks up the wet clothes we'd practically thrown around the room.

"My pleasure, Lady. I'll be off to clean these and pick up the pack in your horse's stall." The corner of Roux's mouth quirks up as she nods. Mary turns to me. "I'll come back as soon as I can with a change of clothes for both of you." I glance down and realize I'm still covered in filth from carrying Roux here along with spots of dampness from cleaning her. My nose wrinkles with intense distaste.

"Thank you, that would be appreciated." She shines at the praise and ducks out of the room, shutting the door behind her and leaving Roux and me alone.

I turn back to her and pop out the cork from the bottle as she reaches for it. Her hand trembles when she lifts it and I gently lower it back to the bed before taking the potion myself. "Why don't you let me do that?" Her sharp eyes scan my face, then she nods once. I'm surprised by the lack of argument but don't hesitate. My hand slides behind her neck to support her head as she leans forward just enough to consume the entire potion, then settle her back onto the pillows. With the pain hopefully fading with the painless potion, it seems all that's left is exhaustion.

"I think you've fought enough battles for today. Don't fight sleep as well." I drag myself away from her to rifle through the cabinet on the other side of the room. Staying in these clothes for another minute isn't acceptable.

"You didn't ask why," She murmurs as I latch onto some long pants and a cream cotton shirt.

"Why what?" I turn back to her as I shed my disgusting clothes. Satisfaction flits through me when her eyes scan my bare chest, my thighs, and the area covered by my underwear. Her eyes sizzle and smolder when they reach mine again and I remind myself she's tired and injured as I shrug on the clothes. They certainly aren't silk, but they're clean and that'll have to do.

"Why I could kill you."

I shrug as I grab a stool, setting it as close to her side as I can get before settling down with an arm laid out next to hers on the bed. "I figured possibly killing everyone is your constant state of being."

A smile teases her lips and her hand coasts over her side as she holds back a laugh. "You didn't tell me you had a goddess-damned swamp monster on your land."

My brows shoot up. "Fred?"

"Fred?" She repeats, deadpan. "You...you named that thing? And you named it *Fred*?"

I hold up a hand to stave off her judgment. "Henry and I had a run-in with it when we were kids. We were wrangling some cattle as punishment for...well, that's a story for another time. Two got stuck in the mud and we were coming up with ways to get them out without entering the pit when Fred showed up." The thought of her facing down that thing and only getting stabbed in the leg fills me with even more respect for her. "Being children, we named it after the most frightening thing we could think of." I grin at her dubious expression. "The old gardener who would wave his spade at us when we messed up his rose bushes."

She shakes her head, but I'm glad to see a smile on her face. "Then you know Banks' fate." A chill slides down my spine at the memory of how those sows died. "But the message was already sent out by bird. Reinforcements will be coming." And the look in her eyes makes me think they won't be any ordinary soldiers.

"Worry about it tomorrow." My fingers graze her arm to call her attention back to me. "You're injured. You need to be well to bring about the end of others." I give her a half-smile. "I'll stay. Bar the door, even, if it'll make you feel better."

"Oh, and where will you sleep?"

"Right here. If you'll let me have a pillow."

"Hm, a lord on a stool. Sounds like a good joke." I laugh softly before the sound tapers off as the levity fades from the room. Her hand turns on the bed so her palm is up and her thumb is skimming my pinky finger. I slide a little closer, letting the longest of my fingers skim her wrist where her pulse beats soft and strong. "I owe you. You saved me."

"No, you owe me nothing." The words come out a bit harsher than I meant, but she doesn't flinch or pull away. I take a breath and steady my gaze on hers. "If you make a choice, if you decide to give me anything, I don't want it to be because you think you owe me. I want you to want to give it." We stare off for a minute and I know she's searching my eyes for a lie or half-truth, but she'll find neither. She nods once and relief floods me. My eyes trail back to our hands as I trace the lines of her palm, the tips of my fingers barely skimming her skin. My mouth opens to ask her something but shuts when I glance up to find her eyes closed. I smile at her peaceful face and sigh as I lean my shoulder back against the bedpost.

I hadn't realized how the events of today have worn on me as well as I slide into unconsciousness.

*   *   *

"Sil. Come on, get up." Henry's quiet voice wakes me and I instantly look to Roux. She's fine. Still sleeping. Blearily, I blink up at Hen as he smirks. "It's evening. You need to eat something. Both of you do, really."

I catch his arm as he moves towards Roux. "Let her sleep a bit longer." He debates the notion for a moment, then relents and tugs me up and over to the small table in the corner. We both settle down with Henry watching the door and me watching Roux. My fingers pick at the rough edge of my shirt collar before I give up with a futile wish for my clothes.

Henry chuckles at my irate sigh. "I told your mother that you're tending to Mr. Geoffrey and kept to the story you told the stableboy about Roux falling off her horse. Telling her everyone is resting kept her away for now, but I wouldn't be surprised if she came over in the morning."

I remove the covers on our food as he speaks and try to store the information in my sleep-addled brain. "Thank you, Hen."

He sighs heavily. "Not a problem. Only two left now."

I raise a brow. "Counting them down? That's certainly a change."

He pins me with a look and I snicker quietly. "She saved our lives." I sober as I recall that far too recent night when the warden's soldiers sought to end us. "And seeing the way she let you help her…she's learned to trust us a little. I can give her some trust in return." His grimace tells me he doesn't find it easy, but his eyes are set as he glances at Roux. I'm proud of him. A soft groan leaves him when he looks back over at me. "Don't look at me like that. I still don't like her. Or the way you are around her."

"What way is that?"

He points at me with his fork. "Careless."

I scoff. "When have I ever been careless?"

He gives me a look that says '*always*', but goes on, "When your father is gone, you usually take the opportunity to go through the books. See what he's messed up and cheated to try to hoard coin for himself. You haven't so much as been in his rooms this time around."

"He'll be gone soon enough and I'll have all the time in the world to fix everything for the estate and our tenants."

Hen hums as I stab the slab of meat in front of me. "And you've actually thought about that? It's not just something you're saying now to give me an excuse?"

My jaw locks. This is the one disadvantage of having lifelong friends. They know you far too well. "Alright, I see your point. I've been a little...preoccupied."

He grins at winning while I throw a bit of garnish at him. "It's good that you've taken a break from worrying over everything, but remember why she's here, Sil. She has a job to do and once done, she'll leave." My gaze wanders over to the sleeping predator who looks remarkably like a young woman at the moment. He's right. He's always annoyingly right. "I don't want you to get hurt." Henry's voice is a bit softer but doesn't draw my eyes away from her. I'm already invested. There's no denying that fact. The question now is whether I reveal all of myself to her, tell her I want her to stay, or that I want to go with her when she leaves. The other option is less likely. Try to remove myself from her as much as I can so that when she does inevitably leave, she doesn't take my heart with her.

I look back at Henry with a helpless shrug. "She's going to hurt me." There's no avoiding it and I won't stay away from her. I can't. "But I think it'll be worth it." Henry doesn't bother voicing his disagreement but leans back in his chair with a goblet of wine.

"Why did she have to be an assassin?"

I smirk, copying his lax position. "Would you rather I spent my time with a lady of court?"

Exasperation flits across his face as he throws his hand up in the air. "Yes!"

I hush him even as I laugh. "Then you should have known better, Hen. I'd never be so boring."

Chapter Sixteen

Old Friends

Roux

I feel like death when I wake up, but at least I wake up. My mouth is coated in a film from those disgusting potions and my body aches with sharp hunger as my body works hard to heal with no fuel. The smell of food lingers in the air and as I wipe the crust from my eyes, I see a silver dome on my bedside table. Light is dim in the room lit only by two candles, one on the table by the door and another on the tray next to me. Night must have fallen an hour or two past.

The soft cascade of water reaches my ears and I turn my head to the tub now hidden by a screen. It's all wood with soft swirls carved out to give me the barest glimpse of what lies behind it. The flaming head of hair gives him away along with long limbs littered with dark freckles. "Hey." There's a soft splat as he drops his washcloth in the water before he yanks the screen aside. All that's visible above the water is his fine shoulders, long arms, and pretty face, but the thought of what's hidden under all the bubbles makes me wish I wasn't injured.

"Hi." He returns, his face and tips of his ears tinted red either from the warm bath water or my discovering him. "Mary brought me some of my clothes so I thought I'd wash before changing. Sorry if I woke you."

"That's alright." He certainly isn't a bad sight to wake up to. "I woke up because I was hungry." I move to push myself up when his hand darts out.

"Wait, I'll help you."

I freeze, raising a brow. "How, exactly? Your clothes and the clean towels are over there." We both look over to the vanity where towels, two pairs of pants, a shirt, and even some clothes for me sit. A smile tugs on my lips as he settles back into the water with hands braced on the sides.

"Don't think that would stop me." I'm fighting a smile now as he runs long fingers through his hair stained darker with water. "I've seen you naked nearly three times. Suppose I owe you."

"The first time didn't count." I was starved when we first met and that body that I washed in the river doesn't belong to me. "Neither does this time."

"One for one then." My teeth sink into my bottom lip as I fight a smile.

"Here I was thinking you didn't notice."

"I noticed." His voice drops and makes my toes curl. "Only a blind man wouldn't notice." Gods, this isn't the time for this. Not when I'm stuck in bed for unfun reasons and can't do anything about the heat pooling in my gut. Still, I'm helpless to resist playing the game.

"How scandalous to think our nights together haven't been as innocent as I thought. If the arrangement was...*hard* for you, you could have told me." There's no stopping my grin now as I watch his throat bob as he swallows. "No doubt you haven't had much time alone to take care of things."

"Roux." I'm not sure if the name is meant as a plea or a warning, but I have no intention of stopping. The dull ache of my pain and hunger has almost completely faded away at having this new, delicious focus. His hands dip under the water.

"Hands where I can see them, Silva." A thrill dances down my spine at the desire that flickers in his eyes like flames.

He leaves them floating on the surface, nudging the small bundles of bubbles still sailing over the water. "And if I were to disobey that order?" My fingers curl into fists and the corner of his mouth lifts at the small victory. "If I were to…take care of things here and now? What would you say to that?"

Do it. I want to say, but my words are stuck to the roof of my mouth. My nails are digging into my palms as I resist reaching under the blankets at the mere thought of what he's suggesting, the images of what pleasure would look like scrawled across his face, what noises he'd make. Gods. "Would you?" My words are barely said and husky. He doesn't answer and instead lets his hands drift below the edge of the tub.

I can't decide which part of him is the best to watch. The glint of the candlelight gilding the water droplets sprinkled over his curly chest hair? The muscles shifting in his arm as his hand descends through the water? Those brilliant, clear, blue eyes fixed on me? Or those pink lips that part with a small gasp as he takes himself in hand? I can't choose. But this is certain—in that huge house filled with precious paintings, sculptures, and jewels, even among the riches offered by this entire estate, he is the most precious and glorious piece of art.

His lids become heavy as his gasp grows along with the soft swish of water around the tub. A knee rises out of the water as he turns slightly to face me more and I'm certain my nails digging into my palms may be drawing blood.

This is the best torture I've ever subjected myself to.

His head falls backward and a few drying waves sway with the movement. Never have I wanted to run my hands through his hair more than this moment. He clings to the edge of the tub with his other hand but keeps his eyes on me throughout every second. Both of our breathing is heavy and I'm about to throw caution to the side, screw my wounds, and go join him when the door swings open.

Henry stumbles in, clearly having rushed here. "A rider approaches on the main road." His wild eyes settle on mine. "A rider cloaked in white." All the heat in the room turns to ice.

"Enhanced," I confirm. Banks practically told me before being dissolved, but I've been a bit busy since.

"Go to my mother. Make sure she's awake for our new visitor." Silva instructs Henry from the bath while his friend furrows his brows at him. "Go. I'll be there in a few minutes." He shuts the door behind him when he goes and Silva releases a long sigh once he's left. The only release he'll be getting tonight. I still get a little satisfaction over seeing his naked body as he walks over to the towels and wraps one around himself, but the moment has lost its spark in the face of a new threat.

"You know to tread carefully."

He nods, padding over and ever so gently sliding his hands under my arms to help me sit up. "Worried about me?" The tease doesn't lighten the mood. It does the exact opposite, actually.

"Worried about the job." I correct as he sets the tray of food in my lap. "We have a mission to complete."

His face falls and I curse the regret that rises in my chest. "Of course." He walks to the door and I struggle to find something else to say.

"Try not to lie. Enhanced can hear your heartbeat." He waves a hand behind him to say he heard me before slipping out the door without a glance backward. "Ugh." I groan and let my head fall back against the wall. Maybe I should have specified that not sleeping with someone you like should also include not having sexy bath time with them either.

I rip the dome off my tray and shove food in my mouth despite not being hungry anymore. My body still wants and needs it to heal. My gashes should turn pink within the day, but my ribs will take days if not a week. The hole through my calf...I'm not even sure about that one. Best lump it in with my ribs just to be safe. I put a hand on my side as I shut my eyes to take a breath, thankful my painless potion hasn't worn off yet. Might as well stretch my legs while I have the chance.

I turn so my feet are flat on the floor and cling tight to the posts at the foot of the bed. As soon as I try to stand it's obvious that I can't put any weight on my right leg. My left thigh aches, but it's manageable. Feeling ridiculous, I hop to the left and snag the nightgown someone brought before hopping back to the bed. My ribs burn along with every breath, but I make it. It's good enough for now. The nightgown is dark royal blue silk that comes down to my knees with quarter-length sleeves. Comfortable, but cool.

I recline back in the bed covered by the thin blanket with a heavy sigh. My eyes shut and I don't even have enough energy to think about how I'm going to walk tomorrow. Not to mention defend myself or the others against Enhanced. My eyes flash open when I hear soft scratching coming from the window and I reach for my dagger that someone has cleaned and put on the bedside table.

Little black paws appear on the window sill and I shake my head as Graves tugs himself up. Silva opened the window, more than likely to not steam up the room with his bath, so the black cat happily flounces over and leaps onto the bed. "Here to guard me while the others are gone? How thoughtful." My fingers wiggle under his chin as he purrs and settles down beside me. "But I doubt I'll need the protection tonight." I keep my dagger tucked close with eyes steady on the door as the night passes by, slow as molasses.

It must be an hour or two before Silva returns. My eyes scan him for distress or injury before relaxing when I find none. He seems unsurprised to find that I'm awake and almost collapses into the stool next to me. "There's only one." My brows pop up.

"The leader that we met in the woods. She's settled in at the house and Henry is staying to keep watch over my mother."

I'm silent for a few moments as I take this in. "You didn't have to come back." It probably would have been better if he hadn't. Less chance of someone following him and discovering us.

He shrugs a shoulder. "I said I'd stay the night and I like to keep my word if I can help it." A half-hearted smile tempts his lips. "Aren't you happy to see me?" The question has a tad more weight than a mere tease.

I look at Graves as I massage his ear. "I'm glad you're not hurt. We should both get some sleep. You'll need to get back to the house before they miss you in the morning." My eyes flick back to his as he nods, rising and blowing out each candle in the room. I'm about to tell him not to blow out the one farthest from us, but he doesn't try. He leaves it burning and returns to me, settling back against the foot of the bed with his arm stretched out on the mattress.

I'd been so busy learning him, I hadn't considered he'd learned me as well. I toss him the pillow beside me before I can think better of it and sink into the bed with my lips pressed against each other. "Goodnight, Silva."

There's a beat before he answers. "Goodnight, Roux." He barely moves, but I feel his hand slip under the blanket covering me so his knuckles brush against the bare skin of my knee. Nothing more. It's this little gesture, the barest touch of his skin to mine for no reason other than to touch me, that has me choking on emotion as I shut my eyes for the night.

I'm in far more trouble than I first thought.

*   *   *

The door knob is jiggling.

I've no clue what time it is, who is outside and wants in, but the knob is moving and that's an unavoidable fact. Sleep slakes off me like water as I go through the most likely culprits and what can be done against each. I brace a hand on my side and slide away from Silva before pushing myself up onto my feet. My right leg nearly gives out before I brace myself on the bedside table. The knob stills. I take a step towards Silva and put my hand over his mouth before giving him a little shake. He startles awake but calms quickly when he sees it's only me. He frowns at seeing me on my feet but seems to know not to make a noise as he stands.

I wrap a hand around his neck and tug him down so I can whisper into his ear. His hands automatically ghost over my hips and gods, I wish I was waking him for another reason. "There's someone at the door. Get in the bed." His eyes dart to the door, but he obeys. I brace myself on the bedframe and lower myself onto my knees, grabbing my dagger before laying flat on the floor. Silva peeks over at me before I vanish under the bed. After a few hand movements to shroud myself in shadow, I still.

The darkness seems to press in close down here. My nose is only a couple inches from the bed frame and the slats remind me eerily of prison bars. I focus on taking deep breaths while my hands clench to prevent the shakes. A soft creak has me holding my next breath before I see little black feet beside me, then glowing green eyes as Graves dips down to crawl under the bed with me. I gather him close and calm at feeling his soft purr against my side.

Silence descends, but it isn't the soft quiet of the night. There are no crickets, no breeze, no shuffle of blankets or breath. This is the quiet of a predator's approach and a silence spell. My hand tightens on my dagger and Graves as I think of a vulnerable Silva above us, but there's no reason why they should harm him. If they try, they'll meet their end the next second.

"Rather rude to slide into someone's window uninvited, but I'll overlook it this time, Huntress." Silva's voice cascades through the room like rustling satin.

A female laugh answers back and I barely catch a glimpse of bare feet as she rounds the bed to stop in front of the door, cutting off the exit. But I know that laugh. I've known it long before now, even before that fleeting moment in the woods after escaping the prison. "There are few who have awoken to an Enhanced sliding through their window rather than the simple, sharp slice of a knife." It takes all my willpower not to move at the threat. Light fills the room and I feel the distinct tingle of magic in the air as she lights all the candles with a spell.

"A privilege then. Especially to see you without your white cloak." My spine stiffens despite myself and I take a closer look at the only part of her I can see. The bottom of her loose pants are white, but I see now that they're only cuffs. The pants themselves are a deep, blood red. A known Enhanced is never to be without their guard of white clothes unless with their troop or immediate family, by blood or by choice. What could she mean by coming here dressed like that? Does she even have her hood up?

Her feet move and my thoughts fall silent again as if she can hear them. "I wanted to speak with you one on one, but it appears we aren't alone." My hand braces on my dagger. I won't draw it just yet; she'll smell it when the steel hits the air. "That purring is loud enough to hear a mile away." She drops to her knees beside the bed as I realize she hasn't discovered me, but Graves. Her hand reaches under with a dark red hood lurking just beyond. I have to make a split-second decision. Give up Graves or give myself away.

The answer is obvious.

I grab onto her hand and pull. Her head slams into the bed and I release Graves as he scuttles out of the way. Her hand turns and drags me out from under the bed in one tug, but I've already drawn my dagger. I roll on top of her and press the blade to her throat as I straddle her hips. Harsh breaths leave me from the expended energy and the pain surging through me, but I've bested her. At least until I feel the soft prod of a knife on my ribs.

"You know I could kill you with a few words. Even slow down time for a second or two so you'd feel the pain a fraction longer." I don't dare glance over at Silva to see his horrified face. This threat demands all my attention.

"You'd be dead before you uttered a word," I growl, letting my blade bear down just a bit harder as she does the same with hers.

The soft glimmer of violet eyes escapes the darkness of her hood. "Mutually assured destruction." My heart seems to skip a beat at the familiar words. It was a lifetime ago when they were last spoken. At least spoken to me by this particular Enhanced. "Sounds like the beginning of a beautiful friendship."

"I'm not a naïve girl anymore."

She laughs, letting her small blade clatter to the floor as she folds her hands under her head. "You never were, querida. Although I see you've gained some trust issues. Nice."

My eyes roll and I lighten the pressure on her neck, but don't remove the blade just yet. "And you're still disregarding war college rules. Only your family—"

"Or your troop should see under the façade, yeah, yeah." She finally dispels the darkness charm around her hood as it drops. The sight of her is achingly familiar, but different all at once. No longer do either of us have the extra pounds of childhood. Her round face has turned square with a jaw sharp enough to cut marble. Her dark, fluffy hair has tints of copper and falls just past her shoulders, half-up and half-down as always. Her body is strong and fit, that's clear, but those vivid eyes and pouty lips…those are the same. "You've always been part of my family, querida."

My head shakes, but I'm fighting a smile. "Much to my eternal torment." I sheathe the dagger at last before she reaches up and plants a full kiss on my lips with a soft muttered word under her breath.

"It is good to see you. Even if you're practically falling apart." She helps me stand while I snort painfully.

"You've got some nerve. What in Under did you do to your face?" I draw a line from my left ear to the corner of my mouth and trace another crossing it over my left eye to copy her scars. They're old enough to only be thin lines across the rich brown of her skin, but they weren't there the last time I saw her.

She plants her hands on her hips. "You're going to comment about *my* scars?" I wave her off as we finally face Silva who seems to be in a state of shock. Only me settling next to him on the bed seems to snap him out of it.

"Can you really slow time?" Of course that would be his first question, but she just grins.

Her mouth opens to reply, but I beat her to it. "No. It's a death spell that only makes it seem that way to whoever is killed. It's just a trick of the mind." She pouts at me spoiling her fun, but I'm afraid he'll never recover if I let her tell him too many secrets at once. "Silvanus Dinnsesk, this is Leader or Lee. Head of the Branch of Pursuit for the Enhanced." Dubiously, he holds out his hand and she shakes it with a teasing grin.

"Leah. I'm not too stingy about my name like most Enhanced. Just don't call me by name in public or I'll have to kill you." Silva pales and her eyes cut over to me when I sigh. Names aren't shared because it's a *law* for them. A smile tugs on my lips at the fact that she doesn't seem to have changed too much. "I don't hold it hostage like this one." I frown when Silva tenses.

"You know her name?" This question is hushed. He'd never asked me for it and I'd never offered, but of course he's thought about it. I certainly have.

Leah glides over to the table and snags a chair, bringing it over before settling down with her feet propped up on Silva's stool. "Sure. We met before she was la Muerte Roja, the Red Death." She glances over at me. "I'll want to hear all your stories, querida. I'm sure you have some good ones." Her eyes stall on the bandages around my calf along with my hand braced against my side.

"Where did you meet? *How* did you meet?" Silva is clearly trying to piece things together and I glance at Leah for what she wants to say. She shrugs. The decision is mine, then.

"Well…" I take a breath, going further back in my memory than I usually like with my hand firmly affixed to my aching ribs. "We went to war college together."

His brows furrow and I can almost see the mounds of questions building behind his eyes. "War college…with Enhanced."

Leah crosses her arms over her chest. "There are a special few that come who aren't Enhanced. Any with magical talent and deep pockets are welcome."

Silva's eyes are still on me and I answer his next question before he asks it. "My parents…" I can't remember the last time I spoke of them, much less their names, even less their positions. "They wanted the best for me. Magic can get unruly in someone not taught to handle it or give it a focus. Even as a child I had more than a regular person, even though it was far less than an Enhanced. The school taught me how to harness it and use it to my advantage."

"Where is this school?" Silva asks and Leah tsks.

"Hidden. No one who goes to war college ever reveals its position and that's one rule I keep." She leans back in her chair, balancing on two legs. "Imagine what people would do to and with a school full of powerful children." Her voice has darkened and Silva doesn't bother asking any more about it. The college did a lot for her and me. Not only when we were children.

"We became allies in school—"

"Family," Leah corrects and my heart squeezes at the word, but I don't correct her.

"We lost touch afterward until I arrived back at the war college with an arrow through my hip and poison flooding my blood." I've no clue how I made it to the great gates guarding the grounds. The pain was excruciating. "The Enhanced are some of the best healers in the world. I knew they'd be able to figure out what the poison was."

Silva shakes his head slightly. "They let you in just like that?"

My eyes lift to Leah's knowing gaze. "It's one of the principles in the Creed." Leah and I say the next words together in a reverent hush. "Once found, taken in, and accepted, one cannot be turned out of the fold. We are the threads in the fabric of the world, we are the letters that form a spell, we are the metal that is hammered into armor. We are pieces that form a whole."

Leah chuckles softly. "There are exceptions that prove the rule. Break the tenants without any excuse and you're cast out."

"But that rarely happens. Maybe twice over the past hundred years."

"Twice is more than enough." Her voice deepens as her violet eyes flash and I know it's a sensitive topic for her.

I look back at Silva whose hair sticks up messily as he runs his hands through it. "They let me in and healed me. That's where we met again." My hand gestures to Leah. "I'd been Roux for a year and Leah revealed she'd been tasked with hunting me down. That's why she'd been at the college. Receiving orders."

"We had a good laugh about it before coming to an agreement." A grin breaks across her face while one tugs at my lips too. "After we left the college, I'd hunt her as I would anyone else. If I caught her, she'd have to take me to dinner and pay the whole tab." Silva's expression is priceless and I let myself laugh softly.

His head shakes. "How could you do that? Wouldn't your superiors—"

"I have no superiors." She interrupts. "The higher-ups at the college send me assignments I can take or reject. As for those who hire me…" Leah shrugs a shoulder. "What can they do to me?" Silva seems to remember that he isn't just talking to a woman or an assassin, but an Enhanced. There are few who could do anything to her and those who could would receive recourse tenfold.

"What will you do here?" I ask finally and Silva's shoulders tense.

She slowly rises onto her feet and I drag myself up as well as she replaces her chair to its original spot. "For now, I will go back to my lovely room," She shoots a teasing glance towards Silva, "and sleep through the night in that comfy bed. In the morning, I'll come over and walk you to breakfast as you tell me what you're doing here."

"After the events of tonight you'll more than likely be carrying me." Soreness already limns my every limb and there's still hours left until morning.

Leah smirks. "As fun as that sounds, the little kiss I gave you will heal those wounds twice as fast. You'll be walking tomorrow. Maybe with a cane, but you'll walk. Unless you want me to carry you." She winks at me and heads towards the window as I blink.

"Thought you didn't believe in that 'healing bullshit'?"

Her smirk widens although her eyes harden. "It seems neither of us were capable of holding onto our naïveté, querida." She straddles the window before tossing up her hood and dropping out like a stone.

Silva sighs softly. "Do they teach you to avoid using doors at war college?"

The corner of my lips lift as I sit back on the bed while withholding a grunt. "Kind of. Less chance of running into someone outside a window." Movement catches my eye as Graves slinks out from under the dresser with a glance to the window as if to make sure it's empty.

Silva stands and offers me a hand. "You should lay down. We both need all the rest we can get tonight." I stare at his clear eyes a moment before taking his hand and tugging him back onto the bed.

"Just stay there. I'll sleep with my bad side towards the wall." I drag myself back and lay down while setting my dagger back on the bedside table. My eyes shut instantly as exhaustion sweeps over me. The excitement of Leah kept me awake, but without her or a threat to entertain me, my very bones feel tired. My lids flutter open when I feel a soft touch on my side and find Silva slipping one of the pillows between me and the wall.

"It would be nice if you could avoid getting another injury for a while," He whispers. I smile as he turns away to once again blow out all the candles but one, then returns to lay beside me. There's something comforting about his form beside me once again. This bed is far smaller than his, so our sides are practically squished together. I slept alone in a filthy cell for so long…I don't look forward to sleeping alone again.

A few minutes pass and I let the silence settle over the room. He'd been subjected to a lot of information today. He'll need far more than a few minutes to absorb it all. "The Enhanced, Leah, said anyone with magic and deep pockets is let into the college." It's not a question, but I know he's looking for confirmation.

"Yes," I murmur, staring up at the spider vein cracks in the ceiling. There's a slight dip in the bed as Graves walks over and decides to settle between my legs.

"You have the speech of someone highborn, you know the manners, how we walk, the way we court. I asked if you'd visited lord's beds, you answered, 'lords, baron's, a prince or two.' You didn't give me any more information than that."

My lips press together at the reminder and what he's hinting at. "Yes."

He turns onto his side to see my face and I reluctantly meet his eyes. "A princess goes missing and people notice. Ours is missing, yes, but you would have been recognized by now if you were her. There are only a few options left."

"Silva," I warn, fingers pinching the fabric of my nightgown from nerves. "You understand…" I swallow, my throat suddenly dry. "The more you know, the more danger you'll be in."

His lips press together, but those clear, bright eyes don't leave mine. There's no hesitation or remorse in his next words. "I'd rather know you and be in danger than be safe and know nothing." The truth of the words ring through the room, leaving my heart trembling like a bell after a hammer strike. "You're a lady. By birth."

I'm not sure if I'm breathing anymore. This is more information than I've shared with someone since…since before I was Roux. The instinct to lie, to run, to defend my secret is strong, but all my defenses shatter with one word. "Yes." He releases a long, heavy sigh before collapsing onto his back once again. "My mother was born a lady and my father a baron. They're both dead now. The warden took them from me at the behest of the person holding her leash." His eyes are shut and I press my lips together as I turn on my good side with my head braced against my hand to see him better. "I have never lied to you, Silva." Not about anything that mattered, anyway.

"I understand why you didn't tell me. It's just hard to feel like I know you when someone can come in out of nowhere and shatters what I thought I knew."

"Why does it matter?" His eyes snap open at my sharp tone. "If you know me, if you don't. Who do we ever really know?"

"Don't bullshit me, Roux. You know me." I pull back at the heat in his voice as he sits up too so we're facing one another. "You've met the most important people in my life, seen my home, my estate, slept at my side, seen my naked body, and saved my life. You know my relationship with my parents and my greatest fear."

"And don't you know mine?" I toss back. "I've told you my greatest fear, you've seen me at my weakest, seen me naked, seen me afraid, seen me cry, seen me hurt, seen me caged. Do you think anyone else out there has seen me like that? Do you think I've let them?" I shove myself up so I'm sitting straight up, not giving a shit about my aching body. "Knowing everything about me isn't knowing me, Silva. Nor does knowing my name mean you know any more than anyone else. I don't know where you went to school. I don't know the name of your nanny or how many bones you've broken or your favorite thing to eat, but I know you. Isn't that enough?" There's too much emotion in my voice, but I'm too upset and tired to care. If I lose Silva, then I'll lose Henry and I'll have nothing. After so long without anyone else…I don't want to be alone.

He sits up too and I try not to notice how the candlelight twists and curves around his copper waves. "What about not really knowing people?" He tempts with a slight smile.

"Shut up. Answer the question." But the bite is gone from my voice.

His smile vanishes, but his eyes are nothing but tender and soft. "Yes. Yes, it's more than enough." My shoulders deflate with relief even as I berate myself for caring too much. This wasn't part of the plan. It only makes everything more complicated and difficult. "I'm sorry." My mind goes quiet at his apology as he runs his hands through his hair. "I got jealous of Leah and doubted myself. It won't happen again."

"Why?" I whisper, energy and anger fading fast. "Why were you jealous?"

Silva glances to his lap and shrugs. "I want to know you. I want you to choose to be known by me."

"Why?" I ask again.

His eyes return to mine and my breath catches at the candlelight swirling inside them. "Because you're the most brilliant, interesting, courageous, and reckless individual I've ever come across. And I know no one will ever make me feel as alive as you do."

All this from the man who practically brought me back to life from the brink of death. "Ironic considering I end lives for a living." A breathless chuckle leaves his lips as he flops back onto the bed and I follow his lead a tad more gracefully. My eyes shut and I spend some time listening to the steady rise and fall of his breath. "V."

"What?" Silva's voice is a bit groggy. He must've been on the cusp of sleep.

"V. It's the first letter of my first name."

His body goes so still that I'm not even sure he's breathing. "V." He breathes with the reverence of a saint calling upon a goddess. "Do I have to earn the rest?"

I don't fight the smile that tugs on my lips. "Yes."

"Good." His response is instant as I feel his knuckles brush mine before our fingers loosely interlock. "I like a challenge."

We fall asleep that way; a smile on my face and our fingers entwined.

Chapter Seventeen

The Beginning of the End

Silva

Morning comes far too soon and I have to greet it earlier than everyone else in order to get back to the house before I'm missed. Roux's fingers are still caught in mine and she'd moved closer in her sleep, so her cheek now rests against my shoulder. I waste a few moments staring at her sleeping face, so much smoother and open with no conscious defenses up. There's even a remnant of a smile on her lips.

"Had your fill yet?" Her voice nearly makes me flinch before her eyelids flutter open to reveal those vivid gold-flecked green eyes.

I swallow and clear my throat softly. "And if I said I hadn't?"

Her husky laugh sends heat shooting down to an already slightly uncomfortable situation. "I'd remind you that you do have a time limit. Wouldn't want your mother or anyone else questioning where you've been." She extricates herself from me before poking my arm. "Get a move on."

"Cruel assassin." I grin as she hums the affirmative while I rise to get dressed. "Excited for your date with the Enhanced?"

Roux snorts and I'm glad to see no hint of pain on her face as she does so. "We're just walking to breakfast. Hardly a date."

I walk back to the bed as I button my pants with my clean shirt over my shoulder. "She did kiss you on the lips."

She pulls herself up into a sitting position and leans against the wall. "That's just how she is."

"She didn't kiss *me* on the lips."

"Jealous again?"

I roll my eyes and slip my shirt on, tucking it neatly into my pants before looking back at her. A frown instantly appears on my lips as she leans over to pick at the bandaging on her calf. "Let me do that."

"You're leaving." She points to the door while keeping a focused eye on her work.

I slip onto the bed and curl my fingers. "I have a minute." She sighs, but leans back against the wall with a hand sliding over her ribs. "How are those feeling?"

"Like I got run over by a carriage." I wince at the image while slowly unwrapping the bandage. Roux only smirks. "Better than yesterday. That damn thing itches like someone shoved bugs in the wound."

My nose wrinkles. "You have a gift for terrible comparisons."

She shrugs a shoulder. "I try."

I unwrap the last layer and do my best not to make a face at what I uncover. "It's…well. It's disgusting." A scab has formed overnight and some clear fluid leaks from the edges here and there. Disgusting, but healing.

"I did offer to do this myself."

"I've got it." I lean over and grab a clean handcloth, gently wiping away the clear fluid before snagging the medical case under the bedside table. "So, what are you going to tell Leah?" Morning sun is starting to filter into the room bringing our breakfast rendezvous ever nearer.

"The truth." My eyes flick up to hers as I press a fresh bandage to the wound, then start wrapping it. "There's no reason to lie. She's from the fold. She may not help me outright, but I doubt she'd thwart our plans either."

"More of these principles that I know nothing about?" I tie off the bandage and she pulls her leg back, tilting it this way and that to examine my work.

"Something like that." Something else she'll tell me in her own time. "I hope you know I told you the truth last night. In fact, I tell the truth far more often than you probably think."

I raise a brow at her. "Oh, so you're actually on the run from your evil uncle?" She tosses a pillow at my face as I grin.

"Obviously not. But my uncle, a very sweet, kindly man, does run my parent's estate."

I blink, almost laughing at the near truth she'd told my mother. "*Your* estate. That'll take some getting used to."

"It's not mine." The sharp edge returns to her voice as I slide off the bed onto my feet. "It hasn't been mine in many years."

Her previously thawing eyes chill and I think for a moment about the question on my tongue before letting it fly. "What happened to your parents?" I lean against the post at the end of the bed. "You said they died, but…" I leave the question open for her to finish.

She takes a deep, steadying breath before her eyes pin me to the spot. "There was a fire." The flames seem to still flicker in her eyes along with the candle across the room. "A tempestuous, riotous fire." There's no emotion in her voice or on her face anymore. Her expression is blank, smooth, and glassy like the surface of a deep lake. "The warden and her soldiers raided the main estate and I can only guess the fires were set to make everyone panic so they were easy to pick off. I was away and came back in time to see my parents one last time." Her fingers knit together and her knuckles turn white as she grips tight to herself.

"Henry asked if I killed them. No. I didn't hold a blade to their throats, toss them from a window, or poison their food. But I am responsible for their deaths. Even if…even if I didn't strike the match." My mouth opens to ask another question, but she holds up a hand. "That's enough for today. You need to get out." And at this moment, I think it's the kindest way she could have phrased it.

I walk to the door before a crazy, fun thought occurs to me and I turn to walk towards the window instead. "Maybe I'll try things your way this time." Her brows furrow critically as I shove one foot through the opening, then scrunch up my spine as I try to duck out.

"Need a little push?"

My face pinches with pain as I peek up to find Roux standing beside me. "Possibly—" Without another word, she picks up my foot and shoves me out of the opening like a cork popping out of a bottle. I've hardly sucked in a breath to scream when I've landed on a surprisingly hard bale of hay. Still, it's softer than the ground. I roll off, frowning at the pieces of straw sticking to my clothes, then look back up at the perpetrator. There's the barest hint of a smile on her face and I return it tenfold. She shoos me away and I take a few steps backward before walking off towards the house just as the sunrise paints the sky.

I've hardly made it up the stairs before I'm being grabbed by the shirt and tugged into the servant's staircase. "What are you doing?" I ask the pair of big hands and brown eyes.

Henry huffs. "You're late!"

I shrug. "By what, an hour? No one is awake yet." I catch his wandering eye and raise a brow. "You just wanted to catch me coming in to ascertain what state I was in."

He pulls back and holds up a strand of straw. "Maybe I was wondering if you'd been romping in the hay." He tosses it to the wayside before crossing his arms over his chest. "So? What kept you so long?"

I go through the long list and wrap an arm around his shoulders. "Quite a bit."

It takes until breakfast to tell him everything. Well, nearly everything. I keep Roux's secrets to myself except for how she knows Leah. We're still whispering like school girls as we come upon breakfast and find my mother absent, but the warden and Deckree are very much present. "Good of you gentleman to join us," Anna comments without even looking up from her plate. She sits on one of the sides of the table in clear view of all the exits and entrances. Typical. "Meira said the morning light was perfect for painting and asks that you excuse her." I risk a brief glance at Henry. He nods in confirmation that's the truth and I release a breath. My mother is fine.

"What a pleasure that you're able to join us, Anna." I walk around the vacant side of the table, feeling Deckree's eyes on my every step. After filling our plates, I settle at the head of the table with Henry on my right.

"Where's that waif you drag around?" Her dark eyes flick to mine, clearly hoping for a reaction.

I give her a charming smile. "Lady Nestra took a rather bad tumble from her horse yesterday. It's no surprise she's sleeping in." I take my time looking around the room just for effect. "Has Banks been similarly afflicted?" I fight my smirk as the warden's back straightens.

Deckree is the one who answers this time. "Banks was sent out yesterday with a message. We've yet to hear from her."

"Oh, how worrisome. I hope no harm has come to her." My brows pinch with concern while Anna's knuckles turn white as she grips her silverware. Henry nudges my foot in warning.

"She's more than competent. I'm sure all is well." Anna dismisses her food to devote all her attention to me instead.

I nod, taking my time to chew a thick slice of ham. "Certainly. Who has ever outsmarted the warden and her band of soldiers, after all?" We stare each other down as I keep that charming smile despite her irritation. "Except for this recent accident, of course, but as you so kindly reminded me upon your arrival, that was the fault of my terrible negligence."

"Yes." Anna spits, hands splaying out over the table as if she'd like to rip it into pieces. Perhaps even use a shard to stab me. "I'll remind you that *I* captured her in the first place. She was in captivity for *years* and I would have kept her there longer, would have seen her rot, if it hadn't been for you. You with your fine clothes and disdain for dirt or evidence of hard work. In your ignorance, you practically handed her the key!" She sits there absolutely fuming as I take a few moments to glance over my shoulder, then look back at her.

"Sorry, I was just looking for who you were talking to with that tone." I lean to the side, resting my arm on the armrest of my chair in the perfect picture of posh leisure. My eyes raise to hers, unflinching. "Because it certainly wasn't me." A loaded moment passes before she vaults out of her seat and I grin at the fury contorting her scarred face. Henry stands too with a hand on the hilt of his sword since it seems like Anna would like to tear out my throat.

"My, my." The two words echo through the room seemingly coming from nowhere and everywhere all at once. We all turn to find the Enhanced, Leah, cloaked in her usual white standing in the doorway. "If I'd known the drama started early, then maybe I would have come sooner."

"To officiate or participate?" Henry mutters under his breath, but stiffens when Leah's hood turns his way. I can almost imagine her smiling under her hood even though her face is once again shrouded by impenetrable darkness.

"Whichever suits me at the time, naturally." A chill slides over the room at her words as each of us ponders what other things might suit the Huntress. A smile tugs on my lips as I realize she's doing much the same thing as Roux. Her hood and white clothes are a hat she dons as an Enhanced just as Roux wears Lady Nestra or the Red Death. A facet of them, of course, but not the sum of them. I smother my smile as I realize what a privilege it is to know more of them and the importance of keeping my knowledge a secret.

"Shall I offer you the seat at the head of the table, Huntress?" I stand as she glides across the room.

"Are you?" Her hood cocks and I note that the warden has settled back into her seat while watching Leah like a hawk.

I step to the side to fully vacate my chair. "It would be an honor to have it taken by you."

She hums, hand brushing the chair beside Henry's as she floats closer. "I wonder if you would say the same thing were I taking your life."

I fight to keep my expression smooth, but I can't help the pebbling of my skin as my instincts scream to run. "I doubt I'd be doing much talking then, Enhanced." Nothing stirs inside the darkness of her hood for a long moment before she laughs, startling Henry so much that he nearly tumbles from his chair.

"No, I'd suppose not. I'll sit here," She places gloved hands on the back of the chair to the right of Henry. "But thank you for the show of chivalry." I incline my head to her out of respect as we all settle back down into our seats. My eyes are now on the doorway, waiting for Roux to come in.

"How is the hunt coming?" Anna asks Leah directly and I believe Deckree withholds a sigh for her warden's directness.

Leah brings forkful after forkful to her hood and the food vanishes into the seething darkness. I'm relatively sure Henry is hypnotized by the motion. Or perhaps my propensity for curiosity is finally rubbing off on him. "The hunt for your suspected murderer or for your compatriot?" Leah's tone is utterly uncaring. The warden's jaw locks and I take a sip of my tea to hide my smirk.

"Either."

"Oh, well, your soldier is dead." Faking shock isn't hard since neither Henry nor I were expecting those words to come out of her mouth. Going off the way Anna's face darkens and Deckree's rapid blinking, they're just as surprised. "I found her sword down the path you showed me along with a trail of blood and mud. There was this too." She tosses the tooth that came out of Roux's leg onto the table, then sweeps her cloak aside to lay Banks' sword on the table as well. "I'd guess there was a tussle. Your soldier lost and was swept away into the mud or eaten while this lucky little assassin escaped with a minor wound." I'm not sure the affection in her voice when she says assassin is intentional, but it makes me shift in my seat slightly.

Anna ignores her soldier's sword completely and instead grabs the tooth. Her eyes gleam with a hunger and possessiveness that I've never seen from the warden, never seen from anyone. I'm instantly reminded of Roux's words about there being intimacy between enemies. Roux considered the connection with cold resignation, but I never paused to think of how Anna would see it. I didn't expect the pure desire and entitlement now on her face, but now that I see it, the expression makes my skin crawl. "And how are you sure both weren't taken by the swamp?" Her eyes flash as she looks back to Leah.

The Enhanced leans back in her chair and twirls her finger with a purple shimmer while the spoon in her tea follows the motion. An idle reminder of her power. "Because I am smart, skilled, and can follow a trail." Her finger stops and the spoon clatters to the side as she lifts the cup to dip it into the darkness of her hood. "Remember who you're talking to, Annaliese." The warden's eyes narrow at the use of her name, but she doesn't dare speak against Leah. Gratefulness floods my chest at having her on Roux's side.

"Of course." She sets the tooth back onto the table and takes a breath as if it pains her to stop touching something that was once stained with Roux's blood. "What's your next step?"

Leah sets her cup back in the saucer with a soft sigh. "My next step is to greet the lovely creature at the door." Our eyes all lift to find Roux hesitating in the doorway as if a lady unsure if she should come in during a charged conversation. She *is* good.

"I don't mean to interrupt." Soft and demure, her voice filters into the room as she takes the few steps to the table. Her limp is noticeable, but not as bad as it should be. Given that she had a limp before a monster bit through her leg, it's a shock she isn't hopping everywhere.

"You aren't. Please, join us." I walk over, looping my arm with hers to hide her staggered step. She smiles up at me so brightly that I almost forget that it's for show. As we pass the corner of the table her hip seems to catch on it and the pitcher of orange juice careens off towards the floor. Roux drags me down with her in an effort to catch it, but seems less concerned with the pitcher than whispering in my ear. "Don't drink the orange juice." My brows furrow, but there's no time to ask what she means.

Leah is there the next moment and handing the intact pitcher to Roux with only a few drops spilled. "Maybe pay more attention to walking than your arm candy." She spins and sits back down before I can figure out if she's talking to me or Roux.

"So sorry." The assassin addresses the room and sets the orange juice back on the table before choosing the seat next to Leah and across from Anna. My steps are slow as I walk back to my place before Mary slips in. She's silent and quick as she fills all our glasses with the bright, sunny liquid before slipping back out like a ghost. The warden watches closely as Roux and Leah both drink. My mind whirs as I try to think through the strange riddle, but things clear when I see Leah's hand clamp down on Henry's arm as he reaches for his drink.

When Anna's soldier's blade poisoned me, Roux took the wound from me saying it wouldn't kill her. She'd practiced something...some art—mithridatism, that allows her to ingest deadly things without dying. My gaze glides to Leah. The two share quite a few similarities. Perhaps there was a class at war college in poisoning and how to avoid being poisoned in return. My eyes fall to my glass of orange juice, then to the ladies across the table.

They're poisoning them.

I've no clue what the poison will do, but I certainly don't want to find out first hand. "How long are you staying exactly, Lady Nestra?" Anna asks as Deckree sips her juice without a qualm.

"Well, seeing as I've no other place to go, as long as my hosts will have me."

"Forever wouldn't be too long." Green eyes meet mine as Roux hears the truth of my words.

"Well," Leah's hood turns to me. "Are we to expect an announcement sometime soon?"

Roux's expression turns scolding, but I only smile. "It would hardly be appropriate to confirm that considering recent events. I'll make sure to send you word when there is something to announce." Her hood dips and I believe I see a flash of upturned lips before there's nothing but darkness again. My gaze turns towards the warden. "And you, Anna? You've more knowledge than me of my father's whereabouts. How long will you be staying?" While forever with Roux doesn't seem like enough, forever with Anna would be a nightmare.

Her lips purse at the clear distinction, but she answers. "Your father should be home by the end of the week. Meira already knows and was planning on throwing quite the soiree." Distaste colors her voice at the mention of a party and I'm suddenly struck by the thought that Anna has never had nor been fun her entire life. "We'll stay to meet with your father and plan what to do from there." This weekend is a mere three days away. I glance at Roux and she nods slightly. That's enough time then.

Being suddenly confronted with the end of our little charade shakes me more than I care to admit. My father's death looms ever closer along with Roux's inevitable departure. I'm not sure what it says about me that I feel no regret for the former while the latter fills my mouth with bitterness.

"It's about time we all got to work. Down your drinks, ladies. You'll need the fuel." Leah stands and sweeps out of the room without a sound. Deckree looks to Anna for instruction and stands only after she does. The warden drinks the rest of her coffee, then walks out leaving her glass of orange juice completely untouched.

"Care to tell me why in Under an Enhanced just used magic to put her tongue in my ear?" Henry's voice rings out first and it may be the only moment where I've seen true surprise flicker across Roux's face. Then she's giggling as I grin. Mary slips back in and begins clearing away the poisoned dishes with far too much normalcy.

"They poisoned the orange juice." I look over to Roux as she raises an eyebrow. "Right?"

Her eyes shine with what may be pride as she nods. "Yes."

Henry sighs and crosses his arms over his chest. "Yes, that's what she said. But Anna didn't drink any."

Roux shrugs. "That's fine. We covered the tooth in poison as well." We both stare at her before she shrugs a shoulder. "Anna is predictable, I knew she'd slide her fingers all over it and this toxin can sink in through skin."

"Reassuring," Henry murmurs while our assassin addresses her partner in crime.

"Make sure to soak those in the solution we discussed." Roux gestures at the various pitchers while Mary smiles as if she'd only commented on the weather.

I lean forward, breakfast forgotten. "What will the poison do? They walked out of here no worse for wear."

Roux waves an unconcerned hand through the air. "It's incredibly slow-acting. Throughout the day, they'll feel their limbs getting more and more stiff. By this evening, they'll barely be able to move. By midnight, they'll be paralyzed."

"Gods," Henry murmurs as his head shakes.

Our assassin makes no sign that she has any qualms about it. "I'm tired of waiting. They both die tonight and I'll rest up for when the real target arrives." She glances to me with a soft sparkle in her eyes. "Despite the minor hiccups, this will make for a very successful trip. I hope I'll be able to return the favor one day." Even though the thought of her leaving makes me feel hollow, her talking about the future, a future for her, fills me with hope. It's far better than her talk of not surviving whatever her plans are when she leaves here.

"Any invitation you send me, I will accept." It's far too wide and vague a promise to make and Henry shoots me a scolding look for it, but Roux smiles.

"I'll keep that in mind." She finally starts eating and I make sure Henry passes her all the food she can take. "But tonight, the two of you should head to your rooms and stay there with the doors locked." Her eyes flick between us. "And get ready to be surprised in the morning."

Chapter Eighteen

Is Death Truly the End?

Roux

I spend the rest of the day simply walking through the grand house. Leah takes Anna and Deckree out to examine the swamp that consumed Banks, so we're free of their odious presence. Henry and Silva attend something boring—paperwork or similar, so I'm on my own. The only sound is the occasional whisper of servants, my feet on the floor, and the rustling of my clothes. It comes as quite a surprise to me that I've managed to find a sliver of peace here. I thought it would wear off, that in the beginning the feeling was because it was the first safe place I'd known in years, but comfort still swirls in my heart as I look around the home.

I drink in all I can. Soon I'll be leaving and I want to be able to think back to this place. Perhaps recall a drop of safety I felt here while I'm on the road. Graves meows down at my feet and I smile as we continue down the red carpet. I won't be leaving completely alone.

The doors at the end of the hall swing open abruptly and instinct has me sliding into the shadows before I see it's only Silva's mother. I resume my previous position in the hall and suppress a smile at the paint splattered or smeared all over her. Her clear eyes, so like her son's, lift to mine before widening in surprise. "Nestra, perfect! I wanted to see you." She grabs my hand and tugs me into her room even as I stumble. When I stand upright again, I'm frozen.

The room is very much like Meira; paint-splattered and joyful. The walls are a soft yellow, like butter, but are covered in flecks of various colors of paint along with the floor. The windows are exactly the same as my room on the other side of the house. They embrace the room with bright light and the white frames reach from the ceiling to the floor. There's barely any furniture in here, however, just easels, stools, drying racks, and mounds upon mounds of canvas.

"I wanted to show you something," Meira says, eyes shining with a happiness I'm not sure I've ever seen, much less known. "One moment." She dances through the mess with ease, poking and peeking behind various paintings. I take my time to look over what's already on display. One gleams gold as stalks of wheat seemingly sway in the breeze as workers harvest the crop. Another shows a belly round with a child, but the chamber is empty and colored in blacks and blues.

"Why don't you hang these around your house?" All I remember seeing are fine works that cost a load of coin, but nothing of these vivid, beautiful, personal paintings.

She sighs from behind a pile of paint buckets. "My husband prefers that I keep my paintings private. In his eyes, if it didn't cost a lot, it's not worth anything."

My head shakes as I continue spinning around the room to take in each work. There's one of a toddler running through long grass with a tuft of flaming red hair on his head with a dark-skinned boy not far behind. It makes me smile and I idly flip through the pile before stalling on one in particular. It's a baby, clearly Silva with that bright hair, but the arms cradling him aren't the paint-dotted slender build of his mother's.

"Ah, yes." Meira comes over to peek at what I'm looking at. "I remember the day I painted that. The week Silva was born.

One night he woke me every hour with his crying, so I decided just to stay up and paint." A fond, melancholy smile tugs at her lips. "The next time Silva cried, I went into his room only to find his father already there, holding him close." She gently takes the painting from me before sliding it back behind the pile once again. "Do you know much about Lord Lurec?"

I hold back my snort. "Enough."

She nods slowly, eyes still on the painting even though it's hidden well now. "Yes, well. He wasn't always as he is now. When we were first wed, not too long after we first met, he was…" She looks at me with watery eyes. I'd been so consumed with Silva, Henry, and the warden, I'd forgotten that I'm not only making Silva a lord, but his mother a widow. I hadn't bothered to think about how she might feel about it. Love, even love long passed or love turned poison, leaves its mark. Silva comes to mind and I wonder how he'll feel about me once the deed is done. The thought leaves a sour taste in my mouth.

Meira blinks and seems to come back to herself. "But that's not why I brought you here!" The sadness slakes off her like water and I wish it was that easy for me. "I hope you won't mind me asking for forgiveness rather than permission, but—" She tugs me in front of a window where an easel holds a large painting. I'm about to ask her what she's talking about before I look at the work and words vanish from my mind.

It's me. That's clear enough to see. I'm facing a window in what looks like my green room. I'm in the black dress Meira first saw me in and gilded in golden light streaming in the window. What surprises me is that Silva stands next to me. While my face is mostly hidden as I stare at the sunrise, his is turned towards me with an indescribable look in his eyes. Something like trepidation, awe, and fondness. His expression is tender, his body language relaxed and loose, and the only part of my face visible is the corner of my mouth tipped upward.

"It's beautiful," I tell her honestly. She'd gotten every detail right, down to the freckles on his face and the neat way his waves are tousled. It's tempting to reach out and touch just to see if it's truly a painting.

Meira sways into me. "That's how he looks at you, you know." I drag my eyes from the painting to glance at her. She smiles, full cheeks swelling. "Like you could rip out his heart while being the reason it beats."

Silva's words from the other night come back to me. "*No one will ever make me feel as alive as you do.*" Well, no one makes me feel more seen than he does and for an assassin, that isn't usually a good thing. He makes me feel alive too. Not just living, not existing, but alive and vibrant and *free*.

"I thought we'd be hearing an announcement soon if I'm honest." Her face is so bright and earnest that it hurts.

I force out a soft laugh and look down as if in shyness. "It's not the right time for such a thing. Besides…I think I'll be leaving soon after the events this weekend." Telling her isn't exactly the plan, but I don't want to vanish from here to leave her wondering what happened. She'll have enough to deal with. Her expression falls and I steel myself against the regret rising in my chest. Leave it to the disappointed hopes of a mother to slide through the chinks in my armor. "With my health returned, it's time I returned to my land. Try to regain what was lost and I'm afraid it's something I need to do on my own in my own way." Not a bit of it is a lie and there is some solace in that.

My body reflexively stiffens when she tugs me into her arms, but I relax the next moment to return the embrace. "I understand, but you make sure to come back some time. And send for help or anything you may need on your journey." The hug is warm and gentle and reminds me far too much of my own mother's embrace. I relentlessly harden my heart against the warmth rising in my chest, chasing it off with thoughts of soot, fire, and screams. "I've always felt like the boys needed a third.

Despite being plenty of mischief on their own. And," she takes a little breath, "I'll admit that I've always wanted a daughter too." My eyes shut as I squeeze her before pulling back.

There's no warmth or chill in my chest. Only emptiness. I give her a smile. "And I hope one day you'll get one. Excuse me." I turn my back on her and that beautiful, vibrant room to head into the blood-red hallway. I've wasted enough time on sentimentality. There's a reason I'm here, there's a reason I've been slowly working my way through the ranks of Anna's soldiers.

Time to get things done.

*   *   *

The only person I bother to see before midnight is Leah. We meet on the roof as agreed this morning on our walk to the house. The sun has just set, but the last vestiges of light still leak into the sky. I'm sitting on the ledge already dressed in my gear, dagger on my hip and knives strapped to the rest of me. "Far cry from your usual gear, but good to see it on you all the same." Her voice drifts over to me and I turn, leaning back against a chimney as she walks over. She'd set aside her white outfit again tonight and has chosen a light gray jumpsuit instead. A white belt wraps around her wide hips as the rest of the fabric flows and ripples around her muscles and curves with each powerful step.

"Thank you for staying with them tonight. The window will be open, so just slip in when you're ready." More than likely it's an unneeded precaution, but I like being careful when I can.

Leah settles beside me with a leg folded under her and the other hanging over the ledge, just like mine. "My pleasure. It's fun to scare the civilians." She grins at me and I barely return the smile. "You seem chipper." My eyes wander to the landscape stretching out in front of me as night falls. "She's almost dead. It's nearly over."

"That's not true." I glance back over to Leah, picking idly at my hands. "She's the dog that was sent after me, not the master. She may have set the fire, but we know who ordered her to do it. Annaliese is only a link in a long chain."

She sighs, leaning back onto her hands. "You always did look on the bright side of things."

A bit of her humor leaks into me and the corner of my mouth barely lifts. "I had so many nightmares in the places they took me. Some were false, some replayed memories, but nothing haunted me like that night. Even in the freezing cold Prison on the Mount I could feel the heat of the flames, choke on the smoke, hear the screams of dying people." My eyes shut as I torture myself with the images once again. How I rode up to my estate with billowing smoke filling the air, people scrambling to run, to escape the towering flames reaching towards the sky like tongues of ravenous beasts wishing to taste the stars.

It was only when I entered the courtyard that I realized the flames weren't the only things to run from. Soldiers, Anna's soldiers, marched around the buildings cutting down any who escaped the fire with grins on their faces. I leapt from my horse and ran towards the house only to be caught up in strong arms. My name shouted in my ear and the arc of a familiar sword with an emerald in the hilt is the only thing that kept me from fighting the embrace. My father set me behind him and cut down three soldiers before turning to me.

Green eyes looked me over for harm before he squeezed my shoulder. "You have to go!" Behind him, my mother wielded two long daggers, dancing through flames and soldiers to keep them off us.

My head shook. "But you! And mom—"

"We'll manage! Go!" He urged me back towards the gates.

"You know what to do!" My mother yelled over and spared me a wink despite the soot and blood smeared across her face.

So, gods help me, I ran. Screams filled the air, people ran in every direction, some on fire and many bleeding. My horse hadn't wandered far, so I slung myself onto her back once I reached the entrance. I risked another glance back at my parents and saw my mother touch my father's arm, then run back inside the burning building. Annaliese shouted from the edge of the mess, pointing after her. "No!" I shouted and made to turn back, but then the soldiers spotted me. They charged and my father dove forward to fight them off.

"Go!" He yelled again and with no other option, I ran. Soldiers came in pursuit and I remember the frantic pumping of my heart to keep in beat with the sound of the horse's hooves. It was so dark that night. No moon in the sky and the stars were blocked out by the smoke. Eventually, I grabbed a branch that my horse passed and heaved myself up into the trees. The soldiers chased after the sound of the horse while I was left behind in silence.

After that, I wandered through the woods. Blind. Cold. Wondering if my parents survived or died in the fight or the flames. When day came, I found my way into the glen we agreed we'd meet in if anything ever went wrong. For days, I waited. A week passed and that's when I knew they weren't coming. And with all that time to spare, I realized that the appearance of those soldiers was no accident. The fire was no accident. I was betrayed just as I...just as I betrayed. And I knew who the culprit was.

My uncle arrived to find me struggling to survive on the berries nearby and the scant wildlife I'd been able to hunt. His clothes were soot stained and I knew he'd already visited the estate. Tears streamed down his face as we crashed together in a tight embrace. Over his shoulder, attached to his saddle, was my father's sword. If he fell, I knew my mother wasn't long after. Neither could bear to be parted from the other.

We stayed in that glen for hours crying. Weeping over the loss of our family. That was the day Roux was born. The day I

251

decided that I would get revenge on all who had anything to do with that day. I was sixteen.

"I never forgot you, you know." Leah's soft voice winds its way over to me and my eyes open to see her vivid, violet eyes. "When I learned that you'd been taken, I searched for you. I left my troop and scoured the jails, then moved to the prisons. I'd get a lead and head out only to hear that you'd been moved." Frustration colors her voice while my mind goes blank at the meaning behind her words.

"I thought they'd moved me to keep me from learning the guard's rounds or the layout, but it was *you*." A joyless laugh leaves my lips at the memory of the mad scramble of the soldiers as they moved me from place to place. Annaliese wouldn't have been able to identify which Enhanced was pursuing me and would have no clue the one she's brought to find me now was pursuing me then.

"More than likely it was a mixture of both."

"Mm. You could have left me in Pearl Prison. It was my favorite." After that, I was on the Mount and that was a nightmare.

Leah rolls her eyes. "The point is that you were never far from my mind and I never would have stopped looking for you. You still have family, querida. And you'll continue to have me when you leave here."

I raise a brow. "I don't believe I invited you to run away with me."

"As if you could stop me."

"And your troop? The jobs you'll be missing out on? I won't be able to pay you in anything but shed blood."

"You know that's my preferred payment anyway. And chocolate." She winks at me and my smile finally breaks through. "My troop can continue individually or split up. Enhanced are adaptable, if you remember. Besides, I'm bored. You always promise excitement."

"At the risk of your life." A little light leaks back into my heart at the sight of her wide grin.

"Just how I like it."

My lips purse as I think about what I can say to change her mind, and then I decide I don't want to. "I look forward to being on the road with you rather than running from you. Although you'll be paying for most of the meals."

"Thank the goddess. You pick shit restaurants." Soft laughter filters through the air and I cling tight to the sound. Despite what I may say, the sound is far better than any scream I could call from my enemies.

"Maybe I just picked the cheapest restaurants since I was normally the one paying." She blinks and my smile grows at catching her off-guard.

Leah stays for another hour before slipping into Silva's room while I slink down to the second-floor hallway. In case anything goes wrong, at least they'll all be safe. Henry has multiple guards at Meira's door and while they seem to be terrible at finding me, they should be able to halt any other problem until Leah can get there. It's a strange feeling to slink through the great house I'd walked through as Nestra. This is more familiar for me even if I haven't done it in a while. The times I snuck into a house far outnumber the times I've been invited in.

Servants mill about accomplishing their tasks, but they're few and far between. I use their staircase and slip out at the end of the hall where my target's rooms are. The guards don't look over as I open Deckree's door and slide inside with barely a click behind me as it shuts. I don't bother hiding the sound of the lock since Deckree's body is laid out on the floor with a hand reaching towards the door. The poison has done its job. "You know…" I start, walking forward so my foot is inches away from her hand. "I've worn my hatred for Annaliese bright and clear ever since we met, but I could never truly decide whether I hated you more."

I crouch, drawing one of my many knives and letting the tip coast over each of her fingers. "You remember when they moved me from that jail, don't you? When they stripped me down and hung me up for any and all to see? You were present for every moment. You watched as Annaliese beat, whipped, cut, and deprived me of any and all relief." Her brown eyes are open and follow me as I stand and kick her over onto her back. I plant my feet on either side of her hips before settling down onto my knees straddling her. Another knife slips into my free hand as her dart around with fear.

"The warden left for a day, I assume to rest since she hadn't left my side, and that's when you made your move. You fed me, gave me water, even laid a blanket over my naked body as best you could." I let the flat side of my blade glide around her face like a gentle caress. "We spoke a little. Inconsequential things. What day it was, how long I'd been there, when she'd kill me. I was almost thankful for you. But it was when she returned that I realized what you were doing."

I slam a knife down into her palm, the blade digging into the wood beneath. To my delight, she can't even scream. "You were caring for me as a farmer does his pigs to ready them for the slaughter." Another knife crashes down into her other palm and tears begin to leak from her eyes. "You stepped back, stripped me of my blanket, and practically presented me to the warden all over again. It was that moment I started planning this. I already knew that I'd kill everyone who had a hand in it, but it was then that I decided to come up with a special end for you. You should feel the effects soon."

I stand above her, careful not to touch her blood. "Banks met a horrific end. I'm sure you found that out today, but it was far too quick for my taste. It was inspiring though." I flick my chin to the knives still pinning her to the floor. "That tooth you saw this morning had enough poison locked inside it for me to extract it and soak those blades in it. Poison that will now be in your bloodstream. Hopefully, it'll travel through your blood, infecting it, then dissolving your body bit by bit." My smile is sharp and bright as her eyes shut for a moment as a wave of pain washes over her. "Although, this is an experiment. Who knows what will happen to you. Or how long it will take."

I sit on the bench at the end of the bed and cross my legs. "I will offer you one last deal, though. Tell me what I want to know and I'll stab you in the heart. Your end will be quick, at the very least." Her eyes strain to meet mine and I take that as a yes. "Don't waste your last breath on a scream." A few hand gestures and a shimmer of magic later—she's gasping for breath and sobbing. The only part I released is her head and neck, so she's still mostly frozen. Ah, the benefit of magic-based poisons. "Where is the book?"

"I don't—I don't know." She gasps. I figured as much, but it doesn't hurt to try.

"Who does the warden answer to?"

Deckree squeaks as she fights the pain and not to scream. "I...I think you already know that."

My eyes narrow as I try to keep my body loose and ready to move. "A royal." She barely nods in answer. Even though I knew it, and suspected it for so long, hearing it confirmed feels like someone is driving a dagger into my heart. "When were you next going to meet?"

"She decides. We don't know until she sends for us." Her eyes shut tight and she slams her head back into the floor. "Gods...please, I can't—" Frustration rolls through me at the lack of information. But she's always been smart. It's no surprise she's playing the game well.

"Do you have any useful information?" My finger perches on the handle of the knife sticking out of her left hand. She may be dying, but there's still plenty of time for her to hurt.

She swallows. "There's a...a messenger we can send for in emergencies. Tolliver. He follows us everywhere just in case. He's never further than the nearest town." I make a mental note of the name as I feel the wear on my energy. Keeping her head and neck unparalyzed is draining my small reserve of magic. What information I've gathered will have to do. "Kill me. Goddess, please...just—" Her voice is cut off as I release my hold on my magic.

Frozen once again, her eyes accuse me as I stand and roll my shoulders. "I lied. Give your compatriots my best when you see them in Under." I glide to the door and look back only to memorize her death, then slip out.

The warden is across the hall and it's a little jarring to see the guards still standing at the end of the hall like no time has passed. I slink to Anna's doors, then step inside. I freeze when I see her sitting up in bed, panic shooting through me before I realize the hands holding a cup of tea in her lap are completely still. The only part of her that's moving is her chest with every breath. Berating myself for that shot of panic, I lock the door and walk to the end of the bed.

"Nice to see you looking so well, Annaliese." The words pour out like honey and I grin when her eyes flash open. The scar on the side of her face looks jagged and warped in the half-light from a candle on her desk. I wonder if she wants the reminder that she's not in that prison just like I do. Fury burns bright in her black eye anyway and I feel nothing but pure satisfaction at the sight. "I'm going to release your voice. I would tell you not to scream or I'll kill you, but I wouldn't mind." Magic shimmers over her and she swallows to wet what I'm sure is a dry throat.

"But then you wouldn't get any questions answered, now would you?" Irritation pulls my brows together, but it was an obvious guess. I'm still in control. "I knew it was you. That waif of a lady was too sharp for her own good."

"Mm, I'll take that as a compliment."

"How fun it must have been to play the part of a lady. An urchin like you, dressed in finery in the big house."

"Not quite as fun as murdering your guards, but fun just the same." Her expression darkens while mine brightens. "Deckree has told me a bit, but I did save some questions just for you." This is where I'll have to tread carefully. Even if she'll be dead within the hour, I'd rather not reveal too much to her. Maybe out of spite, maybe just because I don't want her to know me. "There was an estate that you were sent to destroy. You set it aflame and cut down all those who tried to escape." I round the bed, hand skimming the blankets before I sit next to her. "I want to know if you were sent there to pillage and riot, or for a more specific purpose."

Her eyes give nothing away. "Why would that matter to you?"

"Oh, I think we both know the answer to that. There was something you took from there, then lost like a child." Her face hardens, then laxes and I prepare myself for her next words.

"I thought you had no interest in being a sniffer dog for that book."

"I'm happy to hunt for myself, just not anyone else."

"Really? You showed no interest when we were at Skeleton jail." Her voice softens. "The first place I had you locked up and strung up for me. Such good memories. You remember all the lovely art we did there. The cuts, the bruises, the whip marks, but I wonder if you remember what else we did…"

"*We* didn't do anything." The words grind out of my teeth and I don't know why I don't shut her up. Don't know why I don't take back my magic even if there are questions that I need to know the answers to.

I nearly flinch when her finger barely moves to graze my knee. "I disagree. You certainly drank that whiskey as if you wanted to drown in it." *Yes, because I had no water in days. Because I wanted the pain to go away. Because I wanted oblivion.* But I hold back my words, knowing that this is a game and that I owe her no explanation. "You were much nicer after that. Do you remember how I touched you? The little gasps you let slip—" In a moment, I've slammed her hand down on the bedside table and drawn my dagger. In one swipe, her fingers tumble to the floor without her hand. A hard hit to her throat cuts off her scream and I watch with mounting pleasure as pain ripples across her face.

"You see, Annaliese, there are some people who deserve artistry, but others...others should just be dead." I turn on my heel and march to the door, grabbing a chair and snapping off the leg, then shoving it through the door handles. I don't care if everyone hears the screams anymore. She's going to suffer and no one is going to interrupt me. I'm turning back around when an arm wraps around my neck and tugs me back against her body.

"I wholeheartedly agree." She whispers, but seems to have forgotten that I have a dagger. The blade slices across her thigh, but instead of enticing her to let go, she falls and takes me with her. I turn as we fall and ram my elbow into her ribs, the strike expounded by my bodyweight falling on top of her. Her breath whooshes out of her lungs, blowing strings of my hair into my face. She's still lethargic from the poison, so it's easy to pin her down and press the point of my dagger to her throat.

"Did you really think I wouldn't start mithridatism after realizing you employed the tactic?" She gasps out and it's terribly tempting to just slice through her neck like butter. But that's not how I've imagined it for so long.

"*Still.*" I use spoken magic for the first time in years and instantly feel a heaviness settle over me as it takes its price. It'll be hard for me to stand after this, but it'll be worth it once she's dead. Anna freezes once again and I sag slightly without having to fight her resistance. "I remember each and every moment of our time spent together. The times when we weren't, I planned to do this." My hand has unbuttoned her shirt as I've talked and now I remove my dagger from her throat to her chest. I sink the blade into her chest and jerk it down to slice through skin and muscle then go to work smashing her ribs. She won't die from this, not yet. She's still taking healing potions for her previous injuries and they'll keep working, staunching the bleeding, keeping her on the cusp of death until I deliver the final blow. Once there's a clear enough path through her ribcage, I reach down to pull out her still beating heart. But there's something terribly, terribly wrong with it.

"What did you *do*?" Her heart is no longer red, but shimmers as if made from silver. My eyes lift only to find that she's passed out. "Wake up!" I hiss, slapping her face relentlessly until her dark eyes flash open. She wakes up gasping, but then those gasps turn into staggered laughter.

"Tied...a spell...to me." The words spill out in pieces as I drop her heart back into her chest as I feel a strange tug on it. It wriggles back into her chest as I watch with horror, then her crushed ribs begin reforming piece by piece. "Reanimation. You'll...you'll never kill me." She laughs again and the sound echoes in my head like the screams of Banks in that damned swamp. "You'll never be rid of me!"

Horror settles strong and potent through my every limb. She can't be killed. Reanimation spells, they're tricky. They have loopholes, yes, but most are only temporary while the actual spell can take years to undo. I never would have thought that the Red Death scared her enough to endure the cost such a spell would require. Not to mention the pain of reanimation. The sacrifice of never dying...gods. My mind frantically goes through everything I know and have learned about the spells before settling on something I've learned while being here. My last hope.

Before she heals completely, I rush to press my blade against her neck. "Reanimation spells are powerful, but fallible. You might heal from my cuts, maybe even from a heart split into pieces, but larger body parts take quite a long time to reattach themselves." Her eyes widen. "Now I would love to chop you into tiny pieces and scatter you all over the world, but there's another secret to reanimation spells. There has to be a piece of you that survives to act as an anchor for the spell. Not a hair or piece of fingernail, but something substantial like a limb or an organ. If there's nothing left, then there's nothing to reanimate." There's a grim smile on my face as her lips open and I make my first slice over her throat so she chokes on her own blood. The next is deeper, and deeper, and deeper, until I'm hacking away at bone along with slamming my foot down on her until her head is only connected by a thin strip of skin. All the while her body is trying to heal and I pray to every god and goddess that she can feel every single strike.

It is my great pleasure to make the final cut to sever Annaliese Warren's head from her body.

Her dead eyes stare at me as I drag a bloody hand through my hair. Relief fills me, but there's still work to be done. "Leah." Her name fills the silence and I know she'll be keeping an ear out for me. "Leah, I need some help." I don't bother getting up to unlock the door. Not when there are windows on either side of the bed in front of me.

I'm nearly asleep by the time I hear someone fiddling with the window and open my eyes as Leah swings in quickly followed by Silva, then Henry. I blink at them as if to check they aren't mirages while each reacts in their own way. Leah nods down at the body in appreciation, Henry has turned back to the window and looks to be deciding whether to leap from it, while Silva scans the whole scene with a wrinkled nose, then looks me over with wide, nearly glowing eyes. It's him I look at when I speak.

"Want to help me get rid of a body?"

"Absolutely, yes." Silva agrees as Leah smiles and Henry knits his fingers behind his head as he looks up at the ceiling.

Leah ends up carrying the body while I carry the head and the fingers I'd severed. Silva half carries me. Henry lends us his eyes to watch our backs since he can't stand to look at the rest of us. We walk to the swamp and Leah swings Annaliese's body into the slick while I vault her head and fingers nearby. When green bubbles begin to break the surface, Leah and Henry turn back to the house. I'm fixed to the spot. I won't leave until I see her vanish down that creature's gullet.

"Go ahead. Cover for us if we aren't back by morning." Silva's voice seems very far away and muffled to my ears. I see him settle into the grass next to me and it's only then that I realize I must have collapsed to the ground the second he left my side.

"She had a reanimation curse put on her," I breathe, hardly realizing I'm talking. "The cost of such a spell…" My head shakes. All magic has a price, but most only take energy from you that can be regenerated with time and rest. Magic like that…magic to defy the relief of death would have a cost far higher. She'd have to give up something precious; someone she loved, a complete innocent, her soul.

"Will this keep her?" Silva's voice drifts over to me.

I shrug. "It should. There's no way of telling other than time. And this." My hand lifts to reveal a tooth I'd yanked out of Annaliese's mouth. Not enough to act as an anchor, but enough to act as a warning. "If she comes back, this piece of her will want to return. Then I'll know."

"Charming." His response almost makes me smile. Almost. "Are you…happy? Satisfied, I mean." There's a ripple as the swamp creature lazily flicks its tail in the mud and wriggles forward towards Anna's body. She's swallowed in one gulp and there is relief in that. Relief fills my body so strong and potent that it nearly steals the breath from my lungs.

"The people who once trapped me, kept me, starved me, and put me in those damned cages are dead." The words are the most beautiful music I've ever heard even when I know my work is far from done. "The ones who…killed my family, who tortured me—" Tears cloud my vision and emotion rises in my throat to the point where talking is useless. There's a light touch on my shoulder, then soft shuffling as Silva moves closer with a hand sliding down my arm. I turn to look at him as he sits next to me without a trace of judgement or fear on his face, only understanding and concern. When his hand reaches mine, our fingers entwine and I lean towards him before pausing. Even exhausted, my mind runs through what a terrible idea it is to allow myself even a second of vulnerability. Not when there's still so much left to do. But I'm too tired to think further and I've always liked bad ideas. I give in and rest my head on his shoulder as a shuddering breath leaves me.

Tears begin sliding down my cheeks and I slowly reach up to wrap my arms around Silva's neck. There isn't a second of hesitation as his arms snake around my waist to tug me tight against him, but his embrace doesn't feel like a cage, it feels like he's holding me together. My head buries itself into his shirt as I cry without reservation. Silva keeps me close, accepting me fully into his lap despite the blood covering me like a second skin. He brushes a hand over my hair again and again while whispering to me softly, his cheek resting on my head. "They're gone. All gone. You never broke, Roux. You'll never break."

And even after saying it to myself so many times, this is the first moment I've really believed it.

Chapter Nineteen

Plans

Silva

It kills me to wake her after what must have been a traumatic night, but dawn is on the horizon. We're both covered in blood and she has the added flair of *other* bits that I don't particularly want to name in her hair. She fell asleep soon after her tears were spent and I've been content just to hold her. But all good things must end. "We've got to go. Morning will be here soon." She hums in soft acknowledgement, so I take matters into my own hands. I stand up with her steady in my arms and start walking.

"Dirty." She murmurs.

I glance down at her and marvel at her ability to be cute while covered in blood. "We're not going back to the house. We both look like, well, like we got rid of a body." My chin gestures to a path not too far ahead. "I'm taking us somewhere safe where we can wash up without the prying eyes of my servants or guards." She hums again and I wonder what took so much of her energy last night. But questions can wait. I treasure the trust she's showing me by letting me lead and carry her. Let her rest a bit longer.

When we reach the slow-moving river, I pause. "We're here."

Her eyes peek out at the scenery. "Uh huh." She lets her head rest back against my chest as my heart swells. Instead of setting her down, I simply wade into the water. Her eyes flash open, but she doesn't squirm or try to get away. I carry her out until we're about waist deep and stand there for a few moments as the current washes away some of the blood. "Does your cleanliness obsession include carrying soap?"

I chuckle. "Didn't exactly have time to pack some away when Leah tugged us out of your room."

She raises a brow. "So you do normally have soap on your person?" I shrug and am glad to see it when she smiles. Her arms push her away and she moves so she's floating on the surface of the water, our connected hands the only thing keeping her from flowing downriver. With her hair loose and flowing around her in the water, she could be a mermaid or a selkie. I would happily stand here all day as her anchor if I got to keep watching her. Water cleans the blood off her and luckily she wore black so there's no sign of the stains. I'm in navy, so the same goes for me. Though I'll be throwing out this outfit as soon as I can.

I tug her back to me and slide my arms under her as those brilliant eyes look at me. "There are pieces of flesh and bone in your hair." She laxes into my arms and lets me cling to her as she reaches up to run her hands through the wet mass so the miniscule pieces float down river.

"Our time is coming to an end." The whisper is so soft that I almost don't hear it. Her voice blends so well with the breeze in the trees and the sound of flowing water. "Leah said she'll come with me when I leave. I thought that…that it might be a comfort for you to know."

I swallow and nod, trying to decide if I should release the words sitting on the tip of my tongue. Her hands stop their ministrations in her hair and I turn to the side, wading through the water and setting her on a boulder. Water flows gently over it, but this puts most of her out of it. I remain in front of her with my hands resting on her knees just to stay in contact with her. Her eyes are soft and steady on mine as I war with myself.

Naturally, my mouth wins out. "I know you have things to do. I know you think that you have to leave." My eyes lift to hers. "But you don't. You could stay. Take your mantle as Lady up again with your real name. No one would be able to track down Roux or lay a claim against you." Even as I say it, I know she won't. But there's something about letting her know that seems important. That I would be glad if she could stay here with me. That it would be a privilege if she wanted to.

She looks down at her hands in her lap, flicking out blood and dirt from underneath her fingernails. "I can't…I won't stay." I nod, letting my head fall to look at her hands before they lift to tilt my chin back up. She sighs heavily. "You have to understand. This isn't over." Roux flicks her chin back where we came. "The warden and her ilk killed my family. They set fire to my estate, killed my people, pillaged my home, but they didn't do it on their own. Someone, someone I know, sent them after us and I have to hunt her down. I have to." Her hands slide to my shoulders, squeezing lightly as my brows furrow.

"Her? You know who it is then?"

She nods slowly. "Yes. She was…she was my friend many years ago. My closest friend." Her eyes darken and I see that flicker of guilt I saw before shine out of her eyes. "Until I betrayed her and she betrayed me in return." A thousand questions rise to the forefront of my mind, but vanish when her eyes clear to focus only on me.

"You'll send for word if you need anything? Even a letter every once and a while to tell me that you're alright."

Her hands climb to frame my face, one of them carding through my hair and nearly making my eyes shut with the ecstasy of her touch. "When I can." I move just a bit closer and her legs open so I'm wedged between her knees.

"If you send for me, I'll come." My fingers dance over the outside of her thighs before my hands settle heavy on her hips. Her eyes shimmer and sparkle like the water around us in the early morning light. "No matter where you are. Even across the world. Even in Under or Above."

The skin between her brows pinches slightly as one of her hands trails down to make a fist in my shirt. I bite back a groan as her hand in my hair tugs lightly. "And I'll come if you send for me." She tugs on my hair again and this time I can't stop the grunt that leaves me. She smiles at the sound. "For emergencies only."

I hum, leaning down until our foreheads are centimeters from one another. "What if the emergency is that I need to see you?" I almost couldn't stand not seeing her for two weeks when we were under the same roof. I can't imagine not seeing her when she's hunting her prey across the country.

Something alights in her eyes. "That, I can remedy. For now, we should head back before we're missed." She pushes me back as she stands and wobbles off the rock onto the shore. I'm in shock at being thrown from her closeness so suddenly, but quickly get my feet back under me as I exit the water to move to her side. Her arm wraps around mine and we're silent as we walk back towards the estate. I'm realizing that this may be the last time we're alone together for…for who knows how long. My only hope is that she feels a fraction of the sadness that I do at that fact.

*　　*　　*

It's a riot of activity when we get back to the estate. Dawn has broken her sunny yoke over the world and the golden light revealed Deckree's gelatinous body melting into the carpet in her room. The rest of the house is practically empty, so at least it's easy for Roux and me to slip in to change our still damp clothes. As soon as I come out of my room, I'm pulled into the fray. I respectfully refuse to enter Deckree and Anna's rooms to see what carnage the day reveals, but let my guards talk me through their findings.

With the culprit hopefully resting upstairs, I do what I can to put the rest of my staff at ease. Henry arrives curiously trailing Leah now draped in her usual white. I tell my friend to station any extra guards he may need around the estate before Leah takes over. "I'll be staying a few extra days in lieu of these murders. Hopefully, I can drive off this little assassin before she causes any more damage." A glance at Henry reveals disgruntled acceptance on his face, so I suppose they already planned this.

"It would be our honor to have you stay." I tilt my head to her dark hood while, much to my surprise, relief flashes across my guard's face. Even though Roux has only harmed the warden's soldiers, it seems fear of her has spread to my staff. Something I'm sure she'd be glad to know.

Leah tilts her head back to me. "It's my pleasure. I've never been one to miss a party, anyway." I get the distinct feeling that she's winking at me before she turns and sweeps down the hall with that white cape swirling behind her. My mother apparently hasn't left her room since she heard the news and has refused to let anyone in but her ladies. I'll let her have the day before I try to speak with her. This has all been a lot for anyone to take on, but especially her since she doesn't know what's really happening.

With Henry and Leah taking over security for the estate while Roux rests, I take myself to a place I haven't been since coming home from the Prison on the Mount. My father's rooms are decorated lavishly in red and gold with gaudy baubles covering every flat surface. I ignore it all and head straight to the desk on the right, on the opposite side of the room from the bed. Stacks of gold coins guard the papers underneath and after swiping them into a drawer, I settle down and start flipping through the folders. Today, I'm grateful for the distraction paperwork provides.

This will be the last day that I have to do this. The last day I'll have to look through these papers looking for my father's scheming hand in every contract and deed. Never again will anyone try to pilfer coin from my tenants. Never again will profit be the goal of each and every agreement. Soon, my tenants will come first, tending the land, making sure my mother can walk free through this house without watching her words and keeping to one room all the time.

A hand on my shoulder nearly makes me jump out of my skin before I turn around to find Henry standing behind me. Glancing to the windows reveals that night has fallen. I've worked the day away. "Getting used to your occupation?" He asks with a tired smile that I return before standing and stretching my aching limbs.

"Doing one last check. We'll be in mourning for months, so I won't be able to get started on the changes I want straight away. I'll make plans—"

"I know you will. For now, let's get some food in you, then get you into bed." He wraps his arm around me and I put an arm over his shoulders as we walk down the hall to my room. I scan the space for my assassin, but she's nowhere to be found. "The Enhanced slipped into her room a while ago. I'd guess you won't see her tonight." My stomach twists at losing more time with her, but I let Henry corral me to the table where two trays filled with food already sit. He settles across from me and I smile over at him.

"Thank you, Hen."

He smiles and nods back. "Nearly over, now." There's nothing but relief on his face as he says the words.

My lips press together as I lean forward a bit, forearms on the table. "I am sorry, you know." He raises a brow in silent question. "I know how you feel about this whole ordeal. If it isn't a breach in your morals to let such things happen, then it's certainly close. I am sorry about that." And I mean it. Henry is a good man, always has been, and I'd hate for him to feel like less of one for letting events happen the way that they did because of me.

He sighs and rubs thick fingers over his eyes. "In truth, while I don't think what's happened here was completely right, I don't think it was completely wrong either." Surprise ripples over my face and he rolls his eyes at the sight. "Roux told me a few things and while the two of you were off frolicking over the past few days, I did my own research." He swallows and I wonder what exactly he discovered that left such an impression on him. "She told the truth. They were…well, suffice it to say that I doubt any in their prisons did worse things than them."

"Nothing would have kept them from continuing to do what they've always done. Except death, anyway." Henry shrugs. "It's good that they're dead. No longer can they pillage and torture the people of this world." His eyes meet mine as he takes a breath. "Your father is the same. Nothing can stop him from his greed. He will bleed this land, this house, and its people dry until he's drowning in coin and there's nothing left." His head shakes. "I won't say I approve of what's going to happen, but I certainly don't disapprove either."

I let his words ruminate in my mind for a minute before I wave my fork at him. "Someday, you're going to have to decide one way or the other, Hen. That river may be steady now, but it won't save you from the waterfall. Only choosing a shore on either side will do that." He gives me a deadpan look that has a smile creeping onto my face. "And technically—"

"Oh, shut up with your technicalities and eat your food." He tosses a roll at my face and I laugh before eating everything on my plate. Even the roll.

*   *   *

The three days before my father's arrival pass far too quickly.

I haven't seen Roux at all and I wonder if this is her subtle way of preparing me for her absence. Whatever the reason, it's terrible and I hate it. I'm kept plenty busy with security concerns,

269

the traditional end of life celebration for all the dead that will now double as my father's welcoming party, and my poor mother who is slowly losing that light that she regained the past few weeks. It's as if Lord Lurec is a shadow and the nearer he gets, the more light leaks out of her.

Leah passes like a ghost through the house, so I barely see her, but everyone is present on the front porch when my father arrives. We arrange ourselves in a V leading to the door; me, my mother, and Henry on one side with Roux and Leah on the other. I drink in the sight of the assassin dressed in a gold day dress with her curls down and gleaming with color from days outside. The dress hugs her curves, makes her skin look darker, more sun-kissed, and she hardly has any limp but for the one she had before. She looks absolutely ruinous.

Her eyes flick to mine as my father's carriage pulls up and I note that she has gold dust around her eyes. The corner of her mouth rises before she tilts her head forward to tell me to pay attention. I turn towards the doors opening with great difficulty. My jaw locks as Lord Lurec steps out bedecked in gold brocade, shimmering gold pants, gold rings on every finger, and gold clasps on his shoes. He looks up at the house first, blocking the sun from his sapphire eyes, before he surveys the group in front of him.

"Welcome home." My mother's voice wavers slightly and I move closer to her, grasping her hand to hold it tight in mine. He glances over at her with his long, thin nose wrinkling before he turns to me. Temper at his dismissal of her flares in me so hot and strong that I'm surprised I don't catch fire.

"You look well enough." He looks me up and down, his hair not moving one bit from the hardened wax he uses to keep it tamed into one smooth wave.

"A miracle what exercise, fresh air, and your absence will do." My mother tugs my hand in clear dissent, but my father only meets my gaze and laughs.

"Still got that spirit, do you? And no doubt you've meddled with my books." He heaves a sigh and I try to let his disappointment roll off my shoulders. "I'll put that right after the festivities tonight. You," he points to Henry, then the carriage. "Bags."

"That is *not* his job." My teeth grit as he treats my friend like a dog, but he doesn't even respond. He's too caught up in the two ladies he's yet to be introduced to.

I wonder if Leah can hear my heart beat faster as he walks over to Roux so they're less than a foot apart. "And who is this gem?" She curtsies and my mouth goes dry at the way he looks her over, as if he's gobbling her up with his eyes. She shouldn't have worn gold.

"Lady Clytemnestra Sassian." The words barely make it out of my mouth and I know he hears it as he glances over to see my face, then looks back to her.

"Arrived early for the celebration, eh? Have you had a tour yet, my Lady?" Him immediately taking possession of her makes me see red, but the smile she gives him stabs straight through my gut. *An act.* I remind myself. *It's all an act.*

"Not by you, my Lord." Her voice is soft and shy, almost cloying. He offers his arm and she takes it before he tilts his head to the white hood next to her.

"Enhanced." Leah inclines her head back before he begins lecturing Roux on the architecture of the building with not-so-subtle hints at the astronomical cost of paintings and sconces. My mother tugs my hand and I realize I'd been leaning forward as if to go storming after them. Leah waves a hand at me in reassurance as she shadows the couple, but that offers little relief.

"Let her distract him while we get everything ready. More people will arrive soon." My mother pulls her hand from my grasp to go help Henry dismantle whatever my father brought home this time.

"You'd throw her to the dogs?" I crane my neck as they turn a corner and deflate when they vanish.

My mother's scoff has me turning to find her irritated face as she hands some things off to the servants. "Sil," Henry calls my eyes to him. "She can take care of herself." His gaze is pointed and I nod, remembering that Roux isn't only a lady, but a skilled assassin with an Enhanced at her back. Everything will be fine. I start helping them unload the bags while another carriage comes down the road. Guests will be arriving all day before the ball tonight.

Even as I go through the motions of unpacking, greeting, and welcoming, my mind is on that hungry look in my father's eyes.

Chapter Twenty

Harbinger of Death

Roux

It would be pretty easy to kill Lord Lurec.

All he does is talk without paying attention to anything else around him, including the assassin at his side and the Enhanced hovering behind him. We're upstairs and alone within minutes of his arrival so he can show me his grand rooms. He disconnects from me as we enter and shrugs off his jacket as the doors shut. Leah ducks in right behind us and remains at the doors, leaning back against them if she needs to act as a barricade.

I take the brief quiet as a moment to survey Silva's father. He's tall like his son, but not quite as lean. His hair is much darker, more like wine red than bright copper, and there's muscle corded in his arms more like Henry than Silva. He could do real damage to a person if he chose to. After he lays his jacket out on the bed, he settles down on the bench at the end of it before looking at me. "I saw the way my son was looking at you. Are you involved?" The direct question is such a change from his rambling that I nearly let my interested smile slip.

"That's quite a forward question, my Lord." I let a little nervous laughter filter into my voice, but don't let my eyes drop from his intense gaze.

He heaves a sigh and leans back against the bed. "Of course, forgive me, but when I want something, I see little point in dancing around." He pats the space beside him. It's tempting to glance at Leah as I walk over, but I don't dare. I settle on the bench as far from Lurec as possible. Deep-set eyes scan my face before he rubs a hand over his pointed jaw covered in a dusting of stubble. "You see, my son is stubborn. Set in his ways. If I tell him anything, then he'll do the opposite just to spite me." He chuckles. "It's his mother's spirit in him that I can't seem to break." The implication that he's broken Silva's mother has my gut churning, but imagining him headless steadies me.

"If I had someone, someone like you, to act as a go-between, then maybe we would work better together." His voice is smooth and clear like the sharp ring of a bell. "Do well enough and maybe you'd be mistress of this house someday." Shock hits me first. He'd been pretending before with all his talk about paintings and the house. It was all to put me at ease and to satisfy any listening ears before we were here, alone, where he could offer me this. The temptation is clear. It would be a good deal to anyone who didn't care about Silva or the estate. The perfect deal for someone who cared only for status, influence, and coin. Someone just like Lurec.

I smile, sliding a bit closer. "And in the meantime?" He's silent for a moment as I flutter my eyelashes at him. What can I say? It's too tempting to play with him. "If I do this for you, there's no guarantee of my future, so what will acting as your mediator give me?"

He shifts in place as he shakes his head. "Clever girl. Alright, I'll give you a small stipend and keep you dressed in the finest dresses and jewels money can buy."

"Jewels?" I repeat, my tone hungry and deep.

Lurec's smile widens, thinking he's snared me. "Oh, yes. Diamonds, sapphires, emeralds, and pearls." I swallow as if the very mention of them is mouthwatering. He looks up and waves at

Leah as he rises from his seat. "Continue your rounds around the house, Enhanced. We're safe enough here." Her hood shifts slightly as she looks at me and I nod from behind him. I can handle the lord of the house. She doesn't bother dipping her head as she turns and walks out the door without a sound.

Lurec turns back to me and takes my hands in his. My first instinct is to tug them back, but I freeze as he grins down at me. "Close your eyes and I'll give you an advance." I hesitate only a moment before my eyes shut and his hands slip from mine as his footsteps cross the room. I wipe my palms discreetly on my dress while making a few gestures too small to see. A few seconds pass before my eyelids become transparent enough to see through. To anyone else, they look normal, but I can the room in muted tones through the thin skin. It's a simple spell, but won't last long.

Lurec walks to the other side of the room and glances back to make sure my eyes are still shut, then presses down on a section of the chair rail. A long piece of molding moves out of the wall with a soft click and I watch as he lifts a few necklaces from the drawer that shimmer and sparkle like stars. The spell on my eyes begins to fade and I depend on my ears to tell me what he's doing. After a minute, there's another click as he pushes the drawer back in, pulls the piece of molding back out, then I hear his footsteps as he walks back over.

"Hold out your hands, palms up." It takes me a moment to follow his instructions since he could have absolutely anything in his hands. I nearly flinch when something cold settles into my palms and my eyes flash open. It's a necklace. Three red gems are tethered together by gleaming white gems, like drops of blood caught in a spiderweb covered in morning dew. It's breathtaking, I'll admit it. "Rubies from the far south. Very rare." Lurec's voice is like a caress as his hungry gaze is fixed on the necklace.

His eyes flick to mine as he takes a step back. "Wear it tonight to the festivities. Prove to me that you can hold my son's interest and we'll have a deal." I smile and think about killing him for a moment. It would be easy, but I'd have to leave straight away. He'd be found within the hour. And I wouldn't be able to go to the ball tonight.

I rise, straightening my dress with the necklace held tight in my hand. "Most generous of you."

He grins, walking me to the door and pausing in the doorway as it swings open. "My pleasure. Fine art deserves a fine place to hang." Disgust fills my mouth even as I smile and curtsey before walking past him out the door. Just as I cross the threshold, his fingers ghost over my curls and makes the hair on the back of my neck stand on end. "Remember your task." He flicks his chin down the hall where Silva stands nearly shivering with anger. I slip the necklace into my pocket before walking down the hall towards him.

"Did he hurt you?" He asks as soon as I'm within earshot and I raise a brow.

"Silva, remember who you're talking to."

His eyes leave his father to look at me and his posture softens. "Right. Sorry." A little humor returns to his eyes. "It's not like you've been hurt at all while you've been here anyway." I huff a soft laugh as he grins and heaps of tension leave his shoulders. "Do I have any crazy theatrics from poison or toxins to look forward to tonight?"

A real, soft smile alights my lips as I shake my head. "Not tonight. Actually...I was going to wait a bit. Maybe even until tomorrow." Silva's brows furrow and I know I'm not going to walk away from this without answering why. "Well, I...I haven't been to a ball in a while and wanted to enjoy this one." A moment passes before a smile blooms on his face.

"You only had to say so and I would've thrown you a ball every night you stayed here."

I fix him with a disdainful stare even as my heart squeezes. "We were a little busy."

He leans towards me a bit, his hand on the handle of his door as if it's his anchor. "I'm glad you're going to enjoy yourself tonight. You deserve it. Although I will ask that you save me the first two dances."

"The first two?"

"One wouldn't be enough. I'm showing restraint asking for only two."

My lips press together to keep from grinning too widely as I take a step closer so we're a little less than a foot apart. "I'll give you three. How about that?" His eyes brighten and it's incredibly tempting to lean into his arms and feel those hands on my hips again. But the reason I've been staying away from him the past few days is so I *don't* jump his bones. I don't need another temptation to stay. "Not in a row. Spaced out a bit."

His smile doesn't dim as I brush by him towards my room. "Since you're attending the ball, I guess it's a good thing I left a surprise in your room." I turn back on my heel to catch his wink before he vanishes into his room and I hurry into mine to find whatever surprise he's set up. The first thing I find is Mary straightening a garment bag hanging off the canopy of the bed. She turns to face me with a wide smile and hands clasped in front of her.

"Are you ready to start preparing for the party?" She's practically bouncing on the balls of her feet and I let a little bit of her energy leak into me. This is my last night here, after all.

"Yes."

Mary wastes no time. She tugs me over and helps me out of my dress, then into the tub with my usual scents and soaps. It feels good to be pampered for once and I'm grateful that Mary doesn't ask any questions about the tooth in a vial around my neck. For tonight, it'll be tied to my dagger's belt which will wrap around my thigh. Thanks to some consultations from Leah, my injuries are healed. All that's left is my limp from before and I'm grateful for the normalcy. It's also freeing to finally be rid of all the bandages I've been lugging around.

After the bath, Mary wraps me in a soft robe with my hair tied in a towel while I walk over to inspect the garment bag. "Have you seen it?" I ask her as I reach for the zipper. Her smile is so wide it nearly splits her face as she nods. My lips lift and I take a breath before pulling down the zipper and gasping quietly at the contents. "Oh, Silva." My whispered words caress the soft fabric of the dress as my fingers pull it out of its shell.

The sleeves are long and will sit just off my shoulders with gathered folds around the top. The supple fabric falls to the floor with a small train behind and there's even a slit that will come up to about mid-thigh. My head shakes with awed appreciation as I feel the plunging back of the dress that scoop down to my waist. But as I step back with fingers fluttering over my mouth, what brings me to tears is the bottom edge of the dress. The dress is black, a deep black, but fades into a bright red at the bottom. A string of glittering red gems also connects either side of the high slit and looks like a blood-soaked spiderweb.

A conversation Silva and I had rises to the surface of my mind while I blink back tears. *"If you're keen on gifting me things, then I'd like a gown dripping with the blood of my enemies..."*

"And he supplied these as well." Mary comes forward with a small bag and pours the small items into her palm. The small trinkets sparkle and shine in the light streaming in the window as I take one to run my thumb over the green gem. *"...emerald hair pins sharp enough to gouge eyes from the socket..."* My eyes jump to the box sitting under the dress and I rush to open it, my lips parting at the sight of blood red shoes with gleaming silver down the back. *"...and shoes with a blade along the heel."*

He remembered everything I told him from that one tease. All of it. My eyes sting with tears as I pick up one of the shoes and find I can see my wavering reflection in the metal. "My Lady?"

Mary calls quietly and I wipe away the tears that have escaped as I turn back to her.

"After I'm done getting ready, I have a favor to ask of you."

She perks up and nods, gesturing to the stool in front of the vanity. I hand her back the hairpin I took and settle down in front of the mirror with a sigh. "How would you like to look tonight, my Lady?"

My eyes meet the soft brown of Mary's in the mirror as I smile. "Like a destroyer of worlds, if you please."

*   *   *

For the first time in a long while, nerves gather in my stomach. There are more people here than I've been around for two years and I'll have to convince them that I'm one of them. Usually I go in knowing everything about everyone, but there wasn't time to compile research. I've winged things plenty of times. I can do this. Even though parties are something I don't particularly like going in blind on. Too many variables in too small a space.

But I do have allies. Henry, Leah, Mary, and Silva will all be there to watch my back. I take a deep breath and start walking down the red hall with the silky fabric of my skirt whispering against the floor. The necklace Lord Lurec gave me weighs heavy around my neck, but I find the weight steadies me a bit. Along with the feel of soft leather on my right thigh telling me my dagger is close. My curls are piled on the back of my head and my fingers coast over the placement of the emerald pins just in case I need to stab someone in the eye. A few wisps frame my face and tickle my skin as I finally come to the top of the stairs to see the ballroom.

I pause for a moment, my lips pressing together as I hear music filling the room. It's classical of course, mostly strings like violins, harps, and cellos. But when the little trill of the flute and violin build together before everything else joins in a crescendo, I have to blink back tears. It's been *so* long and I underestimated how much I missed music. I don't allow myself to miss much from my old life, longing after things lost gets you killed, but the sweet notes slip through the cracks in the armor around my heart.

"Too fast, too fast!" I giggle as my father spins me in tight circles while my uncle plays his violin in the corner. My music teacher would call the way he plays so recklessly sacrilegious, but all I know is his music always makes me feel like someone is pouring sunshine in my veins. Both are grinning along with me and I'm fearless in my movements, confident that my father won't let me fall. He dips me, then pulls my feet back on top of his as we start swaying again.

"Look at you, already a little dancer. Better at ten than your mother was at twenty," He teases and looks over my shoulder to find my mother leaning against the doorway. She's smiling and shaking her head with a hand pulling her copper-tinted curls over her shoulder.

"If you're referencing the time I stepped on your foot, I'd like to remind you that I did that on purpose," She says and my uncle fudges the next note as he chortles.

My father raises a brow and I can already feel laughter building on my tongue as I recognize the mischief in his eyes. "You mean you didn't find me irresistible the moment we met? Impossible."

"Think anyone who has ever met you would disagree," My uncle comments and my father shoots him a playfully exasperated look. He spins me again so we're both facing my mom.

"What do you say to your mom coming over and showing off her dance moves?" He asks and her smile turns a little crooked as she pushes off the wall before I start eagerly nodding. He presses a kiss to my temple and my mother brushes a hand over my hair when I pass her to hop onto the chair next to my uncle.

He leans down and whispers to me as he starts to play something slower. "I played this at their wedding." The music starts to slowly cascade into the room and when my parents begin to dance, nothing else seems to exist for them. They speak softly to one another but I can't make out what they say, only seeing their smiles, fond looks, and quiet laughs. Eventually, they pull me back up and we dance together, my uncle passing the violin to a servant who can play so we can all spin around messily together.

I take a deep breath, shaking off the memory and not letting myself descend into any more. *This is your last night as Lady Nestra. This is your last night in this beautiful place with these lovely people. This is your last night not as Roux.* I remind myself and force myself to take a step down the stairs as I take in the splendor. Ladies in pastel skirts twirl around the space in unison as men in multicolored jackets follow suit, spinning and lifting them up in the air so they can fly. Firelight gilds the white and gold room with warmth while a cool breeze floats in from the front doors as more guests come in. Movement catches my eye and I spot Silva's mother heading up the opposite stairs with a hand on her head. Perhaps the noise and conversation has proved too much for her after everything.

I continue down the stairs and wonder about her son, but no sooner have I thought of him than I spot that shock of red hair.

He's surrounded by a gaggle of ladies, as I'd guessed he would be, but even as they speak and tug on his sleeves, his eyes are only on me. He's the one in all black tonight with a pop of red as his neckcloth. We match. I smile wide, not bothering to hold back now, as he walks away in the middle of what one of the ladies was saying to meet me at the bottom of the stairs. Crystals and firelight dance in his eyes as he stares, then dips in a low bow. "My Lady."

He offers a hand and I slip mine into it as I curtsey. "My Lord."

We both straighten as he presses velvet lips to my knuckles to send a shiver dancing down my spine. "I believe you promised me three dances." He reminds me and I roll my eyes.

281

"Would you like to claim one now?"

He answers by escorting me out onto the dancefloor and wraps an arm around my waist while I wrap mine around his shoulders. We're practically chest to chest as our fingers entwine and we begin to dance when a new song starts.

"You look fatal, tonight," He murmurs and my eyes lift to his instead of being preoccupied with his lips mere inches from mine. "Tell me, what would it take for you to dance with only me for the entire night?"

I hum a soft laugh and his eyes flick to my blood red lips. "I believe you already negotiated three dances."

"Yes, but that was before I saw you." He's so matter of fact about it that I nearly misstep. "Now, the thought of these people dancing with you—it just doesn't seem right. They don't know who they're holding."

"And who are they holding?" I raise a brow at him, but he takes the challenge in stride as we spin around the room.

"A predator. A flame made flesh. A blade wrapped in silks, satin, and rubies." His finger dances across the gems around my neck and I swallow at the feeling.

"You look…very nice too." Humor dances through his eyes and my lips purse at the poor compliment. Teasing, flirting, and playfulness, I can do, but I'm not talented with genuine compliments. "I mean, you look handsome. Like a lord." His smile soothes my burning cheeks as we pause in the middle of the floor, separating so each lady can walk around her partner.

"At least I look the part, then." He winks over at me as we come face to face again and start the dancing anew. We're quiet for a few turns and I feel the air between us change. "This is it, then." All levity has left his voice and the light has faded from his eyes.

My heart squeezes even as I nod. "Yes."

He nods slowly and looks at the stairs as his father climbs them with languid ease. Seems I've passed his test if he's retiring early. "When will you leave?"

"We don't have to talk about this now."

He gives me a melancholy smile. "I'd rather know than suddenly find you gone."

That stings a little, but it's the logical response. I step back and drag him with me through the crowd and out of the ballroom into the fresh, cold air of the gardens. Better that no one hears this particular conversation. "Probably right after. It'll be better if I'm not here when the real authorities arrive. The palace doesn't care about much, but they'll send someone to talk to all of you after the death of a lord."

"Right, of course." His shoulders are so deflated, I can't resist reaching out and resting a hand on his arm.

"I'll let you know I'm alright as often as I can. And send someone if I need anything. I will." A little bit of a smile returns to his face at that. "Oh, and your father keeps all his jewels in the wall next to his desk. Just press the flower in the molding and a drawer will pop out." They'll need all the money they can get to help their tenants.

He smiles and shakes his head at me. "Of course, you found the jewels. What am I going to do without you poking around the place?" The question is meant as a tease, but I take it seriously.

I squeeze his arm. "Live, Silva." He frowns, mouth opening only for a sudden wail to ring through the air. I automatically step in front of Silva with our backs towards the house and his hand on my hip in case he needs to pull me back. Our eyes scan the gardens for the source of the noise. The music is so loud inside, there's a chance no one heard it but us. Strangely, it isn't coming from inside, but towards the woods.

"What was—"

"Shh!" I hush him as mist gathers around the hedges before I can just barely make out the ghostly shape of a woman.

"By Under." Silva breathes while I take a few steps towards the figure.

I swallow to wet my dry throat before speaking. "Banshee?" The word causes the mist to swirl, then it seems to settle into a semi-solid shape. A woman in a flowing white dress stands before us with pale translucent skin and white hair that blows in an unforeseen wind.

"Vex? Is that you?" Her wavering voice leaks over as pale blue eyes focus on my face.

"Vex?" Silva repeats as I wave him off.

"Another one of my many names. Not the real one." My gaze returns to the banshee. "Ritha, what's going on?" My brows furrow and I cross my arms to ward off the chill that always follows a banshee's presence.

She floats a bit closer and I feel Silva's heat at my back as she smiles. "It's good to see you, Vex, but you know why I'm here. Although, I'm surprised you aren't the one causing havoc."

"What is it talking about?" Silva's voice leaks into my ear while panic wraps its hands around my heart.

I spin on my heel to face him. "A banshee means that someone will die. Mr. Geoffrey, you said he was healing from his wound. A day away from being good as new?" He nods, eyes flicking between me and Ritha. "Is there anyone else in danger? Anyone else who could be a target?"

Worry leaks onto Silva's face. "Henry?"

I glance back at the house before shaking my head. "Leah's with him. Who else?" We both look back to the house where Henry and Leah linger at the back door to watch over us.

Silva releases a pent-up breath, clearly at a loss. "Can't you ask her?"

My head shakes as I immediately dismiss the idea. "They can't tell you, it's part of their nature."

"But we always arrive near a loved one. To warn them of the upcoming grief." Ritha hints and my gaze steadies on Silvanus in front of me. If Henry is safe, then…no. My eyes snap to Lurec's bedroom where candlelight flickers. Ice fills my veins as information floods my brain. Of course. Everything makes sense now. That's why he wanted me to distract Silva, that's why he left so early tonight when he saw I had him in hand. He's going to kill Meira. He's going to kill Silva's mother.

"No. *Gods, no*. He's going after your mom." I shove Silva towards the doors while I pick up my dress, not even taking a moment to lament as I tie the train in a knot on my hip to free my legs. I kick my shoes off and run for the house. It takes me less than a minute to climb the house and slide over to the lord's windows where I see him approaching a prostrate Meira on the bed. The headache earlier—must've been poison. Or at least a sedative. Silver gleams in his hand as he stalks ever closer and I try to open the windows. Locked. Why is he the only one who locks his windows in this house?

He raises the dagger above her and I damn it all to Under. Bracing myself on the stone above the window, I draw my dagger and slam the hilt into the glass. I roll in onto the floor and grit my teeth at the glass cutting into my soft skin. Just as I look up, the dagger falls. "NO!" I scramble to my feet and rush over, but it's too late. Fresh blood is already seeping into the soft cream of Meira's nightgown and the white sheets of the bed.

Yet the blood doesn't belong to her.

Lurec's dagger is buried into the mattress beside her while another blade lies deep between the ribs of the lord himself. He falls to the floor with a final gasp while I watch, shocked. She killed him. Meira Dinnsesk, light of Ayncuarst estate, has driven a dagger into her husband who planned to murder her this very night.

Any other day, I'd congratulate her. If she were anyone other than Silva's mother, I would tell her I'm proud and impressed. But she is Silva's mother. And he hired me to kill his father because somewhere in his heart, he still loved him. Still longed for his approval. Now, his mother is the one with his blood on her hands. I sheathe my dagger and think fast.

I move to Meira and tug the dagger out of the mattress, hiding it under the bed before tugging the other blade out of her husband's ribs. Then I turn to their dresser and yank the drawers open before I find a black cloak that I drape over myself with the hood up. I hurry back to her frozen body as there's a hard knock on the door. "Listen to me. Meira, listen." I turn her head towards me as she blinks and I wonder if she can comprehend anything at all right now.

"He...he started talking about the deaths here. That he knew my plan for when he came home. That...that I planned to kill him so he wanted to beat me to it." Her eyes are wide as she stares in front of her without seeing me. "I didn't...I didn't do any of that. I grabbed the letter opener from the bedside table...it was instinct. I...I didn't want to—"

"It doesn't matter. I killed him. Do you hear me? I stabbed him when he was on top of you and that's why you have blood on you. Do you understand?" Bodies are slamming against the door now and I know I don't have much time left. I grab her shoulders and shake her roughly. "Think of your son, Meira!" She blinks again, eyes focusing slightly. "Good. I did this. An assassin. An intruder. Understand?" I barely get a nod, her brows furrowing as her glassy eyes scan my face, before the doors fall and I barely have a moment to turn and see a few guards with Silva stumbling in after them.

Our eyes meet and we both take a breath before I toss the letter opener at the wall close to a guard's head before vanishing out the window. There's no time for anything else. No time for a goodbye, a word, a wave. I have to get out of here now. I sprint through the shadows to the barn and grab a saddle bag I'd stuffed with dried meat and cheese in case I had to make a run for it.

There's another with a change of black clothes which I slide on with haste, leaving my beautiful dress in a small bag under the hay. Mary will collect it. I slip into the stall with Banshee and toss the saddlebags onto her back before hearing a soft meow.

A glance down reveals Graves twisting around my feet and I hurry to place him in one of the packs before sliding onto her back. The stall door opens and Banshee snorts and stamps her hooves when we see our path is blocked. Mr. Geoffrey stands there in his feeble glory with a bandage peeking out from under his shirt. There's no point in pretending anymore, so I don't try to. "I have to go, Mr. Geoffrey, I'm sorry."

He takes a step forward and squints up at me, then smiles. "Course you do." He holds up another pack and I tentatively accept it. "Blankets and such. You'll be needing them."

My lips press together at his thoughtfulness and I nod once. "Thank you."

He nods once and moves to the side to clear a path. "We'll all be waiting for the day you come back, my Lady." His hand removes his straw hat as he gifts me a deep bow. Tears sting my eyes as I bow my head in return before clicking my tongue. Banshee trots forward until we're clear of the barn, then takes off like an arrow down the main road. I glance back to look at the grand house one more time before looking forward again with a soft pat on Banshee's neck.

"Let me see how fast you can run."

Epilogue

The End of the Beginning

Silva

The funeral happens a little more than a week later at the family graveyard a few miles away. My mother clings to my arm like it's the only thing keeping her standing and while her eyes are red, she sheds no tears. Henry stays by my side as he has through the whole ordeal and I grab onto his hand as my father is lowered into the ground.

Leah left the same night that Roux did under the guise of hunting her down. None of my guards wanted to accompany her but felt reassured enough that the Enhanced would take care of things. The guests funneled out of the house within the hour and at least this will keep us from having to entertain for a while. I take a deep breath as my father's white coffin vanishes into the dark earth. Whatever I thought that I was prepared for when I gave Roux this task, it wasn't what I found. Her crouched over my father with a bloody knife in her hand was somehow a more shocking sight than seeing her pick up the warden's head like it was a purse.

Part of me knows it's because it was a surprise. We didn't know Lord Lurec was going to die that night. We certainly didn't know he was planning on killing my mother. I rushed to her after

Roux ducked out the window and my heart nearly stopped when I saw the blood on her abdomen. But she said she wasn't hurt and just wrapped her arms around me. That's when I got a clear view of my father's body off to the side, vacant eyes staring up at the ceiling seeing nothing.

Those images will live in my mind forever. I know they will. I'm not mad at Roux, she saved my mother's life, but I'm still in shock. It's best she left when she did. Not only to save herself but because I needed the space. Yet, as the gravedigger begins shoveling dirt over the coffin, I wish she was next to me to make some horrible pun about death.

My mother tugs my arm. "It's time to go back." I look around to find the few people who were here have left. It's just us three.

"Of course, yes." I turn and begin escorting her to the carriage.

"Hey, Sil." Henry's soft voice has me glancing up and following his gaze to a white-hooded figure slipping around the side of a mausoleum. I straighten up a bit as a flash of hope zings through my chest like lightning.

Henry takes my mother as my hand runs down her back. "I'll be just a moment longer." My feet carry me towards the figure, dodging gravestones and patches of flowers before I round the mausoleum only to be tugged inside by a hand on my collar. The doors shut behind me as I stumble into the coffin in the middle of the room before the hooded figure turns to me.

"You need to be more careful chasing after white hoods. You're friends with an assassin now. You need to watch your back." Her voice echoes through the space before her hood falls to reveal Leah's face. Something in me deflates, but of course, Roux couldn't come. Too risky. "When and if I come here, I'll have something red on my person. A ribbon on my belt, a pendant around my neck, something. If you see nothing red, do not approach. Am I understood?"

"Yes," I speak at last with a sigh of exasperation. "Did you only come to scold me?"

Her eyes roll, but she reaches into her cloak and pulls out an envelope which she hands to me. "This is from her." I take it and run my fingers over the seal, knowing her fingers followed the same path. "Don't expect such service again. The only reason I came is because she asked me to check on you."

My eyes snap to hers. "She's—"

"She's not here." Leah dashes my hopes with a gentle smile to soften the blow. "But she's close. We're moving as soon as I get back and I doubt you'll hear anything for a while."

I nod slowly. "Where will you go?"

She gives me a reluctant look. "You can't know that, I'm afraid. I'll tell you we're headed east, then south. That's about it."

"Well, that just leaves the rest of the world." I huff, but Leah only smiles crookedly.

"She's fine, Silva. I'll look after her as she'll look after me. We're family, after all." I nod again. There is some comfort in that. She reaches out and squeezes my shoulder with violet eyes looking remarkably soft. "Is there anything you want me to tell her? Give her?"

There are dozens of things that I want to say, to ask, to understand, but they're all things I want to speak and say to her myself. "Tell her that I'll keep all her dresses and slippers safe. Mary is keeping her room spotless. Mr. Geoffrey and Mrs. Geoffrey are keeping Banshee's stall filled with straw. Tell her…tell her whenever she wants a home, she has one here."

Leah grins. "She knows that."

I give her a weak smile back, the first real one since my father's death. "Then just tell her I miss her. And that I wish her luck. Both of you."

She nods and takes a step back to the door, flicking up her hood as the mausoleum opens to let in the fading sunlight. "Good luck to you as well, Lord Dinnsesk." I lean a bit heavier against the stone behind me as I hear the title for the first time. Then she's gone and I'm left with Roux's envelope and a single strand of hope in my heart.

I wait until I'm home to open the letter. Henry and my mother had been waiting long enough and I wanted real privacy to read whatever she wrote. As soon as my mother is safe in her bed and I've seen to it that the guards leave Henry alone for an evening, I waste a moment in my room to change into more comfortable attire. My eyes lift to a painting I found here after Roux vanished. It's clearly my mother's work and has me standing beside Roux as she looks out of the window as I stare at her. There was a tiny note wedged in the back that said, "*Don't miss me too much.*" I couldn't bring myself to get rid of the note, so there it remains, still in the back of the painting I've hung between the two far windows. It's the first thing I see when I come in at the end of the day and the last thing I look at when I leave in the morning.

After slipping on comfortable pants and a lightweight shirt, the green one Roux favored, I duck into Roux's room to dive into the letter. Dismay strikes me first at the few words on the page, but I drink them in any way as I settle down on a chaise in front of the window.

In three months, when mourning is over, you'll receive an offer from me. Make sure you're confident in the answer you give and that your affairs are in order. If you bring anyone else, make sure they're aware of the work. I'm sorry for any complications I may have caused with my leaving. It wasn't intentional.

Hoping to see you soon, V.

There's a drop of ink as if she hesitated before writing one last line.

P. S. I would have danced with you all night.

I read it three times before a smile breaks over my face and I look out the window with hope wrapping around my heart like a warm embrace.

"See you soon."

Acknowledgments

My deepest and most heartfelt thanks to my family. Without their unfailing support and patience, this book and my writing in general would be practically impossible. I'll forever be grateful to them.

To my friends! These are the people who looked over every iteration of my cover, let me nitpick over small scenes, and let me rant when all the work drove me crazy. Your encouragement and excitement pushed me forward even when writing was hard.

Mom. If there is ever a kind, caring, giving mother in my books, know that it's a reflection of you. Words could never encompass how thankful I am for you and everything you've given me. Until then, I'll keep saying thank you in every way I know how. Thank you, thank you, thank you.

My beta readers. This book wouldn't be what it is without all of you. Thank you for loving it as much as I do and loving it enough to make it better. Some of your comments live rent-free in my head and always serve as a sword I can brandish against the thoughts that I might not be good enough.

To all my English teachers over the years who encouraged my reading and writing. (Even if they caught me reading in class) I'll never forget all the times I was told to keep going, to put my voice to paper, and I'll never forget it.

Thank you, as always, to God. He gave me the air in my lungs and the inspiration in my hands. I'd be nothing without Him.

Last, but most certainly not least, my readers. Ultimately this comes down to me telling the story to you. I hope I've made something you love, characters you relate to, and a world you want to get lost in. Thank you for picking up this book. I can't wait to see and hear all that you have to say about it. Hope you like it enough to see what else I have in store for you all in the future.

About the Author

M. Kenzie was born and raised on the East Coast and currently lives in rural Virginia. She loves arts and crafts, drinking various teas while swaddled in a blanket during a thunderstorm, and staring lovingly at her (nearly full) bookshelves. On the rare occasion she isn't reading or writing, she's painting or spending time with family.

Connect with M. Kenzie on social media!
Website: https://authormkenzie6.wixsite.com/my-site-1
TikTok: @author_m_kenzie
Instagram: @author.m.kenzie